WHERE'S YER WILLY NOW?

Jeff Kristian

A MR BINKS MEDIA BOOK

Copyright © Mr Binks Media 2019
Cover design © Mr Binks Media 2019

First Edition
Edited by Robert Ingham

British Library Cataloguing in Publication Data.
A catalogue record for this book is available from the British Library.

ISBN 978-0-9928456-9-8 (Paperback Edition)
ISBN 978-0-9928456-7-4 (eBook Edition)

Mr Binks Media
mrbinksmedia@jeffkristian.com

I DEDICATE THIS BOOK TO MY FELLOW DRAG QUEENS

"What an absolute riot! I wouldn't have missed it all for the world."

www.jeffkristian.com

CHAPTER ONE

Deep in the heart of London's darkest Soho, Madame Fifi's notorious drag cabaret nightclub Sugar Sugar rocked to its foundations. The annual Halloween Spectacular was nearing its end, with the final glittering performance of the night from its three cabaret stars Lulu L'Amore, Chastity Belt and Connie Lingus in full swing. The legendary Madame Fifi herself was centre of attention as usual, but not propping up the bar surrounded by admirers as would be expected. She had just been arrested on stage for first-degree murder in full view of her adoring audience. Handcuffed and dragged unceremoniously through the parting crowd by several police officers, she had screamed her innocence. But Soho's eccentric cackle of heady night owls had just assumed her horror to be part of the show and mercilessly cheered her on.

Hot in the wake of Fifi's abduction was the instigator of carnage himself, back-from-the-dead drag queen, Lettitia Von Schabernacket. Having stolen her name, her club and her money, he had then set her up for the murder of his own twin brother. Now, he was keen to witness the final humiliation of her being thrown into the back of a waiting police van. Still wearing his hideous Phantom Hooker Of Olde Soho costume from the show, he glided grandly out of the club's front entrance, throwing out his arms as though still in sinister character. A small group of smokers huddling together in the bitter cold on the damp pavement gave him a lame round of applause. They watched on excitedly as Fifi faced her vicious nemesis.

'What do you want?' she screamed at him, struggling against her captors. 'Another turn of the knife?'

'You could say that,' smiled Lettie. 'I just want to savour every delicious last moment of the downfall of the magnificent Madame Fifi.'

'You twisted weasel,' she spat.

'Ooh, speaks the trout in the bin liner,' Lettie laughed.

'You will pay for this,' Fifi hissed. 'I guarantee justice will prevail.'

'Oh yes, go on,' he mocked. 'Blame the drag queen.'

'It is your fault,' she yelled. 'You created all of this, you murderer!'

'But there's no evidence is there, bubelah? What's a girl in handcuffs to do? She was rich, but now she's poor. She was famous, now she's just an old has-been.'

'How very dare you!'

'All these Eastern Europeans coming over here taking our jobs,' Lettie gestured to one of the policemen. 'Something had to be done. Know what I mean?' The officer smiled and nodded his agreement, before suddenly remembering his place and looking down to hide embarrassment from his colleagues. Fifi was seething.

'You've been planning this for months. I see it all, now! Every little move, every gesture meticulously designed to steal my life.'

'Yes, the great Madame Fifi is not so great now, is she? Flapping about like a wet fish in her cheap custard-yellow frock... remanded into custard-y, ha ha! Still, it matches your teeth.'

'You know, this is good value for money,' said one of the smokers to his friend. 'They don't usually perform in the street for us fag fags.'

'It's nice to be remembered,' agreed the friend, flicking ash onto the
shimmering flagstones. Meanwhile, Fifi was practically foaming at the mouth.

'I'll get you, Bernard!' she hissed. Lettie's grin dropped.

'Don't call me that!' he snapped defensively.

'Oh yes, Bernard. Look into my eyes, Bernard. What do you see?'

'Cataracts?'

'Revenge!' cried Fifi, theatrically through gritted teeth. 'Diabolical, unmitigated revenge. Is that so wrong?'

'I'm bored, now,' Lettie sighed, looking at his watch. He swished his black cloak and dramatically spun on his heels to go back in to the club. 'Take her away, boys,' he called back. 'And watch your sat nav driving her to prison, her arse is so big it's got its own gravitational pull.' He let out an evil laugh that any Hollywood phantom would be proud of, as he shoved against the glass doors of the club and strode back inside. The once great Madame Fifi's shrill screams could still be heard from inside the police van as it pulled away and disappeared up the street.

The very moment the show's final song was finished, Michael threw off his Lulu L'Amore wig and jumped down from the front of the stage. Shoving and elbowing through the heaving crowd, he ran up the stairs and out through the glass doors into the middle of the street. But he was too late. His hermaphrodite father Madame Fifi was already gone.

Show over, the drunken and disorderly crowd were now leaving. Pushing his way back inside through the throng was difficult. Doorman Daisy held off as many people as possible to help Michael get back in, but it wasn't easy with a soggy tear-laden tissue in one hand and an emergency Mars bar in the other. By the time he reached the dressing room, Chastity and Connie were already out of makeup and dressed. They turned and looked at him as he entered, trying to read his emotions. From behind them, a sobbing Edith ran forward and hugged him around the waist.

'You alright, Dolly?' asked Connie, sympathetically.

'No, I'm bloody not bloody alright, am I?' Michael replied, tears welling in his eyes as he clung tightly to his elderly grandmother. Chastity's heart sank.

'We will get her out,' he encouraged. 'You know that. We'll find the evidence we need and we'll get her out.'

'And get that psychopath Lettie put away where she fucking belongs, in a secure institution,' added Connie.

'I swear on the baby Jesus, if it's the last feckin' thing we do.'

'This is insane!' said Michael, wiping his nose with the sleeve of his costume. 'What are we going to do?'

'We need a plan and we need it fast,' said Chastity.

'But she's already in prison,' cried Michael.

'No she won't be,' said Chastity. 'She'll only be at the police station for now. Then she'll have a brief court hearing, probably tomorrow. Then they'll put her inside on remand, awaiting trial.'

'How do you know all this?' asked Michael.

'I've got the Kavanagh QC boxset on DVD,' Chastity replied. 'John Thaw, it's very good.'

'I wonder if she'll be in a male or female prison when she goes down?' pondered Connie.

'You're not helping,' said Chastity.

'Well, I'm just saying. You know… with a willy and a fanny?'

'Shut up, Connie!'

'Yes, shut up, Connie,' Michael agreed.

'My poor Fifi,' said Edith with a sniff, loosening her grip. 'What are we supposed to do?' She took a small clump of tissue from her pinafore and dabbed her eyes.

'Keep smiling through for now, Edith,' advised Michael, rubbing her back supportively.

'I ain't planning to smile, so I shan't bother putting in me best teeth,' she replied, blowing her nose.

'How do we know if we can do anything at all, anyway?' asked Michael. 'I mean, who are we? We're just a bunch of fuckin' drag queens! What chance do we stand of sorting out this shit?' Connie lit a cigarette and turned to Chastity for an answer. He thought for a moment.

'Fate,' he said, prophetically. 'You've been chosen, Lulu. Like our blessed mother Mary, that's why you're here. It's your fate.'

'But I'm not a good church-going Christian like she was,' said Michael.

'She wasn't a Christian, she was Jewish,' corrected Chastity.

'Well when did that all start, then?' asked Edith. 'Cause that church at the end of my road's been there three hundred years.' Michael gave her another hug.

'I didn't know you went to church, Edith?'

'Well, not religiously,' she sighed. 'I stopped going when they put in a new pulpit. It was too high, it made my neck ache. Though me and Ethel did go to lessons at the church hall when we were kids.'

'Sunday School?' said Michael.

'No, tap dancing. Thrupence a week.'

'Look, we're all tired, we need to rest.' Chastity suggested, wisely. 'A clear head walks a clear pathway, as my auntie Vi used to say. Let's meet at Connie's tomorrow morning and decide where to begin sorting out this mess.'

Suddenly, the door from the customer area flew open to reveal Lettie, now out of drag in a smart, tailored sugar-pink suit and matching tie.

'Ta da!' he laughed, taking a sip of champagne from a large glass. The force of the door had thrown Michael and Edith off-balance, tumbling them to the floor. 'You don't have to fall at my feet. Well, not just yet, anyway. A polite curtsey would suffice for now,' he demonstrated.

'You monster!' growled Chastity.

'Grrr!' Lettie responded with a giggle. 'Now, listen up! I've made a decision. I'm going to make a comeback and re-join the show.' There was a momentary shocked silence.

'What?' gasped Chastity, Connie and Michael in disbelief.

'Yes! Exciting, isn't it?' smiled Lettie, his effervescent demeanour belying the true horror of the evening's events. 'But of course, that means one of you three will have to go.'

Less than a mile away from Sugar Sugar, Madame Fifi was sitting silently on the bed in a small grey cell at New Scotland Yard Police Station in Westminster. Though a little numb, she could still feel the cold emanating from the high walls that enclosed her. She had not had the opportunity to collect her coat before her untimely arrest. Panicking, screaming and striking out had made the job all the more difficult for the arresting policemen. Now her adrenalin had calmed a little, she could feel their bruising grip marks on her arms and ribs. She stretched out her right leg to look at her canary-yellow satin stiletto. Grubby black finger marks were ground into the delicate fabric. In the struggle, she had kicked out and it had flown into the air, hitting a passing bag lady on the shoulder. It had been quite difficult for one of the coppers to convince the unfortunate elderly that the shoe had not been a gift and that she had to give it back.

Glancing into her lap, she rubbed the red cuff marks around her slender wrists. She pulled the rough, taupe standard-issue blanket from the bed and wrapped it around her petite yellow-sequinned shoulders, turning her back slightly against the creeping smell of decaying urine from the stainless-steel toilet bowl in the corner. Though never before accused of murder, she had been through tough scrapes many times before. She remembered fist-fighting for food as a child and having to sell her body as a teenager to avoid being drawn into fatal drug-running. She recalled her Interpol interrogation, the dangers of being smuggled out of communist East Germany and performing night after night at the Vindergurderbreurgenshaftenshitz club in Berlin to pay the blackmailer who threatened to expose her to the authorities. She was tough and she was a survivor.

Standing, she walked slowly across to a small rectangular sheet of polished metal, mounted on the wall above an equally grubby sink. She looked at her reflection through the scratched graffiti, plumping a few rebellious wisps of hair back into place. Her melancholy turned to anger. How could she be so stupid as to allow this to happen? From the moment Lettie began using her name for his drag character, she should have been suspicious. In one spectacular foul swoop, he had conned her out of her club, her money and her liberty. She could perhaps admire his audacity if she didn't hate him so vehemently. And now he'd had her incarcerated, how could she protect her naïve son Michael and gullible Edith? She knew Lettie was capable of anything. She also knew she hadn't yet seen the last of psycho Essex thug Billy-no-nut. She had to find a way to prove her innocence and get out. But how?

Her focus was distracted by sudden footsteps in the hallway outside. As a key rattled in the big metal door, she quickly threw the blanket back onto the bed and pulled back her shoulders, raising her bruised frame to its usual, defiant height. The door flew open and in walked a tall uniformed policewoman. She paused for a moment in the doorway, looking at the small but perfectly formed lady before her; masterfully elegant in her glittering gown with her chin held high and hands on hips. She recognised that glint of fire in the eyes and glanced back up the corridor to check they were alone before stepping inside and quietly closing the door.

'The great Madame Fifi,' she whispered, not wanting anyone else at the police station to hear.

'Do I know you?' Fifi asked, suspiciously.

'I'm Carrie. We have met,' replied the officer, pushing a loose strand of blonde hair behind her ear and sitting on the bed. She signalled for Fifi to sit close beside her to keep their conversation private. 'I met the love of my life at Sugar Sugar six years ago, so I guess you could say I owe you.' Fifi knew she was in no situation to trust anyone right now, but she could sense a window of opportunity.

'I did not commit this murder. I should not be here,' she said, sitting on the bed beside her.

'Word on the street is, you've been set up. Big time! You know some real nasty people.'

'Evidently,' Fifi sighed.

'Look, there's only so much I can do. They're moving you to the Court House in half an hour ready for the morning, so we haven't got much time. Have you been inside before?'

'No, but I know people who have.'

'Why does that not surprise me?' Carrie laughed. 'A few things to remember... don't talk in front of anyone, not even on the prison phone because they

13

listen in. And most cons have got someone on the outside to do their dirty work. You've been arrested as Letitia, not Madame Fifi. I'd keep that quiet if I were you. And for Christ's sake, don't tell anyone we've had this conversation.'

'Right,' nodded Fifi. This was all pretty obvious stuff, but at least the woman seemed to be on her side.

'And you can wear your own clothes on remand, but you'll have to wear something more casual than that!' She smiled, pointing at the shimmering cocktail gown.

'I don't do casual,' frowned Fifi.

'Then you'll have to wear the prison togs till you can get something brought in. Get someone to go in Primark for you, or something.' A cold shudder ran down Fifi's spine at the thought. 'Trust me, be invisible. At least till you know whether or not you'll get out. What else can I do?'

Fifi thought for a moment. She could feel the seed of an idea germinating in her mind. Glancing up at the door to ensure they were still alone, she leaned in closer and whispered, 'I need you to locate someone.'

Back in the Sugar Sugar dressing room, everyone was in deep shock at Lettie's sudden revelation.

'One of us will have to go?' repeated Chastity. 'Go where?'

'That's not my problem,' smiled Lettie, as Michael helped Edith up off of the floor and onto a chair.

'But why do you wanna come back?' yelled Connie. 'Now you've got all that money, you could do anything. But this is all we have!'

'Well, I've thought this through, Connie darling. If I get rid of you, I could have your flat above the club. My own little Soho shag palace!'

'Who'd wanna shag you, you genetic throwback? And where am I supposed to work?'

'Hmm. Perhaps you could get a little job demonstrating in Mattress World?' Lettie laughed.

'But I make all the costumes?' Connie pleaded.

'Like you say, I'm moneyed now. We can do better than that old shmata you run up.' With glee, he turned to face Chastity. 'Or, I could get rid of you?'

'What?' Chastity cried. 'You know nobody else will book me after that incident with Cyril. What am I supposed to do?'

'Well, you're a bit past it, dear. Perhaps you should consider retirement?' Chastity slumped into a chair, rubbing his face in disbelief. 'Keep your chins up, old girl, if your neck can support all that weight.' Michael backed up against the counter top, squirming as Lettie turned to face him. 'And Lulu? I've had what I needed from you now, you're surplus to requirements. You could go back to your little bar job in Essex? I'm sure Billy would be pleased to see you.'

'Eh?' Michael gasped in horror.

'Well come on then,' snapped Connie, grabbing for his cigarettes and lighting up. 'Do your worst. Which one of us is it gonna be?' Lettie paused for dramatic effect, looking at each one in turn. A stunned silence filled the room, broken only by Edith's gentle sobs.

'You do it,' grinned Lettie, maliciously. 'You decide between you who's gonna stay and who's gonna go. You've got a week.' He spun on his heels to leave.

'You poisonous little bugger,' screamed Edith, leaping to her feet and shaking her fist. 'I oughta give you a four-penny one round the earhole.' Lettie paused in the doorway and turned back.

'Oh yes, and Edith?' he smirked. 'You're fired!'

CHAPTER TWO

It had taken Michael a long time to finally get to sleep. In his dreams, he slowly opened his eyes, dazed and confused. He was lying on his back in pitch dark and silence. For a moment, he pondered if he might be dead, but then a pungent smell of damp and mould filled his nostrils, hitting the back of his throat and making his nose itch. He recognised it from the Halloween Special the night before. Why was he back under the stage at Sugar Sugar? He tried to lift his hand to scratch his nose, but he couldn't because his arm was secured with a wide leather strap, as was his other arm and his legs.

He called out, 'Hello? Hello? Help me, please help me!' but there was no response, not even a sound. Panting like a trapped fox, he could feel a further strap across his stomach. He seemed to be lying on a table of some kind. Suddenly, with an uncomfortable jolt it began to move, carrying him silently upwards from the black abyss.

After a few moments, he could sense he was going through the trap door to the stage. Without warning, the dazzling proscenium lights came on. Like hot needles searing into his pupils, they blinded him with their brilliance. Instinctively, he tried to shield his watering eyes, but could not move from the table. His senses further overloaded when deafening, raucous applause broke out from what sounded like a full house. Lifting his head and painfully squinting down past his feet, he could begin to make out the familiar Sugar Sugar audience, laughing and pointing. On the front of the stage to his left, he could see his father, Madame Fifi, struggling to come to his aid but held back by two muscled, topless policemen. To his right, his grandmother Edith and great-aunt Ethel tearfully clung to the blood-red velvet stage tab, helplessly watching on. His mother Verity was nowhere to be seen.

The audience fell eerily silent and parted to create a human corridor, up through which walked the character he himself was supposed to have played, The Phantom Hooker Of Olde Soho. Slowly and deliberately, it reached the stage and climbed the steps towards him. As the grotesque monster stopped at the side of the table, Michael realised exactly who was inside the costume. His blood ran cold at the sight of his would-be executioner.

'Billy?' he cried, desperately. 'Please don't hurt me!'

'Hurt you?' said Billy, through a deep smoker's chuckle. 'I'm not going to hurt you, I'm going to kill you.'

'Please! Please, let me go!' Michael gasped.

Billy pulled away a glittering sequinned sheet covering Michael's torso. The whole room gasped, as Michael realised for the first time that he was naked and exposed. A round of appreciative applause once again echoed.

'Argh! No, please no!' he cried, tears of horror welling in his eyes. Billy reached inside his cloak and pulled out the phantom's huge sword from its scabbard. Michael was mortified. He could feel sweat tricking down the sides of his torso as he held his

18

breath in diabolical anticipation. Running a rough, icy-cold hand slowly down Michael's torso towards his crotch, Billy took hold of Michael's tackle and lifted it to fit the blade snuggly under its base. The audience cooed like two hundred deranged pigeons. He turned and lowered his face closer towards Michael's ear.

'Wanna be a girl, do ya?' he whispered menacingly. 'You won't be needing this anymore then, will you?'

The sound of the Billy's blade dismembering his manhood still echoed in Michael's ears, as he awoke from his nightmare screaming. Panting and sweating profusely, he realised he was in the relative safety of Connie's lounge, on the sofa as usual. Lying in nothing but blue and white striped pyjama bottoms, he had kicked his quilt onto the floor in his desperate dream. He instinctively reached down to grab his crotch and check everything was still where it should be. Calming slightly to catch his breath, he wiped the tears from his eyes and looked up at the clock on the wall above Connie's television. It was only ten past four in the morning.

Through the window came the dim stream of light from Soho street lamps. The usual din of London traffic and the pitter-patter of rain on the flat roof above rang comfortingly in the background, along with the steady drip-drip of water into a bucket behind the sofa from a leak in the ceiling. Completely unaware of any trauma, his cat Nigel was stretched out asleep across the windowsill beneath the net curtains. The room was just as cluttered and untidy as always. Bits of unfinished and abandoned costumes lay strewn across every surface, and magazines of all description littered the corners of the room. An ashtray on the coffee table beside him was piled high with smelly cigarette stubs, their ash overflowing onto its glass surface around several dirty coffee mugs. Random cobwebs of dust swung silently from the ceiling, caught in a gentle draught from the semi-derelict Crittall window.

Suddenly, the door to the adjoining bedroom flew open and out leapt Connie. He too was wearing pyjamas, though his were sugar-pink and covered in small bright yellow bananas. Through large black-rimmed National Health spectacles, he glanced first at Michael's flushed face then down at his wrist tucked inside the pyjama bottoms. Michael quickly retrieved his hand and jumped to pull the sodden quilt cover back over his naked torso.

'What do you want?' he snapped, cynically.

'Well, you were puffing and panting so much, it was either a really bad dream or one hell of an orgasm,' grimaced Connie.

'And?'

'And so I thought I'd better check…. you were OK, Dolly?'

'Well I am,' answered Michael, a little embarrassed. 'It was just a nightmare. Thank you for caring.'

'Did I say I cared?' Connie sighed, losing interest. Michael was riled.

'Anyway… Banana pyjamas? And I didn't know you wore glasses?' He shot back, knowing how vain Connie could be.

'Only when I'm watching porn!' returned Connie, ducking back into the bedroom and slamming the door abruptly behind him.

Chastity arrived early at Connie's later that morning. Like Michael, he hadn't slept well, but it was essential they come up with a plan to avenge Fifi and take back control from Lettie. There was much to do, and quickly.

'Look at my sofa,' moaned Connie. 'He's left an imprint of sweat. And look at this!' He ripped off Michael's sheet and held it up against a shaft of light from the window. 'It's like the Turin Shroud.'

'I'll get some Febreze,' promised Michael.

'You'll get me a new fucking sofa!'

'It's not your sofa, it's Lettie's,' Michael shouted. A sudden lull of realisation fell upon the room. 'I mean… well, it could be Lettie's now, couldn't it?'

'Yes, well. That's what we need to talk about,' said Chastity calmly. 'Just cover it with a blanket for now so we can all sit down.' Connie walked sulkily out to the hall and fetched a few bath towels, laying them across the damp seat cushions. Chastity sat and tapped the seat beside him for Michael to follow. Biting his nails, Connie crossed to the window.

'I'll have to dip these nets,' he said, pulling one into the room and letting it drop. Minute specks of dust drifted through a shaft of light down to a worn patch on the carpet. Still laid out lazily across the sill, Nigel lifted his head momentarily to watch the net fall back into place. 'And get that leak fixed, too. Well, assuming I'm still gonna be living here!' he frowned, reaching down to the coffee table for his cigarettes. 'What am I supposed to do if she throws me out? Live in a cardboard box?'

'Ooh, you have to be careful where you do that,' suggested Chastity, turning to Michael. 'Our friend Anna-Lee Retentive got evicted from her council flat.

She pitched up a tent on Tower Bridge, but not for long. Three times a day, everything slid down to one end.'

'Yeah, she always had delusions of grandeur,' added Connie. 'Like someone else we know, in her pink suit and tie like an estate agent from Teletubbies.'

'But what about Fifi?' Michael yelled.

'It ain't just Fifi, is it Dolly? It's all of us!' screeched Connie.

'I can't go back to Southend!'

'You'd be alright, you can shack up with your grandmother. But what about us?'

'Stop it!' shouted Chastity. 'Stop it, both of you! Can't you see what she's doing here? Divide and conquer.'

'What are you rattling on about, now?' said Connie.

'She's trying to set us all against each other, that's what this is about,' continued Chastity. 'She's got no intention of coming back to the show, you know how lazy she is?'

'True,' said Connie, flicking ash on the carpet and treading it in.

'The more divided we are, the more powerful she is. It's a calculated distraction. Politicians do it all the time… Hitler, for feck's sake!'

'So, she's not gonna sack one of us then?' said Michael.

'I know her so well,' assured Chastity. 'It's a dirty trick. As long as we're thinking about ourselves, we're not thinking about her and what she's done. No, what we have to focus on is proving her guilt.'

'But what about Edith?' asked Michael.

'Nothing's gonna happen to Edith,' said Chastity, patting Michael's hand reassuringly. 'She'll be safe from harm at home, till we can unravel this mess.' Michael was trying hard to supress the butterflies in his stomach.

'OK, so what have we got?' he said, rubbing his forehead and trying hard to concentrate. 'Fifi, whose real name is Lettie, apparently murdered Lettie, who wasn't really Lettie but who we know as Lettie's brother Brian in disguise. But it wasn't Lettie, who we know as Fifi, who murdered the brother that was disguised as Lettie, it was the real Lettie, whose name's really Bernard and not Lettie because he stole it from Fifi in the first fucking place!' Chastity looked at Connie in bewilderment as Michael threw his head in his hands. 'Oh, I don't fuckin' know!' As he began to cry uncontrollably, Chastity moved closer and put his arm around his shoulders to comfort him.

'He's hysterical. Shall I smack him?' asked Connie.

'No! Just stop hitting people,' grunted Chastity.

'There's a surplus of Lettie's, ain't there?' Connie drew back on his nicotine and thought for a moment. 'Shall I just put the kettle on?'

'Perhaps we all need something a bit stronger,' Chastity suggested. 'Is there any of that brandy left from last Christmas?'

'I think so, I'll have a look.' Connie disappeared into the kitchen as Chastity turned back to Michael.

'Now come on love, pull yourself together,' he said gently. 'We can do this. The Sisterhood can do this. We can figure it out together. You're not alone. We're a team. Look, even Nigel's behind you.' Michael lifted his eyes momentarily to see that his faithful cat had stirred from the sill and was now sitting at his feet, watching.

'Miaow,' he rasped supportively, rubbing his head against Michael's leg.

'There, you see, even he knows it'll be alright. And you know how clever cats are?'

Connie returned from the kitchen holding aloft a bottle with a small amount of brandy in the bottom.

'There's not much left, but it'll have to do,' he sighed, crossing to the display cabinet and picking up three glasses in his other hand. Blowing off the thick layer of dust and wiping them briefly on his jumper as a gesture of cleanliness, he placed them all on the coffee table and began to pour.

'I wish my Mum was here,' sobbed Michael.

'Her number will be in Fifi's office somewhere,' suggested Connie. 'If we can get past that deranged trollop.'

'Yes, we should call Verity. I expect she'll be back in New York by now, but we can't fight this alone. Lettie's got it all too wrapped up.' Chastity's mind was racing for an idea. 'We've got to find a way to get Fifi out. What we really need is... a good Solicitor.'

'But we haven't got any money!' Michael cried.

'Hmm, that could be a problem,' sighed Connie.

'Ooh, I feel like Glynis Johns in The Card,' said Chastity, dabbing his sweaty top lip with the sleeve of his cardigan. 'Ooh, erm... what about that barrister you were shagging, Connie? What was his name?'

'Oh, it's me having to prostitute myself again to save the day, is it?'

'But you're so good at it,' encouraged Chastity.

24

'Yes I am, aren't I?' Connie grinned, remembering all his lustful adventures. 'Philip. But he wasn't a barrister, he was a barista. The only thing he'd be good at in court is passing round the cappuccinos.'

'Oh. Well that's no feckin' use.'

Connie thought for a moment. 'But what about that friend of Vernon's? The big leather guy. What was his name? Wasn't he something legal?'

'Yes!' Chastity's face lit up. 'Mister Mark. He did all Vernon's business dealings for him.'

'Oh yes, lovely big Mister Mark. Yummy!' Connie mused. 'I wonder if he's married?' He took another puff of his cigarette. '*Chanson d'amour*,' he sang. 'He looks like that bloke from Manhattan Transfer. The dishy one, not the one who looks like someone's dad getting up and having a go.'

'Who's Vernon?' asked Michael.

'He's a regular at Sugar Sugar, a leather queen. He's about a million years old and absolutely loaded.'

Chastity described to Michael the last time he had seen Vernon, only a few weeks previously. He had been standing in drag on the front step of Sugar Sugar, holding open the glass door as a teenage man in tight rubber shorts and a matching cut-down vest had come bouncing merrily out and jumped into the back seat of a waiting limousine. Behind him, Daisy slowly supported a rather unstable elderly man across the kerb.

'Bye bye, Vernon love,' Chastity had said, grinning at the sight of the loose wrinkly skin from his naked buttocks draping down the rear of his open-backed leather chaps. Daisy had removed the man's Muir cap and chucked it inside before gently folding him into the vehicle. Then, after hanging the man's

25

colostomy bag on the coat hook just inside the car door, he had pulled off his rubber glove and shoved it into his coat pocket.

'Steady as you go, Vernon!' he had shouted, slamming shut the door and banging on the roof.

'Would you look at that?' Chastity had smiled. 'Absolutely no arse, just a hole at the top where his legs meet. No shame. And no teeth... destined to spend his twilight years sucking chicken!'

'Sounds like a character,' said Michael.

'Yes, he is. He'll know what to do, we'll ask Daisy. She knows how to get hold of him, she always reserves his table.' Chastity looked at his watch. 'She'll be arriving downstairs in about ten minutes, we can meet her at the front desk.' He tapped Michael's hand. 'Come on love, pull yourself together, we've got work to do.' Reaching forward, he pulled a couple of tissues from a box on the coffee table and held them to Michael's nose. 'Now... blow!'

At Westminster Magistrates Court, it had been decided there was enough evidence to send Madame Fifi to trial. Refused bail, it had been ordered she be detained at Her Majesty's Pleasure for six weeks until being heard.

The journey in the back of the police van to Holloway Prison had been much more uncomfortable than when Madame Fifi had been arrested. Perhaps it had been the adrenalin rushing through her veins at the time, but stepping briefly out into the bright winter sunshine to cross a small, enclosed courtyard, she could feel every muscle in her back aching. She took in a deep breath of fresh air to recover from the stale

26

smell of body odour she had suffered in the vehicle. As she was led inside the main building, she lifted her cuffed hands to shield her eyes from the glare, glancing back over her shoulder briefly at the high walls topped with glittering loops of razor wire.

Inside, she was led up a long dank corridor and into a stark whitewashed room. After having her cuffs removed, she was left alone. In the middle of the room was a metal chair next to a long steel table. Fifi noticed they were bolted to the concrete floor. In the corner was a rather ominous industrial shower. The whole shocking scene was lit by dull, buzzing fluorescent tubes embedded in the ceiling.

Fifi spun to face the door as it opened. In walked a big-boned middle-aged woman in a bile-green prison officer's uniform holding a clipboard. Her long, wiry black hair with greying roots was pulled tightly back into a ponytail, as if to yank the wrinkles out of her face. Her dull complexion and sullen expression lifted slightly as she saw Fifi in her yellow sequinned cocktail dress.

'Oh, my! What have we got here, then? Ain't she pretty?' she mocked. 'Where are we now then, Ascot?'

'This is not an Ascot dress. But I guess you would not know such things,' Fifi replied sarcastically.

'Oh, sorry m'lady,' growled the woman, lunging face-to-face with Fifi as if to threaten. 'Mouthy cons like you make my job so much more enjoyable.' But Fifi wasn't in the least bit intimidated. She had wiped the floor with vile creatures like this many times before.

'Can we just get on with this?' she moaned impatiently.

'My name is Finch, you will refer to me as Miss Finch. Strip, spread your legs and bend over,' she grinned, taking a pair of rubber gloves from her pocket. Fifi turned her back and did as she was told. Naked, she bent forward and laid her two palms on the table, bracing herself for the inevitable. The gloves snapped on behind her and a big hand reached between her legs to her crotch. There was a moment's shocked silence. 'What's this, then?'

'You didn't expect that, did you?' grinned Fifi defiantly. 'I have both. Male and female.'

'Oh, yes!' said the officer with glee. 'Our ladies are going to love you. A week on remand with me and your life won't be worth living!'

Soho echoed with its usual buzz as Michael and Chastity accompanied Connie out of the alley from his flat and around the corner to the front entrance of Sugar Sugar. People were rushing to and fro, navigating around several delivery vans making their morning visits to local shops and businesses. Across the street from Sugar Sugar's entrance, Michael could see a street cleaner trying to sweep around an elderly tap dancer. Wearing a cheap sky-blue sequinned waistcoat and matching fedora, he happily entertained an imaginary audience from his own little dancing bubble. When Michael had first arrived in town, he would have found this type of behaviour extraordinary. But now, six weeks on, he was getting used to Soho's uniquely eccentric flavour.

About to enter the club, Daisy could see them coming. He raised his eyes at the dancer and grinned as he went in. Finally arriving at the entrance themselves, they pushed against the glass doors and stepped inside.

'He's dead,' frowned Daisy in the entrance lobby, taking off his cerise-pink scarf and matching woolly bobble hat.

'Vernon's dead?' asked Chastity despairingly.

'He died last Tuesday. He was under the weather. Well, he was under two big blokes when he actually died.'

'Good old Vernon,' said Connie. 'Going out with a bang.'

'That's just typical, dying when someone wants something from him. Every time it was his round at the bar he always vanished to the toilet.' Chastity put his head in his hands. 'What are we going to do now? Oh, feck! Feck, feck, feck!'

'What's wrong?' asked Daisy, reaching into his coat pocket for an emergency Mars bar.

'We need to speak to Mister Mark,' added Connie. 'Lulu needs legal advice to sort out this bloody mess Lettie's created.'

'I expect he'll be at the funeral,' said Daisy.

'When?' Michael grasped Daisy's arm in desperation.

'This afternoon, love. Eileen Sideways told me. And he died on his own birthday. Very neat and tidy, Vernon would have liked that. I would have said, but I didn't think you'd be interested.'

'Interested in what?' came a voice from the darkness at the top of the stairs. Startled, they all spun to see who was speaking. As their eyes adjusted to the dim light of the stairwell, they gasped in shock to see Madame Fifi.

'Oh my God! Dad, you're free!' said Michael, ready to run forward and hug. But as she stepped towards them into the light flooding through the glass entrance doors, he realised that it was just Lettie. Dressed as Fifi, in Fifi's clothes. Hair, makeup, jewellery, even the sharpened red talon nails were the same. He was a perfectly immaculate parody of the real thing, if not quite so petit. For a moment, everyone was frozen speechless. It was the first time they'd all seen him since the dressing room the night before. Connie broke the silence.

'You ain't right in the head, you ain't. What are you dressed like Fifi for? You're taking this obsession thing a bit too far, you silly bitch.'

'This is insane!' said Michael, through acute disappointment.

'Silence! Up with this shit I will not put,' Lettie mimicked.

'Oh for feck's sake,' Chastity retorted. 'She's even fecking talking like her, now!'

'I said, interested in WHAT?' Lettie repeated fiercely.

'Well, they wanted…' Daisy began, through a mouth full of Mars bar. Thinking fast on his feet, Chastity interrupted.

'We… err, wanted to know… if you'd said anything to Daisy about the show? Any changes, now you're in charge?' It took all Chastity could manage to muster a fake smile of servitude.

'Yes,' snapped Lettie. Though said in desperation, this would actually be a good way to keep everyone distracted, if only for a week or so until the drama had died down. 'I want a completely new show. New costumes, new songs, the works. You have two

30

weeks!' They looked at each other in disbelief at this further revelation. Connie threw a bitter look at Chastity for opening his big mouth.

'New show? New costumes? How the fuck are we supposed to do all that in two weeks?' He spun to face-off Lettie. 'And you, you venomous old...' Connie was impulsively ready to pounce but Chastity held him back. Lettie was dangerous, and rocking his boat couldn't just make things difficult, it could be fatal. Connie changed tact. 'What I mean to say is, if we haven't decided who's going yet, who do I make costumes for?'

'Do mine first and the others when you decide,' said Lettie impatiently.

'Yes, a fresh start and a new beginning, ready for your glittering return. Sounds like fun. Don't you think, Connie? Lulu? Fun?' Chastity feigned glee, desperately trying to keep the peace. But to his growing frustration, Connie wasn't finished.

'Hold on a minute... If it's me that's fucking off, there won't be anyone to finish making the bloody costumes, will there? You never thought of that, did ya?' he smirked. Lettie frowned thunderously, about to retaliate.

'Best go and start making plans, then,' Chastity interrupted. Grabbing Connie's arm, he yanked him back out through the doors and away up the street followed closely by Michael. Lettie angrily returned Daisy's baffled glare.

'What are you staring at?' he screeched. Daisy jumped with terror and ran off down the stairs, crying.

Lettie walked slowly over towards the glass doors and looked out. This was his manor now. He owned this club, and so much of Soho that he hadn't

31

even had time to assess it all. After months of planning and scheming, he'd finally got exactly what he wanted and was prepared to do absolutely anything to keep it. But he could sense something brewing. He knew Chastity's way of thinking so well that he could almost hear cogs whirring in his head. He'd been one of The Sisterhood himself for too long to miss a trick. His twisted breath misted the glass as he whispered, 'Watch your step, girls!'

At her little terraced house in Bermondsey, Edith reached into the cupboard under her scullery sink and pulled out a duster. She couldn't get the horrific events of the previous night out of her mind. She knew the best thing she could do under the circumstances was to keep busy. Walking through to the parlour, she began dusting her knick-knacks. But her emotions were getting the better of her and, reaching the end of the mantle shelf, she couldn't remember which ones she'd dusted and which she hadn't. Perhaps she should have accepted Chastity's kind offer and spent the night with him at his home?

'You're here now girl, bestest is as bestest does,' she said, trying to pull herself together. But a nagging sadness in the pit of her stomach wouldn't allow her mind to focus. She scrubbed at the patch of damp mould on her scullery wall and re-stuck the Sellotape on her cracked windowpane, but still she felt distracted. She decided to make herself a cup of tea.

Sitting at the small table in her scullery, she blew off the steam and took a sip. 'That's a tonic,' she said, straightening the doily under the teapot. She reached forward and opened the little cash tin she had

32

retrieved from on top of her wardrobe. Opening it, she took a handful of cash and began counting. With no job, she wanted to know what she had left to survive on. But she couldn't concentrate because she was too worried about her three drag daughters and her dear friend Fifi. And there was something else that she couldn't quite put her finger on, something instinctive. What was this ominous feeling welling up inside?

She decided the best thing to do was to head over to Connie's and be amongst family. Chastity would probably be there by now, too. Perhaps last night had all been a silly mix-up and Fifi would be there, as usual?

In the hall, she put a few tissues in her handbag, checking she had her bus pass and her little white paper bag of boiled sweets for the journey. Putting on her hat with the wobbly red cherries and pulling on her coat, she took a quick glance in the mirror to adjust her woollen scarf. As she opened the door, she was shocked to see a female police officer standing on her doorstep.

'Ooh, golly wars!' she jumped. 'You gave me a fright.'

'Are you Edith? Edith Pimm?' asked the officer, gently.

'Yes, why? What's happened?'

'Can I come inside?' the officer said, stepping in through the door. Panic flooded Edith's veins.

'Is it Madame Fifi? What's happened to Madame Fifi?'

'No dear, it's not Madame Fifi, it's your sister Ethel. Shall we go and sit down?'

'Ethel? My Ethel?' This was all too much for Edith. The noise from the street became an overwhelming echo and the little hallway suddenly went blurry. The officer jumped forward, attempting to catch her delicate elderly frame as her knees gave way, slumping her to the floor.

CHAPTER THREE

It was a bitter November afternoon as Michael, Chastity and Connie made their way to Vernon's funeral. Overcast and dull, the journey wasn't made any more pleasant by Connie's continuous ranting about having to make so many new costumes so quickly. Were it not for Chastity and Michael's own stress, they would happily have thrown Connie from the moving bus.

Walking across the frosty graveyard grass towards the chapel, their feet made a dull crunching sound. Connie clung to Chastity's arm, lifting his feet like a dressage horse as he walked.

'What's the matter with you now?' complained Chastity, yanking his arm away.

'We could be treading on dead people, here. Why couldn't we walk on the path like normal people?'

'It's too cold and slippery to walk all the way round there. It's quicker to cut across,' Chastity explained.

'I'm not being buried, I want to be cremated,' mused Connie. 'I've got it all planned. The coffin goes on the conveyer belt to the oven as they're playing, *don't you wish your girlfriend was hot like me*,' he warbled. 'I don't like the idea of going down that hole and being eaten by worms.'

'What makes you think they'd want to eat you?' glanced Chastity.

'But then again,' continued Connie, 'when they burn you, the smoke can't be good for global warming, can it? I have to ask myself, what can I do to improve our environment?'

'Emigrate?' suggested Michael, hopefully.

'Anyway, you didn't need me to come,' Connie whinged. 'It's so boring! I could have been at home in the warm watching Homes Under The Hammer.'

'I need you here in case I don't recognise Mister Mark. If we haven't got a solicitor, then we've no chance.'

'It's too cold, Tit. And anyway, I'm not sure I'd know him if I saw him again.'

'Don't talk rubbish!' said Chastity. 'You had your head up the front of his jumper on stage singing, *something tells me something's gonna happen tonight*.'

'Oh, yes, I did didn't I?' Connie smiled.

As they stopped at the back of the other mourners outside the arched gothic chapel entrance, Connie pulled his black woolly scarf in tighter under his chin and tucked the slack under the lapel of his matching coat before lighting a cigarette.

'Do you know any of these people then?' asked Michael, pulling his knitted hat down further over his ears and blowing warm breath into his clasped hands.

'No. I think Vernon led a bit of a double life, these are probably all from his straight world.' Chastity craned his neck to be sure.

'Bloody Christians,' spat Connie. 'And look at that thing!' He pointed to a life-size statue of the crucifixion facing the church's entrance. 'That reminds me, I must get my nails done.'

'Shhh! Stop it, now,' snapped Chastity. 'Anyway, who are you to criticise? You went to Southwark Cathedral a few Sundays ago.'

'That was different.'

'How was it different?' asked Chastity, impatiently.

'Err... hello? Songs of Praise was there?' said Connie, as though his reasoning was clear.

'Eh?' Chastity shrugged, none the wiser.

'You know... Telly? For my CV?'

'Oh for feck's sake,' sighed Chastity, shaking his head. Michael laughed.

'Was you on the telly then, Connie?'

'No, I watched it back. They boxed me in behind a pillar. Can you believe it? Story of my life. Ooh, talking of boxes...' Connie nudged Chastity in the ribs as the hearse carrying Vernon's coffin pulled up in front of the mourners. The priest stepped out of the church followed by six big, hairy muscle bears dressed head to foot in black leather. 'Ooh... not quite so boring now,' grinned Connie, licking his lips.

As the driver opened the back of the car, the men leaned in to lift out the coffin. Chastity pushed his finger under Connie's chin to close his lecherously gaping mouth, before ripping the hat off of Michael's head as a lesson in respect.

'God bless, Vernon love,' he smiled, dipping into a short curtsey.

Madame Fifi was feeling a little violated, after having been forced to put her clothes and jewellery into a plastic bag before being unceremoniously hosed down in the shower cubicle by Finch. Finally dried off and wearing a grey two-piece standard-issue smock, she was escorted through a long, narrow corridor carrying a folded pile of bed linen, towels and a change of clothing. A cold draught bit into her scalp through damp hair. Reaching the end of the corridor, Finch turned a key in the steel, riveted door and held it open for Fifi to enter. Once through, she ordered Fifi to stop as she locked it behind them. Her huge bunch of keys snapped back against her belt on a retractable chain as she directed Fifi forward.

They were in an enormous central hall lined on either side with cells. Whitewashed brick walls were dazzling after the dull light of the corridor. In the large open space immediately in front of them were recreation tables, at which sat several groups of prisoners; some playing cards; some chatting, and a few reading books and newspapers. The sound of the door slamming shut drew attention from their distractions, noticing for the first time their now not-so glamorous new arrival. As Finch marched Fifi past the tables to one side, her fellow cons began shouting and whooping.

'Look ladies, fresh meat!' shouted a tall muscular woman with shortly cropped greying hair. Several other prisoners stepped out through their open cell doors to take a look.

'Alright, alright. Keep it down,' grinned Finch, as she pointed Fifi in the direction of a wide black-painted metal staircase leading to a wrought iron mezzanine. Until this point, the great Madame Fifi had been confident in her defiance, oozing strength and stamina. But the moment her moccasin-clad foot touched the bottom step, a feeling of dread shivered through her bones. It was the first time she had felt this foreboding since the realisation of her arrest on the Sugar Sugar stage the night before.

'Round to the left,' ordered Finch, as they reached the top of the stairs. Fifi was doing everything she could to prevent the bitch officer from noticing the nerves shaking in her hands and legs as she entered her designated cell.

The room was larger than her holding cell at the police station. The high ceiling was a nicotine-cream brick arch, from which hung a caged fluorescent tube on two heavy chains. A large window high on the back wall allowed streams of bright daylight through a wide steel grid, bolted to the front of its frame. Below it was a steel sink basin with two shelves. The top shelf was tidily cluttered with toiletries: a blue flannel facecloth, a toothbrush with toothpaste in a plastic beaker, a half-used bar of soap and a can of deodorant. The bottom shelf was empty, other than a similar beaker. To one side was a silver toilet with a black plastic seat. The lower half of the room was painted a depressing chocolate-brown colour, framing two single beds, one to either side.

'That's yours,' said Finch, pointing to the left-hand bed which was stripped back to the mattress. 'Welcome home, m'lady,' she smiled sarcastically, feigning a bow. 'Make your own bed. Dinner's in an hour, the others will tell you what to do. We'll sort your toiletries later till you buy your own, once we've sorted your job.'

'Job?' questioned Fifi.

'Oh yes, m'lady. This is a prison, not a hotel. You'll have to work if you want luxuries in here.' She left the room with a cackle.

Fifi sat on the foot of the bed, pulling the pile of linen into her chest protectively. For the first time in her life, she felt a little claustrophobic. The walls appeared to be moving closer as the room seemed to shrink. She closed her eyes and took a deep breath, silently counting backwards from ten as a distraction. But as she reached the end of her countdown, she sensed she was no longer alone. She opened her eyes to a middle-aged woman sitting on the other bed directly in front of her. Scrubbed face framed with badly bleached shoulder length hair, she stared Fifi straight in the eyes.

'Who's a pretty boy, then?' she grinned with an Essex accent, pushing back her fringe with chewed fingernails.

'Oh, she told you,' sighed Fifi. 'I'm not a man, I'm a woman.'

'Suits me either way, Lettie,' said the woman. 'You've got a sexy accent. Nice tits, too.'

'I'm straight,' warned Fifi.

'So is spaghetti till it gets wet. I'm Bunnie.' She reached out her hand to shake, but Fifi ignored it. A snigger from the doorway made them both look up to find two rough-looking cons chewing gum and listening from the walkway. 'Fuck off!' screamed Bunnie, kicking the door shut on their faces.

'Finch shouldn't have told you that. And now thanks to your big mouth, everyone will know,' snapped Fifi.

'Didn't you read the brochure, sweetheart?' grinned Bunnie. 'This is Disneyland, we're all friends here. Or at least... we can be.' Rolls of stomach fat pressed against her thighs as she leaned a heavily tattooed arm forward and put her hand on Fifi's knee. 'Does it work, then?'

'Does what work?'

'Your dick?' Bunnie slid the hand up her leg towards her crotch. Incensed, Fifi stood and turned her back, shaking out the sheet to make her bed.

'That is something you will never know,' she growled.

'Cause if it does, we can make a killing,' suggested Bunnie.

'We?'

'Yeah, I can set things up for you. There's a lot of horny birds in here, we can trade food, smokes, drugs... everything!' Bunnie jumped to her feet, trying to get Fifi's attention. 'You've got to admit, it's a blinder of an idea?'

'It is ludicrous!' Fifi spat, avoiding eye contact by tucking her sheet under the edges of the mattress. 'I will not be pimped out for your cigarettes.'

'You scratch my back, I'll scratch yours.'

'You're not coming anywhere near my back, and certainly nowhere near my front!' Fifi had had enough. It was time to take back the upper hand, if only to survive her first night on remand. 'Let me make something quite clear,' she said, pulling a linen case onto her pillow. 'I wish to be left alone. No friendly chats, no girlie sleep-overs, no sharing, no drugs and definitely no sex!' She spun defiantly back to face Bunnie, but the upper hand was debatable.

'There's two sets of rules in here, sweetheart,' whispered Bunnie menacingly in her ear. 'Their rules and our rules.' She squeezed Fifi's fingers painfully around the edge of the pillow. 'Think very carefully sister, or it won't just be your dick that's stiff.'

After Vernon's ceremony, little sobs could be heard as his coffin was lowered into its grave. From a little way back, Michael glanced up at the crowd to see if this might be a wife or daughter. But it was just one of the leather bears, dabbing a small black laced handkerchief under his eyes.

'That was a nice service,' said Chastity, pulling his gloves back on.

'When the undertaker said he'd never seen a body so well preserved by whiskey…' smiled Connie.

'And they lined the coffin in fleece instead of satin?' questioned Michael.

'That's cause he was laid out in backless leather chaps. They thought satin might be a bit cold on his wrinkly little bum,' said Chastity.

As the priest solemnly bellowed the last rights, most of the crowd of mourners began to move away.

'Right, it's now or never Connie,' said Chastity. 'Which one's Mister Mark?'

'It's hard to tell,' squinted Connie, taking his spectacles out of a small case and holding them up to peer through. Chastity was a little taken aback.

'Since when have you worn glasses?'

'Only when she's watching porn, apparently,' Michael offered, sarcastically.

'I think that could be him with the cowboy boots,' said Connie, pointing to a tall, well-built man near the foot of the grave. 'I need to get closer.' As he went to move forward, Chastity held him back.

'Wait,' he said. 'I think something's happening.'

As the priest stumbled precariously across the frosty grass back towards the chapel, the leather men surrounded the hole, each looking down while fumbling at the crotch.

42

'Oh my God! What's going on?' gasped Michael, as each man pulled out his tackle and began to urinate down onto the lid of the coffin.

'Ahh, now that's lovely! Oh, I'm welling up now,' said Chastity, taking a tissue from his pocket and dabbing his nose.

'That was Vernon's thing,' said Connie, pointing at the steam billowing up from the hole in the ground. 'He liked being peed on. It's a final nod of respect.'

'Really?' Just when Michael thought he had seen everything.

'Yes,' grizzled Chastity, making the sign of the cross on his chest. 'Bye-bye Vernon, love. Rest In Piss.'

'Do you know,' said Michael, 'I was sure that choir was singing, *save all your pisses for me*, instead of kisses. They did, didn't they?'

'Nothing would surprise me,' smiled Chastity, shaking his head and pushing his hankie back inside his coat pocket. 'Right, let's sort this out before they all leave. Come on, bitch.' He looped his arm through Connie's.

'Yes quick now, Dolly,' said Connie, grabbing Michael's arm. 'This bloody cold weather, I could do with a piddle myself.'

Twenty minutes later, Michael, Chastity and Connie sat with Mister Mark in a tatty Greasy Joe's café across the road from the cemetery. The buzz of traffic from the busy road outside could barely be heard above the clatter of the kitchen, as two waitresses in red gingham aprons and matching hats bustled to and fro, taking and delivering orders from a dozen or so hairy workmen. Mister Mark took a sip of his coffee.

'What you need is evidence. Cold, hard evidence. If Madame Fifi's already on remand, they probably already have what they need to convict her. They wouldn't just take Lettie's word.' He put down his mug and took a bite from his sandwich.

'What evidence have they got, then?' asked Chastity.

'That's the million-dollar question,' Mark replied, wiping his mouth with a paper napkin.

'How do we find out?' said Michael.

'She will have had a solicitor for the hearing, but they're unlikely to tell you. They may tell a next of kin.'

'Lulu's her son,' suggested Connie. 'And Fifi's her…'

'It's complicated,' interrupted Chastity through a swig of tea.

'Well, as long as he can prove that, you're fine,' said Mark, taking another sip. Michael's heart sank. He'd only found out Fifi was his father a couple of weeks before, there was certainly no proof.

'Where's my bloody sandwich?' moaned Connie, stretching his neck to look for the waitress. 'Oi! Oi, wench!' he shouted, clicking his fingers in the air. 'I ordered a sausage sandwich about three hours ago. Everyone else got theirs.'

'Yours is the only one that's cooked,' shouted back the waitress.

'You should have just had ham, like me,' said Michael, taking another bite. Connie shot him one of her looks. The waitress walked slowly over and chucked the sandwich on the table in front of him.

44

'There. Happy now?' she quipped sarcastically.

'You've got a lot of attitude for a condiment supervisor. I'm the customer here, remember?'

'How could I forget?' she replied, walking away with as little effort as possible.

'Everywhere we fecking go,' sighed Chastity, shaking his head.

'Anyway, Lulu,' said Mark, trying to lighten the mood. 'Any chance of a fuck?' Caught completely by surprise, Michael spat his tea across the table and over Connie's sandwich.

'Oh that's just bloody perfect, ain't it?' whinged Connie, looking down at his sodden food. 'She gets the soggy knickers and all I get is a soggy sandwich? Just take her, she's getting on my fucking nerves!'

Outside in the street a few minutes later, they said their goodbyes to Mister Mark.

'Thanks for the sandwich,' he said.

'Yes, sorry about Connie, and that waitress throwing us out,' Chastity apologised.

'I burped,' explained Connie. 'It just came out sounding like go fuck yourself.'

'If you find evidence that Lettie was somehow involved in the death of Creighton Cross, you should contact his solicitor directly,' advised Mark. 'He'd need to re-open the case with the police. It said in the papers they think his death was an accident.'

'But that doesn't help Fifi, does it?' asked Michael. 'Can you represent her for us?'

'I can't step on anybody's toes, you should use the solicitor that's already instructed. But call me if you need free advice.' He handed Michael his card. 'Or if you change your mind about that shag?' This wasn't what Connie wanted to hear. He lit a cigarette, spun on his heels and stormed off.

'Take no notice of that bitch,' said Chastity. 'She's on heat. I'll chuck a bucket of water at it later.' Mark laughed. Then thought for a moment.

'You really believe that Lettie killed her own twin brother? She'd need a pretty strong motive to do that. If you can find her motive, it may help you find the evidence.'

CHAPTER FOUR

The atmosphere in the Sugar Sugar dressing room was tense. The first show since the hideous events of the Halloween Special, everyone was a little nervous that something else would happen. As they prepared for their performance, Chastity broke the ice.

'So are you going to call Mister Mark then, Lu?' he said, dusting a swathe of azure blue eyeshadow across his eyelid.

'No. I can't concentrate on a relationship right now with everything else that's going on,' he replied, applying glue to his false eyelashes.

'He only asked you for a shag,' Connie snapped bitterly. 'You've got to open your legs, not your whole fucking world!'

'Connie!' Chastity scolded.

'Well, he's making so much bloody fuss over one shag!'

'And you're not, I suppose?' said Chastity.

'Anyway, you can have him.' Connie stood back, admiring his makeup in the mirror. 'I can do better. That particular knight in shining armour is just a wanker in tin foil.'

'He's a bit Neanderthal for me,' said Chastity. 'Caveman sex, like being shagged up against a wall by Fred Flintstone.'

'It would be my first time,' explained Michael. 'Sorry, but I want it to be special. With someone special.'

'Whatever,' Connie sighed.

'You don't need to apologise,' said Chastity protectively. 'She's just bitter that he asked you and not her. Look at that face,' he said pointing. 'Like a rotting bowl of lemons.'

'It's not just that, I've still got to make a dozen costumes for a totally new show.' replied Connie, pulling on a large blonde beehive wig. 'Although I admit, you're probably right Lettie won't sack one of us.'

'Ah! Well actually, a thought did run through my mind,' said Chastity, unhooking a pink and green rose-patterned dirndl costume from the rail.

'Bet that was a dreary journey,' bitched Connie.

'We've still got two new backing tracks that Slasher gave us a few weeks ago. And there's the ones Lulu's already learned while Lettie was away, she won't know about all of them.'

'True. And the new costumes you've already made for me,' added Michael.

'So…' said Connie, realising Chastity's train of thought, 'we just throw in a couple of new bits and adapt what we've already done?'

'That's it!' smiled Chastity. 'Mix it around a bit, add a few feathers and bows here and there, and Bob's your uncle.'

'And she'll think it's a brand new show? That's genius!' laughed Michael, brushing rouge across his cheekbones.

'It is, isn't it? Giving us time to secretly look for clues.' Chastity held open the dirndl for Connie to step inside. 'But don't rush, oh no, no, no. It's got to look as though we're spending all our time rehearsing. And remember, we've got to look as though we're all at each other's throats deciding who's gonna leave.'

'Yes, you're right,' agreed Michael. 'We're actresses, we can do this.'

'Work on your Judi Dench,' said Chastity.

'At a push,' sighed Connie. 'That woman's only gotta walk past a cinema and an Oscar falls in her handbag!'

'Do your best,' said Chastity. 'If Lettie suspects anything, I dread to think what she'll do next!'

Connie opened the show with his tribute to the swinging sixties, an up-beat song reflecting echoes of Helen Shapiro. Running confidently centre stage, he swung his hips, twisted his feet and arms, and began to sing.

'Every boy I meet I want to play with. Every boy I meet just feels the same. I'm not one to tease and then say no, no, no. So who am I if I deny the boys?' With hand on hip, he leaned towards the audience wagging his finger.

'Every time we touch I get a tingle. Every time we kiss it's just the same. I don't see the harm in what we both adore. So who am I if I deny the boys?' He opened his mouth wide and wagged his tongue, as if French kissing.

'Then if we get to thinking that it's not enough, we loosen up our clothing and see what comes up. We're only playing Mother Nature's game!' He aggressively thrust his groin at the audience several times. They rewarded his efforts with raucous laughter. He turned to focus his attention on a middle-aged woman at the front, by feigning looks of horror

and disgust as though she were the measure of disapproval.

'There's no shame in this type of self-expression, because it's just another form of joy. I don't care if people talk and shake their heads. For who am I if I deny the boys?'

Back in the dressing room, Michael zipped Chastity into his first costume of the night, a red velvet number with long sleeves and a huge puffball skirt.

'Sounds like a nice audience,' said Chastity, looking in the mirror to fasten matching rhinestone earrings. 'Probably a good thing, because this next song isn't the best I've ever sung.'

'I agree, Connie's is a better opener,' Michael suggested. Chastity stopped what he was doing and turned to face him, pausing for a moment to make eye contact. 'What?'

'You know, I'm very proud of you? It was only six weeks ago you left your fingernail marks in the doorframe trying to escape.' He put his hands on Michael's shoulders affectionately. 'But now look at you, a fully-fledged drag queen. And a bloody good one, at that!'

'Thanks,' said Michael, a little lump coming to his throat. 'But I feel a bit wound up tonight. I could really do with a drink.'

'Just ponce a fag for now. Mine's the packet with the scabby tongue, Connie's is the man with the hole in his neck. Have one of hers, I think she owes you.' Michael took one from the pack and lit up.

'She can get an attitude on her, can't she?'

'You know, I read in Woman's Own that the mouth develops much later in the womb than the sphincter,' said Chastity, plumping his wig in the mirror. 'So basically for most of our time in there, we're just an arsehole. I guess some people never grow out of it.'

Back in the auditorium, Connie sat on the front of the stage with his long skinny legs dangling into the customer area. He lifted the front of his skirt and parted his knees at a bashful young man on the front table.

'I'd rather be called easy or a common slut, then have them say I'm cold and frigid or hard up. I wouldn't have it any other way.' Jumping back to his feet centre stage, he twisted into his final verse.

'Every boy I meet I want to play with. Don't tell me that I'm too old for toys. Let me be myself and do the things I like, for who am I if I deny the boys? There may not be a special someone in my heart, but who am I if I deny the boys?'

Chastity's intro music began to play as Connie ran from the stage into the dressing room. Pulling off his wig, he reached for a cigarette.

'Good crowd,' he said, lighting up. Chastity was just about to step up onto the stage when Daisy ran in through the door from the customer area.

'Chastity, come quickly! There's a policewoman waiting for you upstairs.'

'A copper?' said Chastity, concerned. 'What do they want?'

'I don't know.'

'Connie, put your wig back on and get back out there.'

'I'm having a fag!' complained Connie, pointing at Michael. 'Make her do it, I hate this song.'

'You know it better, Lulu hasn't rehearsed this one.'

'Then make the pig wait!' Chastity snatched up the beehive and thrust it into Connie's chest.

'Just feckin' do it, this might be important.' Connie reluctantly yanked it back onto his head, catapulting his lit cigarette at Michael as he ran on stage.

'Is it Fifi?' Michael was concerned. 'Is something wrong? What's happened?'

'I think you'd best wait here,' said Chastity, squeezing his arm before turning to follow Daisy up to the front entrance.

'Can you step outside please, sir,' said the officer, pushing a loose strand of blonde hair behind her ear. Chastity did as he was asked, following her through the glass entrance doors and a little way down the street to a waiting police car. She seemed somehow familiar to him.

'What? What is it?' he asked nervously.

'Special delivery,' she answered, opening the door to reveal Edith. She leapt from the back seat and grabbed him around the waist.

'Oh Chastity,' she cried. 'It's Ethel. She's gone! She's gone!' He wrapped his arms around her shoulders, patting her back as she buried her head in his stomach.

'Oh my darling, I'm so sorry,' he responded gently, looking to the officer for answers.

'She had a little turn. We took her to casualty as a precaution, but she's fine. She wanted to come here?' Chastity nodded.

52

'Don't I know you from somewhere?'

'Carrie. I'm one of your regulars. Listen, I've got a message from Madame Fifi. She's asked me to trace someone.'

'From Fifi? Trace who?'

'Don't know, I had to search covertly through Interpol. For fuck's sake don't tell anyone I've done this, or we could all be in serious trouble,' she warned, glancing about to ensure nobody could hear.

'Of course,' agreed Chastity. Reaching into her trouser pocket, she took out a piece of paper and handed it to him.

'It's a German number, possibly near Berlin. I've got absolutely no idea who this is or what they're capable of, so for Christ's sake proceed with caution.'

'Right,' said Chastity, beginning to get a little worried.

'But she wants you to ring the number and ask for The Extractor.'

'The Extractor? Oh my God, that sounds worrying!'

'And there's a secret code. Tell him: "Fanny whistles by moonlight".'

'Fancy that,' said Chastity.

'Do you know anyone called Fanny?'

'A transsexual friend of ours,' he nodded. 'She's just had a new vagina installed, but I doubt she can whistle through it.'

Hearing the news that his great-aunt Ethel had died greatly saddened Michael. Although he hadn't known her very well, she had none-the-less been a part of his family, something for which he had always longed. He had so desperately needed a drink after the show, but now he just wanted to be spend as much time as possible with his grieving grandmother. Following Fifi's shocking incarceration, Verity's quick return to New York and Ethel's sudden demise, he felt his new family were disappearing almost as quickly as he had found them.

Chastity had advised Michael that it may be too much of a shock for Edith to discover she had a grandson so soon after Ethel's departure, and that it would be better for her to rest at his flat in Kennington for a few days. Agreeing with this wisdom, Michael reluctantly waved them off from the bus stop and returned to Connie's.

On the doorstep, he stooped to give Nigel a rub on the head as he greeted him at the door. Connie was humming to himself in the bathroom. Throwing himself back on the sofa, Michael thought about his mother. He so needed to hold her right now, for her to tell him everything would be alright.

'Come on, get yourself ready Dolly, we're going out,' said Connie, flitting through to his bedroom in a nylon karate dressing gown.

'I'm not in the mood,' moaned Michael. 'Can't we just have a drink here?'

'There ain't none, we finished off that brandy,' called back Connie.   'Anyway, I need to get out of this dump for a while.' He threw a pair of leather trousers into Michael's lap. 'Put them on.'

'Leather? Why?'

'You'll see, just put them on. And wear them Doc Martin boots and that lumberjack shirt you arrived in.' He glided back out towards the bathroom, now wearing an outfit similar to Michael's but topped
54

with a black leatherette cowboy hat. 'We'll drop a few Jagerbombs, have a laugh, let off a bit of steam. See the world in a fresh light tomorrow.' Michael had to agree, Connie was probably right. And he did desperately need a drink. He began to get changed.

'I wanna break in to Lettie's office and get me mum's phone number,' he called out. 'Will you help me?'

'Yeah, tomorrow,' said Connie, squirting perfume around his neck, wrists and crotch. 'Tonight, we're going out to play!'

The wind was biting as Connie led Michael across Trafalgar Square and over the road to a small turning up the side of Charing Cross Station. He could hear the sound of music thudding in the distance as they approached a queue of about fifty men, also dressed in leather.

'Come on,' said Connie, 'we don't have to queue cause we work at Sugar Sugar.'

'Really?'

'Well, that and I've shagged most of the doormen!'

A little embarrassed by whinging from the waiting crowd, Michael followed close behind. As they approached the entrance, he looked up to see the sign Heaven.

'I've heard of this place,' said Michael, a little nervous.

'It's leather night, you ain't seen nothing yet!' Connie grinned, putting his hand on Michael's chest to stop him walking in.

'What?'

'There's a golden rule,' said Connie seriously. 'Never, never, ever, under any circumstances, tell anyone you're a drag queen.'

'Why?'

'It's an instant turn off. You'll end up standing on your own all night, like a pork sausage at a Bar Mitzvah.'

'Well, what should I say?'

'Tell them you're a barman, or a lumberjack or something,' said Connie, treading out his cigarette.

'Lumberjack? Nobody's gonna believe that!' laughed Michael.

'They won't care, just as long as you're not a fucking drag queen!' Connie advised, grabbing him by the arm and leading him excitedly inside.

They walked through a low, dimly lit brick-arched tunnel and under an opening into a large hall with a high ceiling. Michael's eyes were immediately drawn to hundreds of high-tech lights and lasers spinning above their heads, pulsating in time to the almost deafening beat of Donna Summer's I Feel Love. As his eyes followed the beams down, he was faced with a sea of men. Hundreds of them danced vigorously, mostly shirtless or wearing leather chest harnesses, every single one of them gorgeous. Michael thought his heart would stop beating. He had never seen so much gay flesh in one place at one time and the shock was overwhelming.

'Oh my dear God,' he sighed. 'This is insane!'

'It's not your usual night out on the piss in Southend, but I'm guessing you'll cope,' laughed Connie, amused by his friend's bewilderment.

'Connie, it's amazing!' he gushed, eyes twinkling.

56

'Call me Norman, Michael. No drag names, remember?'

'Oh yes, sorry. I was a bit distracted.'

Several of the hunks dancing nearby looked Michael over and smiled. One huge muscle guy wearing nothing but leather shorts and a Muir cap winked at him, sticking out his tongue as if to taste him in the air. As the music and lights went up a gear, so the energy in the room increased, with everybody throwing their arms in the air, gyrating and thrusting at each other. Since working at Sugar Sugar, Michael had got used to looking his audience in the face while on stage in costume, but he still hadn't quite become accustomed to making eye contact with unknown men, preferring instead to keep his line of vision safely away from the risk of questions about his sexuality, for fear of reprisal and the possibility of homophobic retaliation. But this was different, something he had never before experienced. In this strange, new exciting world, eye contact was mandatory.

'Take a deep sniff,' said Connie poignantly. 'What can you smell?' Michael did as advised. The perfume was intoxicating. A heady mix of testosterone, leather, fresh sweat and alcohol almost made his head spin, dulling the music momentarily, as the hedonistic aroma rose in his nostrils and sparkled through his veins to every extremity of his body.

'What... what is that?' he asked.

'Sex,' smiled Connie.

CHAPTER FIVE

After downing several shots, Michael had loosened up a little. Standing at the bar with Connie, he drank in the scenery and found his feet tapping to the heavy beat of the music. Swigging back the last of his vodka and coke, Connie grabbed his hand and pulled him onto the dance floor.

Michael had danced in a club before in Essex with his dear friend Tamara, but nothing could prepare him for this. Around and around he span with his arms in the air. There seemed to be hands all over him as he gyrated with a dozen or so different men. It was exciting, joyous and magical. Everyone was happy, everyone was equal, and there was a feeling of unmitigated unity that Michael had never experienced before. He felt he had come home.

'I can see why they call it Heaven,' he shouted across to Connie.

'What did you say?' Connie yelled back, laughing.

'I said, I can see why they call it Heaven!' As he spoke, he became aware of two large hands on his hips. Then in his ear from behind, he heard a deep whispering voice.

'If this is Heaven, you must be an angel.' Michael turned to see who was speaking. Without warning, the music in the room seemed to fade to a dull thud and the crowd appeared to be dancing in slow motion. He was face to face with the most gorgeous man he had ever seen. Sparkling emerald-green eyes penetrated his very soul as he drew in a deep breath and his heart skipped a beat. Short blond hair cropped at the sides framed the square jawline of his face, injecting Michael with an unexpected rush of adrenalin as it opened into a broad, Hollywood smile. He was in the presence of Zeus.

'Breathe,' the hunk smouldered. His muscular arms reached slowly forward to gently hold Michael's elbows. But Michael couldn't, he was still swimming underwater in the cool, clear pool of those eyes. 'Breathe!' the man repeated, giving him a little shake. Suddenly, the beat of the music became louder again, the dancing sped back up and Michael was back in the room.

'I… err… I'm sorry,' he coughed, gasping for breath.

'It's OK,' laughed the man, pulling him into a friendly hug. 'Is that your boyfriend?' he asked in a raspy Scottish accent, nodding towards Connie.

'Norman? No. Oh God, no!' Michael gushed. 'He's just a friend.' He glanced back to where he had last seen him. Still there watching over Michael, Connie grinned and winked back. He protectively looked the man up and down and gave a thumbs-up. Then with a little wave, he disappeared into the heaving throng.

'Travis,' said the man, holding out a hand to shake.

'Michael,' he responded. Travis grabbed him by the front of his shirt and pulled him into a passionate kiss. The music numbed again momentarily as Michael's feet appeared to lift off the ground. Heart pounding loudly in his chest, he threw his arms around

Travis' broad shoulders, as if to stop himself from floating away. After the longest time, Travis stood back from their embrace and grinned.

'Wow,' he giggled, licking Michael from his lips. 'Can I buy you a drink?'

'Oh God, yes please!' gasped Michael, a little embarrassed for sounding so desperate. Travis took him by the hand and led him through the crowd in the direction of the bar.

Away from the dance floor, Michael could get a better look at Travis. A bit taller and a little older, his shapely nude torso was dusted with cropped golden hair beneath a black leather waistcoat. His muscular right arm had a tattoo sleeve spreading over onto his chest and he had a small pierced ring in his eyebrow. Tight matching hipster trousers over footballer's legs draped twelve-hole Doc Martin boots.

'What do you do, handsome?' he asked, passing Michael a bottle of Budweiser.

'Err… I'm a barman, in Soho,' he answered cautiously, remembering Connie's advice.

'You don't sound too sure?' Travis laughed.

'Oh sorry, I'm just… it's not easy to hear in here, with the music. What do you do?'

'I'm a graphic designer.' He reached forward, undoing another button on Michael's shirt and running the back of a finger gently down his chest. 'But, what I'd really like to do… is you!'

'Really?' Michael couldn't quite believe his luck.

'You know what you've done, don't you?' Travis moved in close and kissed him tenderly on the neck.

'What?' Michael whispered.

'You've got me really horny. Can I take you home?'

The journey to Travis' on the back of his motorbike was both frightening and thrilling. Never having ridden pillion before, Michael clung tightly around his waist, resting the side of the crash helmet against the back of his leather biker jacket as the wind whistled past. Swinging back and forth through the London traffic, Travis called back occasionally to ask Michael if he was OK. Michael had never been more OK in his entire life.

Pulling to a stop, Travis switched off the engine and signalled for him to dismount. They were outside a small block of recently modernised mid-century apartments close to the river. As Michael removed his helmet, Travis gave him a peck on the lips and took him by the hand, leading him inside to the lift.

'Where are we?' Michael asked, as the doors closed and they began to ascend.

'Pimlico,' grinned Travis, unzipping his jacket and rubbing his hand playfully in Michael's hair.

'You're mad,' he laughed, pushing his hair back into place as the doors opened and they stepped back out of the lift into a small, clean corridor.

'That's because I live in Wonderland!' Travis unlocked the entrance to his apartment and stepped back for Michael to enter.

The door led straight into a large, open-plan lounge, furnished sparsely with modern low-level brown leather sofas and armchairs. Cream shag-pile rugs adorned the oak floor under minimalist glass coffee tables, and the white walls were hung with canvases of bold colour splashes to either side of the largest flat-screen television Michael had ever seen.

'It's great for porn!' Travis commented, noticing Michael's expression.

To their left, stark ivory kitchen units ran the full length of one wall, broken only by a steel cooker below a matching extractor hood. In front of them was an entire wall of glass windows overlooking the Thames. Battersea Power Station stood across the river in all its silent majesty, illuminated and glistening in a light shower of rain.

'Fuck!' Michael gasped.

'That's the general idea,' smiled Travis, taking his hand and leading him to a door on the right. 'We're not in Kansas anymore, handsome!' he whispered, throwing it open and switching on the lights to reveal an adult playroom full of every type of sadomasochistic leaning imaginable. Straps, buckles and sex toys lined the black walls on hooks and leather-covered shelves. A set of medieval stocks sat ominously to one corner, over which hung whips and cat-o-nine-tails. To the left was a selection of handcuffs next to a large bowl of condoms atop a small glass table and, centre stage, suspended from the ceiling by thick chrome chains, was a black leather sex sling.

Michael was mortified. He'd never seen anything like this before. He was also a little saddened. For the first time in his life, he'd met someone he really felt was special enough to give himself to completely. But this wasn't the kind of special he had always envisioned, and he could feel his dreams quickly sinking into the pit of his stomach. Having just met his perfect man, he was probably about to be thrown unceremoniously back out into the street. His eyes began to water.

'What's wrong, what is it?' asked Travis softly.

'I... I've never done anything like this before,' he sighed, wiping his eyes.

'We can take it easy at first.'

'No, I mean, I've REALLY never done anything like this before!' There was an uncomfortable silent pause as Michael prepared for the worse.

'You mean...?' Travis asked. Michael nodded, closing his eyes and bracing. 'Oh, man! What am I gonna do with you?' Travis joked in an exaggerated Glaswegian accent, stroking the side of Michael's face and kissing him gently on the lips. 'You're adorable.'

'Really?' Michael opened his eyes. This wasn't the angry response he had expected.

'And dangerous!'

'Dangerous?'

'Aye, dangerous,' Travis grinned, switching off the dungeon light and pulling the door closed. Taking Michael gently by the hand, he led him into the bedroom next door. 'I went out tonight to reel in a quick screw. But I think I've hooked myself a keeper.'

Madame Fifi laid on her bed in the dark. She had found the events of her first day in prison stressful. Although she had stood her ground under pressure, the comments about her unique physical attributes had been quite hurtful.

Growing up as a young girl and then a woman in Eastern Europe, she had for the most part been able to keep herself under wraps, managing her secret successfully. She had considered having her penis removed, until she met her lover Creighton Cross. Though they had not spent long as a couple, he had remained a dear friend, always encouraging her that she was perfect without surgery. He was strong and powerful, she had trusted his wisdom. But now that he was gone, perhaps the time had come to finally go under the knife?

She glanced across the room at Bunnie, snoring on the other bunk. She had a plan to ensure she would not spend very long in prison, but it relied on the loyalty of others. Without Creighton watching her back, she was unsure whether or not anyone capable of carrying out her plan was really on her side. There was now absolutely nothing she could do but wait.

At Chastity's flat in Kennington, he had settled Edith down for the night with a warm cup of Ovaltine. She had slept like a baby in his queen-sized bed next to him, so that he could keep an eye on her. By the time he awoke, Edith was already up and about running a cloth around the kitchen.

'Edith dear, what are you doing? You're supposed to be resting,' he said, gently taking the cloth from her hand and leading her into the living room.

'Well, you know me. I like to keep busy,' she grinned.

'You've got to rest,' he said, sitting her down on the peach flowery sofa. He kicked a small footstall into place. 'Now, put your feet up on that pouffe and I'll make a cup of tea. You've had a terrible shock.'

'I was gonna go home, but I thought I'd wait till you got up, seeing as you've been so kind.' She dabbed her nose with a clump of tissue from her cardigan pocket.

'No Edith, you're going to stay here for a few days,' he smiled, pulling her forward to plump up the cushion behind her back.

'But I feel as though I want to wear something black, you know?'

'Yes dear, I quite understand.' He walked through to the kitchen and filled the kettle, bringing through a tray with two cups and saucers, a small sugar bowl and a jug of milk. 'I'll take you home shortly so we can pack some of your bits and bring them here.' He laid the tea things down atop a large lace doily on his little wooden coffee table. Edith looked up at him and smiled, her crystal-blue eyes twinkling in the sunlight from the window.

'Don't forget to warm the teapot, first,' she advised, lifting her feet onto the pouffe.

'Yes dear, it's all in hand.' He sat beside her. 'Now, we've got a little bit of organising to do. We need to be sure Ethel has a good send off, don't we?' Edith thought for a moment.

'Yes, I'd like that. They pay for the cremation up there. But I'd like to see her in the chapel first, just to say goodbye.' She dabbed a little tear running down her cheek.

'I think that's really lovely, and we'll all come with you,' said Chastity, patting her hand. 'I'll phone the institute later to make arrangements.'

'And I was due to see her this week,' she snivelled. 'Once a year, we used to meet up and watch the fireworks together on bonfire night. It was our special thing, you know?'

'Oh, that's a shame,' Chastity sympathised.

'Won't be doing that no more, will I? Cause I ain't got no family now. If my baby Marvin hadn't died, I'd have someone to go with.'

'Well, try not dwell on that right now,' smiled Chastity. 'You know we're all here for you, we're your family too.' He desperately wanted to tell Edith that her son Marvin hadn't died and that he was in fact Madame Fifi, and that Michael was her grandson. But it wasn't his place, and the shock may be too much for her in this delicate state. Patting Edith on the knee, he returned to the kitchen and brought through the teapot, sitting it on the tray in front of her.

'Shall I be mother?' Edith asked.

'Yes please, I'll have a quick one before I pop over and meet the others. I've got to make a phone call to Germany, so I'll use Connie's phone.'

'Ich wurde gerne nach Deutschland gehen,' said Edith casually, lifting her feet off the pouffe and leaning forward to stir the tea in the pot.

'Eh?' Chastity was worried she may be going into shock.

'I'd like to go to Germany, dear,' she said, giving the teapot a little shake.

'What... how... you speak German?' Chastity was baffled.

'Well a bit, yes,' she smiled. He sat back down beside her.

'How do you speak German?'

'Well, just before I got married, I worked as an under-house parlour maid for a German mafia family. We all had to speak a bit of German, it was the only way to get by.'

'You're a dark horse, Edith!' Chastity shook his head in amazement. 'Where was this, then?'

67

'Ooh,' said Edith. 'It was a great big house. Very, very big, lots of windows.' she screwed up her face in deep thought. 'Oh, what was it called?' Chastity was concerned she may be overstretching herself.

'It doesn't really matter that much, just…'

'Buckingham Palace!' She smiled and began to pour out the tea. Chastity thought for a moment, unsure whether or not Edith was thinking clearly.

'Buckingham Palace? Are you sure?'

'Yes, dear. I was there for two years. Course, when I met Bert I had to end the affair. It wouldn't have been proper.' She tipped a little milk into each of the cups and gave them a stir.

'Affair? What affair?'

'Prince Phillip. I was his porcupine,' she said proudly, handing Chastity his teacup. Bemused, he put it back on the tea tray.

'Hold on a minute… you're telling me you were Prince Phillip's concubine? THE Prince Phillip?'

'Yes, it was all a bit hush-hush,' she grinned cheekily. 'I had to meet him every Tuesday at four o'clock, in the broom cupboard under the servants' back staircase. Ooh, he was a caution! But he was a charmer, gave me little gifts and things. He even drove me home on his pony and trap a couple of times.'

'He races them, doesn't he?'

'Yes, he raced alright. I wouldn't have gone in a car with him, he was all over the road!' Edith giggled.

'And it ended when you met Bert?'

'Well, yes. My father made us marry quick, like. I'd only known Bert a month, but I got pregnant, and you couldn't have a baby out of wedlock in them days. Then of course, six months later I gave birth to baby

Marvin, bless his little heart.' Chastity sat silently in shock for a moment.

'Let me get this straight. So, you're saying you married Bert a month after meeting him, then gave birth six months after that?' He counted on his fingers.

'Yes, dear.'

'So, that means you were already two months pregnant when you met Bert?'

'No, I don't think so. Well, it didn't show.'

'Didn't you have your period?'

'I can't remember whether Aunt Flow came or not.'

'Well then, were there any other men?' Chastity picked up his tea and drank it back in one mouthful.

'Ooh no, dear. I couldn't do that!' Edith laughed, 'Perish the thought.'

'So...' Chastity scratched his head. 'That means that Prince Phillip must have been the father of your baby?'

'No, that can't be right,' she said, 'cause we only ever did it standing up, you can't get pregnant like that. It was only a small broom cupboard, there weren't any room to lie down proper.'

'Edith, that's a myth. Of course you can get pregnant standing up!'

'Ooh, golly wars!' she cried, holding her hands to her face. 'Perhaps that's why Marvin died in childbirth? They're all in-breds up there, you know.'

'Well, it could explain one or two things,' said Chastity. 'Edith Pimm... you gave birth to a member of the royal family!'

Michael couldn't stop smiling. Everything was just so very perfect. Lying in bed watching the man asleep beside him on the crisp white linen, he felt he had finally found where he belonged. The comforting buzz of late morning traffic in the street below made him feel alive, as did the butterflies in his stomach every time he thought about Travis. The tooting horn of a passing lorry stirred the hunk from his slumber. Slowly opening his eyes, he smiled at the sight of Michael watching him.

'Hiya, handsome,' he said, reaching forward to affectionately ruffle his hair.

'Morning,' Michael grinned.

'Did you sleep well?'

'A couple for hours, I think.'

'Aye, it was a busy night, wasn't it?' Travis chuckled. 'I could lie here all day just watching you, but I've got to go into work for a few hours.'

'I've got to get back to Sugar Sugar,' sighed Michael disappointedly.

'That's a drag club, isn't it? I assumed you'd work evenings, as a barman?'

'Erm…' Michael had completely forgotten he'd had to lie about his job. 'Well… there's deliveries, stocking the bar, and I need a change of clothes.'

'Where do you live?'

'Above the bar.'

'That's convenient.'

'Yes, but I have to sleep on Norman's sofa. It's a bit of a dump.'

'Well then, I'm glad you're here in my bed with me.' He kissed Michael tenderly on the lips. 'Oh no, you've done it again!' he laughed, lifting the quilt to look down at his stirring manhood.

70

'What's Glaswegian for sex?' asked Michael cheekily.

'Hochmagandy!' Travis purred. 'Now, get tae shower an gees a swally-gobble!'

Sitting cross-legged on the bed in his underpants, Michael ate cereal as he watched Travis put on a shirt and tie.

'What are you thinking?' asked Travis.

'I was just thinking how my Rice Krispies are only snapping and crackling. There's no popping. Did you get them half price?'

'You're a cheeky little boy,' Travis laughed. 'Sorry, I don't take the bike to work. Can you make your own way back?'

'Sure,' said Michael, taking another bite.

'There's no rush, take as long as you like.' Travis pulled on his suit trousers. 'Can I see you again tonight?'

'Yes please, I'd really like that,' Michael grinned.

'Shall I meet you at work? You could pour me a pint at the bar?' Travis suggested. Michael choked on his breakfast.

'Are you OK?'

'Err… yes. Thanks. I… err…' Michael's mind was racing for an excuse to cover his lie. 'Perhaps we could meet outside? They're a little touchy about boyfriends.' Suddenly, Travis' smile dropped. 'Oh… no, not that I'm saying we are boyfriends, I didn't mean…'

'It's OK.'

'When you said I was a keeper, I…' Michael could feel his face flushing.

71

'You're adorable,' said Travis, 'but the boyfriend thing... it's a bit of a problem for me.'

'Oh,' said Michael. Travis could see his heart sinking.

'I really like you, Michael.'

'It's my fault, I shouldn't have said it.' Michael was embarrassed.

'No, don't apologise, it's fine, but... it's complicated,' Travis sighed, pulling on his jacket. 'Look, I'm going to have to go,' he frowned, glancing at his watch. 'I can't do this now.'

CHAPTER SIX

Chastity arrived at Connie's to find him sitting alone on the sofa with his feet on the coffee table, flicking through the local newspaper in front of the television.

'What you reading?' asked Chastity, throwing his bag on the armchair and taking off his scarf.

'Gok Wan. He's designed a new range of spectacles,' said Connie, drawing back on his cigarette. 'Can't be easy when all you've got to work with is a square, a circle or a rectangle.'

'Unless you're Elton John,' added Chastity, removing his coat.

'And there's this local competition looking for a catwalk costume designer.' Connie held up the page. 'Thinking I might have a go, get me out of this dump.'

'Do you get anything?'

'First prize is five-thousand pounds and a design contract!'

'Ooh, that reminds me, I borrowed a tenner out of your purse yesterday to buy some mascara.' Chastity glanced at the television. 'Good grief, is that Watch With Mother?'

'Black and white telly? That's way before my time.' Connie pointed at the screen. 'What's that thing?'

'That there's Andy Pandy,' Chastity smiled.

'No wonder kids of your generation are all in therapy. Ain't it got fat fingers?'

'That's why Looby Loo was always smiling!' said Chastity, joining him on the sofa. 'Talking of kids, where's Lulu?'

'She didn't come home last night,' said Connie, turning the page.

'What? Well, where is she then?'

'How would I know? I've had the flat to myself for the first time in weeks, it's been absolute bliss. Wish I'd picked up a bit of trade myself, now.'

'Picked up where?'

'Leather night at Heaven.'

'You didn't leave her there? She's too naive!' Chastity was vexed. 'She could be anywhere in the South of England right now. Probably tied up on all fours in a cage, eating from a dog bowl. Connie, how could you?'

'Oh, she was gagging for it, Tit,' said Connie defensively. 'She was dripping like a broken fridge. What am I now, her fucking babysitter?'

'How do we know she's OK?'

'Just text her if you're so worried. Anyway, I saw the bloke she went with,' said Connie, putting the magazine down and standing to switch off the telly. 'He was rather a stud. If it weren't for her, I might have had a go on it myself.'

At that moment, Michael arrived. A little flustered, he grinned like a Cheshire cat as he made eye contact with Connie.

'Well, then? Are we still virgo intacta?' He asked. 'Or did he nobble your fire exit?'

'I'm not discussing my sex life with you,' Michael laughed.

'Ooh, she's got a sex life!' Chastity batted his eyelids.

74

'Well done, Dolly!' said Connie. 'Has he got a big knob? You're not walking like you've got chapped lips.'

'I'm not complaining,' said Michael, sitting next to Chastity.

'See?' said Connie, flicking Chastity's ear as he walked past into the kitchen.

'Well come on then, what's he like?' Chastity asked excitedly.

'His name's Travis, he lives in Pimlico and he's gorgeous,' Michael gushed.

'Ooh, Pimlico? That's quite posh, now. I was worried she'd taken you to a leather night, it can be a bit aggressive if you've never done anything before.'

'Oh it was nothing like that,' Michael smiled.

'They used to have a hanky code,' Chastity explained. 'You wore a different colour according to your sexual preference. A blue one on the left meant you wanted to shag someone. Vernon wore a yellow one on the right. Trouble is, after a while the colours would run the wash, and then suddenly you're into something completely different.'

'Nothing like that happened,' said Michael. 'He was very gentle and loving. He's a wonderful man.' Suddenly, a short wave of intense disappointment washed over him, as he remembered his last conversation with Travis. There was every chance the mention of boyfriends may have frightened him off.

'Is something wrong?' asked Chastity, concerned.

'No. No everything's fine, thanks. Just a little tired.'

'I could tell she'd had a good seeing to,' said Connie, carrying through three mugs and a teapot.

'She's got a bald patch behind each car where her ankles have been rubbing.'

'What?' Michael was still a little distracted by his thoughts.

'Come on Noddy, you're not in Toyland now!' Connie grinned, pointing at the cups. 'Pour the tea.'

'Not jealous are you, Connie?' Michael laughed, leaning forward to pick up the teapot.

'You know, I went out with a bloke called Travis a couple of times,' said Connie. 'He was a lanky streak of piss, but had a great imagination in the bedroom.'

'I think I remember him,' said Chastity. 'He was very artistic?'

'No, I said he was autistic. That's why I got rid. He trashed Greggs cause they ran out of donuts.'

'Anyway, how's Edith?' asked Michael, passing Chastity his mug.

'She'll be OK, I think. I've left her at mine so she can rest. We've got to arrange Ethel's funeral for her.' Chastity looked concerned.

'What's the matter?' Michael asked.

'You know, I really think you should consider telling her you're her grandson, even if you don't tell her about Fifi just yet? I think she's feeling isolated.' Chastity paused. Michael could see there was more on his mind than just Edith.

'Is there something else?'

'You remember that copper who brought Edith back? She gave me a phone number.'

'For who?'

'Someone Fifi knows in Germany.' He reached into his bag and passed the piece of paper to Michael.

'The Extractor? That sounds scary. Do you suppose it's someone who can help us get her out?'

'I don't know,' said Chastity. 'There's only one way to find out,' he said, reaching forward to grasp the phone from the coffee table.

'You're not phoning Germany from here, are you?' Connie whinged. 'I'm not fuckin' made of money!'

'I'll give you something towards it,' said Michael, as Chastity dialled the number.

'It's ringing!' Chastity grabbed Michael's arm for support. 'Hello? Talky English? Can I speak to The Extractor?'

'I don't like the sound of this,' said Connie, taking a sip of tea.

'Shhh! Chastity said, biting his bottom lip. 'Hello? Is that The Extractor? Fanny whistles by moonlight,' he whispered poignantly, taking a pencil from his pocket and writing notes on the piece of paper as he listened.

'What's he saying?' asked Michael.

'You can't be serious?' The colour drained from Chastity's face. 'How the fuck are we supposed to do that?'

'What? Do what?' said Connie.

'OK. Thank you. Have a nice day.' He put down the receiver.

'What did he say?'

'He told me we've got to break Fifi out of prison.'

'What?' Michael was shocked.

'Then take her to the address I've written down, he'll take care of everything else.'

'Oh, that's just fuckin' marvellous,' spat Connie, reaching for another cigarette. 'Can you believe it? I'm not getting involved with this, we'll end up behind bars ourselves!'

As Connie's tirade continued, Michael's mobile phone vibrated with a text from Travis. Fearing he was about to be dumped, he held his breath and cautiously opened the message: "Not mean 2 upset handsum. Can explain. Meet 2nite pizza?"

Billy's bar in Southend-on-Sea had not yet opened for the night. A pungent smell of stale beer and sweat hung in the air, accompanied by the faint music of fruit machines waiting to entice willing gamblers. A dull shaft of light streaming in through the front windows illuminated a cloud of cigarette smoke before casting long grubby patterns on the threadbare red patterned carpet, as if to shine a spotlight on several cigarette butts already trodden into the pile.

'Nobody gets one over on me,' growled Billy, pacing the floor with frustration.

'Why won't you tell me what's going on?' asked Knuckles, sitting at a nearby table with a pint of lager.

'That Soho bitch filmed me. She's blackmailing me and I ain't fuckin' having it.'

'What 's she got a film of?'

'That's none of your fuckin' business,' Billy screamed angrily. He ran his hand across the top of the counter, swiping a collection of dirty pint glasses through the air. As they hit the floor with a loud crash, his new barmaid rushed in to see from the back storeroom. 'Fuck off!' he yelled at her. Without question, she quickly ran back out.

'Billy, you're trashing the place, mate,' said Knuckles calmly, flicking a few fragments of broken glass off of his table. 'If she's got you on film, let's just take the boys in and get it back.'

'It ain't that simple. There's a copy at some security firm or other. I need to get that film back.'

'This is all Michael's fault, fuckin' nonce. I think we should finish him off,' suggested Knuckles, lighting another cigarette.

'But she's protecting him. If we do anything to Michael, she'll use the film to grass me up.'

'Then get another firm to do it. The Burke Brothers, they owe us a favour. Just don't do it at her venue, she'll be none the wiser.' He took another sip of lager.

'Somewhere randomly, in the street.' Billy's eyes lit up with diabolical excitement.

'He's queer, ain't he? Let's give him a bash,' laughed Knuckles.

'Yeah. But don't kill him, not yet. Just damage him, fuck him up real good. I want him to suffer big time before I slit his throat!'

Back in Soho, Nigel coughing up a fur ball on Connie's bed had diverted attention away from his rant.

'I'm gonna shoot that hideous fuckin' creature,' he screamed. Rushing from the kitchen with a damp cloth, he stormed into the bedroom, unceremoniously ejecting the cat and slamming the door shut. With a loud self-pitying miaow, Nigel jumped up onto Michael's lap to lick his wounds.

'Don't worry,' he said, stroking back down the fur on his back and kissing him on the head, 'I'll find us somewhere else to live, soon.'

'Ooh, talking of prisons, I almost forgot.' Chastity took an envelope from his bag and handed it to Michael. 'It's a visiting order from Fifi for next week.'

'It's just for me and you, isn't it?' said Michael, prising it open and looking at the small leaf of paper inside.

'Yes,' whispered Chastity. 'I think only two can visit at a time, like in hospital. Don't worry about Bonnie Parker in there, she won't want to go, anyway.'

'Hopefully, by then we'll have figured a way to break her out.'

'Yes,' Chastity agreed. 'And there's a letter.' Michael pulled it from the envelope and began to read.

'Oh,' he sighed, disappointedly. 'She doesn't say very much, does she?'

'She can't put much because the screws all read it before it's posted,' said Chastity. 'I saw it on an episode of Dempsey and Makepeace.'

'She wants us to take her in some clothes?'

'Yes, we're gonna need the key to her apartment,' said Chastity, wrapping his scarf back around his neck. 'Come on, let's go down to Fifi's office and see if we can find it.'

At that moment, Connie walked back out from the bedroom, holding the soiled cloth aloft with a rubber glove. 'Where are you going?' he snapped.

'Downstairs,' said Chastity.

'Oh that's it, go on. Leave me to breastfeed the fuckin' cat!'

'No, you're coming with us in case Lettie's there. You're in just the perfect mood to create a distraction.'

The staircase from Sugar Sugar's entrance down to the bar was very dark. Chastity, Connie and Michael clung to each other as they tiptoed slowly across the customer area.

'We'll hide behind the bar till the coast is clear,' whispered Chastity, grabbing Michael by the sleeve and pulling him towards the counter. 'You know what you have to do, don't you?' he called back. Connie nodded, continuing onto Fifi's office.

After standing outside for a moment to get his story straight, he threw open the door to reveal Lettie sitting with his feet up on Fifi's desk, eating an enormous chocolate éclair. The room was a mess. Paperwork was randomly strewn everywhere, as were clothes, costumes, empty champagne bottles and bits of half-eaten food. The shock of this unexpected visitor's sudden appearance made Lettie gag on his cake. Taking his feet down, he leaned forward coughing, signalling for assistance by way of a thump on the back. Connie didn't respond.

'All that liposuction won't last if you keep stuffing your fat gob,' he said, shaking his head in exaggerated disgust. Swigging back a drink from his cocktail glass, Lettie caught his breath.

'I could have choked to death,' he wheezed, wiping his mouth with a sheet of blotting paper from the desk.

'Better luck next time, Dolly,' smiled Connie, sarcastically.

'What do you want?'

'There's a leak in my ceiling. Water pisses in every time it rains, you've got to fix your roof.' Connie wagged his finger.

'Why would you worry? You can't drown a witch.'

'Oh, so it's just between Chastity and Lulu now then, is it?'

'What do you mean?' Lettie's eyes thinned suspiciously.

'Well, if I'm not going, you won't be needing my flat, will you?' Connie had him cornered. As Chastity had guessed, Lettie had no intention of sacking anybody and returning to the show. But believing he had all three drags plotting against each other, for the moment, he had to maintain the deceit. Reluctantly, he stood and beckoned Connie to follow, leading him out of Fifi's office and through a door at the end of the small corridor.

As they disappeared up the concrete staircase, Chastity and Michael crept from behind the bar.

'Where does that go?' Michael asked, straining his neck to see.

'It's the fire exit to the roof.'

'If the building was on fire, the last place I'd want to be is on the fuckin' roof!'

'No, all the roofs in Soho are joined by interconnecting metal staircases and walkways,' explained Chastity. 'In an emergency, you just climb across from one building to another until you find a staircase down. It's all very Chim Chiminee.' He looked around the room. 'Look at this mess! I told you she was a lazy bitch. Still, at least there'll be less chance of her noticing anything's missing.' He opened the top drawer of the filing cabinet.

'I'll check in here,' said Michael, jumping behind the desk. In the front drawer on top of a small black book was a big vintage key. He held it up to look at it in the light. Cast in iron, it was very heavy with a gothic barley-twist stem, which wrapped around the handle like the trained branches of a tree. It had a mystical feel, as though emanating with a natural, unearthly pagan energy. Michael instinctively knew it would somehow be important to him. Blowing off the thick layer of dust, he could faintly see a relief of three intertwined letters.

'Look at this. It says, C.A.C.' He held it up. It glinted as the glow from the table lamp reflected off of its bevelled rim.

'That can't be her apartment key,' said Chastity, squinting his eyes for a closer look. 'She doesn't live with The Addams Family.'

'And there's this,' said Michael, flicking through the little black book. 'Here's Verity's number,' he grinned, shoving it into his pocket with the key.

'Here they are,' said Chastity, holding aloft a fob of keys. Michael could see the name Withering Heights stamped into the small brass plate. 'That's her apartment block!'

Suddenly, they could hear Lettie and Connie descending the concrete steps from the roof. Chastity grabbed Michael's hand, as they ran quietly back out across the customer area and up the stairs to the front entrance.

Pausing in the lobby, Chastity held Michael back for a moment. 'I've had a thought,' he said, screwing up his face to think. 'I wonder if the fire escape across the roofs leads to Creighton Cross' office? We could climb over there tonight after the show and break in.'

'I can't, I'm meeting Travis after work,' said Michael. 'I've got to go, it's really important.'

'Don't worry, it's fine, I'll take Connie. She's picked up that many men in the dark, she's practically a bat. We can use her sonar. There must be some kind of evidence in there somewhere.' He noticed the look of concern on Michael's face. 'This Travis... is it love?'

'I can't stop thinking about him. And every time I do, my heart flutters and my stomach goes all funny. It just feels so right, and I want to be with him all the time.'

'Sounds like love,' smiled Chastity, squeezing his hand. Michael nodded his head, sighing dejectedly.

'Trouble is, I'm not convinced he loves me back.'

In the dressing room later that night, Michael stood in shock as Connie rolled on the floor at his feet, hysterical with laughter.

'Prince Philip?' he screamed.

'Get up you silly mare, making a show of yourself,' Chastity frowned.

'Surely it can't be true?' Michael was dumfounded.

'That's what she told me. But then, you know Edith?'

'She's a fruit loop short of a breakfast!' chuckled Connie, climbing back into his chair.

'You wanna watch yourself,' Chastity warned. 'You'll end up in The Tower being pecked at by ravens.'

'She wouldn't look out of place amongst all them Beefeaters,' added Michael, checking his long red corkscrew wig in the mirror.

'Eating beef is what I do best,' Connie sighed, dabbing his lipstick with a tissue. 'So she's a queen and a prince? Hope you're not expecting me to curtsey?'

'You might try,' Michael teased.

'I like Prince William the best,' mused Connie. 'He can land his chopper on my patch any day!'

As Michael's backing track began to play, he hesitated on the steps to the stage. 'You don't suppose it could help us get Fifi out of prison, do you?'

'I doubt it, love,' said Chastity. 'The best you can hope for is a Corgi named after you.'

The music swelled from a drumroll and heraldic trumpets echoed as Michael walked slowly to the front of the stage. Wearing a gothic, long-sleeved red velvet gown topped with a gold medieval crown, he looked every bit Arthurian royalty. Thunder roared and lightning flashed as he began to sing his dramatic ballad, as if chanting his pagan incantation from the parapet of some long lost mystical castle.

'If I fell from a star, would I land in his heart? If I rose from the sea, would he be true to me?' He waved his arms dramatically, as if to awaken the very dead from their sleep.

'Earth, wind and fire, ignite his desire, bring passion to its knees. Lightning and rain, empower me again, and bring that man to me. As trees reach from the land, make love grow in this man.' He span around and thrust his open hands into the air, weaving his witchcraft for the enthralled audience.

'Planets above, infuse him with love, for no one else but me. Potions and charms, bring him to my arms, and make my life complete. Avalon, hear my spell. Pluck wishes from the well. Spin dreams and

make him fall, be mine forever more.' With a loud clap of thunder and a pyrotechnic puff of smoke, as if by magic, the queen had vanished.

CHAPTER SEVEN

Michael paused before walking into Pizza Hut. Standing on the wide littered pavement, he looked around at the hustle and bustle of cars, taxis and busses flooding the streets. People of every colour, religion and nationality were going about their late night business with their own cares, worries and problems. Was he the only one feeling as though his dreams were about to be shattered? Taking a deep breath, he grasped the door handle and pushed inside.

The restaurant was practically overflowing with an effervescent Soho buzz. Customers were eating, talking and laughing. In one corner, a group of inebriated young women in matching schoolgirl costumes were loudly taking selfies of themselves with a brunette girl, who wore learner plates and a faux bridal veil. Right in front of him were a middle-aged couple, staring longingly into each other's eyes and holding hands across the table. They appeared so happy and in love. Could his life ever be like theirs?

In a small alcove at the other end of the room, he could see Travis looking at his watch impatiently. With a gulp, Michael nervously walked along the aisle to the side of the table. Suddenly Travis' face lit up, as he jumped to his feet and pulled Michael into a hug.

'Hiya, handsome,' he grinned, pecking him on the lips. 'I've already ordered for us, but I was so worried you weren't gonna come.' His eyes sparkled as he sat back down.

'Why would you think that?' said Michael, sitting opposite.

'Well, I know I upset you and I'm sorry. I'm really, really sorry.' He reached across to hold Michael's hands.

'I didn't think you'd want to see me again.'

'I do, I really do. Do you forgive me?' Travis feigned a guilty puppy-dog frown.

'There's nothing to forgive,' Michael smiled. 'I shouldn't have mentioned the B word.'

'The thing is,' said Travis, taking a deep breath. 'I came down to London five years ago so that I could live my own life. I'm the youngest of six, the only boy. My father's a bit of a traditionalist. He's not an ogre, but I could never tell him I'm gay. He just wouldn't cope. And I could never lie to him.' He picked up a cardboard beermat and began picking at the side. 'My eldest sister Morag knows, though she'd never say anything. I had to tell someone.'

'It must be very difficult for you,' said Michael sympathetically.

'It is. Do your family know you're gay?'

'I grew up an orphan,' said Michael, biting his lip. How could he even begin to explain his relationship with Fifi and Edith, let alone Prince Philip?

'Aye, I'm so sorry,' said Travis, slapping his own forehead with embarrassment. 'And there's me whinging on, complaining about family to someone who hasn't got one.'

'It's OK, really it is. I want to know everything about you.'

'Since I've been in London, I've dedicated my very soul to three boyfriends,' Travis continued.

'When I fall for someone, I fall very hard. So, for me, it's gotta be all or nothing, that's just the way I am. But then come the lies! I just can't cope with the lies.'

'What do you mean?' asked Michael, fidgeting in his seat.

'They all lied to me. Boyfriends lie and it destroys me every time.'

'Oh.'

'That's why I've got the playroom in my flat. I don't have to get emotionally involved with anyone in there. But you're different. I like you, Michael. I like you a lot. You're adorable! I can't stop thinking about you, you're doing my head in, man!' Travis gushed. 'I've never met anyone like you. In fact, I could so very easily fall in love with you. But, do you feel the same?'

'Yes, yes I do, very much,' said Michael desperately.

'But you've got to promise me one thing? Never lie to me, about anything, however insignificant. Can you promise me that?'

This was serious. He really didn't want to deceive Travis, but he had already lied about his job and quite possibly his family. He knew that right now in this moment, he would without hesitation abandon drag and become a barman just to be able to say he had been honest. They'd only met twenty-four hours before, but already he couldn't imagine life without him. Perhaps he should just come clean and admit everything here and now? Michael's heart would surely break if Travis walked away, but at least he would be honouring the feelings of the man he loved.

At that moment, their pizza arrived. Large and with a deep-crust, it was loaded with pepperoni, tomatoes, sweetcorn and peppers. Michael gasped as he noticed the pizza had been made in the shape of a heart. It was now or never, what should he do?

'I promise,' he whispered, eyes watering with guilt. As the waitress walked away, Travis stood from the table and knelt on one knee at Michael's side. He offered up a small, green velvet ring box.

'Will you be my boyfriend?' he grinned impishly. Michael took the box and tipped open the lid. Inside was a small white button-badge of a red heart with the slogan Boyfriends R Us. Seeing Travis on one knee, the other customers in the restaurant applauded with delight. The waiters and waitresses stopped what they were doing and cheered in support, even the hen party whooped and whistled.

Overwhelmed with contradicting emotions at this unexpected proposal, Michael finally began to cry, as he uttered the words, 'Yes, I will.'

Chastity and Connie had been hiding in Sugar Sugar's dressing room toilet for nearly an hour, waiting for the venue to close. As everything finally fell silent, they crept slowly out and into the darkened customer area.

'Thank fuck we're out of there, it stinks,' whinged Connie, taking several deep breaths. 'You can tell Edith's not been here lately with her toilet duck. It smells like the green room on Last Of The Summer Wine.'

'I didn't think we'd be in there as long as that, but I think everyone's gone,' said Chastity, shining his torch around the venue. Both dressed head-to-foot in black like two deranged cat burglars, they crept silently across the room to the fire escape door and up the concrete stairs.

Pushing open the door onto the roof, Chastity grabbed hold of the doorframe, holding his stomach in distress.

'What's the matter with you?' asked Connie, unsympathetically.

'Heights! You know I can't do heights without a few drinks inside me, it makes me giddy.'

'You've always been giddy, come on!' Connie pushed him from behind, out into the middle of the roof. With a loud tearing sound, Chastity plunged to the floor with a thud. 'Now look what you've done,' Connie screeched, pointing his torch. 'You've torn the felt right off! That's my lounge under there, it's gonna be like Niagara Falls next time it rains.'

'Yeah well, you shouldn't have pushed me. Help me up, you emaciated clout!' Chastity reached out his hand, but Connie just stepped over him and lit a cigarette.

'I've bought the fireworks for our Bonfire Night display, so you owe me twenty quid. We can set them up there by that parapet, like we did last year.'

'Twenty quid?' groaned Chastity, climbing painfully to his feet.

'Well, I'm not inviting Lettie this year,' said Connie, glancing over the side of the roof at the bustling street below. 'Mind you, if Lulu comes, we could split it three ways as usual, thirteen quid each. And if he brings that bloke he's rogering, it'll only be a tenner.'

'Perhaps we should invite Edith? Apparently, every year she'd watch the fireworks with Ethel. It was the only thing they ever did together, I think she's gonna miss it very much.'

'Hmm,' said Connie, flicking his cigarette ash over the side.

'Mind you, it doesn't look secure enough up here anymore, not for setting off gunpowder.'

Chastity shone his torch around the platform. A loose patchwork of lead, felt and temporary plastic sheeting moved with the breeze, and several bricks across the front of the parapet were missing cement, merely balanced on the narrow ledge above the heads of unsuspecting passers-by in the street below. Clumps of slimy brown and green moss peppered the floor, and several huge tree-like weeds were growing out of the stair dormer.

'That's what I told Lettie. But she don't give a fuck, so long as she's got a chocolate éclair stuffed down her screech.' Connie trod his cigarette out and zipped up his jacket. 'Anyway, let's get this over with, come on.'

Chastity followed him onto a narrow metal walkway, leading across the flat roof of the adjoining building.

'I don't like this at all,' groaned Chastity, edging sideways past a section with a missing handrail. 'Bits have dropped off, it's not safe!'

'Just don't look down, keep looking ahead,' encourage Connie.

'This better be worth it!'

'She should be here doing this, not us. Sitting there eating pizza in the warm, it's her father that's in prison and it's her inheritance,' said Connie, springing over a small gap in the platform to the next building.

'It's our problem, too. We've got to get rid of Lettie, we need evidence.' Chastity gasped with horror as he looked down the gap at the thirty-foot drop to the alleyway below.

'Just jump,' said Connie. 'You'll be alright.'

'How can you think that?' panicked Chastity.

'Because you wouldn't fit through that hole! Just got for it... imagine you're trying to reach for pie and chips.'

'Aargh!' cried Chastity, lurching to one side and grabbing the handrail.

'What?'

'A gust of wind threw me off balance.'

'Must have been a very big gust,' smirked Connie. 'It wouldn't be the first time I'd been blown off on a rooftop.'

'Can you just get your mind out of the guttering and help me come over it?' said Chastity.

'That's exactly what he said to me at the time!' Connie smiled, grabbing Chastity by the arms and yanking him unceremoniously across the abyss.

Reaching a small platform at the back of Creighton Cross' office, Chastity could finally catch his breath for a moment.

'I'm not fit enough for this malarkey anymore,' he said panting, sitting on a wooden crate. Connie put his fingers behind a sheet of plywood covering a window to one side. Putting his foot on the wall below for leverage, he managed to rip it free, nails popping through the rotting grain.

'This'll do,' he said, lifting open the sash window and climbing inside.

'Help me in,' Chastity gasped, dragging across the crate to stand on.

'Can't you do it yourself?' Connie sighed.

'We're supposed to be working together. When I becomes we, illness becomes wellness,' preached Chastity.

'Ah, fuck off!' said Connie, grabbing him by the lapels and pulling him inside.

Creighton's office was a mess. Old abandoned cupboard doors and drawers lay open, and paperwork littered the top of a large mid-century desk. There were light patches on the heavily varnished wood-panelled walls where pictures had been removed, and a pungent musk of damp hung in the air.

'The smell in here's worse than that toilet,' said Connie, covering his nose with his woollen scarf. 'And you can tell Lettie's been here, look at all this clutter.'

'She's a clutteris,' Chastity smiled. 'Where do we start?'

'Gawd knows,' said Connie, opening a drawer in the desk. 'What are we looking for, exactly?'

'Just anything that looks like it may be relevant.'

'Look at this.' Connie held up a large vintage cast iron key. 'It says, C.A.C.'

'Ooh, that's just like the one Lulu found in Fifi's office!'

'What's it for?'

'I don't know, but I think we should keep it,' said Chastity, pulling a folded plastic Waitrose bag from his inside pocket. As he laid his torch on the desk to put the key into the bag, something caught his eye. 'Look at this,' he said, reading the front of a tatty box file.

'What?'

'This here. It says, Creighton Cross Holdings versus Cohen Property Services.' Chastity opened the lid and glanced inside. It contained a singular sheet of typed paper, torn at the corner where it had been ripped from a larger file.

'So?'

'That's Lettie's surname... Cohen. Perhaps it's got something to do with getting her claws on Creighton's will?'

'Stick it in the bag,' Connie nodded. Opening the door of a long cupboard, he noticed something that made his blood curdle. 'Argh!' he jumped.

'What? What is it?' Chastity said, running to join him. Connie pointed at a large clump of matted black fur lying in the bottom corner.

'It's a dead cat!' he cried. 'Oh, I feel sick now.' Chastity poked at it with the butt of his torch.

'It's not a cat, it's a wig,' he said, lifting it up for a closer look.

'Perhaps it's one of Lettie's? We know Creighton liked cross-dressers.'

'No, it can't be Lettie's. There's no way a Jewish woman would ever let a wig get into that sort of state.'

Shuddering off the shock, Connie crossed to a large window at the back of the room. He wiped dust from the pane with his sleeve and looked out. 'This must be the one he fell out of, there's still some police tape stapled to the frame outside.' Chastity darted across to look.

'That's creepy,' he said. 'This is where he actually died!'

'No, this is where he fell from, he died down there.' He lifted the sash to look into the grey back alley two floors below. 'I'm still convinced Lettie

95

pushed him. The sill's too high to fall out accidentally. Probably just after he signed his will over to her, the silly old bugger.'

There was a morbid silence, as they pondered what Creighton might have suffered. Though he had been known for being a shrewd and tough business tyrant, he had always been very friendly and kind to everyone who worked for Fifi. An icy shudder ran up Chastity's spine.

'Mary, mother of the blessed drag queen... I think he's here!' he said, crossing himself and kissing an imaginary rosary.

'Ooh, don't say that. He ain't, is he?' whined Connie, eyes darting around the darkened room. 'It was her idea, not mine,' he called out to the shadows, pointing at Chastity. 'I didn't want to come!'

'Do you think we should go?' Chastity turned to leave, but Connie caught his sleeve.'

'Wait a minute,' he said, pointing out of the window. 'Across there, that building at the back, the arched skylight window... where is that?'

'I don't know,' said Chastity. 'Why do you ask?'

'Because I think I've seen it somewhere before!'

Michael had decided to walk back to Soho from Pimlico. Despite the cutting breeze, the morning sun was warm on his face, and he still had a glow in his chest from spending another dreamy night with his new boyfriend. Having thought he would be rejected in Pizza Hut the night before, he hadn't bothered to take clean clothes. Over breakfast, Travis had suggested he use something from his wardrobe. He'd chosen a distinctive lime shirt with contrasting red stripes and a matching green baseball cap. They felt comforting against his skin, as did the borrowed Calvin Klein underpants. Pinned proudly to the left lapel of his jacket was the badge that Travis had so romantically given him.

Walking beside the Thames, he pushed in his earphones and searched his iPod. He really wanted to play something sugary and romantic, but instead thought it a good idea to begin learning one of the two remaining songs. Chastity was right. It was essential they convince Lettie that a completely new show was being created, if only to prevent any further disasters. Although he was looking forward to his drag performance that night, it served as a reminder of the lies he had told Travis. Perhaps Chastity's wisdom would also help him find a solution?

Turning into Old Compton Street, he decided to listen to the backing track one more time before reaching Connie's. As he approached the side alley to the flat, he didn't notice Billy's Daimler, parked at the kerb opposite Sugar Sugar's entrance. Oblivious to any danger, he hummed away and bobbed his head back and forth to the music, as Knuckles cunningly took several photographs of him from the driver's seat.

'I can't make head nor tail of this,' said Michael, sitting on Connie's sofa staring at the typed sheet of paper from Creighton's office.

'Who's Edna Tail?' asked Edith, taking a sip of her tea.

'It's all herein, forthwith and ipso facto. And what does demurrer mean?'

'That's what I thought,' said Chastity.

'And we found that,' said Connie, looking up from his sewing machine to point at the old key on the sideboard. Michael jumped up and grabbed it from the shelf, holding it in the light from the window.

'That's exactly the same as the one I found in Fifi's office,' he gasped, reaching into his holdall to pull out the other. 'C.A.C. But what are they both for?'

'Keep them together, only time will tell,' said Chastity, lighting a cigarette.

'Is anything organised for Ethel's send-off yet?' Michael asked sheepishly, sitting back down.

'Yes, it's at The Woolwich Centre crematorium early next week.' Chastity grasped Edith's hand. 'We're going to see her in the Chapel of Rest just before.'

'Sorry I've not been here for you, Edie,' said Michael.

'That's alright, duck.' She beamed at him, eyes twinkling. 'You've gotta chase romance where you can, you don't know when you'll get another chance.'

'That's right, love,' Chastity agreed.

'It must be love,' Connie chipped in. 'I've not seen that shirt before, Dolly?'   'Ah, wearing his clothes? That's a good sign,' Chastity smiled.

'I only borrowed it,' Michael blushed.

'Anyway, Edith's got some news,' encouraged Chastity.

'I've got a budgie!' she grinned. 'Chastity bought him for me to keep me company. He's got lavender-blue feathers with a little white smudge on his head.'

'Oh, congratulations!' said Michael, leaning across to kiss her on the cheek. 'What are you going to call him?'

'Caligula.'

'After the Roman Emperor?' Michael was baffled. 'Wasn't he a bit of a tyrant?'

'No, duck,' Edith laughed. 'After my greengrocer's dog! He had a lovely temperament, always wagging his tail when you went in. He didn't have any eyelashes.'

'The dog?'

'No, the greengrocer! Cause he used to light his fags on the toaster,' she giggled. 'Happy days! Trouble is, I don't think he likes heights.'

'The greengrocer?'

'No, Caligula! All he does is waddle around on the carpet. Every time I put him up high, he just jumps back down again.'

'A budgie that don't like heights? I've heard it all now,' Connie sighed, jiggling around his worktable.

'What's wrong?' asked Chastity.

'This thing's wobbly. It's like Heather Mills McCartney, it needs a couple of beer mats under one leg.' He picked up a magazine from the sideboard and knelt to fold it under the front leg, but something on the page caught his eye. 'Here it is!' he said, passing the magazine to Chastity. 'That arched skylight window we saw from Creighton's office, I knew I'd seen it somewhere before.'

Chastity rested his cigarette on the rim of the ashtray and looked at the picture. It was a photo-shoot of a young female with pink hair and a matching silk dress, draped dramatically across the sill of the window inside a large minimal white room. She elegantly held out one hand, upon which sat a white dove. Behind her through the glass, he could see the back of Creighton's building.

'Well, would you look at that?' he said, scratching his head. 'Do you suppose someone might have seen something from this window?'

'It's possible,' said Michael, craning his neck to look. 'Perhaps we should go round there and find out where it is?'

'I'm not coming if you're going now. I've got to finish this,' said Connie, reaching for a different magazine and jamming it under the leg.

'Don't rush making things for a new show,' said Chastity.

'No, it's a costume for that fashion competition on page six,' he said, running another length of orange fabric under the needle. 'I've got to make three fabulous outfits, one for each of us. I've got it all planned.' He lifted off the fabric and cut the threads. 'I'm trying to get it done while lover boy here's off shagging.'

'One for each of us?' said Michael. 'I'm not doing no competition!'

'Yes you are,' said Connie. 'I've been babysitting Nigel! You bloody owe me, so you're gonna sing and Chastity's gonna pick up after me.'

'No change there, then,' Chastity sighed.

Hearing his name mentioned, Nigel awoke from his slumber under the television. Looking up, he noticed Michael and ran to jump on his lap.

'Miaow!' he rasped, rubbing his head in his chest.

'Ah, he's missed you, bless him!' said Edith. 'I'll have to introduce him to Caligula.'

'I'm not sure that's a good idea, Edith,' said Chastity. As Michael stroked Nigel's back, he noticed a gritty black substance stuck to his fur.

100

'What's this?' he said, holding it up and sniffing his hand. Chastity gasped.

'Ooh, I think it's gunpowder. Connie, was one of them fireworks leaking?' Leaving the machine, Connie looked around the carpet and noticed a pile of black grains in front of the dresser. He reached behind his bedroom door and pulled out the vacuum cleaner. As it hummed loudly into action, Michael leaned in to whisper to Chastity.

'I need your advice about Travis?'

'If it's anything to do with sex, you're better off asking Connie, love,' Chastity whispered back.

'It's her advice that's got me in this bloody mess!'

'What mess? What's wrong?' Chastity was concerned.

'The drag queen thing, I've made a terrible mistake,' Michael sighed, looking down into his lap as Connie poked the nozzle into the ashtray and sucked its contents.

'I was still smoking that fag,' shouted Chastity over the noise.

'What?' Connie yelled. As he switched off the machine, he noticed the sudden realisation of horror creeping across Chastity's face.

'You... you've been Hoovering gunpowder? And... and you've just sucked up a lit fag?'

'Shit!' Connie screamed, grabbing his cigarettes from the sewing table and dashing into his bedroom.

'Bugger! Chastity cried, pulling Edith swiftly from her chair and running her out to the kitchen.

'Fuck!' Michael threw Nigel over the back of the sofa then bounced off the cushions to join him.

BOOM! The walls of Connie's flat shook as the vacuum cleaner exploded into a thousand pieces, piercing ornaments on the sideboard, smashing the glass coffee table and throwing all of the furniture backwards. Pictures flew from the walls and lampshades were knocked from the ceiling pendants, as the room billowed with a massive cloud of dust, dirt, paper, sequins and remnants of costume fabric.

A few moments later, Chastity poked his head round the door, spluttering as he waved the dust away from his face.

'Oh my God! It looks like the tram crash on Coronation Street!'

'Bloody hell, Connie!' coughed Michael, climbing from under the overturned sofa. Connie stepped out of the bedroom, lighting a cigarette as he looked at the absolute carnage that used to be his lounge.

'I hated that old Hoover, anyway,' he sighed. 'What I need is a nice little Goblin.'

CHAPTER EIGHT

Even with Daisy's help, it had taken several long hours for Michael, Chastity and Edith to help Connie clear up his apartment. They had filled a whole roll of bin bags with rubbish, which Michael had covertly distributed between the dumpsters of several nearby restaurants. Edith had wisely advised to start dusting at the top and work down so the dirt would settle on the ground, and Daisy had carried up the vacuum cleaner from the bar to suck up the last of the mess. As cleaning progressed, the stack of grubby linen next to the washing machine had grown higher and higher, including most of Michael's clothes.

But despite the camaraderie of everyone chipping in and working together, there was sadness and worry in the air. The moment the front door had been opened for the first time since the loud bang, Nigel had bolted down the stairs and away up the alley. Michael had walked around the whole of Soho calling out his name, searching in every conceivable hiding place, but to no avail. By the time they had finished clearing up, had a wash and something to eat, it was already time to prepare for that evening's show and Nigel still hadn't returned.

The mood was understandably solemn in the Sugar Sugar dressing room, as Michael, Chastity and Connie prepared for their performance.

'I quite like it, actually,' said Connie, trying to lighten the mood. 'I've got uncluttered surface and clean lines, very minimal.'

'Like an STD clinic,' smirked Chastity, stepping into a tatty, torn dress adorned with faded pink bows and dirty lace. 'Anyway, it's about time the place was cleaned, even your dusters and polish under the sink had cobwebs on them.' He turned to Connie to zip him up.

'My ears are still ringing,' said Michael, poking in a little finger and wiggling. 'We could have been killed.'

'It was my tribute to the great Dusty Springfield, the patron saint of dust,' Connie smiled.

'I'm so worried about Nigel,' Michael sighed. 'He's not used to living on the streets. Anything could happen.'

'Edith's upstairs in case he comes back, and Daisy's looking out for him on the door. There's not much else we can do for now, love.' Chastity pulled on a large matted wig. Ginger, grey and brown, its split ends stuck out in every direction, as if caught in a hurricane.

'He'll be alright, he's a fighter,' said Connie, sympathetically. Despite his allergy to cats and his constant whinging about Nigel, he had actually become quite fond of him over time.

'Tell you what,' said Chastity. 'If we've not heard anything by the interval, why don't you finish early and go look for him again? We'll do the second half, won't we Connie?'

'Sure, go find the little bugger,' Connie smiled. Michael was moved by the support of his dear friends,

104

especially Connie, who he'd have expected to react quite differently.

'OK I will, thanks,' he said, applying glue to his eyelashes. 'I'll see if I can find out where that arched window is on my way round.'

As the dirty rock n' roll saxophones of Chastity's opening backing track swung out from the loud speakers, he shuffled his grubby moccasins aimlessly to the front of the stage. With a vague, deranged expression across his Baby Jane Hudson face, he looked as if he'd just stepped out from the epicentre of Connie's untimely explosion.

'She's a mess, my friend. She's got tits right down to there. She's a wreck, my friend. Things are growing in her hair. She looks like road-kill in a frock. A puppet made from some old sock. Eyes like marbles, skin like slate. Teeth like some old garden gate,' he growled, chattering his molars at the laughing audience.

'*She's a mess, my friend. She's got ears like dinner plates. With a droopy head, like a ball that won't inflate. Her nose is twisted to one side. She smells like something that's just died. Her breath could strip paint from a door. Her toenails chisel up the floor.'* He pulled at his grey ankle socks.

'She's a mess, my friend. Her knuckles drag the ground. Her bum's so big, that her arsehole can't be found.' Thrusting his hand up his skirt, he pulled at his knickers and shook his leg out to one side, as if to release some loose bit of canker.

'To see her face could send you mad. She has to wear a plastic bag. From my mirror, I despair. She looks back with a vacant stare. My friend!'

105

Having left the show early and checked with Edith that Nigel had not returned, Michael wandered around Soho again. Very worried and close to tears, he began by checking all the places he had searched earlier in the day before extending further out. Although still not too late in the evening, there were already drunken revellers shouting and falling about, which he found more disturbing than usual. The thought of what any one of them may have done to Nigel if he had gone to them for help didn't bear thinking about.

His expedition made him realise he had never before really explored the vast array of vintage buildings squeezed so tightly together in this relatively small footprint of central London, from the busy shopping parade of Oxford Street in the north to theatreland's very own Shaftesbury Avenue in the south. Layer upon layer of history, flourishing in a divine harmony of adventure and vice. It was as if he could feel the beating heart of the city beneath his very feet. He finally arrived at its centre, the dark open greenery of Soho Square. Wondering if Nigel might be hiding somewhere in the bushes, he pushed at the black metal gates but they were locked shut for the night. Walking around the paved perimeter, he called out his name through the spiked railings.

'I'd give up if I were you, love,' shouted a pink, fluffy old drunk from the other side of the road. His equally inebriated friend gave a thumbs-up in agreement.

'What?' Michael called back. Leaning his friend gently against the wall, the man teetered across the damp cobbles and took hold of Michael's arm.

'This Nigel?' he slurred, pointing at the hedgerow. 'If he's in there love, Willy Wonka's probably already entered the chocolate factory!'

'Nigel's my cat,' said Michael, pulling away.

'What did he say?' called out his friend.

'Don't you see?' the man whispered poignantly, tapping the side of his nose as if to accentuate his wisdom. 'You think you've found the love of your life, but in reality, you can't trust no one.'

Already deeply upset by Nigel's disappearance, a sunken despair filled Michael's chest as his mind turned to his own betrayal of Travis.

'What did he say?' the friend repeated impatiently.

'He's looking for a pussy!' the old drunk screamed, the exertion of his loud response throwing him momentarily backwards against the railings.

'Oh, I can't be bothered with breeders!' came the reply. 'Come on, Doris.' Wobbling precariously towards each other, they managed to meet in the middle of the road, clinging on and laughing as they made their way off towards the bus stop.

As he watched them disappear beyond the corner, a tall thin Victorian building next to a scaffolded works site suddenly caught Michael's attention. The red brick of the lower level reflected the streetlights, while the upper floors faded into the darkness above, roof silhouetted against moonlit clouds. He stood and stared for a moment as his eyes adjusted to the shadows. Just above the light of the front elevation was a big arched window like the one he had seen in Connie's magazine. He crossed the road to get a closer look at the big brass nameplate beside the front entrance.

'Armitage Photographic Studios,' he muttered to himself. 'This must be the place that overlooks Creighton's office.'

Suddenly, he heard a distant raspy voice call him from somewhere nearby. His attention turned to the site next door. Squeezing himself between the scaffold and plastic security sheath strapped all around the outside, he climbed in, squinting to see in the bright orange glow from street lamps shining through the white sheeting.

'Nigel?' he called back, grabbing the scaffold pole in anticipation.

'Miaow!' came the response. Having heard his voice, his beloved cat raced excitedly up from behind a pile of cement bags to greet him. Michael picked him up and hugged him close to his heart.

'Where have you been? I've been so worried about you. Why didn't you come back?'

'Miaow!' he purred loudly, rubbing his face around Michael's neck and chin.

'You're so cold and wet, let me get you back home.' Climbing back out, he stopped momentarily to look at a large plastic sign strapped to the front of the scaffold. "Three brand new luxury apartments and a penthouse available soon." Michael chuckled. 'It's a lovely idea Nigel, but we're never gonna be able to afford to live somewhere like this!'

As soon as Michael had put Nigel inside Connie's front door, he had darted into the corner behind the television, and there he had stayed for the best part of a week. Venturing out only briefly for food and to use his litter tray in the bathroom, the shock of the explosion seemed to have stayed with him, despite everyone's best efforts to encourage him otherwise. Although Travis had invited Michael to stay every evening, he had spent a few nights on Connie's sofa in an attempt to support his cat, but with no success.

'I can see its little beady eyes staring out at me,' said Connie, beavering away at his sewing machine. 'Like The Pussy of the Baskervilles.'

'He probably thinks it's your fault,' said Chastity, picking at his finger.

'It was her fault!' said Michael. 'We could have all been killed.'

'You don't have to live here,' Connie snapped. 'Why don't you move in with your grandmother?'

'Nigel can't live there because of Caligula,' Michael explained.

'Just put him in a different room,' said Connie.

'I can't stay there,' said Michael, defensively. 'The roof leaks in the spare bedroom, Ethel told me.'

'Use a bucket,' snapped Connie.

'You'd know more about that than me,' Michael bitched.

'Stop it you two! Michael's right,' said Chastity. 'I took Edith home last night to pick up some things before the funeral. Her house is falling apart, there's mould and damp everywhere. No bathroom, and I can't believe she's still using an outside toilet. I'm not even sure she should be living there.'

'If she's shagged royalty, get them to bloody sort it out,' said Connie. 'Take it to the papers, I fucking would!'

'She is going to need someone living with her before too long, if we can just find a way to get her house repaired,' Chastity continued. 'You know, last night she put three Cup-a-Soup sachets in one mug. It was like plaster of Paris, I had to scrape it out with a knife. And she puts a teacloth over the budgie every time someone swears on telly.'

'It's easy. Get the place fixed up, then he can lodge there and look after her instead of getting up my fucking nose,' said Connie, standing from the table and holding up a black and white costume. 'Here, try this on,' he said, pulling Chastity from his chair.

'I don't see why not.' said Chastity, putting his arms into the sleeves. 'She has got a point.' He smiled sheepishly at Michael. 'Her sister's got a different lodger every week.'

'Yeah, she's up the gut again,' added Connie, pinning around the left cuff.

'Again? How many kids is that now?'

'Six, if you include Nobby, though he's the runt of the litter. She lost the last one.'

'Oh, that's really sad,' said Michael, trying to be sympathetic.

'It's not sad, it's careless. She left it outside Asda in its pram and forgot the bloody thing was there.' Connie stood back for a moment, admiring his handy work. 'Every one of them's got a different father. It's cause we used to have sleepovers when were kids, it's a hard habit to break. Now she's always got some bloke or other sleeping over.'

'Like sister, like brother,' Michael whispered under his breath.

'What happened to Nobby after he wrecked the ice cream van?' asked Chastity, lifting his other arm.

'They dropped the charges, but he got fired. So he's got another job, fuck knows how,' Connie shook

110

his head in disbelief. 'Apparently, he's a bulb technician.'

'What does he do, sit on the grass and wait for daffodils to grow?' Michael smirked.

'He operates one of them lorries with the long arm on the back that lifts him up to street lamps in a little cradle.'

'That's it!' Chastity cried. 'That's how we can get Fifi out of prison. Hang a rope off the cradle and yank her over the wall!'

'We can't do that... can we?' said Michael.

'How else are we going to do it?' said Chastity. 'I can't smuggle her out in me handbag, can I?'

'You haven't even got room for your gargantuan knickers in there,' smiled Connie sarcastically, lifting off the costume and laying it next to the sewing machine.

'Not spotty Nobby Banister?' Michael threw his head into his hands. 'This is insane! He's too dangerous. Someone could get killed, remember last time? He's depriving some village of an idiot.'

'I don't see we've got any choice,' said Chastity, biting his lip. 'We can tell Fifi when we visit on Friday. Then I'd better phone back The Extractor. Meanwhile, let's walk round and take a look at this photographic studio. Come on, you two.' Brushing a few loose strands of fabric from his sleeve, he reached for his coat.

'You go, I've got to get this finished for the competition,' said Connie, sitting back at the sewing machine. As Chastity and Michael closed the front door behind them, he tiptoed into the hall to check they had gone. Then picking up the phone, he dialled enquiries. 'Hello? Give me Buckingham Palace Press Office.'

Chastity and Michael made their way across a cold and windy Soho Square to the photographic studio.

'Take no notice of Connie,' said Chastity, taking Michael's arm supportively. 'She's a hard-faced bitch, but it's just how she copes with stress.'

'Well actually, when I told Travis about Nigel, he suggested we move in with him.'

'Oh, that's wonderful news, why didn't you say so?' Chastity smiled, pulling him into a hug. 'It'd be good for Nigel I think, and misery guts will be over the moon.'

'Please don't mention it to Connie just yet, it could spell disaster.'

'Why not? Ooh, I feel like Helen Capel in The Spiral Staircase.'

'Because there's a big problem,' Michael sighed, 'and if Connie thinks I'm moving out and it doesn't happen, she'll make my life hell.'

'Are you not going to move, then?'

'I don't know. I've been trying to get you on your own all week to ask your advice.'

'Oh yes, you said. What's wrong?'

'It's Travis. I lied to him. Connie told me not to tell anyone I was a drag queen, so I told him I was just a barman.'

'That's not such a big deal, is it?'

'For Travis it's a really big deal. I haven't even told him the truth about Fifi and Edith. If he finds out I've lied to him, he probably won't want to see me again.' Michael bit his lip, trying not to get emotional.

112

'But I love him, I really do love him. I don't know what to do.'

'Oh, Lulu love, you poor thing! You definitely have to tell him the truth before you make that kind of commitment, especially if that sort of thing is so important to him.' As they crossed the road to the studio's front entrance, Chastity could see the shame on his face. 'Come on chin up, it might not be so bad. So, when do I finally get to meet the man that's captured our Lulu's heart?'

'He's gonna be waiting for me outside tonight after we've finished the show, to help me collect the other half of my stuff. I guess I need to explain everything to him then,' Michael sighed, pushing against the heavy door. 'But there's a real chance he might just tell me to fuck off.'

Inside was a narrow hallway leading to a flight of stairs, at the top of which was the large white room they had seen in Connie's magazine. Photographic lighting umbrellas on metal stands, reflector shields and digital cameras cluttered the room, all flooded with dazzling natural sunlight from the giant arched window. They navigated over the mass of black wires trailing across the wide wooden floorboards to look out at the back of Creighton's office through the mottled vintage glass.

'That's it. That's the window he fell from,' whispered Chastity.

'Can I help you?' They turned to see a short stout man in a pink shirt and white trousers, peering out from a wooden door to one side.

'Ah, yes,' said Chastity, walking forward to shake his hand. 'We're looking for the owner?'

'That's me,' grinned the man. 'Giles Armitage at your service, though my friends call me Bruce.'

'Fancy that!' said Chastity.

'Armitage, like the sanitary ware manufacturers? Our names are in toilets all over London.'

'So is Connie's!' Chastity giggled.

'We were hoping you might be able to help us,' said Michael, pointing through the window. 'A man fell from the back of that building up there. We need to find out if you saw anything?'

'No dear, I'm just back from Sitges,' said Bruce, taking hold of Michael's chin and turning it from side to side. 'Have you ever done modelling?'

'No,' Michael answered, a little embarrassed.

'Take your shirt off, let's have a look at you.'

'I'd rather not,' said Michael.

'Err… it was a while ago,' interrupted Chastity. 'Around the end of August?'

'Oh, I remember that! All the police in the background, what a pain in the arse,' said Bruce, looking at Michael and licking his lips. 'It was a really busy time for us, we were shooting a new fashion line for Eva Minge.'

'Police in the background?' said Chastity, the seed of an idea sprouting.

'Yes dear, they kept getting in shot. We had to stop several times.'

'Do you still have any photos from that time?'

'Yes, we have an archive.' said Bruce, a little vexed. 'But I haven't got time to trawl through all that lot. I'm a busy man.'

'We could do the trawling,' said Chastity, hopefully.

'It would really help us... get to the bottom of things?' flirted Michael, unfastening an extra button on his shirt.

'Well, if you put it like that,' said Bruce, scratching the back of his head. He spun on his wooden clogs and swished across the room to a pile of cardboard folders stacked behind a large white editing bench. Pulling out a file, he placed it on the table. 'Only be quick, I'm meeting someone for lunch in ten minutes,' he snapped, heading back through the wooden door.

Michael opened the folder and spread out the stills. Beyond the glamorous models in fabulously expensive clothes, they could see dozens of police surrounding the back of Creighton's building, taking photographs and measurements, collecting forensic samples and fixing crime scene tape. But Creighton himself was nowhere to be seen.

'Time up,' said Bruce, reappearing in a brown suede jacket and matching fedora.

'These are all photographs of the police,' said Chastity. 'We were hoping for something a few hours earlier, of the incident itself?'

'We have digital files on the computer. But like I say, I've got to go out,' whinged Bruce, taking perfume from his shoulder bag and squirting it around his neck. Chastity looked to Michael in desperation.

'Perhaps just five more minutes? I'd really like to see your laptop,' Michael grinned, taking off his jacket and pushing back his fringe. 'Jesus, it's so hot in here, don't you think?' He unbuttoned the rest of his shirt and flapped the front, creating a breeze across his exposed toned torso. Throwing back his head, he rubbed a hand across his chest down to his abs.

115

Chastity smiled knowingly as Bruce stared in open-mouthed wonder.

'I suppose five minutes late could be fashionable,' he gushed excitedly, throwing his bag onto the table and pulling out his iPad.

There were dozens of photographs stored on the computer. Each was very slightly different from the other, as though many shots had been taken in fast succession. Despite flicking through very quickly, it was beginning to feel that their efforts were futile. Then suddenly, something caught Chastity's eye.

'Stop!' he shouted, pointing at the screen. 'Look there!'

Michael leaned in closer, pushing his forefinger and thumb out across its surface to enlarge the picture. There was Creighton, staring out of his office window with a very angry look on his face. Chastity flicked rapidly across to the next photo, and then the next, watching the story unfold as if in slow motion. Creighton appeared to be arguing with someone. Suddenly, he lunged forward, losing his balance and flying out of the window, shot by shot plunging towards his death in the alley below.

'Oh my God!' Chastity gasped.

'Bingo!' Michael shouted. There in the window above the falling body was Lettie, grinning from ear to ear with arms outstretched where his hands had shoved Creighton violently from behind.

CHAPTER NINE

Travis was really excited about Michael moving in. Since he had first arrived in London, he had dreamed of meeting someone he could care for and look after, someone he could finally trust enough to fall in love with.

After tidying around his apartment and clearing some wardrobe space for Michael's things, he pre-prepared a candlelit dinner for their return later that night. He had spent the afternoon shopping, especially to buy Nigel a brand new fluffy cat bed, which he had decorated with a giant red ribbon bow as a surprise. After taking a shower and dressing in clean clothes, he poured a little cat litter into a new tray in the bathroom and put water and some freshly grilled chicken pieces into two small ceramic bowls next to Nigel's bed. He unwrapped a glorious bunch of red roses and stood them in a glass vase on the coffee table, with a card welcoming Michael into his home and his heart.

Sitting at the kitchen island with a coffee, he looked around the room at his handy work. Everything had to be finished just perfectly for their arrival, and it was. He looked at his watch. There was still two hours to go before their arranged meeting time. He tapped his fingers on the counter.

'Where's the harm in being a little early?' he smiled to himself, gulping back the rest of his coffee and pulling on his jacket.

In the Sugar Sugar dressing room preparing for that evening's appearance, Michael's stomach was in knots. He'd been over and over in his mind how to explain to Travis why he had lied but, unlike his pending performance, no amount of rehearsal could really prepare him for the enormous task that lie ahead. For the moment, the best he could do was to stay focused and concentrate on the show.

'I must shave my ears tonight,' said Chastity, yanking out a long dangling strand with a pair of tweezers.

'You look like Yoda,' Michael grinned. 'Shave ears I must.'

'Only do it with gel this time,' said Connie, 'because that cheap shaving foam from the market's shit. You'll cut yourself again… and I can do that for you!'

'The trouble is, I shave off a few wisps of hair and it grows back as stubble. It's a never-ending battle.' Chastity pulled his earlobe forward to check he hadn't missed any. 'Last week, I got a long hair caught in one of my quick-change earrings. When I pulled it off, it smarted and made my left eye water. So then my eyelashes came unstuck and disappeared down my cleavage. I can't feckin' win!'

'Get one of them nose trimmer things,' Michael suggested, stepping into a petrol-blue sequinned jumpsuit.

'And I've got a little mole coming up on my face,' Chastity sighed.

'Which one?' Connie smirked, dabbing glitter on his lipstick.

'Perhaps it's just a beauty spot?' encouraged Michael.

118

'What, like Chiswick Park?'

'Your looks will change too as you get older,' Chastity warned. 'If you're lucky!'

'I'll have you know, I came fifth on a Facebook DILF list,' said Connie, pouting at himself in the mirror.

'DILF?'

'Yes… Drags I'd Like to Fuck.'

'Oh, that's just marvellous, ain't it?' snapped Michael. 'You told me men don't wanna shag drag queens? It's because of you I'm in this fucking mess now!'

'What fucking mess?' said Connie, slamming down his glitter pot.

'Because of you, she fibbed to Travis,' Chastity explained. 'So now there's a chance he's gonna dump her.'

'I lied about drag, lied about my family… I've lied about everything! God, I feel like such a fake,' Michael cried, throwing his head in his hands.

'If you'd told him you were a drag queen, he probably wouldn't have took you home in the first place, so don't fucking blame me!' Connie shouted.

'Lulu's gonna tell him when he comes here after the show tonight,' Chastity continued. 'So when you meet him, for feck's sake don't mention drag before she's told him. I've warned Daisy, too.'

Suddenly, Lettie swung in through the door from the customer area. Dressed head to foot as Madame Fifi, he snapped his fingers in the air aggressively to draw their full attention.

'Takes more than two fingers to make me come,' said Connie under his breath.

'Listen up! I've been telling everyone this is a brand new show tonight,' Lettie growled. 'I demand you don't let me down.'

'We've been working like buggers all week on this,' said Chastity, crossing his fingers.

'Yes, it's all in hand,' said Michael smarmily. 'You gave us that push and we made it happen. But then, you're good at pushing people, aren't you?'

'I don't like being pushed back, so watch your step, young man!' Lettie slammed the door shut behind him as he left.

'Patronising wanker,' spat Michael.

'Don't worry about her shouting her big fat mouth off, Dolly,' said Connie, fastening a diamante bracelet around his wrist. 'You could get two hands in her gob and still have room to peel a potato!'

Connie's right Lu, we've got her!' Chastity grinned, fluffing the side of his wig with a hairbrush. 'All we've got to do is wait for the appropriate time to present the incriminating photos to Creighton's solicitor.'

'But that doesn't help Fifi, does it?' said Michael.

'Right. So first, we need to try and find evidence of Lettie killing her own brother, proving Fifi's innocence. Then we can hit her with a double whammy and she'll be out of our rather fabulous hair forever!'

With a constant smile and a spring in his step, Travis stepped from a black cab onto Old Compton Street and paid the driver, checking his reflection in the door's glass before it pulled away. He looked at his watch.

120

'Still an hour to go, do I look too eager?' he laughed to himself, walking across to a café. Grasping the door handle to enter, he paused for a moment. 'I could really do with a proper drink,' he said, rubbing a hand over the butterflies in his belly. With a self-assured nod, he shoved his hands in his pockets and headed towards Sugar Sugar.

After pulling on a long black wig, Michael climbed the steps to the stage as the show's opening music began to play. The crowd cheered in recognition, as he flicked back the hair with his finger and began his best Cher impersonation.

'Do you believe I'm made of plastic? There's a seem down here and a zipper right up the other side. Do you believe I'm made of plastic? Don't you get too close with that camera, I've got things to hide.' He rocked his shoulders as the club music pounded from the speakers.

'There's not much left of the me I used to know. It's all been changed around somehow. Cause I believe in staying always young. It's stretched so tight I can't sit down.' Legs apart, he squatted as if to demonstrate, much to the delight of his audience.

'And I can't dance the way I used to do. I have to bob from side to side. Cause there's a little seepage now and then. I even piss formaldehyde. Do you believe I'm made of plastic...'

Standing in the street outside, Travis turned his back to the bitter breeze and blew hot air into his clasped hands to warm his fingers. Seeing no sense in facing the cold, he pushed against Sugar Sugar's glass doors and stepped into the warm.

'Evening, Sir,' said Daisy with a smile. 'You're just in time, the show's just started. That'll be ten pounds, please.' He took Travis' hand and stamped a black ink entry mark above his knuckles.

'Oh, I'm not here for the show,' said Travis, 'I'm meeting someone. Your barman… Michael? I'm his boyfriend, Travis.' Daisy was shocked.

'Oh… err… you're early…' he panicked, glancing at his watch while padding his pocket to check he had an emergency Mars bar on standby.

'I know they don't allow boyfriends at work, so I'll be discreet. I promise.'

'Eh?' Daisy didn't know what he was talking about.

'I'm supposed to wait outside, but it's so very cold.'

'Erm… if you could just wait here?' Daisy feigned a little laugh. 'I'll… I'll… Aw, my Gawd!' Taking the Mars from his pocket, he ran for the stairs.

Back on stage, Michael was giving it everything he had.

'I always wear a wig when I go out, to hide the carcass underneath. If not you'd see how everything's attached. My face is bolted to my teeth.'

The door to the dressing room flew open with such force as Daisy entered that it threw Chastity backwards, landing him unceremoniously in a large box of wigs beneath the costume rail.

122

'Jesus, Daisy,' he moaned. 'Watch what you're doing!'

'He's early! He's early!' Daisy cried through a mouth full of chocolate.

'Who? Who's early?' said Connie.

'Travis! He's only in my lobby, ain't he?'

'Oh, feck, feck, feck, feck!' said Chastity, reaching out his arms. 'Quick, help me up.' Daisy and Connie took a hand each and yanked him from the box. 'Daisy, stop him coming down here, for feck's sake! And Connie, we need to get her off stage.'

'How?' Connie shrugged.

'I'll bring him back in here, you just finish the feckin' song!'

With no one to stop him, Travis decided there was no harm in taking a distant peek at his boyfriend in action behind the bar. Smiling to himself, he followed in Daisy's wake down to the customer area. Standing at the bottom of the stairs, he grinned when he saw the cabaret in full swing before glancing along the bar to catch sight of his lover through the buzzing crowd. But suddenly, his mouth dropped and a frozen shiver ran the full length of his spine as he looked back at the drag queen. To his horror, he recognised Michael. His first instinct was that of pride, he wanted to sing and dance along with his boyfriend... he was fabulous! But this was very quickly overshadowed with a dark, intense sinking in his stomach and a flood of sour emotions, as he realised the guy he had wanted only moments before to spend the rest of his life with was nothing but a deceitful liar. The reality quickly began to sink in that in fact, he didn't really know this stranger at all.

Unaware, Michael continued. *'Say all you want about this thing I've done. Perhaps the things you say are true. They'll always talk about my cunning stunt. Cause no one does it like I do!'*

Spinning around, his eyes flitted momentarily towards the bottom of the stairs. Doing a double take, he was suddenly mortified as if hit by a bolt of lightning. There was Travis. Looking angrily back, he shook his head in disgust before turning and walking slowly back upstairs. Michael was rooted to the spot, as his friends ran on supportively behind him. Connie snatched the microphone from his hand.

'Do you believe she's made of plastic...' he continued, as Chastity led Michael slowly from the stage, holding him under the arm as if to help Cher as an elderly pensioner. Michael's shocked stiffness only served to emphasise the rapidly improvised play-acting. The audience squealed with glee.

In the dressing room, Michael's senses snapped back into play. Lunging towards the door to run after Travis, he accidentally knocked Chastity flying back into the wig box. Connie watched from the stage, as he leapt up the stairs three at a time towards the front entrance.

'Where did he go?' he panted.

'Over there,' sobbed Daisy, pointing as he held the door open for Michael. He took off his wig and threw it on the lobby floor before running up the street after Travis, stilettos clacking on the cobbles.

'Wait! Please wait!' he shouted with despair. Travis ignored his cries, as he tried desperately to thumb down a black cab. Reaching his side, Michael grabbed his arm. 'Please, let me explain,' he pleaded.

'Leave me alone,' growled Travis, shrugging him off.

'I'm so, so sorry. I should have told you I'm a drag queen.'

'I don't care!' snapped Travis, turning to face him. 'Don't you see? I don't care whether you're a drag queen, a road sweeper or a fucking rent boy. But you lied to me!'

'I know I did, but Connie said…'

'And I don't care about anyone else. I loved you Michael, I really, really loved you. But you're just like all the rest, only thinking about yourself. You're nothing but a selfish little liar!' He shoved him away as a taxi pulled into the curb beside them.

'Please, please don't go!' Michael sobbed desperately. Travis' eyes filled with tears.

'Just feck off and leave me alone,' he cried, climbing into the back of the car. As it pulled away up the street and off into the distance, Michael fell to his knees on the wet pavement with his face in his hands, nails digging punishingly through the makeup into the flesh.

'No, please no! You stupid, stupid fool, what have you done?'

At his bar in Southend, Billy-no-nut sat next to his henchman Knuckles. Gazing defiantly across the table at Jed and Archie Burke, he took another puff on his thick cigar, flicking ash onto the carpet. His arch rivals in crime stared back, both sides attempting every nuance of menace to gain the upper hand.

After the longest silence, Billy pushed forward a large brown envelope. Taking it in hand, Jed took out several large colour photos of Michael, walking down Old Compton Street wearing Travis' green shirt and cap.

'Faggot?' snarled Archie.

'Yep,' said Billy. 'Damage him. Don't kill him, that's mine. Just fuck him up.'

'Four grand,' said Jed, putting them back into the envelope. Billy thought for a moment, before giving Knuckles the nod to reached into his pocket and place a stack of fifty-pound notes on the table. Archie picked them up and counted.

'There's only two here?' he growled.

'Half upfront, half when the job's done,' said Billy.

'Yep,' said Jed, his poker face belying the hideous nature of the job.

'Take a photo,' said Billy. 'I wanna see it for meself.'

'You'll know when it's done,' sniffed Archie, as they stood from the table to leave. 'The little queer won't know what's hit him.'

Michael was heavily distracted the following afternoon, as he stood against the wall in the Chapel of Rest holding Edith's hand. In the middle of the room in front of them was Ethel, peacefully reposing in an open-topped coffin. He imagined himself lying there. Without Travis, his life was as good as over.

126

'Are you ready yet, love?' asked Chastity gently, taking Edith's other hand. 'Yes, dear,' she nodded, pulling them forward to Ethel's side. Connie put down his bag and hugged Daisy, who was sobbing uncontrollably near the doorway.

'Ah, she's smiling,' said Edith tearfully, taking a white rose bud from her lapel and placing it gently between Ethel's clasped hands. 'Night night sweetheart, God bless,' she said, kissing her on the forehead.

'She loved you very much, you know?' Chastity whispered, putting his arm around her. 'Didn't she, Lulu?'

Chastity had noticed that Michael's mind was elsewhere, but he had to snap out of it. Ethel had also been his great aunt, and in this moment, Edith needed her family more than ever. He was so hurt that Travis had called him selfish, but now was the time to be putting others first.

'She really did, Edith,' he said, squeezing her hand. 'When you were mistaken for her and taken to the hospital, she was very worried about you. You meant so much to her.'

'Here, here!' Connie agreed.

A tall, thin man in a black suit and tie entered from a side door. With a nod from Chastity, he solemnly held out a hand to guide everyone from the room towards the church. As they walked through the long corridor, soft organ music could be heard ahead.

'Oh dear, I appear to have forgotten my bag,' said Connie unconvincingly, leaving the group to run back.

'What are you up to?' scowled Chastity.

'Nothing, I'll catch you up.'

127

The service was soft and simple. Michael and Chastity sat either side of Edith in the front pew, while Connie and Daisy sat immediately behind. Two late arrivals walked quickly ahead of the coffin as four bearers carried it in from the chapel. One of the young ladies gently placed a hand on Edith's shoulder and smiled down at her, passing her a small bunch of white carnations before taking a seat a few rows back.

'Who's that?' said Chastity.

'It's two of Ethel's nurses,' she sobbed, moved by the unexpected support.

'Ah, that's lovely.'

Following a few kind words from the priest, they stood to sing All Things Bright and Beautiful from a hymn book, as the coffin moved slowly back on a conveyor and out of sight behind a small red velvet curtain. Within ten minutes, it was all over.

Leaving the church, they walked to the end of the path and stopped beside the gate to the graveyard. The light was beginning to fade and dark clouds hung high above their heads. Daisy leaned down to give Edith a hug.

'Thank you, dear,' she said, wiping a little tear from her eye with a clump of tissue.

'Come on, then,' said Chastity, looking up at the sky. 'Let's see if we can get home before it rains.'

'No, just wait here a minute,' insisted Connie.

'Why, what's going on?' asked Chastity, cynically.

'Trust me!' Connie glared.

'Well, that's it then. I'm on me own now, ain't I?' said Edith, holding back her feelings by tightening her
128

woolly scarf. Michael looked wistfully across to Chastity, who nodded his approval.

'I've got something to tell you, Edie,' said Michael. 'You're not alone. Your son didn't die in childbirth, he's still alive.'

'What, my little Marvin?' she gasped, a huge smile spreading across her face as she began to sob with happiness.

'And I've got something else to tell you.' He took a deep breath. 'I'm Marvin's son. Edie, I'm your grandson.' She threw her arms around his waist, pulling him into a hug for the longest time. Then she pulled back, looking up at him lovingly.

'You've always felt special to me, since the day you came. Perhaps that's why?' she grinned, pushing back his fringe and standing on tiptoe to kiss him on the cheek. 'Look at you darling boy, you've got my eyes,' she smiled.

The suppressed rollercoaster of emotions from the past seven weeks finally caught up with Michael as he began to cry like a baby, holding onto his grandmother as if he had just met her for the very first time.

'There, there,' she comforted, patting him on the back. 'Everything will be alright, now.' Chastity's bottom lip wobbled as he glanced across at Connie and Daisy.

'Ooh, I feel like Elsa Lanchester in Lassie Come Home,' he said, wiping away a tear. Daisy was already in floods, even Connie looked a little emotional.

At that moment, the two nurses joined them by the gate. One of them took Edith's hand.

'She was asleep you know, when it happened?' she said gently. 'And she was talking about you just before she closed her eyes. Something to do with Bonfire night?'

Suddenly behind them, there was a thundering bang. They all turned to look.

'What the fuck?' said the other nurse, as the side doors of the crematorium flew open, bashing against the wall either side with a loud thud. Out ran three men in white overalls, sheltering the tops of their heads with their hands and glancing behind, as they desperately made their way across the graveyard. There was a terrifying rumble from the building, as the ground beneath their feet appeared to shake.

'Aw my Gawd, it's only a bloody earthquake!' Daisy cried, grabbing the gatepost as he yanked a packet of chicken crisps from his pocket.

Suddenly, what seemed like a million fireworks began shooting from the top of the giant chimney. They soared across the sky in all directions, highlighting the solemn clouds with every colour of the rainbow. A kaleidoscope of flashes lit the faces of the surprised onlookers.

'Ooh!' Edith cooed excitedly. 'It's our fireworks, Ethel. And this is my grandson,' she said proudly, holding Michael's hand up for her to see.

'You put them in the coffin?' Chastity grinned at Connie. 'Perhaps you're not such a hard-faced bitch, after all!'

'Well, they were leaking. And we had to give her a good send off, didn't we?' Connie laughed.

'Perhaps you and me could do this every year, duck?' Edith grinned at Michael, eyes sparkling in the lights.

'Yes Nan, absolutely,' he said, putting his arm around her shoulder. 'In loving memory of our Ethel.'

130

CHAPTER TEN

After her sister's funeral, Edith wanted to go home.
Chastity took a cab to collect her things from his flat
then dropped her back in Bermondsey. The next
afternoon, he arrived at Connie's to find him at the
sewing machine, while Michael sat with paper and pen
atop a book on his lap, writing a letter. Strewn around
him on the tatty carpet were a dozen failed attempts,
screwed up into tight little balls. Chastity noticed a
half-empty bottle at his feet. Michael was already
quite inebriated.

'Christ on a bike... Absinthe? Where did he get
that?'

'He went out and bought it this morning.' Connie
lifted his eyebrows.

'What's that, then?' Chastity asked, pointing at
his letter.

'I'm writing to Travis. He won't answer any of
my texts, I don't know what else to do.'

'I've told him, men are like buses,' said Connie,
pinning a zip to a swathe of bright orange organza.
'There'll be another one along in a minute.'

'I don't want another one, I want Travis!' he
hiccupped.

'Do you think you'll get him back?' asked
Chastity sympathetically, taking off his coat.

'I don't know. But I can at least pololagise,' he
slurred.

'It's just a fellah, Dolly. If she's not careful, she'll end up a scraggy old spinster like you,' Connie said, nodding to Chastity.

'Can't you go and see him?'

'He basically told me to fuck off and leave him alone.' He screwed his face as if to cry, though nothing came out. 'So I think the pissabolity is out of the question.'

'You've got a point.' Chastity bit his lip. 'Perhaps you've had enough of that now, missus?'

As he stooped to remove the alcohol, he saw an envelope already addressed to Travis. Without Michael noticing, he picked it up and slid it into his pocket. 'I'll make some strong coffee.' He walked through to the kitchen and put the kettle on.

'Good job we ain't got a show tonight, ain't it Tit?' Connie called after him. 'Can you see that in heels? Wobbling about like a tit in a dodgem car?'

'I've brought my car today. I was gonna suggest we go to Fifi's apartment and collect some of her clothes to take. We're supposed to be going to visit her the day after tomorrow.'

'I'm not going, I don't wanna see her,' Connie whinged.

'There's only two allowed anyway,' Chastity explained. 'I'll take Lilly Lush here, if we can keep her off the monkey juice.'

With a groan, Michael screwed up another piece of paper and began writing on a clean sheet.

'Were gonna have to do something,' Connie sighed, shaking his head. 'I can't live with her in this fucking state, let alone work with her!'

'You-know-who had asked her to move in with him,' whispered Chastity, carrying through three
132

mugs. 'If I can convince him to forgive Lulu, you might get your sofa back.' Handing Connie his drink, he discreetly lifted the envelope from his pocket and showed Connie the address.

'Good luck with that, then!'

'How do you spell soubrette?' said Michael, his bottom lip wobbling.

'Keep it simple, love,' Chastity advised. 'It's a billet-doux, not a job application.'

'Trouble is, you know men?' said Connie. 'This Travis is probably back out there already, walking around town with some chicken.'

'What… on a lead?' gasped Michael.

'Yes, dear.' Chastity lifted his eyes as he handed him his coffee.

'I want to live in a world where a chicken can cross the road without its motives being questioned!' Michael thrust his fist in the air with solidarity.

'For feck's sake, he's getting philosophical now!' Suddenly, Chastity's mobile rang. 'It's Edith,' he said, answering. 'Hello love, how are you today?' The confused look on his face told Connie something wasn't quite right.

'What's she saying?'

'Are you sure? All right dear, just go and make a cup of tea.' His eyes widened with horror. 'No Edith, in the name of all that's holy, don't climb up on the roof! Just wait for us, we'll come over right away.' He hung up.

'What's happening?'

'Apparently, there's a man in a yellow suit leaning against her chimney whistling Raindrops Keep Falling On My Head.'

'Is there?'

'I doubt it! She wanted to take him up a cup of tea. I expect it's the shock of Ethel's funeral? You're gonna have to go over there and shoo the squirrels out through her earhole.'

'Why is it always me?' Connie moaned.

'Because I've got to go find this Travis and you're the only one left. We can't send her, can we?' Chastity pointed at Michael swaying from side to side on the sofa.

'And they called it puppy love,' he sang tearfully into his biro, before slumping backwards unconscious.

'Look at her, poor cow,' said Chastity, taking Michael's half-written letter from his lap. 'The life and soul of a party that nobody wants to go to!'

Chastity pulled the collar of his coat up to shield him from a light drizzle as he crossed Soho Square to his car. Turning the key, he opened the door and climbed inside, throwing his bag onto the seat beside him. There was a strange musty smell that he hadn't noticed earlier. He leaned across to turn the handle of the passenger window a little for some ventilation and noticed it was already half way down.

'I'm sure that was closed,' he said, turning the ignition key. Switching on the radio, white noise blared from the speakers. 'What's the matter with that fecking thing?' he sighed, turning it back off and pulling out from the parking bay.

As he entered the side street to head south, he was shocked to hear a loud voice from the back seat.

'Where are we going?' it shouted aggressively. He glanced in the rear-view mirror to see a tatty little woman staring back at him.

'Aargh!' he cried, accidentally bumping the kerb before pulling over. He turned to look at her.

Black beady eyes glared from a rugged scrubbed face, framed by greying matted hair poking out from either side of a dark blue quilted anorak hood. Rolls of warming newspaper jutted up from the front of her jacket zip, and she had a large, strangely stained fleece blanket around her shoulders.

'What… who the feck are you?' he shouted, grabbing his bag and holding it defensively to his chest.

'I might ask you the same question,' said the woman, grasping her junk-filled plastic laundry sack. She seemed frightfully well-spoken for a bag lady.

'This is my car! I'm supposed to be here.'

'Well, this is where I live,' she answered snootily, 'so I'm supposed to be here, too!'

'How did you get in?' Chastity was baffled.

'There was a metal coat hanger sticking out of the bonnet, I undid the lock through that window,' she smirked proudly.

'That was my aerial, no wonder the radio don't work!' He put down his bag and scratched his head. 'You can't stay here.'

'I move from vehicle to vehicle. Today, I live here… and I'm staying!'

'Well you can't!' Chastity got out and opened the back door. 'This is not a car pool.'

"Isn't that what they give babies with croup?'

'No, that's Cowpol, you deranged elf. Get out! Get out now!' he gestured.

'You wouldn't throw a defenceless woman out in the cold and rain, would you?' She began to cry. 'I haven't eaten for two days!'

135

Chastity's mothering instinct began to kick in. He wasn't at all happy she was there, but he could at least wait until it stopped raining before evicting her, especially if the poor unfortunate was starving. Several cars stacking up behind them began tooting their horns impatiently, unable to get past on the narrow street. Reluctantly, he slammed the door shut and climbed back in behind the wheel.

'Well, just for a little while, then,' he said, pulling away up the street. The woman instantly grinned. She hadn't really been crying at all.

'Fantabulosa,' she laughed, pulling a sandwich from her pocket and taking a bite. Glancing back at her in the mirror, Chastity shook his head in despair. 'I've seen you before,' she chewed. 'You work in Sugar Sugar, don't you?'

'How do you know that?'

'I know everything and I see everything. I'm a very observant woman. I saw you climbing in the back of that building, where the man got pushed from the window?'

'Oh my God, did you?'

'He threw a file out, you know? That man who pushed him?'

'Did he? That could have been what we were looking for. So you were a witness to the murder?' Chastity was dumbfounded.

'Yes. Diabolical business! It fell between the back of the building and the fence, that's where you'll find it.'

'Thank you very much for telling me,' said Chastity.

'Are you an actor, luvvie?'

'Kind of,' said Chastity, turning onto the main road towards Pimlico.

'I'm a character actress, I've done Shakespeare,' she beamed, feigning a regal curtsey in her seat. 'Would you like to see my Desdemona?'

'I'd rather you kept your Desdemona where it is for now, if you don't mind?' Chastity screwed up his face at the thought.

'Don't be cocking a snoot at me!' she snapped, returning his angry stare in the mirror.

'Cocking a what?'

'Haven't you ever been down on your luck?' she said seriously. 'I had my own flat in Covent Garden, a social circle. I was celebrated for my work.'

'Really? What happened?'

'I was playing Arcati at The Garrick. My understudy slept with the director, the producer and the leading man, snatched the very role out from under my feet. I lost my home, my career and everything.' She shook her head sadly. Chastity soberly recalled what Cyril had done to him. It was all too viciously familiar.

'Ooh, I bet you felt like Bette Davis in All About Eve,' he said sympathetically.

'Precisely. Pretty young blonde thing, she was. We could have been friends, if she hadn't been such a rampant, manipulative, back-stabbing little slut.' She pushed the hair gracefully back from her face. 'I was utterly discombobulated,' she frowned.

'Fancy that!' Chastity nodded.

'Gerry,' she said, reaching forward a fingerless-gloved hand to shake. 'Geraldine Braintree.'

'Chastity Belt.' Glancing back at her dirty fingernails, he decided to keep his hands on the wheel.

Steering off of the Embankment, he drove onto Travis' riverside estate. Referring again to the address on Michael's envelope, he pulled into the car park, stopping alongside his motorbike.

'If you're still here when I come back, I'll get you a jacket potato or something,' he offered, taking his keys from the ignition and climbing out.

'A potato in a jacket? What a hoot!'

'You're not going to nick anything if I leave you here, are you?' Chastity asked. She glanced around the battered old car sarcastically, as if there was anything worth stealing. 'Point taken.'

'What are we doing here?' she said, looking out of the window expectantly. Chastity took a deep breath and bit his lip in nervous anticipation.

'Just another mission of mercy!'

By the time Connie reached Bermondsey, Edith's house was a hive of activity. There was indeed a man on the roof in bright yellow high-visibility clothing, repairing and replacing broken and missing tiles to stem any leaks. Two skips piled high with discarded household materials sat against the kerb to the front, and a guy in dungarees stood up a ladder painting the upstairs window frame. In the narrow hallway, Connie had to squeeze behind decorators, beavering away stripping paint and sanding down woodwork. Passing her parlour doorway, he glanced inside to see her furniture covered with white sheets, as another young man painted her ceiling with a roller on a long pole. A buzz of construction, maintenance and repair filled the entire house.

He finally found a very excited Edith in what used to be her scullery. She was watching as three workmen were busy installing brand new fitted cabinets, electrics and plumbing, and a young lad was smearing adhesive onto the back of shiny cream wall tiles.

'Ooh, Connie!' she beamed widely, pulling him into a hug.

'Hi Edith, what's going on?'

'I'm having a sixty innit makeover, duck!'

'Wow, that's fabulous! And about time too,' Connie smiled, knowingly.

'Here, I've got house full of boys!' she grinned mischievously, jabbing him in the ribs.

'Sounds like my place before that cat and his friend move in. So what happened?'

'A man came to the door and said I'd won a competition. Very posh, he was. I had to stand outside next to a big black car with dark windows, so they could get a look at me.' She pulled back her shoulders and stood up straight to demonstrate. 'I suppose they wanted to be sure I was the right one.'

'Yeah, I'll bet fucking they did,' Connie smirked.

'I asked him if I was gonna be in the paper, he seemed very upset by that.'

'Why does that not surprise me?'

'He told me to promise not to tell a soul. Then all these builders turned up. Ooh, isn't it exciting?' she gushed, dabbing her nose with a screwed-up bit of tissue from the front pocket of her pinny. 'I've even got a new inside toilet next to the back bedroom. And a bath!'

The expression on her face suddenly turned a little remorseful. She took Connie by the cuff of his jacket and pulled him into the cupboard under the stairs. Looking up and down the hallway to check they were alone, she pulled the door closed behind them.

'The thing is,' she whispered, 'I ain't done no competitions. Don't say nothing, in case they take it all away again.'

'You needn't worry about that, Dolly,' said Connie, patting her hand. 'It's probably just something to do with being a loyal bingo customer.'

'Do you think?' she asked hopefully. 'Only, I've been going up that Mecca for thirty-odd years.'

'Whatever the reason, one thing's certain… you've most definitely earned it! Just keep it to yourself like they said, don't tell anybody.'

'Mum's the word,' she smiled, patting the side of her nose with her finger. Connie gently took her by the hands and looked her in the eyes.

'You don't always have to enter a competition to hit the jackpot!'

After stepping from the lift, Chastity paused to brace himself before tapping on Travis' front door. There would probably be only one shot at this, so he had to get it right. It took a while to get an answer. When Travis finally responded, Chastity could clearly see that he had been suffering as much as his ex-boyfriend, unshaven with scruffy hair and bloodshot eyes. Wearing just a vest and jeans with bare feet as if he hadn't bothered to dress, he looked Chastity up and down.

'Yep?' he snapped.

'Erm… I'm Chas, a friend of Michael's?' Without hesitation, the door was slammed shut in his face. He
140

knocked again, and again, finally getting another answer, this time more aggressive.

'Look, I told him to fuck off and leave me alone!'

'I know you did, he told me. But he didn't send me. In fact, he doesn't even know I'm here,' explained Chastity.

'Then what do you want?' Travis glared, cynically.

'To explain why you're possibly making the biggest mistake of your life!' Chastity put his hand on the door to stop it being slammed again. 'Michael's been crying a lot, too,' he added. Travis looked away momentarily to hide his red eyes, before finally standing back and allowing him to enter.

Tear-soaked tissues were screwed up on the coffee table amongst half-a-dozen dirty mugs, and several discarded fast food containers were scattered across the kitchen island. The redundant candlelit dinner sat where it was first laid out. In the far corner of the room was Nigel's new cat bed. Still adorned with its big red bow, it was scrunched against the wall where it had landed after being kicked in frustration. Glancing up at the enormous television, Chastity could see Michael grinning with happiness in a paused still-frame from some magical moment with Travis captured on his iPhone.

He gestured for Chastity to sit, swiping the table's clutter into a plastic waste paper bin before switching off the screen with his remote. Perching on the end of the coffee table, he waited.

'He's in a bad way, you know?' Chastity began. 'Connie… I mean Norman told him quite categorically not to tell anyone he was a drag queen. It can be a real

141

turn off for some men, and she should know... she's been through enough of them! She was just trying to encourage him to get out and meet somebody. Who knew he was gonna fall head-over-heels in love with the first bloke he ran into?' He shook his head and sighed. 'It was stupid I know, but Michael trusted his advice. You have to admit, our darling boy's streetwise but a little naïve in matters of love.'

'Even bairns know the difference between the truth and a lie,' said Travis angrily.

'Michael's not a liar!' Chastity defended. 'In fact, he's one of the kindest, sweetest, most honest people I've ever met. Knowing he lied has been torturing him. He came to me for advice, he wanted to tell you the truth before he moved in.'

'What fucking stopped him, then?'

'You did, by turning up too fecking early!'

'He's had plenty of opportunities to tell me,' Travis yelled.

'He's been too afraid something else will go wrong in his poor little life. It's been a hideous rollercoaster, and the ride's not over yet.' Chastity reached into his pocket and took out Michael's half written letter. Travis looked at it and smiled, water welling in his eyes.

'He wrote this?'

Well... kind of, just before he ran off with the green fairy. I don't expect we'll get him back until tomorrow afternoon! So swallow your pride mister, get over there and put that bloody kettle on!'

Travis listened intently as Chastity explained how Lettie's twisted plan had conned Michael reluctantly into drag and how Billy-no-nut viciously came after him. He told him about his oppressed life

142

in Essex as an unwanted orphan, the shock of finding his father Madame Fifi, his mother Verity and his grandmother Edith, and the extraordinary hurdles he was prepared to jump just to save his newly discovered family.

'He needs someone to look after him and to love him,' said Chastity, sipping his coffee. 'And he's chosen you. He's crazy about you!'

'I'm just defensive because I've been hurt so many times before,' said Travis tearfully.

'Yes, but this isn't like all those other times,' said Chastity, passing him another tissue. 'I understand your doubts, but for you two not to be together because of some silly misunderstanding wouldn't just be sad, it would be tragic.'

Travis wiped his eyes and sat quietly for a moment. This was indeed different to what had gone before, Chastity had made him see that much. Michael's story had made his yearning to hold him in his arms and protect him stronger than ever. He had never been so much in love with anyone as he was with him in this moment. Looking back at the desperate words Michael had taken such pain to write, he sighed.

'Oh man, what am I gonna do with you?'

CHAPTER ELEVEN

The following day, Michael awoke with a start to the sound of Connie's front door slamming shut. The morning sun through the lounge window was blinding, it took a few seconds for his eyes to adjust. Looking down, he could see that he was lying on the sofa under a blanket. Pushing it back to sit up, his head began to pound like thunder, and there was a nasty dry taste in his mouth. Looking around the room, he appeared to be alone except for Nigel, who was curled up asleep under the television. In the relative quiet of the empty apartment, he suddenly felt painfully lonely as his mind turned to Travis. Would he ever see him again?

Rubbing his bleary eyes, he suddenly realised he had a sock on one hand. At some point during his drunken dreams he must have taken it from his left foot, though he couldn't remember why.

'Oh God!' he rasped, pulling off the other sock and unbuttoning his sweat-soaked shirt.

He walked through to the kitchen and filled a pint glass with tap water, gulping it down in one. Putting the empty glass in the sink, he noticed a note taped to the kettle: "Lu. Don't go anywhere, visitor at 11. Chas x."

A visitor? Who could that be? Perhaps someone to repair Connie's leaking ceiling? Glancing up at the clock, he could see it was already after ten. Taking off his shirt, jeans and underwear, he threw everything into the washing machine and walked through to the bathroom for a shower.

Driven out of the flat by Michael's cavernous snoring, Chastity and Connie did a little shopping before settling in a nearby café. They stared at menus as a middle-aged waitress stood poised with pen in hand awaiting their order.

'I'll have a skinny latte with extra skinny and a double lard-arse for my friend, here,' Connie began. 'And what's Sherlock Holmes soup?'

'It's a mystery,' grinned the waitress with glee at her own inventiveness.

'Well, as long as it ain't got onions. I hate onions.'

'Oh,' she said, her face dropping.

'It's onion soup, isn't it?' Connie sighed.

'Erm… I'll ask chef if we've got a different flavour,' she frowned, walking off towards the kitchen. A young man on the next table had overheard their conversation.

'I never enjoy my dinner,' he said, staring down at his food.

'What?' said Chastity.

'I always leave the best bits till last, but then they're always cold,' he continued, raising his eyebrows with disappointment.

'Well, why don't you just eat the best bits first?'

'Oh, I never thought of that!' he smiled, turning his plate and pulling his favourite selection forward. Chastity shook his head in bewilderment.

'They all find their way to Soho, don't they?'

146

'Hmm, we get all the waifs and strays,' Connie agreed.

'Anyway, what did you buy?' Chastity pointed at Connie's bag.

'A baby monitor,' said Connie, pulling out the box. 'I wanted walkie-talkies for us to use backstage at the fashion competition, but they'd sold out.'

'Good idea,' said Chastity, reaching into his own bag. 'I had a snoop around this morning and I found this.' He handed Connie the missing file from Creighton's office. 'It was chucked down between the wall and the fence at the back of the building.'

'What does it say?' said Connie, flicking through the pages.

'I'm not completely sure, but it looks as though he had some kind of legal battle with Lettie and her brother. Something to do with property?'

'Perhaps that's why she pushed him?' Connie bit his lip. 'We could ask Mister Mark to take a look, he did say we could if we needed advice?' Chastity nodded, quickly taking the file and shoving it back into his bag as the waitress eagerly returned to the table.

'We've got oxtail soup?' she suggested hopefully.

'I ain't eating nothing that's been near an animal's arse,' Connie whinged. 'Just do me an egg sandwich.'

Despite freshening himself up, Michael's head was still thumping. He looked in the bathroom cabinet and through the kitchen drawers but could not find any painkillers. Throwing on his coat, he looked down at the Boyfriends R Us badge Travis had given him pinned to its lapel, before looking at his watch. It was five minutes to eleven. He scribbled: "back in five" on the reverse of Chastity's note and taped it to the outside of the front door before heading down the metal steps and up the alley to Old Compton Street. Pushing hair back from his throbbing forehead, he walked up the middle of the road towards the chemist through the throng of tourists and shoppers, jumping onto the pavement to avoid a large black Bentley as it pulled tightly into the kerb.

As he pushed the shop door and entered, he didn't notice Travis stepping from a black cab further up the street. Chastity had given him directions to Connie's flat above Sugar Sugar, telling him that Michael would be there at eleven. Purposely wearing his boyfriend's favourite distinctive lime shirt with the contrasting red stripes and the matching green baseball cap, he nervously checked his reflection in a storefront, wanting to set a good impression on his surprise visit. Feeling a little nervous of how his lover might react, he made his way towards the alley up the side of the club.

The Bentley pulled forward slowly, its sinister blackened windows shielding the crazed occupants within.

'That's him,' said Jed Burke from the driver's seat, pointing at Travis while referring to one of the photos that Billy had given them.

'Let's go,' agreed his brother Archie, pulling on a black knitted balaclava and picking up a baseball bat. Handing Jed a thick length of metal chain, they leapt from the car and quickly followed Travis into the alley.

148

'Oi, Michael?' called out Jed.

As Travis instinctively turned, Archie's gloved hands whacked a bat into his solar plexus. Taken completely by surprise, he bent forward, severely winded as pain surged across his ribcage like a bolt of lightning. A fracturing swipe of chain across the back of his legs dropped him gasping to his knees, and a steel toecap hammering up under his chin cracked his teeth and sent him flying backwards, knocking his head hard against the cobbled pathway. His mobile phone flew from his pocket and smashed into a hundred pieces against the brickwork. Fighting for his life through a relentless onslaught of kicks and punches to his face and body, he rolled onto his side and pushed up to get on his feet, but another hideous swipe of wood across his back threw him painfully against the wall. In severe shock, dazed and unable to see through red-stained eyes, he desperately threw out his swollen fists in all directions in a brave attempt to defend himself. A final stunning blow to the side of the head ended his torment. As everything faded to black, he slid slowly down the wall and slumped forward into the middle of the path.

Less than twenty seconds after the vicious attack had begun, the masked strangers had reduced him to a motionless broken heap, lying in a pool of his own blood.

Connie and Chastity had decided to take their sandwiches and coffees to Soho Square. Though there was a slight autumnal chill in the air, it was warm in the sunshine, and the scenery was quite nice towards midday when all the local men took their lunch in the open air. Entering through the black metal gates, Chastity spotted a sunlit empty park bench to one side. As he stepped on the soil to cut across under the trees, Connie held him back.

'Don't walk through there,' he frowned. 'That's where that rich bitch with the pink sports car takes her dog. She don't look the type to pick up shit with a plastic glove.'

Walking the long way around the path, they saw a blind man with his harnessed guide dog reach the bench before them.

'For feck's sake, we've lost our seat now,' Chastity sighed. As they approached, Connie dipped into his paper bag and broke off a piece of egg sandwich, tossing it on the green opposite the bench. The dog leapt forward for his treat, abruptly yanking the man out of his seat and across the grass behind him.

'There we are, Dolly,' said Connie casually as they sat.

'You are awful,' Chastity smiled, sipping through the lid of his coffee.

'I can guarantee you that we saw this bench before he did,' Connie smirked, lighting a cigarette.

'Now, about Fifi? I'm driving Michael to see her tomorrow afternoon, but we need to go to her apartment and collect some of her clothes first.' Chastity took a bite of his sandwich. 'Have you spoken to that dopey nephew of yours yet about borrowing that light-truck-thingy?'

'Yeah, Nobby's up for it. We just need to know when, and what bit of wall we're yanking her sorry old carcass over.'

150

'If I park my car nearby, we can just lower her down and chuck her in the passenger seat. Then I can drive her straight to the address The Extractor gave me, drop her off and we're done.'

'Sounds straightforward enough to me,' said Connie, glancing over his Foster Grant sunglasses at two young men playing volleyball.

'Yes, it does, doesn't it? What could possibly go wrong?' Chastity unwrapped his sandwich and took a bite.

'Do you want mine?' Connie offered. 'She's made it with that fuck-awful granary bread. It's like eating parrot food.'

'Does it keep repeating on you?' grinned Chastity, taking the bag.

'What about showing that file to Mister Mark? We could go there now, he only lives down towards Trafalgar Square?'

'How do you know that?'

'I went to a party there once,' Connie smiled as he reminisced. 'His flat overlooks the theatre where they put on that play, The Vagina Monologues. For six months, his entire panoramic front window was filled with the word vagina in big eight-foot letters. Worse still, it lit up at night and flashed!'

'I hope he didn't have the vicar to tea,' Chastity laughed. 'Let's do it another day, I'm getting a bit chilly now.' He looked at his watch. 'I wonder if it's safe to go back yet?'

'Them lover-torn wonders don't wanna be shagging on my fucking bed, I've just changed the sheets!'

Suddenly, their attention was drawn by the sound of police sirens in the direction of Old Compton Street.

'I expect they're rushing back to the station before their fish and chips get cold,' said Connie ironically, stamping out his cigarette.

'No, wait,' said Chastity, standing to crane his neck at the glimmers of blue light flashing off the surrounding buildings. 'I think they've stopped outside Sugar Sugar.'

'You could be right,' said Connie, taking off his sunglasses to see. 'With any luck, Lettie's dropped down dead!'

Billy-no-nut sat in the tatty little office above his bar in Essex. With his feet up on the desk, he puffed on a fat cigar, blowing thick clouds of rancid smoke towards the nicotine-stained ceiling.

'You can't just keep hiding away up here every time the bar's open, people are gonna know something's wrong,' said Knuckles, rummaging through a stack of invoices.

'I ain't coming back down until I've got that fucking security video off that Soho bitch.' Billy reached inside his shirt to scratch his armpit, sniffing his fingers and wiping them on his trousers.

'But look at these fucking invoices!' Knuckles threw the stack on the desk in front of him. 'You used all the money in the safe paying the Burke Brothers. They're gonna be back for the other half soon, where are we getting that from?'

'It was worth it. We'll make it back,' Billy coughed.

'Not while you ain't showing your face downstairs. They're not coming in, mate. Everyone thinks there's trouble coming, they don't need it.'

'I ain't fucking doing it!' Billy yelled, kicking the papers from his desk.

At that moment, Knuckles' mobile bleeped. Grinding his teeth in frustration, he took it from his pocket and looked. A broad grin shone across his face.

'They've done it!' he laughed, passing his phone.

Taking his feet off the desk, Billy leaned forward and shielded the screen from the sunlight to take a look. It was a snapshot of Travis, lying unconscious on the alley cobbles soaked in his own blood. Billy tipped back his head and let out a loud, gravelled smoker's laugh.

'That's Michael sorted... for now. Next we go after Madame Fifi.' He took a swig of lager from a glass on his desk, wiping his spit with the back of his arm. 'First, I'm having that tape. Then I'm gonna finish them both off, once and for all!'

Michael followed fellow customers out of the chemist to see what was causing all the commotion. Several police cars with lights flashing had brought traffic to a standstill in Old Compton Street, and right in front of the alley to Connie's flat stood an ambulance with its back doors wide open. He had the most ominous feeling in the pit of his stomach, as though this was more than just another ordinary Soho drama.

Crossing the road, he walked cautiously towards the crowd and pushed his way through to the police crime scene barrier. It was difficult to see what was going on with so many officers and paramedics

153

crowding the undercover walkway. He could see the legs of what appeared to be a man lying on the ground, and he could see blood... lots of blood. A broken baseball bat lay to one side just inside the alley.

'He must still be alive, poor devil,' commented the woman squeezed next to him. 'Otherwise they wouldn't still be working on him.'

'Move along now, please,' said a tall officer, standing in front of him with arms outstretched to push back the crowd. To one side, another policeman was taking a statement from a young man in a Parker coat carrying a little Pekingese dog. Michael strained over the din to hear what he was saying.

'There were two of them. Big they were, wearing masks. They drove off up there in a black car.' As he spoke, a white forensics van pulled up behind one of the squad cars.

'I said move along now, please,' repeated the tall officer.

'I live here, up the alley,' said Michael.

'Of course you do, mate,' said the copper sarcastically.

'No, I really do, I live above Sugar Sugar.'

'Well then, you'll need to take another route or come back later, Sir.'

As the officer moved further along the line, one of the paramedics next to the body stood up, revealing a small glimpse of a lime shirt with a distinctive red stripe. As he moved his medical bag, a green baseball cap stained with splatters of blood came into view behind it on the cobbles. Michael gasped with horror.

'Travis!' he shouted, ducking under the barrier tape and pushing past the tall officer into the alley.
154

Taken by surprise, the ring of protection had been unable to stop him. Standing at the feet of the injured man, he looked down upon an inconceivably monstrous sight.

The man's whole torso was red with blood and the swollen, bloated face was unrecognisable. For one sweet moment, Michael thought that perhaps it wasn't Travis lying amongst the mass of tubes and medical equipment, and that he had merely made a mistake. That the man he loved more than anything in the world was safe and well somewhere in London, and that this was just someone else with the same shirt and hat. But then he saw the matching Boyfriends R Us badge, pinned to the lapel of the man's jacket.

Suddenly, the noise around him dulled to a faint echo, over which he could hear nothing but his own rapidly beating heart. Just as in the moment he very first met Travis, everything around him turned to slow motion.

'Nooo!' he screamed, as his knees began to give way beneath him. Momentarily startled, the paramedics looked up as two policemen grabbed him by the arms and took him to one side.

'You know this man?'

'Yes,' Michael cried. 'He's my boyfriend!'

At that moment, Connie and Chastity arrived at the front of the barrier. Seeing them, Michael ran into Chastity's arms.

'What's going on?' he asked, looking beyond his shoulder to the man on the alley floor.

'It's Travis! It's Travis! It's Travis!' Michael sobbed uncontrollably.

'Oh my God!' said Connie, grasping Michael's hand.

155

The paramedics lifted Travis onto a stretcher and wheeled him to the back of the ambulance. Panicking he would be left behind, Michael run to his lover's side as the tall officer held him back.

'Travis, it's me, Michael? Can you hear me? I love you!' Noticing his matching Boyfriends R Us badge, the paramedic nodded for the copper to release his hold. Michael climbed into the back of the ambulance, the doors were pulled closed and, with lights flashing, it sped away.

Chastity and Connie clung onto each other in silent shock for a moment. As the sterile-clad forensic team moved in and cameras began to flash, Connie lit two cigarettes.

'This is like Kate Adie in Beirut, this is,' he said, passing one to Chastity. 'And in our alley, can you believe it? What do we do now?'

'Lulu needs us more than ever. They'll have gone to St Thomas' from here, we should go and be with her,' said Chastity soberly.

'Yes... yes we should.' Connie drew back nervously on his nicotine. 'He's not gonna die, is he?'

Chastity and Connie arrived at St Thomas' Hospital to see Michael sitting alone on a bench at the other end of a long wide corridor, next to the accident and emergency department. Stark and white, it echoed with activity as nurses, doctors and orderlies rushed to and fro in front of him. Every passer-by drew up his gaze from his lap, desperate for news and assurance.

'Would you look at that?' Chastity bit his lip. 'Poor soul, he looks like a little boy outside the headmaster's office.'

'I think I spent more time doing that than I did in class,' said Connie.

'Before you got expelled?' smirked Chastity.

'Shall I get him a coffee or something?'

'Yes, good idea. With lots of sugar for the shock, I'll let him know we're here.'

As Connie disappeared off up the corridor, Chastity walked up to Michael, sitting beside him on the bench.

'What's happening?'

'I don't know,' Michael rasped. 'It's bad, really bad. They've taken him for a scan, they said they'd tell me.'

'How about you, are you alright?'

'I don't understand it, this is insane!' Michael cried. 'Why was he there in our alley?'

'That's my fault, I'm afraid. I invited him, he was coming to see you,' explained Chastity sheepishly.

'What? Why? How?'

'I went to see him to tell him he'd made a big mistake. Sorry I didn't tell you, I didn't want to build your hopes up.' Chastity squeezed his hand.

'What happened?'

'He understands. Lulu. He loves you. He wants to spend the rest of his life...' Chastity bit his tongue. It was questionable exactly how much life Travis had left. Michael put his head in his hands and began to sob. Wiping away a tear, Chastity put his arm around him as a young woman in a green scrubs approached.

'Michael?' she said, holding the bottom of her stethoscope. 'I'm Doctor Carlisle from the trauma team. It's not brilliant news, I'm afraid. Travis has several broken bones, but thankfully his lung doesn't appear to be pierced as we first thought. But he's lost a

157

lot of blood and we think there may be a little internal bleeding, so they've taken him straight down to surgery.'

'Will he be alright?' Chastity asked.

'It's a little too early to tell,' she answered sympathetically. 'It's his head we're mostly worried about because it's taken a lot of beating. I'm sorry to say, we are going to have to induce a coma.'

CHAPTER TWELVE

Sitting in the corridor of accident and emergency at St Thomas' Hospital, Michael found it hard to comprehend what the doctor had just told him.

'Oh my God! A coma?' he gasped.

'He's with a very good team,' smiled Doctor Carlisle, sadly. 'It can really help in cases of head trauma and would give his brain time to recover. Although of course, we won't really know the long-term damage until he wakes up.'

'What kind of damage?' Michael was horrified.

'Well… speech, memory, motor and cognitive skills.' She crouched down to look him directly in the eyes. 'I'm sorry to say, there is a slim chance he may never wake up.' She rubbed his arm. 'Sorry it's not better news. We'll know more once they've had a look. Someone will let you know, OK?'

'Yes, thank you very much,' said Chastity, hugging Michael as the medic stood and walked back up the corridor. 'Ooh, I feel like Helen Vinson in Beyond Tomorrow.'

Suddenly Connie appeared, wobbling up the corridor precariously carrying three plastic cups between his hands. Handing one to Chastity, he sat next to Michael.

'Aright, Dolly?' he smiled, passing him a coffee.

'They said he might never wake up!' Michael was in a daze.

'Eh?'

'The doctor's just been round,' Chastity explained, looking to Connie for moral support.

'Nonsense, a big fit strapping lad like that?' Connie grinned supportively. 'They're very good here. This is where they brought lard-arse Lorraine.'

'Oh yes,' Chastity remembered. 'She had a mastectomy after that bondage accident?'

'Having your nipple chewed off by some skinhead under the influence of poppers is one thing, but having your whole boob starved of oxygen for six hours with a nylon rope by someone you don't even know is another thing altogether,' Connie nodded.

'Imagine losing a tit to a total stranger?' Chastity agreed. 'She had all them piercings in her nose, lips and eyebrows.'

'Yeah, I remember. Her face was covered in punk.'

They turned to look as a policewoman pushed through double doors at the end of the corridor, stopping momentarily to speak to a man in a white coat. He pointed down the corridor at Michael. Watching as she approached, they realised it was Carrie.

'She's coming over here,' Chastity whispered. 'Remember what Mister Mark said, don't mention the Creighton Cross photos to the filth.' Drawing closer, Carrie grinned with recognition.

'I thought it might be you,' she said, leaning down and patting Michael on the shoulder. 'So, Travis is your boyfriend?' He nodded. 'How is he?'

'We don't really know just yet,' said Chastity.

'Witnesses say they saw two men driving off in a black car. There's a Bentley on CCTV but we can't see the number plates. It's an old trick; they're set at a funny angle so they refract the light. Have you seen a car fitting that description there before?'

'Sorry, no,' Chastity frowned.

'It could just be a random homophobic attack, but a couple of things are a little odd,' she said, pushing a long blonde strand of hair behind her ear.

'Like what?' Michael asked.

'His injuries are quite specific. More like a hit than a fight, they knew what they were doing. Can you think who might have done this to him? Any enemies or problems in his life?'

'No, I haven't known him long.' Michael shook his head. 'But his life seems very organised and happy.'

'OK, sorry to have to ask right now. It may come to you later. So call me?' She handed Michael her business card. 'Meanwhile, be vigilant just in case it is homophobia, especially on Old Compton Street.'

'We will, thanks,' Chastity smiled. About to walk away, Carrie paused.

'Oh, by the way, Travis was carrying a donor card. We've contacted his next of kin.'

'Who's that?' said Michael.

'His parents, I think. They're going to drive through the night from Scotland. They'll be here early tomorrow.' With a smile, she turned and walked away.

'Oh God!' Michael groaned. 'They don't even know he's gay, let alone anything about me!'

'Hmm. That's a worry,' said Chastity.

'And what about the show tonight?' Michael sighed.

'Travis needs you here, dear,' Chastity smiled caringly.

'We could get Fanny to stand-in?' suggested Connie.

'And we're supposed to be going to see my dad tomorrow.' Michael was beginning to flap.

'Calm down, love! Don't worry about that, I'll take Connie,' said Chastity.

'Oh. Lovely!' Connie whinged.

'What about my Nan? Have you seen her?'

'Ooh yes, she's having her whole house renovated! Connie phoned Buckingham Palace press office,' Chastity chuckled.

'Really?'

'They were round there like a shot,' Connie laughed. 'Though I don't suppose you'll be moving in with her now you're back with Travis?'

'I don't know,' Michael sighed tearfully. 'If he ever comes out of the coma, he might not even remember me.'

At that moment, a bespectacled white-haired old lady in a red apron rushed in at the top of the corridor.

'That's the bastard!' she screamed, pointing at Connie as two burly security guards rushed towards them.

'Oh for feck's sake, what have you done now?' Chastity sighed.

'The thieving bitch tried to short-change me on the coffees,' Connie explained. 'So I kicked her biscuit stand off the counter.' He took out a cigarette and lit it, puffing smoke towards the ceiling.

'You can't do that in here!' Chastity growled.

'Oh, dear,' he smirked sarcastically, picking up his shopping bags and slipping on his Foster Grant's. 'What will they do, throw me out?'

That night in the dressing room, Chastity and Connie were nearly ready to begin the evening's performance with their special guest Fanny the tranny. She had been shocked to find out about her dear friend Fifi's sudden incarceration, and just as saddened by Michael's desperate situation. But most of all, she was annoyed at the carnage created by murderous Lettie, someone she had once considered a close friend.

'I'm so angry, it's making my new tits hurt,' she said, wobbling them about with her hands to ease the tension.

'We're beginning to piece together all the evidence,' said Chastity, zipping her into a long white hospital gown. 'We've just got to get something on her killing her brother, then we'll go to Creighton's solicitor.'

'Didn't you say Lettie stole Fifi's car before you bought it off her?' Fanny asked.

'Yeah, she fucked it up,' said Connie, pulling on a pair of sling-backs. 'It broke down on the way to our hen show.'

'Well, she must have taken it from outside Fifi's flat, surely? Can't you have a look at the CCTV?'

'Are there cameras?' asked Chastity hopefully. 'We're going there tomorrow.'

'Yes, I remember it well,' grinned Fanny. 'That nasty little security man gave me a wheel clamp a couple of weeks before I wrecked my car.'

'You wrecked it?'

'It fell down a hole on the Brompton Road. Late one night after a party, I drove down the wrong side of the traffic cones. Got a driving ban.'

'Really?' Connie grinned.

163

'Yes. The copper said I couldn't concentrate properly while I was texting. I said to him: Derr… why do you think I took coke?'

'Ha ha! That's my girl!' Chastity laughed. 'So this security guard, will he have footage of the car park?'

'I expect so, but he's very cap and keys, ex-military. Corporal Richard Taylor.'

'Dick Taylor?' smirked Connie. 'Does he do circumcisions?'

'I think they threw away the wrong bit!' said Fanny, pulling on a short black wig. Chastity fluffed the back of it with hairspray. 'Ooh, I look like Isla St Clair!'

'Isle of Sinclair? Where's that?' Connie asked.

'It's not a place you dopey trollop, it's a malt off the telly!' Chastity chuckled. 'With Larry Grayson on The Generation Game? Purdey bob, floaty chiffon, scores on the doors?'

'Whatever!' Connie shook his head in despair at their seemingly pointless knowledge of archaic trivia.

'And poor Lulu! How absolutely awful for her, she must be in pieces?'

'It's not looking good, Fanny,' Chastity bit his lip. 'The trouble is, she's had to cope with so much over the past few weeks. I'm really worried this might just tip her over the edge!'

As crazed piano music began to tinkle from the giant speakers, the lights came up and Fanny stepped onto the stage to perform in Michael's place.

'People said I must be mad, to love someone like you. But love can bloom despite, thirteen years of
164

respite, at a secure institute,' she sang sweetly, holding her head in her hands and crossing her eyes.

'I remember with fondness how we met, when our gurneys became entwined. The lights of the corridor danced on your face, as they tightened your straps and wheeled you away. Your twinkling eyes entranced me, as your medication got high. I knew I was there, in your vacant stare, in the padded room next to mine!' She skipped delicately around in a circle.

'A spark ignited my passion, when you told me you'd been through, Electroconvulsive Therapy, I knew that you were meant for me. Your crazy screams were exciting, your unhinged ramblings divine. I found it erotic, when you got psychotic, in the padded room next to mine!' She sat on the front of the stage, dangling her legs down into the customer area and swinging them from side to side.

'We weaved our baskets together, in the grounds, whatever the weather. We laughed and played, every single day, till the nurse un-padlocked your tether.' Dropping into the delighted audience, she threw her arms around the neck of a fit young man and lifted herself up, wrapping her legs around his waist as she sang, nose to nose.

'I found your schizophrenia, filled me with desire. I adored your split personality, because both of you were meant for me. My love grew deeper every day, as you plunged into decline. I lost my reality, as you lost your sanity, in the padded room next to mine!'

The following day, Connie accompanied Chastity to his car in Soho Square. Padding his pocket to be sure he had the keys to Fifi's apartment, he stamped his cigarette out on the pavement.

'I had a text from Lulu, this morning,' he sighed. 'Travis is stable, it's just bruising and broken bones thankfully. But they're still not sure whether or not he'll wake up from the coma.'

'Only three things in life are guaranteed,' said Connie. 'Tax, death and paying five p for a plastic carrier bag.'

'And they said that even if he recovers, he could be blind!'

'I don't think I could cope with that,' Connie frowned.

'You remember Duncan Biscuit when he had that stroke? He talked really slowly like his batteries were running down?'

'He didn't have a stroke, he was just lazy,' said Connie. 'When he bumped into that Jobcentre woman outside Poundland, he was running like a fat bird with a buffet voucher!'

As Connie climbed into Chastity's car in Soho Square, he noticed a large pile of rubbish on the back seat.

'What's all that?' he said, holding his nose. 'And what the fuck's that pig-awful smell?'

'Oh yes,' Chastity sighed, sitting in the driver's seat and turning the ignition key. 'I've got a squatter!'

'A what?'

'Morning all,' said Gerry, springing up suddenly from amongst her worldly belongings.

'Aargh!' Connie screamed, lunging down into the foot well. 'What the buggery fuck is that?'

'Gerry!' she smiled, holding out a hand to shake.

166

'You're having a laugh, ain't ya? I'm not shaking that, you've probably wiped your arse a dozen times since you last washed it!' Connie screwed up his face at the thought.

'That's a little ignominious, isn't it?' Gerry frowned.

'Igno-what?' said Connie. 'Have I just stepped into the Twilight Zone or something?'

'Sorry, I forgot to tell you,' said Chastity.

'Forgot to tell me? Forgot to tell me? Just throw the bitch out!'

'I can't throw her out, she's got squatters rights,' said Chastity sheepishly.

'Stop the car, I'll fucking do it!' Connie looked back at Gerry acidly.

'He's very aggressive, isn't he?' she said, tapping Chastity on the shoulder.

'Aggressive?' Connie spat. 'If you don't get out of this car now, I'm gonna lamp ya!'

'Leave her alone,' said Chastity, pulling Connie back into his seat. 'She's a fellow actress, just a little down on her luck. It's my car and she's staying… for a while.'

'Thank you, dear,' said Gerry, glancing back at Connie defiantly.

'Besides, she's a very useful lady,' Chastity smiled. 'She sees everything that goes on, it was her who told me where to find Creighton's missing file. She's like an oracle.'

'Yeah, I can smell her oracle from here!' Connie snapped on his seatbelt and opened his window, gasping in a mouthful of much needed fresh air.

'And she's a witness to his murder. She saw Lettie push him!'

'Then why didn't the silly bitch tell the police?'

'They wouldn't listen to an old bag lady, would they?' Gerry explained.

'But if we clean her up, they will,' Chastity grinned.

'Hmm,' Connie sighed, resigning to the situation. 'Anyway, I'm not even supposed to be here. I should be rehearsing for the competition.'

'It's only cos Michael's in the hospital,' said Chastity.

'Is that the poor man who got attacked?' asked Gerry.

'How do you know about that?'

'I saw it happen. Diabolical business!' Gerry shook her head sadly. 'They shouted out his name, he turned and they pounced.'

'How did they know his name was Travis?'

'No, they shouted Michael. Who's Travis?' Gerry was confused. A stunned silence of realisation filled the car as Chastity pulled over into the kerb.

'Oh my God! You know what this means, don't you?' he gasped.

'Billy-no-nut's back!' Connie pulled out another cigarette. 'It wasn't just a random homophobic attack. They thought Travis was Michael!'

Michael sat beside Travis' hospital bed in a private room. Having been awake all night, he was very tired despite being wide-awake. He watched as a pretty young nurse took readings from a machine to one side. Her bright pink hair had dark roots pulled back beneath a small blue hat, held in place with several Kirby grips. She had a dozen piercings in each earlobe
168

and tattooed calligraphy on the side of her neck. As she leaned forward across the bed, he could read the words: kiss here. He imagined her dancing and laughing with her partner in a mosh pit at some grunge concert, happy, healthy, free and in love.

'You could try talking to him?' she smiled. 'It's possible they can hear you, even if they're in a coma.' Putting her pen in her top pocket, she hooked an aluminium clipboard over the bottom of the bed frame and left the room.

Michael sat silently for a moment. There was so much he wanted to tell Travis and yet, somehow, he could not think what to say. A gentle steady bleep rang out the rhythm of the heart that had fallen so in love with him. He could feel his own heart beating in unison.

'Erm...' he began. 'Travis? It's me, Michael.' He cleared his throat, trying not to get too emotional. 'I don't know whether you can hear me or not... but I want to tell you that I love you. I love you so much, I really do.' He paused hoping for a response, but there was nothing.

He looked up at the bruised face wrapped in swathes of bandage with eyes swollen shut. A sticking plaster across his nose secured a tube up his nostril, and a white foam neck brace held his head steady on the pillow. The tattoos on his grazed wrist disappeared underneath a plaster cast that ran the full length of his arm. On his bare chest, a small inked sparrow appeared to be holding one of the little round cardio stickers in its beak, as if to help Travis get better. Michael was surprised that something so simple could bring a tear to his eye.

'I, err… I'm so very sorry that I lied to you. I know Chastity told you, but I think you should hear it from me,' he swallowed back. 'I was so afraid of losing you, but there really was no excuse for not saying anything, and I'm sorry.' He took Travis' hand, gently entwining their fingers.

'When you wake up, there's a chance you might not even know who I am. So I want to say here and now while I've got the chance… thank you. For making me feel as though someone really wants me. And for making me the happiest I've ever been. And even if you don't remember me, I just want you to know that.'

'What's going on?' came a sudden voice. Michael jumped, for a moment thinking it was Travis speaking in his familiar Glaswegian accent. But then he realised it was coming from the doorway behind him. Quickly letting go of Travis' hand, he turned to look. A tall rugged middle-aged man dressed in a fawn tweed suit and green tie stared back at him sternly. Michael could see straight away the family resemblance to his lover. A shorter, matching woman stepped out from behind him and rushed forward to the other side of the bed, gasping in shock at the sorry sight of the broken man before her.

'Travis? It's your ma. We're here for you, bairn,' she cried tearfully.

'Who are you?' growled his father.

'I, err… I'm his best friend, Michael,' he gasped.

'You were holding his hand?' the man questioned suspiciously.

'The nurse,' said Michael, thinking on his feet. 'She told me touch was important… in his condition?'

'Hmm,' he huffed, walking to the bottom of the bed and looking at his son. 'Is he asleep?'

'No Hamish,' said his wife. 'He's in a coma, they told us.'

'Hmm,' he repeated. 'They said this was from a queer battering. Who was he hitting? They must have provoked him.'

'No,' said Michael, a little rattled. 'Travis isn't like that, he was just in the wrong place at the wrong time.'

At that moment, the pretty nurse returned.

'Are you Mr and Mrs McBradey?' she smiled. 'We've been expecting you, the doctor will be round shortly to brief you.' She walked across to Michael and rubbed his shoulders. 'And you mister, I think you should go home and get some sleep.'

'No, I want to stay here with Travis. I'm fine, really I am.'

'That cute boyfriend of yours will be asleep for quite a while yet – really you should rest and come back later.'

'Boyfriend?' Mr McBradey growled. 'What are you saying? That my son's an arse bandit?' Acutely embarrassed by her accidental indiscretion, the nurse quickly left the room.

'Yes if you must know,' Michael snapped, 'though there are kinder things to call us. He wouldn't have wanted you to find out this way. But yes, Travis is gay and I'm his partner,' said Michael bravely.

'You're screwing my son?' his father frowned, clenching his fists as if ready to punch him.

'Hamish! Haud yer wheesht,' his wife shouted at him with frustration.

171

'What kind of a sick perverted monster have you turned him into?'

'Being gay isn't a choice, it's a realisation,' defended Michael. 'But when Travis realised he was gay, he knew the choices he made would be very important to him.' He stood defiantly from his chair. 'He chose to move to London, chose to be himself and chose to live his own life. And as much as it might piss you off to hear, Travis chose me!'

'I think you'd better leave,' threatened Hamish with a deep sinister stare. 'And keep your buftie arse away from my fecking son!'

CHAPTER THIRTEEN

As Chastity reversed his car into Madame Fifi's parking space at her deco apartment building, a short man in a black top hat and trousers with a gold-buttoned red doorman coat stepped from the front entrance. Walking with shoulders back and a slight limp, he ceremoniously marched his way across the tarmac towards the car.

'Oh, here we go!' Connie puffed on his cigarette. 'We've arrived on the set of Camberwick Green.'

'Ooh yes, Captain Snort from Pippin Fort!' Chastity laughed.

'Once you've been in the army, it stays with you,' Gerry observed.

'I don't know why he's limping. Fanny said he was only in the Catering Corps.'

'What did he do, suppress the enemy with egg and chips?' Connie smirked, as the man tapped on the driver's window.

'Corporal Richard Taylor, at your service,' he yelled, standing to attention and saluting. Connie covered his mouth to hide his grin.

'Good morning, that man,' said Chastity, trying to sound official. 'We're here to collect some items on behalf of Madame Fifi. Lead the way!' With a nod and another salute, he turned and marched his squeaky boots back off across the car park. Connie and Chastity climbed out to follow.

'Come on Company, no lollygagging. And the best of luck on your mission!' Gerry joked. Connie and Chastity climbed out to follow Corporal Taylor.

'Lolly what?' said Connie. 'I didn't think people talked like that no more!'

As the doors to the lift opened on the fifth floor, Corporal Taylor gave them another salute.

'Turn right, fourth door,' he directed, as they walked up the deeply carpeted corridor.

'I expected us to come out the top of a music box,' giggled Connie.

'No, that was Trumpton! Camberwick Green was the little clown turning the handle.'

'You live in a different world you do, don't you?' Connie stared with dismay.

Turning the apartment key, Chastity pushed open the door to a plush entrance hall. Elaborately framed gold-leaf mirrors and pictures decorated imperial blue walls, and an ornate hand-carved Italian side table adorned with a huge bunch of pink and white silk peonies stood elegantly between two floor-standing mahogany candle sconces. A long hand-woven Moroccan rug ran the full length of the room, and a large sparkling French crystal chandelier with white porcelain cherubs hung silently from the high ceiling. They stood in wonder for a moment, stunned by the sheer brazen opulence of it all.

'Aw my Gawd, it's like the Moulin Rouge!' Connie gasped.

'Once a showgirl, always a showgirl,' agreed Chastity.

They pushed through double doors at the end of the hall into a gloriously spacious salon. Ivory leather and silk furniture highlighted with baroque gold was conveniently positioned around a large white and grey marble fire surround to one end. Above it in pride of place, a gold art deco frame contained a large Tamara de Lempicka portrait of Madame Fifi herself, wearing an elegant emerald green gown and a matching wide-brimmed hat.

'Do you reckon that's an original?' Connie squinted.

'I don't know. But it's definitely her, so someone sat and painted it.'

'How do you know? They might have been standing up!'

In a large, bright bay window to the left, organza silk curtains created a stunning backdrop to a cream grand piano, the lid of which carried several dozen uniquely framed photographs, portraits and sketches. They walked across the thick golden carpet to take a look.

'Look at this one of her with Creighton,' Chastity sighed, holding up a snapshot of them touching hands across the bonnet of a vintage Rolls Royce. 'Isn't it romantic, they look so much in love?'

'This is how I like to think of her,' smirked Connie, holding up a younger picture of Fifi, somewhere in Eastern Europe wearing dungarees and a straw hat, driving a tractor.

'Aah, remembering her roots! Don't knock it, potatoes make good vodka.'

Through another set of double doors, they entered her matching boudoir. A massive canopied bed sat majestically atop a carpeted raised platform next to mirror-fronted wardrobes.

'Here we go,' said Chastity, pulling open two of the doors.

'You can do her undies, I'm not touching her rank knickers,' Connie whinged, fanning his nose in mock disgust.

Rummaging through Fifi's clothes with unbridled glee, they selected several items from the rail and chucked them on the bed ready to take, unaware of the tall thin woman covertly approaching from behind.

'Stop right there and don't move!' she growled, grabbing Connie from behind and thrusting a large kitchen knife against his throat.

Michael sat on a plastic chair in the large entrance hall of the hospital. Crouching forward, he slowly sipped the coffee he had bought from the machine. As soon as he had heard about the police contacting Travis' parents, he knew they would naturally get priority over him. However he hadn't quite expected such a cruel and frosty first meeting. Regardless, he was for the moment still reluctant to leave the building where Travis lay fighting for his life. His distant thoughts were suddenly interrupted.

'Michael, isn't it?' said a soft voice. He looked up to find Travis' mother standing in front of him.

'Yes,' he rasped, jumping to his feet and looking around with caution.

'Don't worry, I've left his da upstairs,' she smiled awkwardly. 'He's got a heid full o' mince right now, it's all been a terrible shock.'

176

'For all of us, yeah,' Michael nodded politely.

'I'm Jeanie. Do you mind if I join you?' she said, gesturing to the next seat.

'I would really, really like that,' Michael smiled, waiting for her to sit before he followed. She hesitated for a while, gathering her thoughts.

'When Travis was a wee lad of about six, I noticed he was a bit different from other boys his age. He still played with soldiers and guns and that, but he was somehow gentler.' She smiled with melancholy as she remembered. 'He would get emotional about things at the drop of a hat. I thought it was just the influence of his older sisters. You see he's the youngest of six, my only boy?'

'Yes, he's told me,' said Michael.

'His da was always strict with him, but he didn't mean any harm, he was just trying to toughen him up. But… do you think there's something I could have done to make things better for him?'

'Better?'

'Well… different?' She sighed, fiddling with the front of her jacket.

'Travis was born gay, we all are. There's no say in the matter, we just have to bloody get on with it. I guess it's what we do with it that counts.'

'You said he chose to move to London, to live his own life?' Jeanie took a tissue from her pocket to dab her eyes as they began to well up. 'What I'm trying to ask is… was he desperate to get away from us?'

'You've got to understand he loves you both, he really does. And he would have told you eventually. He's told Morag.'

'Morag? That doesn't surprise me really, they're the closest of all my bairns.' She blew her nose and thought for a moment. 'How did your mother react? Was she a blubbering old hen like me?'

'I grew up in an orphanage. I've only just found my real mum and dad,' said Michael.

'Oh, I'm sorry to hear that, really I am.' Wiping her eyes dry and putting away her tissue, Jeanie breathed a big sigh. 'So, you're in love with our son?'

'Yes. Yes, I am!' Michael beamed proudly.

'And does he feel the same?'

'Very much so, yes.'

'Then I guess you're family,' she said, patting his hand. 'But I would suggest you stay away for a wee while, just to give his da a chance to adjust.'

'Oh,' Michael frowned disappointedly.

'Travis has returned to the womb, and that's my job. When he's reborn I can hand him back, so that he can live his own life with you. But I promise, the moment anything changes, you will be the very first to know.'

Michael sat silently for a moment, contemplating having to pull himself away from Travis' side. The very idea made his heart ache, but he had to get back to work to support himself, and he still needed to find time to save his own father from Lettie's fiendish plot.

'OK, I understand,' he agreed reluctantly. Borrowing a biro from a passing nurse, he jotted his number on the side of his paper cup and tore it off, handing it to Jeanie.

'We'll be staying at Travis' home while we're in London. His keys were with his things. It could be a long haul for a hotel, and they've already told us we can only wait here until tomorrow night after visiting hours. So go on home yourself and get some rest.'

178

Giving his hand a final squeeze, she stood. 'Pray for him,' she smiled, before returning to the ward.

As Michael finished his coffee, he thought about his boyfriend's apartment, and how they should have been living there together right now. But suddenly, his daydream was interrupted by a terrifying thought.

'Oh my God!' he gasped. 'They're gonna find Travis' playroom!'

Back at Madame Fifi's swish apartment, Connie was frightened for his life as the tall thin woman's blade pressed tighter against the skin of his neck.

'Aargh!' he gargled.

'Don't move, keep perfectly still!' cried Chastity, himself rooted to the spot.

'It wasn't me, it was her!' Connie panicked, pointing at his friend.

'Don't blame me, I haven't done anything!'

'Who are you? Why are you here?' shouted the woman.

'We work for Madame Fifi, we're here to collect some of her clothes!' Chastity cried.

'Where is Madame?' The woman squinted her eyes with suspicion.

'She's been accused of murder. She's in prison awaiting trial, we're just trying to help her!' The woman looked hurt by this revelation.

'You're not burglars then?'

'No, no, we're her friends!' Connie gasped. 'Well, sort of.' The woman released her hold and stepped back, hand still clenched defensively around the handle.

'And neither of you are Lettie?'

179

'God no! I'm not Lettie, I'm Connie,' he said, rubbing his neck with a sigh of relief. 'And this is my sister Chastity… don't laugh.'

'How do you know Lettie, then?' Chastity asked.

'Madame has warned me never to let him step over the threshold,' she said. 'I'm Madame's housekeeper. I'm Hortense.'

'I'm all tense meself, after that!' said Connie.

Panic slightly over, they noticed she was wearing a short but plain black linen dress with black lace tights and shoes. A small white lace-edged apron hung in front. Long grey hair was pulled tightly back from her worn face into a bun beneath a small matching hat.

'We work for her too. We're drag queens at Sugar Sugar, so we're on the same payroll,' said Chastity, looking at the knife. 'So, why don't we just put that thing down now?'

Hortense placed the knife on the bed next to Fifi's clothes, picking up a jacket and holding it to her chest adoringly before slowly straightening out its crumples and laying it gently back on the bed. Connie and Chastity looked at each other, baffled by this odd behaviour.

'Do you live here, then?' Chastity asked.

'I don't live anywhere.'

'Then, where do you sleep?'

'I don't sleep… I wait. On a chair in Madame's kitchen,' she said, lovingly folding another garment. They watched with bemusement as she took a suitcase from the top shelf inside the wardrobe and began meticulously packing the garments that lay on the bed. 'The police came,' she said, walking to a mirrored chest of drawers to fetch underwear and stockings. 'They went through Madame's clothes.'

'Why would they have done that?' said Chastity.

'They were looking for her red Dior evening gown, but I told them they wouldn't find it!' Hortense smiled, admiring her own fanatical efficiency. 'Madame must have removed it between two and six on the fifteenth of August, while I was out shopping.' She paused for a moment, looking ahead dreamily. 'When Madame walked her Dior, the chiffon flowed like fairy gossamer on a summer breeze. And the golden rhinestones sparkled like the evening sun reflected in a lonely brook.'

'Eh?' Connie was getting nervous.

'Did you know, the song More Than A Woman was written about Madame?'

'The Bee Gees must have known her intimately, then,' Chastity mused.

Shaking her head with awe, Hortense took an empty toiletries bag from the bedside drawer and walked through to Fifi's en suite.

'That is one creepy fuckin' bitch!' whispered Connie.

'Ooh, I feel like Joan Fontaine in Rebecca!' Chastity shivered.

'How could you sleep, knowing that was sitting in the kitchen waiting for you?'

'And that feckin' great knife? Did your whole life flash before your eyes, Connie love?'

'Yes, it did,' he nodded. 'And I remembered... you still owe me a tenner for that mascara!'

'Talk about Lettie? Hortense is like one of those nineteen-fifties serial killers you see on Unsolved Mysteries.'

181

'And black lace tights? It looks like she's been splashed by something driving through a muddy puddle.'

'Well then, let's get a wiggle on,' Chastity sighed. 'The sooner we get out of this mausoleum, the better!'

Corporal Taylor vehemently refused to allow Chastity and Connie to see any recorded CCTV footage of the car park without Madame Fifi being present. Frustrated, and realising they could not spend any more time trying to persuade him, they threw the suitcase into the boot of the car and climbed back in. Leaving him on the tarmac shaking his fist, they headed off towards Holloway Prison.

'He appeared frightfully vociferous,' said Gerry.

'Why can't you just speak proper English like what normal people do?' Connie snapped.

'I'm proud of my diction!'

'Oh, you've got one of them too, have you? I thought she reminded me of someone,' Connie quipped.

'That's it!' Chastity cried, slamming on the brakes. Connie shot forward into the foot well.

'Aargh! What the fuck are you doing?' he screamed.

'We dress Gerry as Fifi! That'll persuade Captain Snort to show us the footage.'

'Eh?' Connie climbed back into his chair and fastened the seatbelt.

'She's a character actress, she can do it! We'll slip her a costume out of the suitcase before we go in the prison. She's about Fifi's size.'

'Sounds like a jolly jape,' grinned Gerry. 'Would be wonderful to get back into the harness!'

'And you can do her wig and makeup, Connie?'

'Maybe. If she has a fucking wash!'

Michael stood at the entrance of the alley to Connie's flat. It had been jet-washed down after the crime scene had been dismantled. A cold shiver ran down his spine as he stared morbidly at the unusually clean cobbles and walls. There was not a single trace from the horrific event just the night before. It had been quickly swept away into a vague memory while Soho continued to buzz all around. It was as if nothing had even happened, as if Travis didn't really matter.

As he remembered the floor covered in blood, Daisy spied him from the front entrance of Sugar Sugar and ran to greet him.

'Oh, Lulu,' he sighed, pulling him into a hug. 'I'm so, so sorry! How is he?'

'I think he's stable thanks, but he'll be in a coma for a while to protect his brain.' His eyes welled with tears.

'Oh my God! Anyway, come on, don't dwell,' said Daisy, looking up and down the street cautiously. 'Let's go have a cup of tea, I've got gossip!' Taking Michael's arm, he led him swiftly up the metal stairs to Connie's.

As Michael sat down on the sofa, Nigel jumped up and snuggled him under the chin.

'You've finally come out from behind the telly?' he sighed with relief, kissing his head and stroking his back.

'Ahh! That's cause you're upset,' said Daisy, switching on the kettle before joining them on the sofa. 'Cats have a mystical connection to the cosmos, they know these things.'

'Do you think?'

'Yeah, I saw it on Oprah. This woman couldn't have a baby, so she had a kitten. One day she went to the supermarket, but she was so depressed she just kicked the shelf and bought what fell off. Trouble is, it was a microwave and it landed on her head!'

'That's insane,' Michael laughed.

'Straight up, on my mother's eyes! The kitten sensed her pain through the cosmos and walked five miles all the way to the hospital to be with her.'

'Ah, that's really sweet. What happened?'

'Someone ran it over in the car park, but the thought was there!'

'Anyway, you said you had gossip?' Michael asked.

'Yeah, Lettie was right on one last night.'

'Again? What was it this time?'

'About you not doing the show. Well, you know what I'm like with my nerves, but I stood up to her.'

'What did you say?' As the kettle clicked off, Michael lifted Nigel onto the seat beside him and walked through to make the tea.

'I just told her you had a migraine. But she's nervous, she's really nervous,' Daisy called after him.

'How so?'

'Fanny stood in for you, and she's Fifi's friend best, ain't she? Lettie's terrified she's spying, so she pounced on her in my lobby.'

'What happened?'

'She told her to fuck off and not come back, and that I'm not allowed to let her in ever again or I'll get the sack!'

'Really?'

'Well, you know Fanny? She's not frightened of anyone. She just laughed and got her tits out,' Daisy grinned. 'She's the spit of my friend Mandy up bingo... trouble's her middle name, an'all.'

'I'd like to meet this Mandy,' smiled Michael, handing Daisy his drink.

'Last week, she was trying to dance The Macarena at a party. It looked like sign language, and a deaf woman in the corner thought she was telling her she'd slept with her husband,' Daisy laughed. 'My life, you should have seen Mandy's black eye! She looked like Chi Chi the Panda in sling-backs.'

'Thank you Daisy, you've really cheered me up,' said Michael.

'But that's not the important thing what I wanted to tell you.' Daisy's smile dropped. 'I had a text from Chastity. She tried to get you, but you were in the hospital. She's told me to shadow you till they get back from seeing Fifi.'

'Shadow me?' Michael slowly sat back down.

'It's a technical term we use in the security trade. I had to do training and everything. I got a certificate.'

'I know what it means Daisy, but why?'

'You're not gonna like this,' he replied, biting his lip. 'When the villains ran at Travis in the alley, they called out a name. But it wasn't his.'

185

'Who's was it, then?'

'It was yours. That vicious beating was meant for you!'

CHAPTER FOURTEEN

Arriving at Holloway Prison, Chastity and Connie handed over the visiting order and Fifi's suitcase before being frisked by a burly male warden. Connie's request for a second go fell on deaf ears, as they were herded through to a long wooden communal bench in a large dank waiting area.

'You're treated like a criminal yourself just visiting,' said Connie, looking around uncomfortably at the array of fellow arrivals.

'It's like being gay,' Chastity nodded. 'We're all tarred with the same bigoted brush!'

'Mind you, that guard can knock the hinges off my cat-flap any day!' grinned Connie, licking his lips.

After a while, everyone was redirected along a corridor to a cavernous Victorian hall. Standing just inside the entrance on a platform at the top of several concrete steps, they could see a row of barred windows high up on one wall, a stark reminder that they too were now on the inside. Through the dusty glass, light flooded in across a score of grey Formica tables with bright orange plastic chairs bolted to the slate floor on either side. From intertwining brick arches across the high ceiling hung enormous fluorescent tube lights, draped with swaying strands of dust.

'Aw my Gawd, it's like something out of Oliver!' said Connie.

'It is a bit Dickensian, isn't it?' Chastity agreed, biting his lip.

'*As long as he needs me*,' Connie warbled in his best Nancy, as a shove from behind pushed them both further down the steps.

'Oi, watch it!' Chastity cried, swinging round the bottom of the black metal handrail.

'Aw, shut up!' grunted a ratty-haired plump woman, climbing over him to be first at the nearest table.

'And where were we when the Manners Fairy handed out talent? Eating from a pig trough?' bitched Connie as he glided past.

'Piss off, you wanker,' the woman responded with disinterest.

Settling at a table on the other side of the room, they heard keys turn in a lock as a metal door at the far end screeched open. Under the watchful eye of Miss Finch, several inmates filtered out and took their seats around the hall. Last in the queue was Madame Fifi.

'Oh my God, is that her?' said Chastity. 'She looks like shit! And is she walking with a lilt to one side?'

'How the mighty have fallen,' Connie mused. 'Lovely smock! Isn't it marvellous what they can do with polyester, nowadays?'

'The beds are like concrete,' Fifi moaned, arriving at their table and sitting painfully on the chair in front of them. 'So now, I have a bad back.'

'Yeah, and the front's pretty fucked up, too!'

'For once I agree with you, Connie,' Fifi sighed, pulling at her fringe. 'I need a haircut, but I'm going nowhere near anyone with scissors in this zoo!'

'Not what you're used to?' Chastity smiled sympathetically. 'We met Hortense when we got your clothes.'

'The woman is deranged but desperately in love with me,' Fifi gestured dramatically. 'The floor needed scrubbing, what could I do?'

'Touché, Dolly!' Connie laughed.

'How are my family?' Fifi had concern in her eyes.

'Edith's fine,' Chastity assured, 'though Lettie's sacked her. But it's for the best she's out of his way till we sort all this out. And the rest will do her good.'

'And Lulu?'

'There may be a problem there,' Chastity said, furrowing his brow.

'Billy-no-nut's back!' Connie raised his eyes.

'But we're looking out for her, Daisy should be with her now.'

'I'm going to destroy Lettie for what she has done to us!' growled Fifi.

'We've got photographic evidence that she pushed Creighton from the window,' said Connie with glee.

'I knew it!' Fifi screwed her hands together.

'We're just trying to find a way of proving you didn't kill her brother, then we can hit her with a double-whammy!' Chastity grinned excitedly.

'By Christmas, it will all be over. We'll finally be able to kiss her arse goodbye once and for all, under the mistletoe.'

'I wouldn't kiss her arse under anaesthetic!' Fifi cringed.

'Then the great Madame Fifi can return!' Connie added brashly.

'Shhh! Keep your voice down,' Fifi warned, looking around. They hadn't until then noticed her scheming cellmate Bunnie, listening from the table behind.

'Oops,' Connie whispered.

'I spoke to The Extractor,' said Chastity quietly. 'I have to confess, the thought of meeting him scares the shit out of me!'

'Gunter? He makes air vents for office buildings.'

'Oh!' Chastity breathed a sigh of relief. 'We're gonna break you out.'

'How?'

'We need to lift you gently over the wall and drive you to a secret location. Gunter's got you a fake passport. It's a special delivery through the back door.'

'That's normally my line of business!' chuckled Connie.

Frustrated that she could no longer hear their conversation, Bunnie signalled across the hall to her cohort Finch. Hands behind her back and chest out, she wandered slowly towards their table, as if on inspection.

'Thursday,' said Fifi, a wry smile forming across her face. 'There's a water tower in the recreation yard, you'll see it from the road. I'll be under it at three o-clock sharp.' They looked up as Finch nosily stopped at their table.

'So I just opened the lid, and there they were… three tiny little kittens!' Chastity feigned with joy. Shaking her head knowingly, Finch kept walking.

'Now listen!' Fifi leaned in closer. 'Lettie thinks she's conned Creighton out of everything, but she hasn't… he was nobody's fool! He will only have

190

signed over the Soho estates to her, including my club. They're my inheritance, and he will have done it knowing I could find a way to get them back.'

'Blimey,' said Chastity.

'But there is more money, much more!' Fifi took another glance around to guarantee their privacy. 'Creighton kept diaries. They will provide evidence that he believed he was Lulu's father. Get them and she'll inherit the rest.'

'Where are these diaries?' Chastity asked.

'In Berlin.' Fifi continued. 'They're in an antique safe that has three big vintage keys.'

'We've already found two of those in Soho,' Connie winked.

'Good. Verity holds the third. We must all meet in Berlin at the Vindergurderbreurgenshaftenshitz club.'

'How the fuck are we supposed to do that?' Connie whinged. 'We ain't got no money!'

'And what about missing the show? If Lettie suspects anything, she might kill us!' Chastity bit his nails.

'You're forgetting how long you have both worked for me,' Fifi smirked. 'I know all about your Sisterhood and its crafty, cunning, scheming, underhand, clever little ways. You, Connie... sneaking off before the end of a show to screw one of my customers? And you, Chastity... faking a tooth abscess to spend a weekend in Margate with your friend Frenchie?'

'How do you know about that?' Chastity gasped.

'Creighton's solicitor is a crook, so he'll agree to anything for a fee. But the henchmen in Berlin who guard his legacy won't be so easy to convince. So just drop all your pathetic little excuses, get Lulu to Berlin and make this happen!'

Preparing for the evening's performance in Sugar Sugar's dressing room, Michael was wracked with guilt.

'This is insane! That should be me up there in that coma,' he said, throwing his head in his hands. 'I thought Fifi had scared Billy off?'

'Apparently not,' said Connie, lighting a cigarette.

'It can't have been Billy himself who attacked Travis, he knows you too well to make that kind of mistake.' Chastity put his hand on Michael's shoulder supportively. 'So, if he's got a couple of his lackeys to do the deed, he probably believes it is you in that coma. At least you're safe for now, cos he won't be coming back to Soho any time soon.'

'It's all my fault. If I hadn't met Travis...'

'You can't blame yourself, Dolly! It's just fate.'

'Connie's right.' Chastity sat at the counter and began to apply foundation to his face. 'The best you can do is look after him until he recovers. Now, come and get your makeup on, we've only got half an hour.'

'How can I look after him if his dad won't even let me near him?' Michael slumped into his chair.

'Can't you just visit when he's not there?' suggested Connie.

Chastity tipped his head back in the mirror. 'We've been so busy today, I've not had a chance to pluck my nose hairs,' he said, screwing his face to get a better look.

'Here, try this,' said Connie, flicking the button on his cigarette lighter and thrusting it under his nostrils.

'Aargh!' he cried, slapping Connie's hand away and grabbing for a wet wipe. 'You've burned me, you stupid bitch! What are you, some kind of sadist?'

'Oh my God!' Michael gasped. 'I almost forgot. Travis' playroom!'

'Playroom?' Connie asked with glee.

'He's got a leather dungeon in his flat. Whips, dildos, the lot. There's even a sex sling.'

'No wonder your cheeks are so rosy!'

'This is serious, Connie! His parents are gonna be staying there, I can't let them find it.'

'But they know he's gay now, don't they?' asked Chastity, dabbing inside his nose with a cotton bud.

'Yeah, but there's gay… and there's GAY!'

'Stop panicking Dolly, it'll probably do them a favour,' Connie laughed. 'They sound a bit uptight to me, they might learn something.'

'Not this, it'd devastate Travis!' Michael grabbed Chastity's arm. 'They're gonna be there tomorrow night. Please, you've got to help me?'

'Let's just go round there tomorrow before they arrive and take it all out,' Chastity suggested.

'I haven't got a key!' Michael was desperate.

'I could pretend it's mine, say we rent the room?' Connie grinned. 'I'll take one of me boys, haul meself in that sling.'

'Oh, that'd be just fucking perfect,' Michael growled. 'Letting them think it's rented to a queer hooker!'

'I said haul meself, not whore meself!'

'Really? Speaks someone who's knickers go up and down more often than Selfridge's lifts,' Michael bitched.

'I'm trying to fuckin' help, here!' yelled Connie.

'Stop it, you two!' Chastity shouted. 'This won't solve anything.'

'His dad can't even cope with the gay thing. If they thought Travis was into sadomasochism, they'd probably never speak to him again.' Michael scratched his head, trying to think. 'You said to look after him, that's what I'm trying to do here!'

'Then what do you suggest?' Connie snapped sarcastically. 'Only, I don't want to state the obvious, but we're all gay as a stick of rock. Snap us in half, it says queer right the way through!'

Michael sat quietly for a moment. Travis' parents would find the playroom. There was no denying the facts and there was nothing he could do about that. If he could just think of a way to distract them from thinking so badly of their son, he might just be able to protect his future relationship with them. Travis was in this situation because of him, it was the least he could do.

'There's only one way to solve this,' he said decisively. 'We've got to let them think the dungeon is rented to a straight couple.'

Holloway Prison was on midnight lockdown. As Fifi lay asleep in the darkness of her cell, she didn't hear a key turn in the lock, or the door swinging quietly open. Bunnie slid silently from between her sheets and slipped on her shoes. Glancing over at Fifi in slumber, she tiptoed out of the room.

'She's dead to the world,' she whispered with a smile.

'She soon will be,' smirked Finch, snapping the door closed.

Creeping along the walkway and down the metal stairs, they crossed the darkened recreation hall and through another locked door into the corridor. As they arrived at a wall-mounted telephone, Finch glanced cautiously up at the security camera then down at her watch.

'Three minutes,' she instructed, as Bunnie lifted the receiver and inserted a phone card. Finch looked up and down the empty corridor to check the coast was clear as she dialled a number.

'I wanna talk to Billy,' she said into the mouthpiece. 'Alright Bruv? This Madame Fifi you was telling me about? She's in here with me... yeah, short-arse, funny accent, big tits? She's topped someone... she's on remand.'

'What's he saying?' asked Finch.

'It's definitely her!' Bunnie nodded. 'You want me to finish her off?' A broad grin formed on her face. 'No probs Bruv, consider it sorted. It'll look like suicide. Thursday night after lights out, it's all gonna get too much for the poor little bitch,' she said sarcastically. 'We're gonna string her up!'

Meanwhile, in the smoke-filled office above his bar in Southend-on-Sea, Billy threw back his head and laughed into a gruff smoker's cough.

'What's going on?' grinned Knuckles, swigging from a brandy glass.

'Fifi's in nick!' he answered, handing the receiver back. 'Me sister Bunnie's gonna take her out.' He leaned forward, rubbing his hands excitedly across the surface of the desk. 'We've had Michael and now we've got that vindictive slut. Oh yes, my plan's coming together nicely.'

'So, what's next?'

'It's time for a trip to Soho.' He drew back deeply on his soggy cigar butt. 'I want them fucking security tapes!'

The following evening, Chastity sat with Michael in Connie's flat watching commercials on television.

'It's all a con, this!' said Chastity, sipping his coffee.

'How so?'

'Well, they always use supermodels to advertise these elasticated body shapers. I mean, look at her?' He pointed at the screen. 'It took me an hour to get into mine. It promised I'd look like Kylie Minogue, but all I saw when I looked in the mirror was Hylda Baker.'

'Really?' Michael giggled.

'Yes, I bent forward quick to tie my shoelace and it sprung me into a backwards somersault, luckily there was a chair behind me.'

They heard the front door slam as Connie breezed into the room, taking off his jacket and throwing his bag on the table. Looking up, they stared at him in disbelief. His skin colour had changed to a dark mahogany brown.

'Oh my God, what happened to your face?' Michael gasped.

196

'It's fake tan. I just had my photo done for the fashion competition. I'm gonna be in the paper!' Connie grinned. 'What d'ya think?'

'You look like a coconut with alopecia!' laughed Chastity.

'It's a bit too dark, isn't it?' Michael asked wryly.

'I got the strongest one they had, don't you like it?'

'No, but it'll have to do,' said Chastity. 'We need that five-thousand pound prize money to get us to Berlin.'

'What?'

'It's the only hope we've got to raise the cash,' nodded Michael.

'Oh, that's just fucking marvellous, ain't it?' Snatching up his bag, Connie lit a cigarette and stomped tetchily into his bedroom. 'You already owe me a tenner for that mascara!' he called back.

At that moment, the doorbell rang.

'That'll be them!' said Chastity, jumping to his feet and running into the hall.

'Now, who the fuck's that?' said Connie, poking his head back around the door.

'Frenchie and her husband,' said Michael excitedly, reaching for the remote and switching off the television. 'They're gonna pretend they rent Travis' playroom.'

'Come in, love,' said Chastity, leading the way. 'Where's Shaun?'

'He's got a kickboxing exhibition, babes,' said Frenchie.

'Ain't he here?' Michael panicked. 'But we need a straight man as well, it's gotta be a couple!'

'Oh, I thought you just needed me?' Frenchie sighed.

'No! Oh God, no!' Michael threw his head in his hands as Connie walked back in from his bedroom.

'New dress, Frenchie?' he asked sarcastically, drawing back on his nicotine.

'No, I've had this ages,' she smiled proudly.

'Oh yeah, I can see that now,' Connie bitched. He suddenly jumped back with shock as a young toddler looked out from behind her legs. 'What the fuck's that?'

'My nephew. You met Shaun's sister at my wedding? He's her'n.'

'Hello, Ern!' Chastity smiled at him sweetly.

'No, his name's Cameron,' Frenchie laughed. 'I look after him while she's at night school. She's doing brick-laying and roofing so she can build her own extension.' At the sudden sight of Connie, the toddler began screaming frantically.

'What's the matter with him?' Chastity frowned with a start.

'He's frightened of black men.'

'It's not black, it's Caribbean Sunset!'

'You look like an inflatable bodybuilder with a puncture, babes!'

'Where are we gonna find a straight bloke at this short notice?' Michael cried. 'Travis' parents are gonna be there in an hour!'

'You can do it, can't you?' said Frenchie, jabbing Chastity in the ribs. 'Don't you remember that hotel in Margate? Mr and Mrs Smith?' She reached into her bag and took out a dummy comforter, shoving it into Cameron's mouth to quieten his tears.

198

'We shared a double room to get it cheaper,' Chastity explained.

'Do you think you could do it?' Michael grovelled hopefully.

'Yeah, me and the wife?' he said feigning a deep macho voice. 'We've always been into that there kinky stuff, ain't we bitch?' He grabbed his crotch and pretended to draw back and spit, as if to demonstrate.

'Don't put Frenchie in Travis' swing,' Connie smirked. 'She'll have his fucking ceiling down!'

'Fuck right off, babe,' she grinned.

'Thank you for doing this, Frenchie. I am very grateful,' said Michael, giving her a hug.

'You was my bridesmaid, weren't ya? I owe you one,' she winked.

'I'd like to go to this kickboxing exhibition. Where is it?' Connie licked his lips. 'All those tasty boys with their shirts off... more abs than a Hollyoaks audition!'

'You can't go, you'll have to wait here and mind Cameron,' said Chastity.

'You're having a fucking laugh, ain't ya?' Connie stomped his foot. 'Let Lulu do it, it's her bastard boyfriend you're saving!'

'I can't, I'm going up to see Travis while his mum and dad aren't there.'

'And you can't smoke around a baby,' Chastity growled, snatching the cigarette from Connie's mouth and stamping it out on the carpet. Cameron began screaming uncontrollably again, as Frenchie passed him to his new babysitter.

'Why is it always me?' he frowned, holding him out in front like a sack of potatoes.

'Please, Connie? Pretty, pretty please?' Michael batted his eyelashes. 'I'll sing at your fashion show for you?'

Connie shot him an acid glance. 'Do I have a choice? Anyway, it can sweep the chimney while it's here.'

'And then he'll be the same colour as you!' Michael chuckled.

'I'll warn you though, he's obsessed with light switches,' Frenchie advised. 'He'll be flashing them on and off like a brothel, but I expect you're used to that, Connie?"

'You needn't worry, all the switches here are too high up on the wall,' assured Chastity. 'It was re-wired in the seventies when we all wore platform-shoes.'

'But I'm not breast-feeding, and I ain't doing no shitty nappies,' Connie whinged. 'And if it don't shut up by the time Coronation Street starts, it's going in the fucking microwave!'

CHAPTER FIFTEEN

Stepping from a taxi in Pimlico, Chastity and Frenchie paused and looked up at Travis' apartment block. Framed by bright moonlight, the building looked dark and ominous, casting a long sinister shadow across the car park. Having been told all about Travis' obstinate father, a cold shiver ran down Chastity's spine at what may lie ahead.

'Looks creepy, doesn't it?' he gulped.

'Is it a full moon?' said Frenchie, pulling down the tight hem of her short skirt.

'Either that or a pigeon with a big torch,' he mused, taking her by the hand. 'Come on wife, let's get this over with.'

In the silent entrance lobby, they nervously walked across to the lift.

'Shhh! You're so noisy, can't you tiptoe?' Chastity whispered.

'In these shoes? I don't think so.'

'I've seen stilettos leave marks on woodblock, but never on granite!'

'Fuck right off, babes,' Frenchie grinned, pushing the button on the lift.

Inside the apartment, Travis' parents took off their coats and draped them over their two suitcases just inside the front door. Having stopped for shopping on the way from the hospital, Jeanie emptied the plastic carrier bag onto the kitchen worktop. She filled the kettle and turned on the cooker before searching through the cupboards for a frying pan.

'You said bacon sandwich?' she called across.

'Perfect, hen,' Hamish replied, trying to work out how to open the doors to the balcony. 'It's awful stuffy in here, if I can just… ah, here we are.' Flipping the lock, he slid back the glass door a small way and took in a deep breath of fresh air.

'This is a lovely stove,' Jeanie smiled, laying several bacon rashers in the pan.

'Aye, our lad's done good,' Hamish sighed proudly. But his pride tarnished slightly when he remembered what had happened at the hospital. 'You spoke to this Michael?'

'Aye. He's a nice boy. I can see why Travis likes him.'

'He's led him astray, that's what he's done,' Hamish frowned. 'It's this town, Jeanie. Full of vice and corruption, we need to take him home.'

'He's a grown man, Hamish,' she said forcefully, slamming a loaf of bread on the island and taking up a knife. 'He has his job and this home, you're just going to have to accept this is the way he is now.'

'Never!' Hamish slammed his hand against the doorframe. 'As long as there's breath in my body, my son will not be queer!' He marched across the room and threw the coats aside on the sofa, picking up the suitcases and carrying them through the open door to Travis' bedroom. 'And another thing,' he spat angrily. 'If that Michael or any other pervert comes anywhere near my family, I swear I'll kill them!'

He threw open the door to the playroom and switched on the light. 'I tell you Jeanie, I…' He paused, open-mouthed at the extraordinary sight before him.

'What is it?' she asked, walking across. He pulled the door closed to block her view.

'You don't need to see this.' He stood in front of the closed door.

'Yes, I do!' she huffed, pushing past him and shoving at the door. 'Oh, my!' she gasped, holding her hands to her face.

At that moment, there was a loud rap on the front door. Hamish leaned forward and pulled it open.

'Hello there, mate,' said Chastity in a butch deep voice, reaching a hand forward to shake. 'I'm Chas and this is the wife, Frenchie.'

'Hi,' she curtseyed. 'Is Travis home?'

'And who might you be?' said Hamish, eyes narrowing with suspicion.

'We rent a room here for our fun and games,' Chastity grinned nervously. 'Ah, I see you've already found our playroom!'

'Vice and corruption,' Hamish repeated, looking at his wife.

'We're Travis' parents,' said Jeanie, reaching forward to shake Chastity's hand. 'He's poorly at the moment in hospital. We're staying here whilst we visit.'

'Oh, that's a shame,' said Frenchie. 'We was hoping for a bit of a sesh tonight, but it looks like you're gonna have dinner?'

'Oh, the bacon!' Jeanie remembered, running across the stove.

'A bit of a what?' Hamish growled.

'Well, you know how it is, mate,' grinned Chastity, leaning an arm against the door frame. 'When the wife's willing, give it top billing!'

Hamish wasn't impressed by his strangely brash behaviour. 'Whatever you two do, you're not doing it while we're here!'

'Wouldn't dream of it, Hamish mate,' Chastity said, with a knowing wink.

'Perhaps we should just go?' Frenchie jabbed Chastity in the ribs.

'Just hold your horses a wee moment, pal!' He grabbed Chastity by the front of his shirt and pulled him inside against the wall. 'How did you know my name was Hamish?'

'Erm… I err…' Chastity bumbled.

'Travis. It was Travis who told us,' Frenchie gushed nervously.

Hamish stared them both in the eyes intensely. 'You're lying!' he snapped. 'That Michael sent you here to do this, didn't he? You're one if his merry band of arse bandits!'

Knowing Mr and Mrs McBradey were at the Pimlico apartment in the capable hands of Chastity, Michael made his way to see Travis. After visiting hours, much of the hospital was falling into darkness as patients began to settle down for the night. Walking onto Travis' ward, he tiptoed quietly towards his room.

'Excuse me?' called a nurse from behind. 'Can I help you?'

'I'm here to see Travis McBradey,' said Michael sheepishly, squinting his eyes in the dim light to see where the voice had come from.

'Oh it's you, Michael,' said the nurse with the pink hair. 'It's after hours, you're not supposed to be here.'

'Please, just for a short while?' he pleaded. 'His parents won't let me come here in the daytime, I just want to see him.' The nurse looked up and down the ward and checked her watch.

'That's partly my fault really, isn't it? I am very sorry,' she sighed, rubbing his arm supportively. 'Luckily my shift was just changed, I'm not supposed to be here tonight. Go ahead.'

'Thank you so much!'

'But keep it brief. His father's left instructions, I'm supposed to call security if I see you.'

'Is Travis OK?'

'Yes, everything's as we would expect right now. Go on, hurry!'

Michael pushed in through the door, gently closing it behind. He stood sadly for a moment, looking at Travis lying unconscious on the bed. Dull whirring and steady bleeps from the electrical equipment in the corner made Michael's own heart race, a reminder of the dire trauma his boyfriend had suffered. A plastic lung breathed slowly through a pipe to his lungs, and blood filled tubes surrounding him reminded Michael of the red pool on the alley cobbles. Taking a deep breath, he took a seat at the side of the bed.

'Travis? It's me,' he gulped, holding his hand and intertwining fingers. 'I haven't got long, I'm not allowed to be here. But if you can hear me, you probably already know that.' He glanced up at the door to check they were alone. 'I just wanted to say I love you, and that I'll be here for you as much as I can.' He kissed the back of Travis' hand.

Bright moonlight shone through the window, illuminating shiny grey tiles on the floor. Michael looked out at the night sky.

'Do you remember when we laid under that blanket on your balcony, looking up at the moon? And you said, it was like the stars had come down from the sky to kiss the rooftops?' His eyes began to water a little. 'Well, I remember that. And Alvin the Super Pigeon? Trying to make his nest in your barbecue? I remember that, too. I just wanted you to know that.'

Suddenly, he felt Travis' finger twitch. 'Oh my God!' he gasped, jumping from his chair to fetch the nurse.

'It's probably just a nerve,' she said apologetically, checking Travis' vital signs. 'But talking to him is good.'

'Can you tell his Mum it happened? But please don't tell her I was here?'

'Will do,' she nodded. 'You need to go now, another nurse will be on shift in a minute.' she looked at her watch again before walking back out to her station.

'I've got to do a few things to help my dad.' He sat and took his hand again. 'I'm singing at Connie's fashion show, the prize money's paying for us to get to Berlin. So I don't know when I'll be able to come back. But get well and I'll see you as soon as I can. I love you.' He stood to leave, pausing at the door to look back. 'And when you wake up, Travis... please remember me?'

Back in Pimlico, pinned against the wall by Hamish, Chastity could feel anger welling in his chest.

'Arse bandits?' he said, dropping his macho pretence. 'Don't forget, you're talking about your own son, here?'

'Keep your sick nose out of this, it has nothing to do with you,' Hamish snapped back.

'That's where you're wrong,' Chastity returned the snap. 'You're not just insulting my dear friends Michael and Travis, you're also insulting me.'

'Oh, so you're one of them too, are you? Do you hear this, Jeanie?' He took his arm from Chastity's chest and stood back. 'I told you, this whole town is infested with buftie-arsed perverts!'

'Haud yer wheesht, Hamish!' she yelled, taking the pan off the heat and rushing back across. Pulling Frenchie inside, she looked up and down the hall before closing the front door.

'Time and again I've had to bite my tongue around bigoted arseholes like you, but now I've had enough!' Chastity straightened his shirt as his blood began to boil.

'The bible says...' Hamish preached, waving a finger in Chastity's face.

'Don't fecking start all that with me, I grew up Catholic,' said Chastity angrily, swiping the finger away. 'And you won't feckin' win!'

'The bible says, Adam and Eve not Adam and Steve,' Hamish continued.

'Where d'ya get that, off a church beer mat?' added Frenchie.

'Why are you like this?' asked Chastity. 'What exactly is it you don't get?'

'What you queers do to one another, it's fecking disgusting,' frowned Hamish defiantly. Chastity was having none of it.

'You so-called Christians are obsessed with sex. Well listen up, mister! This is not just about sex, this is about love. All that matters is love. I didn't choose to be gay, none of us did. We were born like this, and I have to believe that God wanted me this way. He designed it so that I am exactly what I am.'

'Don't talk shite,' smirked Hamish sarcastically.

'If I'd been born with two legs missing, I'd have to assume that was His plan too and make the best of what I'd got. That's just how it is, and the sooner you get your shrunken head around that, the sooner you and your family's lives will be better.'

'The bible says, man should not sleep with man,' commanded Hamish.

'And it also says man should not eat pork. Is that bacon you're cooking?'

'Does it?' Jeanie was shocked at this revelation.

'It's a sacred text, you can't just cherry pick the bits you want and ignore the bits that don't suit you! Jesus said, love one another. That's all he said. Love one another. What are you, thick?'

'How fecking dare you?' threatened Hamish, raising a fist.

'How dare I? Would you listen to yourself? It's not any wonder Travis ran away from home. HE'S YOUR SON!' Chastity screamed. 'You were born straight and blessed with a child. A wonderful, creative, talented, caring son. Do you know how many gay men yearn to have children of their own? But we can't, because God didn't make us that way. That wasn't the plan he had for us. But like all his children,
208

he gave us each other and he gave us the capacity to love. And for us, that has to be enough.' His eyes welled with tears. 'How dare you deny your son the love he deserves?'

Jeanie held her husband's arm. 'Please, Hamish?' she pleaded.

'And now, he's in a coma.' Chastity continued his impassioned tirade unabated. 'He might die... there, I've said it! He might die and you'll have lost your chance to be the father God planned you to be. How feckin' dare you?'

Frenchie was in awe. She had never seen Chastity like this before. 'Come on, you beautiful man. Let's go,' she suggested, taking his arm.

'Jesus died for you, so you could be like this?' Chastity sobbed, pointing in Hamish's face. 'You're an utter bastard. He's your son! How feckin' dare you!'

An uncomfortable stony silence filled the room as Chastity wiped his eyes with his sleeve. Frenchie opened the front door and pulled him gently out into the hall.

'He's right you know,' she sighed supportively. 'I'm not gay, and I'm certainly not religious, but God be my witness... he's bloody right!'

'I'm sorry, Jeanie love,' said Chastity, shaking his head before turning back to her husband. 'Thank God for Michael. That your son has someone who loves him with all his heart. Just feckin' think about that!'

Returning to Connie's flat, Chastity had calmed down a little. But they were shocked to find Cameron with a full face of drag makeup, strutting around the lounge in court shoes, wearing a wig with an offcut of sequinned fabric wrapped around his torso. He kicked his legs and thrust his arms in the air as Diana Ross sang I Will Survive from the hi-fi.

'You wanna keep an eye on that one, Frenchie,' Chastity laughed.

'It's the only way I could get him to shut the fuck up,' Connie sighed, wiping his brow. He pulled a cigarette from his packet, opening the window and leaning out to light it. 'I'm exhausted!'

'What's that funny smell?' said Frenchie, sniffing around the room.

'You said he liked playing with Febreze?'

'No, Furbies, you dim wit! They're in the fucking bag,' Frenchie grinned. 'Did you give him his Kinder Egg?'

'Yeah, but it made him cry cause I took the toy out.'

'Why did you do that?'

'Well, he wanted a surprise, didn't he? And he keeps talking to someone who ain't there? It's creepy!'

'Ahh, bless!' Chastity smiled. 'Didn't you have imaginary friends when you were a kid?'

'No, we didn't have Facebook back then!' Connie drew deep on his nicotine.

At that moment, Michael arrived back from the hospital. Throwing his coat over the back of a chair, he laughed at the sight of Cameron giving it his all.

'It's like they made a little Connie from all the bits left over after plastic surgery!'

'He's very Cleopatra coming at ya, ain't it?' Connie chuckled. 'He just needs a drag name?'

'His mum and dad live in a caravan,' said Frenchie. 'You could call him Winnie Bago?'

210

'How did it go with Travis' mum and dad?' asked Michael nervously.

'Oh Lulu love, I'm so sorry,' Chastity frowned. 'I did try, really I did. But it all went tits-up. I think there's a chance I may have just made things worse!'

By the following morning, Michael still hadn't decided how best to cope with Mr and Mrs McBradey. He knew his dear friend Chastity had done what he could against all odds, there was little more he could do himself before his partner awoke from the coma. So for the moment, he had to concentrate on finding evidence to free his father.

With a plan underway, it was now Gerry's turn to get a drag makeover from Connie. Having had a bath and washed her hair, she sat on a chair at the table in his lounge as he applied makeup to her face.

'Hmm… I'm not sure,' he squinted, standing back to take a look while lighting a cigarette.

'Make her nose a little thinner,' Chastity agreed. 'And Fifi's cheek bones are higher, I think?'

'Unlike her arse!' bitched Connie under his breath.

'Play the tape for me again?' Gerry asked, taking a sip of her tea. Sitting next to her at the table, Michael re-started a YouTube clip on his phone. It was of Madame Fifi at the bar in Sugar Sugar, laughing and chattering with a few of her admirers as one of her bar staff opened another bottle of Champagne. The actress stared at the film intensely, studying her movements and mannerisms. She gestured along with it, rehearsing every little nuance.

'What about the voice?' said Michael.

'Up with this shit I will not put!' she mimicked, throwing her head back defiantly.

'Ha ha! That's it!' Chastity laughed as Connie continued shaping and contouring.

'Her vocal tones are quite mellifluous, really,' Gerry noted. 'Quite grandiloquent.'

'If that means she sounds like a bitch, you're spot on!'

'And we've got this fabulous Chanel two-piece for you to wear.' Chastity held it up on its hanger. 'I think it will fit.'

'Urgh!' Gerry growled. 'Never did trust Chanel.'

'Eh?' Chastity was confused.

'Chanel number five. What happened to the other four? Did they tell us? No, very cunning.'

'It must be difficult for you, having to put up with French couture after being so used to Draylon,' Connie quipped, pulling her into a shoulder length black wig. As she stood from the chair and threw her shoulders back, they all grinned. 'I think we've got it!'

At that moment, Edith arrived. At the sight of Gerry, she dropped her bag and ran at her, pulling her into an affectionate hug.

'Oh, Mrs F! Mrs F! You're home at last,' she cried.

'You've fooled Edith, that's a good sign,' Chastity nodded.

'Edith?' Shocked, Gerry pushed her back to take a closer look.

'It's not Mrs F, it's Mrs B!' Edith gasped, pulling her back into a hug.

'You know each other?' said Michael.

'Yes! I know Mrs Braintree. I used to do for her twice a week.'

212

'When I had my flat. But you must call me Gerry, you don't work for me now.'

'We had a lovely time, didn't we? Edith gushed. 'I'd do all me bits, then we'd have tea and cakes, and we'd laugh and laugh. Then one day I turned up and you wasn't there anymore?'

'I have missed you, Edith. But I lost everything, I live on the street now,' Gerry shook her head with shame.

'Well, she lives in my car, actually,' added Chastity.

'I asked my neighbour Valentina to tell you? The Hispanic woman?'

'Oh, her accent was too strong for me. She did say something, but I'm fucked if I know what it was!' Edith turned to Chastity and whispered, 'Who's that Asian man?'

'Ha ha! That's Connie.' Chastity could not help but laugh.

'I don't know why everyone keeps taking the piss,' defended Connie.

'Oh, it's you! You're black as Newgate's knocker, I thought you was one of them wogs.'

'Edith Pimm! You can't say that,' Chastity scolded.

'Why not?' Edith whined innocently. 'I think they're lovely, with their nice suntans married to all them footballers.'

'Oh, you mean WAGS? Wives and girlfriends?'

'That's what I said, ain't it?' Edith proudly took Michael's arm, turning back to Gerry. 'This is my grandson, Lulu.'

'He's very handsome, isn't he?' Gerry winked.

213

'Someone asked him to do modelling the other day,' Chastity added.

'My sister did that,' grinned Edith.

'Modelling? Was she a good looker?'

'No, she made Big Ben out of lolly sticks. We cremated her last week.'

'Your Ethel? Oh Edith, I'm so sorry,' Gerry took her hand supportively. 'What was wrong with her?'

'She was dead.' Edith took a tissue from her pocket and dabbed her nose. 'Why are you dressed as Madame Fifi?'

'She's going to help us with a little errand, Edith,' said Chastity.

'You can't be living in a car, dear. Why don't you come and live with me?'

'Oh, Edith?' Gerry looked to Michael for his approval. 'I don't want to impose?'

'I think it's a blinding idea!' he beamed, shaking her hand to seal the deal. 'She shouldn't be living on her own, now.'

'Well, as long as you let me pay rent? I just need a chance to get back on my feet.'

'Ooh, it'll be luverly!' Edith held her face excitedly. 'Tea and cake duck, just like old times. I'll bake one on my new cooker, and we can do some tea-bagging tonight!'

'Edith love, that doesn't means what you think it does,' Chastity giggled, looking at his watch. 'Anyway, come on now.' He removed the Chanel skirt from its hanger and held it up for Gerry. 'Force yourself into this hideous costume, we need to get back up there to Captain Snort. Getting that CCTV footage from Fifi's car park might be the only way we'll ever prove her innocence!'

214

Chastity wasn't the only person in Soho with incriminating CCTV evidence on his mind. At the front of the club downstairs, Billy-no-nut pulled his Daimler into the kerb on Old Compton Street. Climbing from his car and crossing the road, he took a last long drag on his cigarette and dropped it onto the tarmac. Looking up and down the street with a gruff smoker's cough, he pushed against Sugar Sugar's glass doors and stepped inside.

CHAPTER SIXTEEN

Billy paused at the bottom of the stairs inside the club, allowing his eyes to adjust to the dim light. With no-one around, he walked quietly across to Madame Fifi's office. Listening at the door, he turned the handle and stepped inside to pitch dark. He grappled across the wall to the side of the door, flicking on the light switch. Opposite the desk, he stood and stared at the bank of CCTV screens. Suddenly noticing Lettie arriving at the bottom of the stairs, he momentarily froze, but it was too late. Within moments, they were face-to-face.

'Who the fuck are you?' Lettie growled defensively.

'Don't I know you? You used to sing karaoke at my bar in Southend?'

'Ah, you must be Billy! I've got rid of the bitch, I own this bar now.'

'I heard. I was filmed in that safe room on these cameras and I want that footage destroyed.' He pointed at the screens.

'How much?'

'Five hundred?'

'You've come all the way from Southend?' Lettie thought for a moment. It was of no consequence to him what was on the footage, but it was clearly very important to Billy. 'Why do you want it?'

'She stitched me up.'

'And why is that my problem?'

'Don't underestimate her, she'll do the same to you. You ain't safe just cause she's in nick.' Billy jabbed his finger into Lettie's chest. 'The only way to stop her is to finish her off once and for all.'

'How?'

'It's sorted, I just need that footage.'

'Make it two grand and we have a deal.' Lettie held out his hand. Billy had anticipated having to negotiate. Pulling a large wad of cash from his trouser pocket, he counted a pile of fifty-pound notes into Lettie's palm.

'And I want the security firm's copy as well.'

'She lied,' Lettie grinned, snapping his hand shut around the cash. Walking across to the filing cabinet, he pulled open the bottom drawer to reveal a stack of videotapes. 'This is all there is.' Taking a large black bin bag from a roll on top of the cabinet, he began to fill it with the cartridges. Billy rubbed his hands together excitedly.

'Time to finally say bye-bye to the great Madame Fifi,' he grinned maliciously. 'Cause this time tomorrow, she's gonna be swinging from the ceiling!'

At Madame Fifi's apartment block, Michael pushed against the door to the entrance lobby, holding it open for Chastity to enter. As they walked towards the security desk, Corporal Taylor stepped from his office to greet them. He looked annoyed to see Chastity again.

'I told you, only residents can view the security film from the car park!' he said forcefully. At that moment, Gerry made her grand entrance as Madame

Fifi. Thrusting the door ahead of her, she marched defiantly across and slammed her hand on the desk.

'What is the meaning of this?' she shouted.

'Oh… err… yes, Madame.' Taken by surprise, Taylor jumped to attention and saluted.

'I want to see this footage… immediately!'

'Yes, Madame. Right away, Madame!' Harassed, he lifted the desk flap and sheepishly led them into his office.

'Very good!' complimented Chastity.

'Not too bombastic?' Gerry whispered back.

'I'm guessing not.'

Sitting in front of his computer, the doorman looked at the time and date on the piece of paper Chastity had handed him. He typed the information into his keyboard and pressed go. Standing behind him, they watched as the picture on his screen fuzzed into view. From above the entrance, the camera showed a wide shot of the car park down to the main road.

'That's it,' said Chastity, pointing at his car in a space to one side. 'Can you fast forward it?' Taylor tapped the shift key as the film sped ahead, showing the comings and goings of various residents. Suddenly, there was Madame Fifi herself, wearing the flowing Dior gown as described by Hortense.

'Stop!' yelled Michael, leaning in closer. 'Go back.' Taylor slowed the film in reverse and played it in real time, as Fifi wobbled precariously from the lobby and climbed into the car.

'Play it again?' said Chastity.

'It really does look like you,' said Michael, nudging Gerry.

'That's clearly what the police must have thought when they saw this.' Chastity bit his lip.

'But we know it isn't me,' Gerry replied, remaining in character. 'It's Lettie.'

'But that can't be Lettie, look at the way she's walking.'

'How do you mean?' Michael asked.

'Look, they're having trouble in those shoes. Lettie never had trouble with stilettoes. Only a drag queen would notice that.'

'But there was a heel stub missing, you found it in the car when you got it back from the police?'

'Yes, but that was after the hit and run, not before. No, whoever this is it's not Fifi, and it's certainly not Lettie.'

'Could it be Hortense?' Gerry added.

'No, it's definitely not her!'

'Can we wind it back further?' Michael suggested. 'Perhaps we can see them arriving?' Taylor did as he was instructed.

'Try between two and six,' said Chastity. 'This is the fifteenth of August, isn't it?' Taylor nodded. As the tape sped through, they watched intensely. 'Stop!' Chastity cried. 'That's Hortense,' he advised, pointing as she walked across the tarmac and away up the street. Suddenly, a man stepped from behind the wall. He paused for a moment to watch as the maid disappeared into the distance before walking cautiously towards the entrance lobby. 'Pause it,' Chastity gasped.

'What? Who is it?' said Michael.

'Oh my God! The wig in his office… I should have guessed!'

'Guessed what?'

'Who killed Lettie's brother, Lu,' said Chastity, holding onto Michael's arm. 'That there is your murderer. That there is Creighton Cross!'

Early the following morning, Madame Fifi queued for her breakfast in the prison canteen. Her mind was racing at the thought of being lifted over the prison wall. She had to be sure she would be under the water tower at exactly the right time for this plan to work. There would only be one chance at this. She sighed with despair at the sight of a large dollop of porridge as it blobbed from the ladle into her bowl, before taking a seat under a tall barred window.

Across the hall, Bunnie sat alone. Above the din of fellow cons chatting and laughing, she stared at Fifi poking at the grey stodge with a plastic spoon.

'Tonight's the night, Billy,' she said to herself under her breath.

Standing on the other side of the room by a large grey metal door with her hands behind her back, Finch could see Bunnie's mind racing with anticipation. She nodded knowingly as their eyes met, a wry smile forming across her sour rugged face.

Michael struggled to climb into a set of orange overalls in the back of Chastity's car as they made their way through the winding streets of north London. Already wearing a matching costume, Connie sat in the front seat looking at a street map while smoking a cigarette.

'Not far now, Nobby should already be waiting in position.'

'Good.' Chastity pulled to a stop at a red traffic light. 'Now, we all know the plan, don't we?'

'You and Connie in the cab, me in the cradle,' said Michael, finally managing to push his shoe through the tight leg of the trouser. 'I throw down the rope ladder and pull the lever up.'

'That's right. Then we just drive round the corner to the car, lower her down and we're away. What could possibly go wrong?'

'And wear this,' added Connie, reaching into a plastic carrier bag and pulling out three baseball caps. Putting one onto his own head, he passed another back to Michael.

'Light Fantastic?' he said, reading the logo across the front.

'That's who he works for, Dolly,' Connie grinned. 'If we've all got the uniform on, we're less likely to be noticed. Here, Tit.' He handed one to Chastity.

'I'm still not sure about this,' Michael groaned. 'If we've got evidence that Creighton Cross killed Lettie's brother, why have we still got to break her out?'

'It's what Gunter told us to do, there's a much bigger plan afoot,' Chastity confirmed. 'Besides, even with new evidence it would take an age to get her out, and we need her to be in Berlin when we get there.'

'That's assuming the police see it as new evidence at all,' Connie added.

'She's not wrong,' said Chastity. 'But then, why did Creighton kill Lettie's brother?'

'Perhaps it's got something to do with that property deal?' Connie suggested.

'But that still doesn't explain why he dressed as Fifi to do it. Why not just send henchmen, like Billy did with Travis?' Chastity was baffled.

'Yes, I see what you mean,' agreed Michael. As the traffic lights changed, Chastity pulled onto Holloway Road.

'No not that way, you dozy old goat! Go back,' yelled Connie.

'Sorry, I'm just so nervous,' said Chastity, pulling over to turn around.

'Why? It's not you we're breaking out.'

'Ooh, I feel like Constance Dowling in Boston Blackie And The Law.'

'Are you sure Nobby will be there?' asked Michael, sealing the Velcro up the front of his overalls.

'I wrote everything down for him.'

'When did he learn to read and write?' Chastity spun his car around into the opposite direction.

'Stop panicking, I drew him a diagram. Though he is a bit distracted at the moment.' Connie flicked his cigarette stub out of the window. 'He's got himself a little girlfriend,' he laughed.

'She won't be here, will she?'

'I doubt it, she's got an ankle tag. She got caught shoplifting, silly bitch. I told her, if you're gonna take the risk, do it in John Lewis not fucking Poundland!'

'And she loves Nobby?' Michael chuckled. 'Is she deranged?'

'It is a bit like someone's dropped a scaffold pole on her head. And she's got those big boggle eyes, as though she's been squeezed too hard in the Heimlich Manoeuvre. Every time I walk past, I'm tempted to throw fish food.'

'Ah, bless!' Chastity laughed. 'Everyone deserves someone to love, even Nobby. He needs compassion.'

'He needs a wash!' Michael quipped.

As they approached the prison wall, they could see Nobby's truck parked in position adjacent to the water tower. Spotting the car, he waved excitedly at them from inside the cab as they drove slowly past in the traffic. Chastity signalled to turn into a side road just past.

'It's a lot busier than when I did that recce the other night. I hope we can get parked?' he sighed. Driving around and around, it looked to be an impossible task.

'That one!' shouted Connie as they drove past a space.

'We can't park there, it's disabled only.'

'I am disabled,' Connie snapped. 'My iPhone's on charge.'

'It's ten to three, we need to stop soon,' said Michael, looking at his watch.

'Yeah, we're running out of time, we'll just have to go in here.' Chastity pulled through the entrance to a B&Q Superstore car park. 'Come on!' he said, jumping from the car.

In the prison recreation yard, Madame Fifi discreetly glanced at her watch. With just a few minutes to go, she looked across to see Finch standing by the entrance chattering with another guard. Bunnie meanwhile, was kicking a soccer ball against the far wall.

224

She took a tennis ball from her Gucci tracksuit pocket and bounced it on the brick paving at her feet. Looking back once more to check that nobody was watching she lobbed the ball into the corner of the yard. After rolling a little way, it settled directly underneath the giant water tower. Looking up at the sky feigning a daydream, she walked slowly and casually towards her secret pick-up point.

By the time Connie, Chastity and Michael reached the truck from their distant parking space, they were quite out of breath.

'The car's too far away!' gasped Michael.

'What choice did we have?' Chastity panted. 'Quick, we've only got two minutes.' Michael climbed onto the back of the truck and into the cradle, as Connie and Chastity joined Nobby in the cab.

'Hello, uncle Connie,' he grinned goofily. 'Hello, Chastity.'

'Hello, Nobby love. Now, you know what to do, don't you?'

'I've got a girlfriend. She's beautiful, ain't she uncle Connie?'

'In a gargoyle sort of way!'

'Well, try to imagine we're rescuing her today.' Chastity created a picture. 'She's Rapunzel locked in the tower and you're the handsome Prince who's come to save her.'

'I'm the handsome Prince?' Nobby rubbed his hands together excitedly.

'At a push, yes,' Chastity smiled kindly. 'You shout: "Rapunzel! Rapunzel!

Let down your hair!" Then Lulu throws over the rope ladder and we pull away.'

'But her name's Beyoncé?'

'Just do your best, love.' Chastity patted him on the knee.

'Do I get a prize?'

'I brought this for you,' Connie replied, pulling a banana from his pocket.   'But you can't have it until we've finished.'

'OK, uncle Connie, thank you very much.' Nobby licked his lips in anticipation, placing it gently on the dashboard.

'Ooh, I can't remember the last time I had a banana,' Chastity smiled.

'You wanna undo the padlock on them out-sized knickers. Even spotty Nobby bannister here can manage a fuckin' sex life!'

Squatting low in the truck's cradle, Michael checked his watch again. With just thirty seconds to go, he looked at the three levers jutting from the handrail. The explanatory wording on the metal plate below each lever was so worn that it was impossible to read.

'Bollocks!' he sighed with frustration. 'Oh well, let's try this one.' Pushing at the big black knob on the left, the truck's long arm jolted into action and the cradle shot abruptly ten feet into the air. 'Argh!' he cried, grabbing desperately at the handrail as his legs fell through between the bars. He hung for a moment, feet dangling above the bonnet of the Mercedes parked behind. Hauling himself back in, he pressed at the middle lever. The cradle shot sideways, bashing against the prison wall fifteen feet above the pavement. An elderly lady beneath picked up her
226

walking frame and ran to save herself from fragments of masonry dust raining down on her feathered hat. Tapping the lever in the opposite direction, he came a little away from the brickwork before lifting himself higher. Finally level with the top of the wall, he glanced discreetly over the parapet through the razor wire. Shielded from view of the guards by the water tower, he could see a few prisoners in the yard below but he could not tell whether or not his father was waiting in position. The sound of a local church bell chiming three o'clock gave him his signal.

'It's now or never!' he said to himself, lifting the cradle higher and lobbing the rope ladder over the parapet.

In the yard below, Fifi was relieved to see her escape route drop down beside her. Glancing back to check nobody was looking, she rested her foot on the bottom rail and grasped tightly, tugging twice. However her relief was short lived as Michael shoved against the lever and she shot into the air like a rocket, bouncing off the barbed top and swinging widely out, across the top of the truck and into the path of a passing double decker bus. As shocked as the passengers at the front of the top deck, she braced for impact.

With a cry of horror, Michael hit the final lever and the cradle span around in a full circle, over car roofs away from the bus and across the top of the cab. The momentum of the swing threw Michael outside the cradle, holding onto the handrail for dear life just a few feet above his father's head.

'That's it!' said Chastity at the sight of Fifi's splaying legs flying past the windscreen. 'Go! Go! Go!'

'Beyoncé! Beyoncé! Shave off your hair!' Nobby cried. Throwing the truck into gear, they jolted violently forward directly into the flow of on-coming traffic. Connie and Chastity screamed, thrusting their feet against the dashboard.

'Turn right, you nonce!' Connie demanded, covering his eyes and peeking through his fingers.

'Prince Nobby to the rescue!' his nephew bellowed, pulling hard on the steering wheel and missing a large articulated lorry by a hair's breadth. As the rebellious arm of the truck twisted back around, Fifi's ladder hit the side of the lorry, dragging her unceremoniously across its lumpy cargo and through the branches of a sycamore on the street corner. Startled pigeons flew out in all directions.

'Ha ha! Yeah!' Nobbie laughed hysterically, tearing up the narrow avenue.

Fifi barely had time to spit the leaves and feathers from her mouth before the cradle hit a second tree with a loud clang.

Still hanging below the cradle, Michael lifted his legs as high as he could to avoid the roof rack of a passing van, before ricocheting back across to the other side of the road. As wind whistled past his ears, he desperately attempted to pull himself towards the control knobs, but the truck's arm clanging against a metal lamppost sent a vibration through his body like an electric shock. Stunned, his teeth chattered as the arm swung back across towards yet another tree. Cradle smashing against its trunk, he was finally thrown back inside.

Fifi's heart skipped a beat, momentarily losing her grip with a jolt as the bottom of the rope ladder caught on a car wing mirror. Ripping it from the door,
228

it bounced across the tarmac behind the truck, shards of broken mirror reflecting the chaos.

Michael soon realised that the ringing in his ears was the distant prison alarm. They had undoubtedly now realised Madame Fifi was missing. Taking a deep breath, he pulled frantically at the levers, managing to finally secure the arm into a fixed position behind the cab. But jamming his hand against another knob, the arm shot sharply upwards, swinging the rope ladder upside down over his head like a trapeze to the back of the truck. Fifi's panoramic scream ended abruptly as she hit the metal deck just behind the cab.

'Look out, look out!' Chastity gasped, as a small terrier suddenly ran into the road before them. Nobbie slammed on the breaks, throwing Connie and Chastity mercilessly into the foot well. They looked up to see Fifi's face squash against the back window, g-force contorting her angry expression.

'We've just got her out of nick, you'd think she'd look more grateful,' said Connie, yanking Chastity's foot from inside his overalls and climbing back into the seat.

As Nobbie slammed his boot on the accelerator once more, Fifi flew backwards through the air like a rag doll, landing in the cradle with Michael. They clung to each other desperately as Nobbie negotiated a forty-five degree turn into the B&Q Superstore car park. The arm of the truck hammered violently against the overhead height-barrier pole, bringing the vehicle to an abrupt stop as its steel frame ripped from the concrete base. Michael and Fifi shot over the top of the handrail and landed on the flatbed platform, while Connie and Chastity flew back down into the foot well.

There was a moment's stunned silence, broken only by the pole clanging against the truck's windscreen as it swung on its chains. Its three strikes on the cracked glass mimicked the church bell only minutes before.

'Are we dead?' Chastity quivered.

'No, we've arrived,' said Connie, kicking open the door and jumping out. 'Quick, let's get the fuck out of here!' Dragging Chastity out onto the path by his collar, they ran towards his car followed closely by Michael and Fifi.

'Bye bye, uncle Connie,' Nobbie laughed after them with a wave, as several burly superstore security guards ran towards the truck. 'I'm gonna eat my banana now!'

'Prince feckin' Nobby's blocking the bastard exit,' Chastity cried, turning the ignition and tearing the car from its space.

'Erm... go that way! Go that way!' said Connie, pointing. Cutting through a vacant parking space, they tore across a large decorative flowerbed, bouncing down onto the pavement on the other side and off the kerb to the main road.

'Well, I think that went OK,' sighed Connie, lighting a cigarette as Chastity sped through the traffic.

'You think?' groaned Fifi sarcastically, shoving a hand up her top and pulling a clump of sycamore branch from her cleavage. 'Connie dearest, why are you posing as an immigrant?'

'Will everyone just stop going on about my fuckin' tan?'

'Will Nobby be alright?' asked Michael sympathetically, looking back through the rear window.

'He's got multiple lives, like some psychotic pussy,' said Chastity. 'Diminished responsibility will save him, like it did with the ice-cream van.'

'At least he didn't get his cock out like he did last time,' Connie quipped.

'Oh, there's good news,' Michael gushed, turning to Fifi. 'We've got evidence that Creighton killed Lettie's brother. So you're finally off the hook!'

'Creighton?'

'Yes,' added Chastity. 'But the bad news is, he did it dressed as you. I think he wanted you to take the blame.'

'He set me up?' Fifi was stunned. 'But I thought he loved me?'

CHAPTER SEVENTEEN

After dropping Madame Fifi at the safe house given to them by Gunter, they made their way back to Soho. As Michael and Chastity headed to the apartment above Sugar Sugar, Connie walked down to the newsagent to collect a copy of the local paper. He was excited to see an article about his fashion show. Turning the corner from Old Compton Street, he was shocked when a man spat at him.

'What the fuck?' he shouted back, jumping out of the way. Several passing people stared at him angrily, and a woman in the cake shop he had said hello to every day for years turned her back sourly and ignored him. 'It can't be the tan, I don't look that different?' he sighed.

Arriving at the shop, he grabbed a copy of the paper from the stand and took it to the counter.

'Alright, Fred?' he grinned at the stout man by the till. 'Give us twenty Rothman's too, please Dolly.' Fred's reaction had never been so cold.

'Bastard,' he uttered under his breath.

'Eh?' Connie was baffled. 'What's going on?' Fred took the paper and turned to page seven, throwing it open on the counter. Connie's eyes widened with disbelief as he saw what lie before him in print. Shock turned to anger as his blood began to boil. 'I don't fuckin' believe this!'

In the apartment, Michael picked up the phone and dialled.

'It's ringing,' he confirmed, as Chastity put the kettle on. 'Hello, Mum? It's Michael.... I miss you, too.' He could feel a lump in his throat. 'Listen, I've got a problem and I need your help. Can you meet me in Berlin?'

Hearing a tap on the front door, Chastity walked through to the hall and answered to find Edith on the doorstep with lots of carrier bags.

'Hello love, let me get those for you,' he said, taking her shopping and peeking inside. Each of eight carriers only held one item. 'This is a lot of bags?'

'I don't put so much in each bag, then it's not so heavy,' she frowned.

'But you've still only got two arms, love?' She seemed a little rattled. 'Is something wrong?'

'My dogs aren't half barking,' she sighed. 'These new shoes are pinching and it's getting on my wick.'

'Can't you take them back? When did you buy them?'

'Erm...' Edith grasped her chin in deep thought. 'It was a Tuesday. September... nineteen-eighty-four.'

'Then how can they be new?'

'Well, I've only wored 'em once.' She took off her coat and hat, hanging them on the hook behind the front door. 'I went past the shoe shop today. The sign said: "buy a pair and get one free". What am I supposed to do with a third shoe?' Chastity shook his head despairingly.

'The kettle's just boiled, come and have a cup of tea.'

Michael put down the phone as they walked through to the lounge. He stood and gave Edith a hug before sitting next to her on the sofa.

'Are you alright, dear?' she asked, noticing the emotion on his face.

'Yes, Nan. I've just been speaking to my Mum, she's going to meet us in Berlin. And she's bringing the third key.'

'That's good,' said Chastity, bringing through the tea things on a tray. 'How's Gerry settling in?'

'Oh, it's loverly! I've put her in my back bedroom, now they've repaired the leak so she won't get rained on. It's so nice having a bit of company.'

'I expect so, I'm very pleased for you.'

'How did you get on with Mrs F?' said Edith, blowing across her cup and taking a sip.

'Ooh, quick! Put the telly on, let's see if anything's on the news,' said Chastity.

'Yeah, have a look, see who's died,' Edith added.

Michael picked up the remote and turned to the BBC. They watched a report about a coach plunging down a precipice into a ravine. A rather frantic woman explained how she was so grateful that God had saved her.

'It was probably Him who pushed her down there?' Chastity smiled. 'Ooh, here it is!'

The next report told of a break out from Holloway prison, though it didn't name the escapee. But it did mention several accomplices wearing orange overalls that police were hoping to identify on CCTV.

'Oh my God!' Michael threw his head in his hands. 'They're onto us!'

At that moment, the front door slammed and Connie stormed into the lounge.

'Look at this, can you fuckin' believe it?' he cried, throwing the open paper at Chastity.

'Oh for feck's sake!' Chastity gasped, looking at the page.

'What is it?' asked Michael.

'They've mixed up my photo with a granny basher!' Connie unwrapped his new cigarette pack and sparked up. 'His ugly mug is on the article for the fashion show and mine says I kicked the shit out of an old lady. People are gobbing at me in the street out there!'

'That's insane,' said Michael, as Chastity passed him the paper.

'What's that?' Connie took the remote and turned the television channel. 'Put it on Ultimate Fighter Championship. Gay porn at tea time, I need cheering up.'

'We was just on the news,' said Chastity, biting his lip. 'They're trying to find out who we are.'

'Are you famous?' Edith gushed.

'Infamous, more like,' groaned Chastity.

'And look at this.' Connie snatched the paper from Michael's hand. 'It says here: "he did it because he was antagonised by his anal cyst". So not only do people think I kick pensioners but they think I've got a scabby arse, too. How am I supposed to manage a sex life with that all over the press?' Chastity looked over Connie's shoulder at the article.

'It says analyst not anal cyst, you silly bitch. Put yer glasses on!' Chastity snapped. 'It's cause of your fake tan. The attacker's black, that's why they got you mixed up.'

236

'Well at least I ain't got dumpy white legs like two milk bottles on a doorstep,' Connie quipped. 'I had a psychoanalyst at junior school. They sent me to see him cause I kept making willies out of Plasticine. He was my first sexual experience.'

'And I had a pervert living next door to me,' Edith laughed. 'He poked his willy through a hole in the fence every Thursday.'

'Really? Why?' Michael asked.

'Cause it was his day off.'

'Did you report him?'

'No, it didn't bother me. I used to hang me peg bag on it.'

'You've got to win this competition, Connie. We need that money to get us out of London as soon as possible. A grand each should just about do it, what with flights and a hotel.' Chastity handed him a cup of tea.

'A grand each?' Connie was confused.

'Yes, we need to take Edith because she speaks a little German.'

'I'm hoping to find a little German when we get there!'

'What if he doesn't speak English?'

'I wanna fuck him, not talk to him!'

'And we need to take Daisy for protection,' Chastity continued. 'We're gonna be dealing with the mafia, anything could happen.'

'But how are we gonna get away from the show?' said Michael. 'You know how unhinged Lettie is, it could be dangerous.'

'You're right.' Chastity's mind was racing. 'We need to shut Sugar Sugar down for a while. Connie, we need a plan!'

237

In Southend-on-Sea, Billy's Bar was still closed to the public. Knuckles paced the customer area in frustration.

'We can't keep on like this,' he whinged. 'There's hardly any money left. I can't go on without wages.'

'Oh, shut the fuck up,' Billy yelled. 'I've got the footage from Soho. As soon as I hear from Bunnie that the manipulative fuckin' bitch is dead, we can finish off that wanker Michael and get this place up and running again.'

'I fucking hope so!'

At the sound of the phone ringing, Billy jumped to his feet and ran behind the counter, grabbing at the receiver. 'Yep?' he coughed. Knuckles watched as the colour drained from his already sullen face. 'What?' His hand tightened into a fist. 'You stupid fuckin' whore, you'll pay for this!' he bellowed, throwing the phone violently across the room. With a loud aggressive scream, he took a large bottle of Bacardi from the back shelf and slammed it violently across the optics with anger.

'Billy mate, what is it?' Knuckles was shocked.

'Someone's had her away over the fuckin' wall.' He ripped the phone wire from the socket and wrapped it around his fists, pulling the cord tightly between his hands. 'Whatever it takes, I'm gonna find her.'

'Why are you so obsessed? You've gotta let this go or we're gonna be finished.' Knuckles' frantic frustration went unheard.

'And when I do, I'm gonna wrap a rope around her neck and throw her off the end of the fuckin' pier!'

Late the following afternoon, Connie stepped from a black taxi outside a large red brick building in East London. He looked at the giant poster on the front wall.

'At least they've used the right picture on there,' he said, taking two large bags from Chastity as he followed Michael out of the cab. As the vehicle pulled away, they walked across for a closer look.

'Fashion Extravaganza,' Michael read aloud. 'It looks quite posh, don't it?'

'Are you nervous, love?' asked Chastity, taking Connie's arm.

'I wasn't till that thing in the paper, but I am now.'

'It's gonna be fine.' Michael patted him reassuringly on the back. 'We're all rehearsed, and your costumes are amazing. You're gonna win this.'

'D'ya think?' Connie bit his lip.

'Of course you are! What could possibly go wrong?' Chastity pulled a worried face at Michael as they followed Connie in through the front doors.

The plush entrance lobby was a hive of activity. Competitors and organisers rubbed shoulders with rapidly arriving members of the audience, as Connie checked in at a busy counter across the back wall.

'I think this must have been a cinema in its heyday,' whispered Chastity looking around. Mostly deco in style, the red carpet echoed the ruby flock wallpaper, trimmed in gold leaf panels around the walls. Shiny brass-framed stained glass adorned imposing double doors to one end, and a massive crystal chandelier hung elegantly from the centre of a cream dome in the ceiling.

'Camp, ain't it?' Michael grinned.

239

'Appropriately so,' Chastity nodded.

'This way,' said Connie, returning from the table. He picked up a bag and led them across the foyer, through a gold door to one side.

Shell-shaped glass wall lights lined a long narrow corridor, which opened out into a large changing hall at the back of the main stage. Dozens of people bustled with costumes of every shape and colour, talking and laughing loudly with excitement as they prepared for the evening's event.

'Over here,' shouted Connie above the din, pushing through to a table at the far end. Framed by two clothing rails and several chairs, the counter top was mounted with a large mirror across which in large red letters read the sign: "Maison Connie". Laying the bags on the table, he unzipped and began handing costumes to Michael and Chastity, who hooked them on to the empty hangers provided.

'How many competitors are there?' Michael asked, moving one of the empty bags under the table.

'Ten,' Connie sighed, looking around the room. 'It's gonna be tough. How bad is this spot on the back of my neck?' he said, giving it a poke.

'It looks like the thing we hang you up on the back of the door with has fell off,' Chastity grinned, taking a stick of foundation and dabbing it on the red mark.

A middle-aged bald man with a clipboard approached. His attempt at dressing fashionably for the occasion made him appear more a victim than a trendsetter.

'Good afternoon, Maison Connie. I'm Will Grant and I'm your stage manager. Just checking in to make sure everything's OK for tonight?'

240

'Yes, thank you,' said Connie confidently.

'So, we have...' he checked his list. 'Connie Lingus, Chastity Belt and Lulu L'Amour?'

'That's us,' Chastity confirmed.

'Lovely!' He moved in closer. 'I'm not supposed to influence the competitors, but can I make a suggestion?'

'We're always open to anything that might help,' Michael nodded.

'One of the judges is a bit prudish. Delilah Flambais-Dubois, she's a magistrate in real life,' he whispered. 'You'll see her sitting in the middle with the Astrakhan collar. She makes Mary Whitehouse look like Cynthia Payne. Can we drop the Lingus?'

'Eh?'

'Let me just put you down as Connie? One name... like Madonna? I think it may help.'

'Yeah, if you like,' said Connie. 'Makes no never mind to me, Dolly.'

'Only, we had the same problem last year. When I announced Maison Faircastle she thought I said Feck Arsehole.'

'Fancy that!' Chastity giggled.

'It didn't go down too well, she thought they were taking the piss. Nil points, if you know what I mean?'

'Thanks for the advice.' Michael shook his hand to seal the deal. With a smile, the man rushed over to the next alcove.

'Will Grant?' said Connie, unzipping his makeup bag and tipping its contents onto the counter. 'Sounds more like a promise than a name.'

They all jumped as a skinny man with spikey jet-black hair suddenly swished back the costumes on the rail and stepped through. He tugged at his tartan bolero jacket as if to draw attention.

'Well, well. If it's not the pensioner-puncher himself? Connie Lingus.'

'Theodora Simpkins,' snapped Connie, spinning on his heels. 'I might have guessed you'd be here.'

'And yet I'm surprised you are. But then, I expect you're used to humiliation, working at that dive in Soho?'

'I beg your pardon?' Chastity frowned.

'You might try begging,' Theodora smirked. 'This your little team, is it?' He looked them up and down sarcastically. 'And how sweet, you've come dressed as one of Bros,' he bitched, poking at Chastity's leather jacket. 'Oh no, my mistake... you've come dressed as both of them together!' As he threw his head back and laughed, Chastity somehow had a feeling this wasn't the first time they'd met.

'Fuck off, Simpkins,' Connie demanded.

'This what you're wearing, is it?' he said, pulling at the organza costume on the rail. 'Dale Winton orange? How sophisticated. Oh no, sorry... I mean elasticated!'

'Why don't you just go back to your own corner?' said Michael.

'And what's your role in this whole charade?'

'Don't tell her!' said Connie. 'She's a thieving bitch, she'll pinch all my ideas like she normally does.'

'Why the fuck would I want to steal ideas from a two-bit backstreet drag queen with such limited talent?'

'Because you're so fuckin' two-faced, and both of them are ugly!'

'Yeah, I'm not sure which one to smack first,' said Michael supportively.

'I'm a star, do you hear me? A star!' Theodora stamped his foot tetchily. 'I've sung with Jane McDonald, for fuck's sake!'

'Yeah, another one that can't hold a tune in a bucket!' came back Connie.

'D'you know? It's taken me a few minutes, but now I know who you are.' Chastity was beginning to remember. 'You're a friend of Cyril's... Buck Rammer! The eighties porn star.' Theodora gasped with horror, grabbing the clothes rail to steady his stance.

'Eighties?' Connie grinned. 'Just how old are you?'

'I'm thirty-two!'

'You're fifty-two, if you're a day,' Chastity shouted loudly for all to hear. Several people turned to look. 'She's had it all pulled back, that's why her eyebrows are above her earholes. She's nothing but an aging backstreet slut trying to re-invent herself as a fashion icon, but a leopard doesn't change its spots. I bet the label in her knickers still says Next.'

'Slut?' Theodora was horrified at his past returning to haunt him.

'It's in the dictionary between prostitute and tart,' Michael contributed.

'I don't have to put up with this,' he growled. 'I'm warning you Maison fucking shite, this is war!' He punched at Connie's costume before stomping off.

'What an absolute bitch!' said Michael.

'Yeah. Trouble is, she's a rich bitch. Daddy left her shed loads of cash, so she can afford a shit-hot team.' Connie looked across at Theodora's table,

243

where he was being fussed over by a hairdresser, a manicurist, a stylist, a makeup artist, a dresser and an assistant tapping away at several social networks. 'She's got no original ideas, but what she does do is good. Really good.' He slumped in the chair dejectedly.

'What kind of look is she?' said Chastity. 'Prada? Gucci?'

'She's a Quant!'

'Take no notice, I think you're brilliant!' Michael smiled.

'He's right, you know,' said a pretty young woman. She flicked a few sequins off her hand and reached out to shake. 'You must be Connie? Fabulous tan! I'm Kat… Maison KitKat?'

'Hello,' said Connie, responding to her warmth.

'He's been really spiteful to everyone all day. I've been here since seven this morning as I've had a lot to set up. He's very vain, he even writes his name in capitals so it has to be shouted. He's really quite vicious.'

'You're not wrong, love. I'm Chastity.' He shook her hand.

'O.M.G. Are you Irish? And Gay? You must know Karen O'Leary?'

'Erm…'

'She's a friend of mine from Donegal. She's a lesbian, she lives in Muff.'

'I expect she would,' Chastity nodded.

'I'm Lulu.'

'Connie, Chastity and Lulu? That's just so marvellous!' she gushed, pulling her long chestnut hair back into its scrunchie. 'I'm a fashion student at tech, I'm hoping this might help launch my career.'

244

'Well, I wish you the best of luck,' said Connie kindly.

'And you, too. It's so exciting, isn't it? I can't wait to see what you do, you gays dress so well.'

'It's all those years in the closet,' Chastity shrugged.

'I love fashion so very much. I guess you could say it's my whole life. Mad isn't it?' Blowing a big kiss, Kat flitted back to her alcove.

'She seems nice?' said Michael, looking over at her moderate team scurrying about in preparation.

'Hmm,' Connie sighed, distracted in deep thought.

'I said she seems nice?' he repeated.

'Oi, Mowgli?' Chastity shouted, snapping his fingers in Connie's vacant gaze. 'Come on, snap out of it. There's five grand on the line here as well as your reputation. We can't let Bitchodora Pornslut win this. So get your act together and put on some slap, we've got a show to do!'

CHAPTER EIGHTEEN

An hour later, Chastity peeped through the stage tabs at the audience. A glorious buzz rang through the hall as people took their seats and discussed the contents of their programmes.

From the dressing alcove, Connie called him on the baby monitor. 'How's it looking? Over.'

'It's going to be fabulous!' Chastity gushed excitedly from the other end. 'Lovely crowd, very busy. Over.'

'Come back, going for a fag. Over and out.'

'That's a relief,' said Michael, dabbing concealer under his eyes. 'It's gonna feel odd singing as a man for a change.'

'Remember to keep it butch,' Connie advised. 'The complete opposite to drag, elbows and knees out, shoulders back, chest forward.'

'Right,' he replied, adding just a touch of light mascara. 'I really wish Travis was here to see this, especially singing as a geezer.' A small wave of melancholy flooded his heart.

'I'm sure he would be if he could, Dolly.' Connie patted him on the shoulder sympathetically. 'Have you heard anything?'

'Not yet.'

'They'll be putting it on YouTube, they always do, so you can show him later. You'll blow him away!' He began limbering up, jogging on the spot and stretching his neck from side to side, pushing his arms above his head.

Chastity returned to the alcove. 'Are you trying to get fit, or just having one?' he grinned, checking himself in the mirror. 'Does my makeup look OK? I've tried a stronger foundation.'

'Should help with the subsidence,' Connie smirked, grabbing a cigarette and lighter.

'I should have had a haircut.' Michael picked up a pair of scissors and snipped gently at the edge of his fringe.

'Eh up, stand by your beds,' Chastity warned. Connie quickly hid his cigarette behind his back as the three judges approached, each holding a clipboard against their chest. Looking up at the sign on the mirror, they glanced at their lists and gave a little tick with a biro.

'I'm Connie, thank you for inviting me,' he smiled sweetly, nodding his head with respect. 'I really hope…' Suddenly, he was rudely interrupted.

'Hello, I'm Theo Simpkins. You might recognise me?' The judges looked a little confused as he rushed to greet them. Now in costume, he wore a faded rose-pink leather jacket heavily beaded with pearls, sequins and rhinestones. Matching shoes with a slight Cuban heel were draped with black and gold trousers, belted with dangling gold chains. 'I was second runner up last year? Although I was here in more of an advisory capacity, really.'

'Excuse me?' Chastity frowned. Theodora continued unabated.

'I'm so pleased to be sharing the spotlight this evening with my dear friend Connie Lingus. I heard you had him down as just Connie, but it's actually

Connie Lingus. As in oral sex?' Connie shot him an acid look. Delilah Flambais-Dubois scowled disapprovingly, grasping at her pearls defensively before making a note on her pad and leading the other judges further into the changing hall.

'Oh, that's just the fuckin' cherry on the bastard cake, that is!' Connie scowled. 'What did you say that for?'

'Like I said, this is war. You're not going to win, I'm just saving you from wasting your time.'

'You've had your pound of flesh, now just feck off!' Chastity snapped.

'He's wearing it,' said Michael, poking at Theodora's jacket. 'What is that, human flesh? Made from your last sad little conquest? What did you do with his white stick?' Simpkins just laughed, unaffected.

'Sorry it didn't work out for you in our glamorous world of Beau Monde. Best just crawl back to your sad little drag show. Bye bye!' he bitched. Turning to walk away, he paused momentarily to stare disapprovingly at Maison KitKat's costume rail. It was all Michael could do not to slap him up the back of the head, but then he noticed an almost invisible chord running from under his jacket to the back of his trousers.

'I wonder what that's for?' he said, instinctively snipping it with the scissors.

'Ha ha! What did you do?' Chastity whispered with glee.

'I don't know. But I expect we'll find out!'

As the lights finally dimmed in the auditorium, the tension of anticipation was at fever pitch. Maison KitKat opened the show, with an innovative pastoral tableau against a big-screen backdrop applauding Gaia, Mother Earth and Save The Planet. A flurry of sky blues, grass greens and daisy yellows, Kat walked slowly forward to pastoral music, scattering flower petals ahead from a small wicker basket. Pausing to place it on the catwalk, she removed her hooded cloak to reveal a beautiful blue gown adorned with crystals, giving the impression of a cool mountain waterfall. On her head she wore a fluffy white cloud with hanging glass beads, emulating a gentle rainfall. A delighted intake of breath rang from the crowd.

'That's beautiful,' Chastity gasped from the wings.

'Yes, it is,' Connie sighed with a little disappointment.

Next up was Theodora Simpkins. As diva club music blared from the speakers, he marched cockily forward down the catwalk, flicking back his hair and pouting as he waved his arms in the air.

'Bad choice of music... techno techno techno notice!' Michael frowned. 'And listen to the lyrics... I've got to sing with my baby, dance with my baby, laugh and sleep and cry with my baby?'

'Sounds like she could do with decent childcare,' Connie quipped.

'And look at the way she's swishing,' Chastity added. 'There's enough mince there for a shepherd's pie!'

As the music reached its climax, Theodora dramatically threw off his jacket and reached behind for the cord... but it wasn't there. A little shocked, he

250

laughed with embarrassment and grappled further to find it. The movement of his reach yanked the remaining chord through a loop in his collar. Suddenly, the front of his shirt fell off to reveal a secret hidden corset holding in his rather flabby stomach. As the panel dropped, so did the gold chains around his waist, pulling the front of his trousers open to reveal his underpants. Screaming with anger, he kicked at his jacket and stormed backstage with much laughter from the audience. Bumping into Connie, he covered his face and growled with humiliation before pushing through to the changing hall.

'I knew that chord was meant for something, but I bet it wasn't that!' Michael giggled.

'Ha ha!' Chastity cried. 'She deserved it, pretentious little mollusc.'

'Coming at us with all her Nutbush City Limits hanging down... disgusting!' laughed Connie.

'It was like that music video, when Madonna tears Justin Timberlake's shirt off, and then he rips off her corset and her tits drop to her knees!' Michael grinned.

'OK, this is us,' Chastity panted nervously, plumping at his big ginger bouffant. 'The Sisterhood must prevail. Are we all ready?'

As the lights dimmed and Maison Connie's tribal drum music began to blare, Michael stepped forward onto the back of the catwalk. Flames of fire filled the big-screen backdrop, filling the auditorium with a warm glow. The lights rose to reveal his sharp suit in shades of orange, yellow and red with a low-buttoned jacket showing the middle of his toned torso. Miniature gold sequins lined satin flames, which licked up from his ankles and cuffs. Walking confidently along the catwalk, he began to sing into a radio mic.

'There's a fire in my heart, where you lit me and let me burn. Then you laughed and walked away, and now there's nowhere to turn.' He span and returned to the back of the stage, positioning himself to one side of the screen. Then, with a cheer from the audience, Connie stormed fiercely onto the scene. Staring defiantly through fire-flashes of makeup spiking to his temples and across his slicked back hair, he threw back his head seriously with his hands on his hips. His jacket was a mass of glowing satin drapes in burning colours, which swung from side to side as his six-inch block-heeled red shoes strutted arrogantly along the catwalk, one in front of the other towards a hidden sunken grill. Stopping to pose above the metal mesh, he spun around with outstretched arms.

'I can't control this fever, it flames out of control. Cause every time I see ya, it melts right through my soul. Inferno! Inferno!' Suddenly, a fan beneath the grill blew a jet of air up Connie's body. The drapes of satin flapped violently upwards, lit by ultraviolet light. He had become a glowing fireball. The audience cooed with admiration. Chastity ran on from behind dressed as a French maid in tangerine satin with a daffodil lace apron, hat and co-ordinating stilettos. With a look of feigned horror, he flapped his hands comically at the back of Connie's jacket, as if in an effort to put out the fire. Stepping forward ahead of the grill, Connie ripped off his jacket and threw it on the floor, to reveal a short yellow shirt with long baggy sleeves. A ruby jewel glistened from his belly

button. The maid loyally picked up the jacket and followed further along the catwalk.

'*When you're turning up the heat, is it Heaven or is it Hell? As your lips set mine aflame, it's so hot that I can't tell.*' Stopping once more and striking a strong pose, Connie ripped off his orange flared trousers to reveal strawberry Lycra shorts. Picking up the trousers, Chastity covered his eyes to the rudeness of it all. Stomping further on, Connie ripped off his shirt to show a rouged leather chest harness, through which was threaded a matching whip. He pulled it out and swung it around and around above his head, cracking it against the floor in front of him. With a cry, Chastity ducked to avoid being hit, much to the delight of the onlookers.

'*You started this explosion, with a spark of pure desire. Now I don't have a notion, how I'm gonna stop this fire. Inferno! Inferno!*' As pyrotechnics exploded at the back of the catwalk, the lights dimmed and the flaming spectacle was finally over. The audience jumped to their feet, clapping and cheering as Michael, Chastity and Connie took a bow and returned to the changing hall.

They were asked to stay in costume until the end. As the final entry drew the competition to a close, everyone from all teams waited patiently in the changing hall for the judges' decision. The tension in the air could be cut with a knife. Even Theodora Simpkins was quiet, after some time spent looping his costume back together again.

'I can't bear this, I'm going for a couple of smokes,' said Connie, grabbing his cigarettes and heading for the fire exit.

'Take this in case they call us,' said Chastity, handing him a baby monitor.

'What if we don't get the money? How are we going to get to Berlin?' Michael sighed.

'I'm a great believer that you should try not to worry about things until you know whether or not there's something worth worrying about,' Chastity replied, biting his lip. 'Trouble is, I'm not very good at taking my own advice.'

'But then, even if we can convince Creighton's henchmen that I'm his son, it all seems so pointless anyway if Travis doesn't wake up.'

'You're right, but you've got to keep the faith.' Chastity took his hand supportively. 'All that money's just sitting there. Someone's got to get it.'

'But it's all a con. I'm not really his son, am I?'

'It's only money! The chances are Creighton might have left it to Fifi, so you would have inherited anyway. Think of what you've been through since you arrived in London, you deserve some kind of compensation.'

Michael thought for a moment. 'Do you believe in destiny?'

'I do. It's destiny that gave you Travis, that's why I know he's going to be OK. You'll have a long and happy life together, whether or not you get the money. You've got him and you've found your long lost family, those are the most important things. The cash is just a nice little bonus, so if you can get it you may as well have it.' Pulling up the back of his skirt, Chastity sat. 'I had a friend called Lisa Shop. She won
254

a little on a scratch card, so she decided to get it all done. After having her tits, arse and pelvic floor lifted, she had just enough left to get her eyes, nose and cheekbones altered. But she ran out of money before they did her lips and chin. From the nostrils down, she looked like Bagpuss! So she sold her flat and all her jewellery to finish the job but it bankrupt her. She spent three weeks living behind the bins of The Savoy Hotel, but she looked absolutely feckin' fabulous!'

'Really?'

'Yes, but she never lost sight of what was important. When she died two years later, all the surgery and money spent was no longer relevant, she'd lived her little dream. At that crucial time breathing her last, she was laid on that gurney surrounded by her family and friends. And at the end of the day that's all that ever really matters, that you loved and were loved in return. Whether we believe it or not, that's the only destiny that counts. Rich or poor, never lose sight of that, Lu.'

At that moment, Connie returned to the alcove looking a little rattled.

'You were quick, I thought you'd be chain smoking?' Chastity asked.

'They were pissing me off, keep pretending to get a light off my fireball jacket,' he whinged.

'Oh for feck's sake, what have you done?' Chastity knew Connie too well.

'I padlocked the fire escape.'

'How are they going to get back in?' Michael grinned.

'They'll have to walk round the front.'

'But they'll be calling us back out for the results any second?'

As if on cue, the announcement for all teams to return to the catwalk was announced loudly through the tannoy.

'They're gonna have to fuckin' run then, ain't they?' Connie smirked. To the sound of frantic banging on the fire exit door, he checked his makeup in the mirror and headed for the stage.

At the safe house in North London, Madame Fifi sat with her dear friend Fanny. The lounge was very basic, with two overstuffed vintage sofas and a nineteen-fifties wooden table and chairs on a cheap flowery rug. The curtains had remained drawn as advised by some instructions on a small sheet of paper, which she had found upon arrival sitting in the middle of the table with a fake Eastern-European passport, plane tickets to Berlin and some disguise props. Hortense had been notified and had been waiting for Fifi at the hideout with some clean clothes and a hot bath already prepared. Having had a while to recover from her frantic escape ordeal, Fifi was now ready to focus on the task ahead.

'Vladimir Tickleykoff?' she said, looking at the passport. 'Surely, they could have thought of a more convincing cover than that?'

'It'll do just fine,' Fanny chuckled, looking at the photo. 'Dressed as a man is a perfect disguise. I don't like you with that beard, though. It looks like a nineteen-seventies porn minge!'

'Coffee, Madame?' asked Hortense from the door.

'Yes please,' Fifi replied. Her faithful servant curtseyed and left for the kitchen.

'She's very odd, isn't she?' said Fanny. 'Her face is a bit like a minge, too. There is another word for it, but I'm too much of a lady to say!'

'Actually Fanny, that's what I wanted to talk to you about.'

'Minge?'

'In a manner of speaking. After Berlin, I've decided to have the operation to remove my penis. Perhaps at your clinic in Istanbul? Will you help me?'

'Of course I will, darling. I can highly recommend it.' She grabbed her hand affectionately.

'Chastity's found the evidence to prove my innocence. And that Lettie killed Creighton.'

'Wow! That's brilliant news, good old Chastity!'

'But if I want my life back, I know I will have to face the music and return to prison at some point until the whole sticky mess is sorted out. I can't live on the run forever.' Fanny could see the sombre look of foreboding on her face. 'I will cope much better if I return truly a woman in every way.'

'I'm the one person you don't have to explain that to,' Fanny smiled. Hortense returned with the coffee and began to pour.

'The problem is, I don't have any money until Lettie is convicted.'

'I have a little put away should Madame need it?' Hortense offered.

'Thank you, but no,' said Fifi. 'It's yours, you keep it. But I do want you to run an errand for me.' Tearing off a strip from the small piece of paper, she scribbled a few lines before handing it to Hortense. 'Get this to Chastity. Go now.'

'Yes, Madame.' She put the note in her pocket and left the room.

'I'll book the snip on the credit card,' Fanny suggested. 'You can pay me back when it's all over.'

'You are a good friend, thank you.' Fifi was clearly moved. 'I will pay you back.'

'I know,' grinned Fanny impishly. 'Cause if you don't, I'll come round and cut your tits off, too!'

Arriving back in Soho after the competition, Connie, Chastity and Michael were a little shocked to find Hortense standing silently in the dark outside Connie's front door.

'Argh!' Connie cried. 'What are you doing here? I thought you was a fuckin' ghost!'

'A message from Madame,' she replied pallidly, handing Chastity the note before walking down the stairs and away through the alley.

'Is that Hortense? I see what you mean, she's freaky ain't she?' said Michael.

'Yes, but useful.' Chastity read the message. 'It says, find the Vindergurderbreurgenshaftenshitz Club in Berlin.'

'That must be our point of contact?' Michael suggested.

'Come on,' said Connie, unlocking his front door and throwing the bags inside. 'Let's go somewhere. That deranged munter's given me the fuckin' creeps!'

In a nearby late night coffee bar on Old Compton Street, Connie brought a tray of drinks and cake to a small table by the window.

'Second place is not so bad, you should still be proud,' Michael said, sipping his frothy cappuccino.

'It was that Theodora's fault, the spiteful bitch,' Chastity added.

'Disqualification can be so depressing!' Connie smirked.

'I wouldn't stoop to piss on him if he was on fire,' said Michael.

'I expect he couldn't stoop to do anything with all the flab squeezed into that corset. That wasn't a washboard under that shirt, it was a feckin' launderette!'

'Actually, I didn't mind losing to Maison KitKat. Her design was very good, and it will help launch her career. I've already got one.' Connie poked at his carrot cake with a fork. 'Trouble is, now we've only got fifteen-hundred second prize instead of five grand. How the fuck is that going to pay for us all to get to Berlin?'

'I've just paid my rent, so I've only got about thirty quid,' frowned Chastity.

'You owe me ten pound of that for the mascara!' remembered Connie.

'I've got about fifty,' said Michael.

'We've just spent fifteen quid on these bloody coffees!'

'You've got the prize money, Connie. Book the flights for the day after tomorrow, and try to get a cheap hotel near that club. Just do your best with what you've got.' Chastity took a swig his tea. 'Now... tomorrow night's show? We've got to think of a way to shut down Sugar Sugar for a few days so we can go to Germany. Any ideas?'

'It'll have to look like an accident or Lettie'll get suspicious,' said Michael.

'We could poison the old trollop?' Connie grinned. 'Put her to sleep for a few days?'

'Why stop at just a few days?' Chastity giggled.

'Fire!' Michael gasped suddenly. Several people in the café jumped and looked around expecting to see smoke.

'Shhh! Keep your voice down,' Chastity whispered. 'We can't set fire to the place. We won't have a job to come back to.'

'No, not a big fire, just enough to set off the sprinklers. It'll take a few days for everything to dry out.'

'Actually, that's not a bad idea,' Connie agreed. 'And I remember just the song we can do it to!'

CHAPTER NINETEEN

Stepping from a taxicab in the afternoon sunshine, Madame Fifi looked at her reflection in the glass-fronted check-in hall at Gatwick Airport. A beige overcoat hung from broad shoulders, padded from inside the jacket of a three-piece pinstriped suit. A fat bodysuit disguised her ample breasts, strapped against her chest under a blue shirt with co-ordinating tie. Beard, glasses and slicked back hair tied into a small ponytail under a black Trilby hat finished the ensemble.

'Don't worry, it's the perfect disguise,' Fanny smiled, joining her from the back of the car. 'It's the glorious and glamorous Madame Fifi the police are looking for. They won't be expecting you to be in drag as Vladimir Tickleykoff!' She handed her a small suitcase. As Fifi's shortly trimmed, unvarnished nails curled around the handle, she sighed despairingly.

'It's not that. It's the realisation that for the first time in my life, I'm actually wearing beige!'

'Go girl!' Fanny whispered. 'See you when you get back.' She glanced across to a police car parked at the end of the taxi rank. Two officers watched all arrivals and departures suspiciously from their vehicle. Pulling a hanky from her cuff, she held it to her face. 'I'm just dropping my beloved husband off for his long business trip, I think just a few tears?' Grabbing Vladimir around the shoulders, she kissed him passionately on the lips before running back to the cab sobbing.

'It's been a while since I did anything like that!' Fifi uttered under her breath as she smoothed down her moustache and headed into the hall.

The ticket desk was a simple task. Nothing to declare, the contents of her suitcase had been prepared with absolute caution and precision, and she really did look like the man on her fake passport, whoever he was. It was the anticipation of trying to deceive the airport's rigorous security that was making her nervous.

'Empty your pockets and all metal objects into here, please,' said a tall woman in a guard's uniform, passing her a plastic tray. She did as she was told and handed it back. 'Now step through the barrier.' Taking a deep breath, Fifi walked under the metal arch. Suddenly, the alarm began to ring loudly. Her heart skipped a beat as the woman and two other guards took her to one side. What could it be? The fat suit and costume had been made specifically to not draw attention.

As the woman ran over her body with a small hand held detector, the problem seemed to be coming from her crotch.

'There's something not quite right down there, Sir,' the officer said.

'I've been told that before,' Fifi replied, deepening her voice and strengthening her natural Eastern European accent. She grappled with her tackle, pushing it visibly to one side to demonstrate her manhood. The woman ran the device back over.

'Ah… it's just the button fly on your trousers,' she confirmed. 'Thank you, pass through.' With a discreet sight of relief, Fifi quickly took her belongings from the tray and walked towards the refreshments lounge.

That night in the Sugar Sugar dressing room, Chastity, Connie and Michael prepared for the evening's performance.

'Everything's booked, but I didn't have enough money to take Edith. So it's just us three and Daisy,' said Connie, smearing azure-blue eyeshadow from his lids to his temples.

'Perhaps it's for the best,' said Chastity, pouting his lipstick in the mirror. 'She's getting a little frail, I'm not sure how she'd cope on a plane. I'll call and tell her in the morning.'

'And we're not leaving her alone, she's got Gerry now,' Michael agreed. 'Perhaps she'll babysit Nigel?'

'That'll impress Caligula!'

'I Googled it, the hotel's just round the corner from the club,' said Connie. 'And I booked a parking space at the airport for your car, Tit.'

'That's good, well done.'

'Right, let's get this tatty old thing ready.' Pushing back the chairs, Connie lifted the side of a large heavily patterned rug from the floor. Between them, they yanked it from beneath the costume rail and leaned it against the toilet door.

'What's it for?'

'You'll see,' said Connie, handing Michael a large black costume. 'And you're wearing this.'

'What is it we're doing?' he said, holding it up to see.

'Just copy whatever I do from the other side of the stage,' Chastity advised, unhooking a matching outfit from the rail. 'We did this last year with Lettie. You and me carry a large torch flame for dramatic effect. Fifteen seconds under the smoke detector above the stage and the sprinklers will set off everywhere except in here and Fifi's office.'

'She was seething last time,' Connie laughed. 'But the firemen were gorgeous!'

'I expect Lettie will be none too pleased this time. Mind you, the place could do with a feckin' wash!'

'Shouldn't we do it at the end of the show?' asked Michael.

'What? Are you mad? No Dolly, do it right at the beginning. One number, then we're all flying off to fashionable Berlin for three days!'

Erotic rhythmic Arabian music began to boom loudly from the speakers, as Michael and Chastity entered the back of Sugar Sugar's stage. Both wore black jumpsuits, baggy on the legs, arms and torso. On their heads were large gold turbans, from which draped black scarves across the lower part of their faces, accentuating their mysteriously-staring eyes. Gold slippers with long curled toes marched slowly and deliberately across the boards, as they carried between them the rolled dressing room rug. Laying it gently on the floor they pulled at the back, unravelling it towards the audience. Inside was Connie.

Comically flying forward as if to shoot off the front of the proscenium, several audience members jumped forward to catch him, much to their delight.

Brushing himself down, he stood centre stage and posed. The audience whooped and whistled at the glamour of his exotic costume. Sheer pink and purple strips of fabric hung from his bejewelled waist, joined at his ankles by a gold band above matching slippers. Chains and coins glistened around his gold knickers, illuminating enticing glimpses of bare legs through the slits of the pantaloons. His golden bra was emblazoned with sparkling rhinestones, also draped with chains and coins. From the shoulder straps ran further strips of fabric to gold bands at his wrists. Atop his pony-tailed blonde wig was a glittering gold pillbox hat, with a violet veil to the waist behind. His toned naked midriff was decorated with a fuchsia jewel in his navel. Head to foot, he was every inch a luscious harem belly dancer.

As his loyal Arabian knights stood to attention with arms crossed to either side, he shook his hips and began to sing into his head mic.

'*I am your genie. Here to obey you. You are my master. I won't betray you.*' Lifting his arms with elbows out, he positioned his hands in prayer and jutted his head from side to side beneath.

Holding court at the bar, Lettie glared his disapproval at their choice of song. He could recall performing this very spot himself with Connie and Chastity, and he remembered its disastrous outcome.

'*As the sun, sets on the horizon, I am here. To grant you three wishes in your ear. Succumb to the power of your dreams, and tell your desires now.*' The chains and coins tinkled as Connie twisted and spun to the back of the stage, picking up two large wooden clubs. Handing one each to Chastity and Michael, he took a cigarette lighter from inside his bra and ignited

265

them, creating flaming torches. Chastity glanced up at the smoke sensor above their heads, signalling for Michael to move a little closer underneath. Kicking his legs in the air, Connie spun back to centre stage.

'*I am your genie. Here to adore you. You are my master. I am beside you. As we fly, on my magic carpet through the air. To far destinations, we will share the journey to strange exotic lands. So tell your desires now.*' Turning his back to the crowd, he looked at Chastity in bewilderment. They had expected the venue to be flooded with water by now. Chastity shoved his torch directly under the sensor, but still nothing happened. Lettie smirked at their failure.

'*I am your genie. Here to entrance you. You are my master. I will enslave you.*' Connie thrust his hips forward, rolling his belly and curling his hands at the wrists. As the song drew to a close, he turned back to Chastity.

'What's going on? Why isn't it working?' he whispered.

'Perhaps Fifi disconnected it after last time?' Chastity bit his lip. 'We need to get the flame underneath the other one. Quick, do something!'

'Erm…' Connie was thinking quickly on his feet as he addressed the sea of faces. 'As some of you may remember, I usually do a dance with Cuthbert… the eight-foot boa constrictor? But sadly, he's gone missing from the dressing room.' The audience gasped with horror. He snatched the torch from Chastity's hand and walked down the steps at the front stage into the customer area. 'So if you wouldn't mind just looking around your feet, check your coats and bags?'

Panic ensued. Amid cries and shouts, everybody ran in every direction in an attempt to get out of the

266

venue. Seeing Connie carrying the flame towards the other heat sensor, Lettie lunged forward to stop him. But the maddened throng carried him backwards and down onto the floor.

'Cuthbert? Cuthbert? Here snakey-snakey?' Positioning directly beneath the sensor, Connie lifted the torch high as if to hunt for his imaginary pet. Suddenly, the sprinkler system activated and cold water began to spray from the ceiling throughout the club. It showered across the bar, ringing against the brightly coloured bottles on the back display shelves. Screams whistled as loudly as the fire alarm as people slipped and slid on the sodden carpet, climbing over each other in desperation to reach the exits.

Lettie finally managed to fight his way back onto his feet. Wig dripping in his eyes like a drowned rat, he stared viciously as if to kill.

'Oops!' Connie grinned back, throwing the extinguished club on the floor and wading back to the stage.

Back in the dressing room, Michael, Connie and Chastity clung onto each other, jumping up and down excitedly.

'We've done it! We've actually done it!' Michael laughed.

'Fabulous, gorgeous, wondrous Berlin, here we come!' Connie gushed. Suddenly, the door from the customer area flew open to reveal Lettie, soaked to the skin with a face like thunder.

'Look what you've done!' he screamed above the alarm siren, ripping off his wig and throwing it at Connie. 'You planned this, you spiteful little slut!'

'It was an accident,' Connie defended. 'And don't call me spiteful.'

'Sugar Sugar's due for its annual fumigation anyway, this'll just save you having to wash the carpets,' Chastity quipped.

'It's going to cost a fortune to clear this up!' Lettie bellowed.

'And just who's fortune is that, exactly?' said Michael bitterly.

'I could sue for this!'

'That sensor above the stage wasn't working,' said Chastity. 'If we report you to Westminster Health and Safety, they'll shut you down anyway. So I guess we're even?'

'No, we're not even. I have an empire and you're unemployed. You're all fired!' Lettie turned and stormed away, as quickly as he could in a heavily sodden gown.

'Look at the back of that frock all hanging down with the water. Your arse is dragging the carpet like a dog with worms!' Chastity shouted after him.

'Fired? Aren't you worried?' said Michael.

'Well yes, but I don't want her to know that. I just hope the evidence we've got is enough to get her arrested for Creighton's murder.' Chastity bit his lip. 'We'll get on to it as soon as we get back.'

'Right,' said Connie, checking his makeup in the mirror and dabbing his chest with a towel. 'Now for some supper!' He minced out through the door to the customer area and posed elegantly at the top of the lower staircase, looking down at several firemen securing the area. 'Eeny, meeny, miny… moe!' he gushed, pointing to a broad-shouldered hunk with a spiked blonde fringe poking below his helmet. The man looked back up at him, breaking into a broad white grin.

'She isn't?' sighed Michael in disbelief.

'She is!' smiled Chastity, with fascination. Connie walked sexily down the steps and flitted across to the fireman. Feigning a collapse at his feet, the stud instinctively grabbed the genie in his strong arms.

'Hi, I'm Connie. I've got a magic carpet. Fancy a ride?'

Later in Connie's flat after Chastity had left for Edith's with Nigel, Michael began packing his case for their trip abroad. He switched on the radio in an attempt to block the sound of Connie having loud sex with the fireman in his bedroom, but as he folded his clothes into organised piles, it was difficult not to be distracted by all the grunting and gasping. Connie shouting his desire to be squirted at by the big hose was the last straw. Grabbing his coat, Michael left for some fresh air.

After some time, he found himself walking across Westminster Bridge towards St Thomas' Hospital. Stopping by the side of the Thames, he looked up at his boyfriend's window.

'Hi, Travis. It's me. I hope you're OK? Sorry, I can't come in cause I've been barred. I guess you probably know that?' He sighed, wiping away a small tear. 'I've got to go away for a few days, so I won't be in London. We're going to Berlin. Not work, just something I've gotta sort out. I'll tell you about it later.' He took a tissue from his pocket to dab his nostrils. 'I miss you, more every day. And I love you. Wake up soon.'

269

He turned to walk back to Soho, pausing momentarily to look back up. 'Please remember me, Travis?'

Several storeys above his head, Travis jolted and gargled in his hospital bed. Through the silence of the late night ward, two nurses at their station heard his struggle. Running to his side, they checked his vital signs.

'He seems to be responding to something,' said one, looking around the room. 'I think he's trying to breathe on his own.'

'I'll call the duty doctor,' said the other, taking a pulse reading. 'He's fighting the sedation. Perhaps it's time for him to come off the ventilator.'

Early the following afternoon, Chastity studied the aeroplane safety booklet as they sat on their aeroplane at Heathrow Airport waiting to take off. Beside him, Michael grappled at his chest to check that the two vintage keys from Fifi and Creighton's offices were still safely on the strings around his neck. Across the aisle next to Connie, Daisy was flapping and close to tears.

'I'm so frightened. I've never flown before,' he gasped, stuffing his face nervously with a third bag of crisps.

'It's nothing to worry about,' Chastity smiled kindly. 'It takes off, they bring you food, then before you know it, you're landing again.'

'Flying on a plane's like doing drag, fun while it lasts but a relief when the undercarriage comes back down!' Connie quipped.

'I nearly didn't come. This morning as I left home, a magpie flew past. One for sorrow, that's really bad luck. But then a second one flew by. Two for joy, so I should be alright?'

'Perhaps it was the same one flew by twice, so double the bad luck?' teased Connie.

'Ooh, don't say that!'

'Connie, you're not feckin' helping!' Chastity scolded. 'Why don't you come and sit next to me, Daisy?'

'No! It'll be too much weight on one side, it might tip up!'

'Anyway, you should worry. I'm missing the international bike race on telly. Meals on wheels!' Connie licked his lips. 'I've set my Virgin box to record.'

'I would have thought your virgin box is out of living memory by now!'

'Assuming your flat's still there when we get back,' said Michael. 'We've all been sacked, remember? Lettie might throw you out.'

'She wouldn't, would she?' Connie bit his lip.

'Don't worry, she's too lazy,' said Chastity. 'We're only gonna be gone a couple of days. Nothing will happen that quickly.'

'Am I sacked as well?' Daisy asked, biting into a large chunk of fruitcake.

'It won't be long before Fifi's back at the helm, there's nothing to worry about,' Chastity assured. 'What could possibly go wrong?'

'I'm just looking forward to stepping off that plane and drinking in all those sexy European men,' Connie grinned. 'I shagged a German bloke once. His dick was so big, I didn't know whether to sit on it or put on a balaclava and rob a post office with it!'

'If dick's were aeroplanes, Connie's mouth would be an airport!' Chastity giggled. Looking across the aisle, Michael laughed.

'What?' said Connie.

'You. With your dark tan sitting next to Daisy. You look like a negative of Laurel and Hardy!'

'What is this, have a fuckin' go at Connie day?'

'I don't wanna spend my life being a colour,' quoted Daisy.

'Ah, fuck off and eat your cake!'

Once the plane was airborne, Daisy had calmed down a little. They had kept him distracted with chat and by constantly passing him food. By the time everything was devoured, they were on the tarmac at Berlin Tegel. Although the weather was overcast, they were quite excited as they jumped into a taxi. However, their enthusiasm dulled as they arrived at their destination.

'Where the feck have you brought us?' sighed Chastity, stepping from the car.

'It looked really nice on Google,' Connie frowned.

The road was narrow and dark with a post-war industrial tattiness, highlighted by rubbish littering the street, and random graffiti on the walls and pavements. Overflowing rubbish bins stood outside every building and there was a faint rancid smell from

272

the drains. Chastity looked up at the hotel with disappointment. A tall, thin redbrick establishment with dirty windows and drab curtains, the illuminated sign above the door flashed from a faulty bulb.

'Big Dick's Halfway Inn?' he read. 'Trust you!'

'It sounded like fun,' said Connie, holding his case defensively against his chest.

'Fun? It looks like the sort of place you'd come for an abortion!'

'Well, we're here now, we may as well just check-in,' said Michael, pushing at the door. They all looked up to see two men begin fighting the end of the street.

'Quick! Quick!' Daisy gasped, hurriedly following Michael in.

'They should have pulled this down when they did the wall,' said Chastity under his breath as he entered.

Inside was no better than the hotel's exterior. Dark and grubby with a single bare light bulb hung high in the large entrance lobby, a wide wooden reception counter to one side seemed the only part that had seen a duster in years.

'Yoo hoo? Bonjour?' shouted Connie, banging his hand on the desk.

'It's Hallo. We're in Deutschland, not feckin' Patisserie Valerie!'

A small, thin weatherworn man appeared from behind a curtain. Wearing grey trousers and waistcoat over a matching shirt with rolled-up sleeves, he peered suspiciously at his guests through gold-rimmed spectacles.

'Ja?'

'I'm Norman. I booked a room for four?'

'Herr Norman?' said the man, licking his fingers and slicking several wisps of grey hair against his bald shiny head.

'Guten Morgen?' Chastity offered.

'Guten Abend,' the man replied, looking at his watch.

'I'm guessing he's not Big Dick?' whispered Michael.

The man pointed at a large brown leather registration book on the counter. 'This,' he said, handing Connie a pen. Nervous of this strange little creature, they all silently signed in as he joined them in front of the desk. 'This,' he said again, gesturing up a long wooden staircase.

'We're locking the feckin' door tonight,' said Chastity as they followed him up the steps.

Reaching the third landing, the man led them along a dark corridor to a panelled door. 'This,' he smiled toothily, turning the big brass handle and steering them inside.

The room was quite large with a high ceiling, though very old-fashioned and basic. A large wooden-framed double bed sat in the middle of the room, with a faded pink and brown quilted eiderdown folded over at the bottom of ivory sheets. On the back wall were two single bunk beds with similar linen. In the corner was an enormous mahogany wardrobe. They could see several metal coat hangers through the partly opened door. Worn wooden floorboards surrounded a giant Persian rug. Just inside the door were four chairs around a kitsch yellow Formica drop-wing table, atop of which were several folded bath towels. Under a little window with beige curtains was a small hand basin with a half-used bar of soap.

274

'Abendessen? Supper?' the man offered.

'No, thank you,' Chastity shook his head.

'Danke euch allen,' said the man, closing the door behind as he left.

'Yeah, you an'all,' called Connie after him.

'Why did you say no to supper?' Daisy moaned. 'I'm starving!'

'He looks like John Christie! He might poison us and bury us in the back garden,' Chastity gulped, turning the key in the door.

'We'd better have the bunk beds, Lu,' Connie grinned. 'Them two would be through the ceiling downstairs. I'm going on top.'

'That's a change for you,' said Michael.

'Me and Daisy'll be fine in the double.' Chastity threw his case on the bed and unfastened the catches. 'You know, when I was young, I always imagined I'd live abroad. The idea of being a foreigner appealed to me. Now I'm older I realise that as a gay man, I've been a foreigner all along.'

'What the fuck is that smell?' said Connie, looking under the bed.

'I think it's coming from the wardrobe,' said Michael, walking cautiously over and opening the door wider to peer inside. 'What's that?' he said, pointing to something wrapped in a grubby pink blanket in the bottom corner.

'Aw my Gawd,' Daisy cried, holding his nose. 'It's the severed head of the last person who stayed here!'

'No it's not,' said Michael, giving it a kick. 'I think it's a dead hedgehog!'

'Ergh! I'm gonna be sick,' Connie retched.

'Get out of the way,' said Chastity. He wrapped his hand in a towel from the table and pushed past Michael, cautiously picking up the suspicious package. Holding it aloft, he walked across to the window, lifted the sash and threw it down into the street. 'There,' he said, rinsing his hands in the sink. 'I'll leave the window open for a while. At least right up here we're away from the smell of the drains. Just leave our clothes in the cases for now.'

'It's not quite the impression I got from David Bowie's videos. Berlin looked so cool.' Connie slumped on the bed dejectedly. 'I was expecting Freddie Mercury, Marc Almond, Depeche Mode. You know... neon lights, wild parties, mad excitement and kinky sex? This fuckin' dump's more like a stay in Broadmoor.'

'I like that German singer from Aha,' Daisy gushed. 'Norman Hartnell? Ooh, I think he's lovely!'

'That's Morten Harket,' Michael laughed. 'And he's from Norway.'

'Norman Hartnell is fashion designer to The Queen,' Connie advised. 'He can run up a twinset with matching shoes, hat and handbag but can he hit those high notes? I think not!'

'And that one with the sunglasses who sounds like a dog biscuit?'

'Bono?'

'Yes, he's lovely too! But my absolute favourite is Lady Ga Ga.'

'Ooh, her with the beef curtains?' said Chastity.

'It was a meat dress,' Connie smiled. 'Though that was quite a long while ago, I expect it's rank by now. Her wardrobe probably stinks like this one!'

276

Suddenly, they could hear the sound of thunder through the window. A cold breeze began to build, billowing the curtains above the sink.

'Come on,' said Chastity. 'Let's get ourselves sorted and out of here before rain sets in. We've got to look for the Vindergurderbreurgenshaftenshitz Club. Though, Lord knows what we'll find when we get there!'

CHAPTER TWENTY

After some time attempting to follow Connie's scribbled directions, they finally arrived outside the Vindergurderbreurgenshaftenshitz Club. In the same district as their disastrous hotel choice, the building didn't look much more upmarket. A frontage of reinforced concrete appeared to be holding together several much older buildings, which could be seen squeezed against each other above the signage. Every window across the entire front had been boarded up. It was unclear whether this was to shield the view of the run-down street or to prevent prying eyes from spying the goings-on inside. It was also hard to tell whether its baron industrial look was on purpose or a result of regional disparity.

'Very wide, isn't it?' said Chastity.

'It'd have to be with a name that long on the sign,' Michael suggested.

'What does that say?' said Daisy, walking across to a promotional sandwich board standing outside the entrance. 'Psychisches Ereignis? What does that mean?'

'Judging by the picture of the crystal ball and tarot cards, I'd guess it was some kind of mystical faire?' Chastity sighed. 'Perhaps we should come back later?'

'Ooh no, please can we go in?' Daisy gushed. 'I love psychics. I wanna have a reading!'

'I wouldn't mind having a go,' said Michael.

'They probably won't speak English anyway, Dolly,' said Connie.

'Well, can't we at least have a look?'

Pushing through the riveted steel entrance doors, they found themselves in a large dull lobby. To the right was a coat-check counter with a rail full of empty coat hangers. Black walls with very little decoration showed signs of wear and tear from a very busy venue.

'It's bigger but not as nice as your lobby, Daisy,' said Michael.

'It's very dark in here. You could see me putting up with that with my nerves?'

'They're all a con,' said Connie. 'I went to see a psychic in Basildon once. She was a hippy. She told me I was gonna have three kids.'

'What about them triplet brothers you shagged? They were only seventeen,' Chastity grinned.

'Then she told me her sofa cushions were stuffed with her own pubic hair, I couldn't get comfortable after that!'

'My mate Mandy at bingo went to see one,' said Daisy. 'She told her that she was gonna have trouble with her hands.'

'And did she?' asked Chastity.

'Yeah, her washing machine blew up. She had to do it all by hand, her fingers were red raw.'

Following directions from a sign opposite the cloak-check desk, they walked down a long wide carpeted staircase lit on either side by metal-framed bulkhead lights. Vintage ceramic tiles in brown and cream lined the walls and ceiling, creating a slight echo from the hustle and bustle of the venue below. Reaching the bottom of the stairs, they stood for a moment in awe at the sheer size and tatty extravagance of what lay before them.

It was exactly as they had imagined from Verity's description of Heinz and his extraordinary nightclub just a few weeks before. There was the dark wooden cocktail bar running the entire length of the rear wall, the long raised stage with its catwalk jutting between dozens of round tables and chairs, the private alcoves and sticky carpet. The nineteen-thirties mirror balls adorning the ceiling. And there was the hole in the wall with the unexploded war time bomb behind a glass screen.

'Aw my Gawd, I'd forgotten about the bomb!' Daisy groaned, taking an emergency Mars bar from his pocket.

'I thought Sugar Sugar was eccentric,' said Chastity. 'But this is like another world! Ooh, I feel like Liza Minnelli in Cabaret.'

'It is a bit Sally Bowles, ain't it?' Connie agreed. 'Look at the size of that stage.'

'My mum and dad have performed on that,' smile Michael proudly.

They looked around at the small throng of people sitting at the tables drinking and chatting. In the alcoves, psychics and mystics gestured dramatically as they told the fortunes of their enthralled visitors.

'That one!' said Daisy excitedly, pointing to a kaftan-wearing medium to one end. 'Look at her sign, it's written in English. Mystic Mavis!'

'She's with someone already. You and Lulu wait in the queue, we'll go to the bar. We need to find out if Fifi's here – come on Connie.'

281

At the servery, a large hairy man with a shaved head stood with his back to them, pottering on the back counter.

'Excuse me? Do you speaky Englishy?' Connie called out.

'Yes, I am English,' the man answered, turning to face them. The sight of this hairy bear in his white shirt and black trousers made Chastity gasp with shock, his eyes watering with tears. Connie grabbed him as his knees gave way.

'Chas?' The man was himself a little taken aback.

'Nicky? What are you doing here?' said Connie, plonking his friend onto a bar stool.

'I work here.' He reached forward to touch Chastity's hand. 'You're still wearing my ring?'

'Of course I am,' Chastity blubbered. 'It wasn't me who left to go find myself. And did you?'

'Did I what?'

'Find yourself?'

'I've missed you, Chas,' he grinned, lifting his hand and kissing his fingers. Pulling it away curtly, Chastity turned to leave. 'No, please wait!'

'Where are you going?' said Connie, grabbing Chastity's arm.

'I can't do this!'

'Well, I think you should.' He pushed Chastity back down on the stool.

'I finish in ten minutes, can we at least talk?' Nicky smiled hopefully.

As Mystic Mavis finished her reading, Daisy and Michael approached her table.

282

'Do you speak English?'

'Yus, love. I'm from Birmingham,' she answered in a broad accent.

'Oh, thank Gawd for that!' Daisy grinned, taking a seat in front of her. Michael sat next to him.

'Do you live here?'

'Yus, I've been in Berlin twenty years. I came here with my boyfriend, but he met someone else and left me. Another fellah! I suppose you're gonna say I should have seen it coming, ha ha?' she laughed, loudly and raucously. Daisy and Michael looked at each other surprised. This wasn't how they had expected her to be. 'It's twenty Euros for ten minutes, do you want to go separately or together?'

'Oh, err... together, please,' said Michael, reaching into his pocket and putting ten Euros on the table. Daisy did the same. Mavis folded the cash and slid it inside her headscarf before laying her hands flat on the table and closing her eyes, taking in a deep breath through her nose.

'Tealeaves for you, I think,' she said, placing a small teacup in front of Michael and pouring a little dark liquid from a purple teapot. 'Drink that down,' she advised, holding her fingers to her temples in contemplation.

'What is it?'

'Welsh tea, love. It's the same blend Shirley Bassey drank as a child in Tiger Bay.'

'Yes, I can taste the tiger!' said Michael, screwing up his face at the bitter taste. Taking the empty cup, she turned it upside-down on its saucer and spun it three times. Then she looked inside, staring diligently at the pattern made by what remained.

'You're going to die! You're going to die!' she cried. Michael's heart skipped a beat. 'Ha ha! Just my little joke to break the ice,' she laughed.

'Break the ice?' Michael gulped. 'I nearly shit meself!'

'For Gawd sakes, please don't do that to me!' Daisy took another emergency Mars bar from his pocket.

'Seriously though, you've had a mad couple of months,' she said, squinting for a clearer look.

'You could say that,' he sighed.

'And a lot of sadness just lately? Someone you love is going through illness?'

'Yes, that's right!' Michael gushed excitedly.

'But she's going to be OK… no… I'm wrong, it's a he?' she smiled, looking him up and down. 'He's calling your name.'

'That's insane! How could you possibly know all that?' Michael was gobsmacked.

'It's all there in the leaves, love!' She shrugged her shoulders knowingly. 'And I can see bells. Is he a Morris dancer?'

'No, he's a graphic designer.'

'Then there must be a marriage around him.'

'His mum and dad are with him now?'

'That'll be it then, love! Go with peace, love and light with blessing from above,' she chanted as if from a script, before handing Daisy a pack of tarot cards. 'Give 'em a good shuffle, love.' He did as instructed. After a while, she took them from him and laid them in a pattern across the table.

'I don't want any bad news! Don't tell me bad news!' he panicked.

284

'You're going to meet a tall and dark stranger,' she said mystically, waving her hands in the air.

'Just tall and dark?' Daisy was disappointed. 'What about handsome?'

'Hmm,' she grimaced. 'Well, you're going to like him. But…' she hesitated, looking a little concerned.

'What?'

'No, there's nothing more,' she snapped, drawing the cards into a pile and covering them with a black silk cloth.

'What is it? You were gonna tell me something bad, weren't you?' Terrified, Daisy's eyes welled with tears.

'You can't not tell him now!' Michael insisted.

'This tall dark man?' she frowned, eyes widened with horror. 'He has a past. He's involved in some dangerous, sinister things. You must beware! Beware!'

In his bed at St Thomas' Hospital, Travis was restless. His legs juddered and his hands twitched as his eyes shot back and forth beneath his comatose eyelids.

'What do you suppose he's doing?' said his mother Jeanie, grasping his wrist protectively.

'He's a fighter. He'll be awake soon enough, you'll see,' said his father.

'Should we call a nurse?' She glanced out at the corridor to see if anyone would come.

'No, he's not an eejit. Let him figure it out for himself.'

Suddenly without warning, Travis spoke. 'Michael! Michael!' he called out, before settling back quietly.

'Oh my God! Did you hear that, Hamish? He's calling for him.'

'Aye, that I did,' he nodded resignedly.

'Do you think I should phone and tell him?' Jeanie was worried how her husband might react to this suggestion.

'No, don't raise the poor lad's hopes just yet,' he sighed. 'He's suffered enough of late, wait till Travis wakes. Then you can call him.' Jeanie had expected a more aggressive response.

'Why, Hamish McBradey? You've changed your tune?'

'He's our son, Jeanie. I love him. And aye, so he's gay... what can we do?' He walked around the bed to put his hand affectionately on her shoulder. 'I'm an honest, hard-working man. I can be a stubborn beast like my da, but I'm not a monster.'

'Oh Hamish, of course you're not!' she gasped tearfully, touching his hand.

'Our bairn's grown up to be a good, strong man with his own mind and I'm proud of him, make no mistake. If this is how it must be, I'll stand by him.'

Kissing his hand, Jeanie stood to hug him. 'And I'm awful proud of you too, Mister McBradey.'

'Besides,' he grinned. 'We can't just abandon him, not after re-mortgaging the house to pay for all that dental work!'

While Connie stepped outside into the bustling street for a cigarette, Chastity reluctantly sat with Nicky at a table to one corner of the club. Looking down at his lap, he fiddled uncomfortably with the ring on his finger as Nicky tried to explain himself.

286

'I'm sorry I just disappeared without telling you. I had to get away and clear my head. I did it because of you.'

'Because of me?' Chastity didn't understand. 'Did you hate me that much?'

'No! No! I don't hate you, and I didn't back then.' His remorseful brown eyes gazed lovingly at his lost partner. 'When my dad died and my sister vanished into thin air, I had to do it all myself. There was the house, then the funeral and all his gambling debts. People knocking on my door day and night wanting their share, I just couldn't cope alone.'

'You weren't alone, you had me!'

'I know, but I couldn't make you suffer all that, it was too much. And then I had a breakdown, I didn't want you to see me like that.'

'Why not?' Chastity lifted his head. 'I would have given everything to be at your side helping you. For better or for worse?'

'I know, I should have shared that with you.' Nicky reached across and took Chastity's hand. 'I realise that now. But I was ill, I couldn't see straight.'

'You're not wearing your ring?'

'After drifting around Europe for a while, I got mugged in Austria. They took everything! I was destitute, sleeping in doorways. Then suddenly I got a message from Madame Fifi.'

'Fifi?' Chastity was confused.

'Yeah, she had me hunted down.'

'Why?'

'She said that I needed to be where you'd be able to find me. It was her that got me the job here, helped me find a bedsit. Got me back on my feet.'

'She did that for me? I had no idea! After all those years of me thinking she was a hard-faced bitch.' Chastity began to cry.

'It was a bloke she knew from Interpol. He found me in the street, I thought he was going to shoot me!' Nicky grinned. 'She told him you were her adopted daughter.' As Chastity sobbed uncontrollably, he moved his chair around the table for a comforting hug. 'I waited to hear from you, but it never happened.'

'Why didn't you just come home?'

'I assumed you'd met someone else and moved on with your life?'

'There is nobody else, there never has been.' Chastity hugged him back. 'You know me… chaste by name, chaste by nature.'

'Me neither. I still love you, cuddle bunny!'

'I never stopped loving you, daddy bear!' He pulled him into a kiss.

'Cuddle bunny?' Connie laughed, arriving back and pulling up a seat beside them. 'I'm never gonna let you live that down!'

'Ah, feck off!' Chastity smiled.

Behind them at the bar, a large heavily built man with grey curly hair stared at them intently. Walking to the end of the counter, he picked up the phone and dialled. 'Es ist Heinz,' he said in a low dark tone. 'They are here!'

As they made their way slowly through the dank streets of Berlin back towards the hotel, Chastity was in a dream.

'So what's Nicky gonna do?' asked Connie.

'He's going to tie up his loose ends here and come home when he can. He hasn't really got the money to just leave and I can't afford to support him, so it may take a while.' Chastity smiled. 'But I can't quite believe Fifi has done this. All those years we thought she was a tyrant when actually she was looking after us.'

'I thought she would be there with my mum,' said Michael disappointedly.

'Perhaps they've not got here yet?'

'I'm starving,' moaned Daisy. 'Shall we get a Chinese from that little takeaway we passed?'

'I'm not sure that's a good idea,' frowned Connie. 'You notice there's no cats around here?'

'Yeah, it does look like the sort of place where you'd have to catch your own chicken!' Chastity grinned. 'Perhaps we could find a McDonald's? At least you know what you're getting.'

Lightning flashed ominously in the sky, followed shortly by the deep roar of thunder. Looking up at the clouds, Daisy removed his earrings as a precaution against being struck then began to count.

'One Gawd blimey, two Gawd blimey, three Gawd blimey…'

'Eh?'

'When it flashes, you count until you hear the thunder. That's how you know how far away the storm is. Each Gawd blimey is one mile.'

'Perhaps it's not the same in Germany?' said Connie, stopping to light a cigarette.

'Don't stand still in a rough district like this or someone will pinch your shoes,' Chastity advised, looking around cautiously.

'I'm not looking forward to sleeping in that bunk tonight,' whinged Connie, drawing back on his nicotine. 'I'm gonna try and dream I'm staying at Claridge's.'

'Good luck with that then,' Chastity smirked.

'Suddenly, a large shiny van with blacked-out front windows screeched to a halt beside them. Before they knew what was happening, two big men in dark clothes and balaclavas jumped from the front and ran at them. They all screamed with fear as one took out a gun and pointed it at their heads. They instinctively threw their trembling hands in the air.

'What the fuck's going on?' Connie cried, dropping his cigarette.

'Do something, Daisy!' Chastity yelled.

'What, on me own?' he sobbed, reaching into his pocket for an emergency Mars bar. Thinking he was about to pull out a weapon, the man stepped forward and pressed the barrel against Daisy's forehead. 'It… it… it's just chocolate!' he mumbled with horror, dropping it on the floor. The man took another step back as the second opened the back of the vehicle.

'Steig in den van! Steig in den van!' yelled the first, waving the gun towards the opening.

'What's he saying?' Connie gasped.

'I think he wants us to get in the van,' Michael nodded nervously. 'Just… just do as he says!' Without taking his eye off the gun, he climbed onto a long wooden bench inside. Shaking with utter fear, one by one the others followed. As the doors slammed violently behind them, they sat huddled together in the pitch windowless dark, desperate to know what was happening.

290

'What do you think they're going to do to us?' said Connie, fumbling for another cigarette.

'I don't know,' Chastity whispered. 'But whatever it is, it can't be good!'

CHAPTER TWENTY ONE

It was quiet for quite some time in the back of the van, broken only by occasional sobs from Daisy. Awash with absolute terror, their minds raced with every possible horrific outcome as the vehicle tore through the endless streets. Connie finally broke the ice.

'Why don't you have some chocolate, Daisy?'

'I can't, that was my last one I dropped on the floor. The rest are in my suitcase.'

'How many did you bring?' said Michael.

'Forty-seven. I didn't know if they'd sell them here.'

'We've been driving for an awful long time,' Chastity sighed, biting his lip. 'Where do you suppose they're taking us?'

'I don't think we're in the city anymore,' said Connie. 'I heard a cow mooing back there.'

'I heard something. Are you sure it wasn't a horse neighing?' said Chastity. 'I liked horses when I was young.'

'Well, it's what you saw when you looked in the mirror!'

'I really need a wee,' Daisy whined.

'Kidnapped by two big men in balaclavas?' said Connie. 'Under any other circumstances, I'd be halfway to an orgasm by now.'

'Do you suppose we're still in Germany?' Michael asked. 'We haven't got our passports or anything.'

'I've got a really bad feeling about this,' said Chastity. 'Perhaps they're going to sell us to the white slave trade?'

'I'm not white,' said Daisy.

'Neither is Connie,' Michael quipped.

'There it is again! That cow.'

'Deja moo!' Chastity attempted to crack a smile.

'We should have been taking notes in case we have to tell the police. I
saw it on Yesterday Plus.'

'Yesterday Plus? What would that be then... today?' Michael was confused.

'A woman in the boot of a car said she could hear a waterfall,' Daisy explained. 'They found her round the back of a sewage pumping station.'

'Surely she could smell that?'

'She could, but she thought it was where she'd shit herself.'

Suddenly, the van stopped.

'Whatever happens, we stick together. Right?' advised Chastity. They all agreed.

The doors flew open and the two men gestured for them to climb out. As their eyes adjusted to the bright moonlight, they could see they were on a dust track in the middle of nowhere. Dark rugged moorlands stretched as far as the eye could see in all directions. The only movement was swaying grass, as a cruel bitter wind whipped across the landscape. Insects from a nearby bog were the only life.

'Aw my Gawd,' Connie cried. 'This looks like where Myra Hindley brought them kids!'

'There's a lot of midges,' said Chastity, spitting a tiny creepy-crawly from his lips.

'Perhaps there's a dwarf epidemic?' said Daisy.

294

'I said midges, not midgets you silly mare!'

As the van doors were slammed shut, they saw a large wooden shack to the other side of the road. Despite its ramshackle and dilapidated appearance, the warm glow of lights and smoke from a crooked tin chimney were inviting, if not a little frightening. The prospect of what could happen to them within those tatty walls was unthinkably scary. The two men signalled for them to walk across to the hut, not an easy task across uneven clumps of grass and earth in the dark. As they approached, one of the men called out.

'Luther?' The door swung open to reveal a massive, muscular black man with a shaven head in black and grey army fatigues. They were horrified to see that he too carried a gun. They cautiously squeezed past into a large lobby. Worn wooden planks made up the walls, floor and ceiling, lit by a single bare bulb swinging from the breeze above their heads.

'Is there a bathroom, please?' Daisy asked politely, putting his hand up to speak. Luther pushed open a door opposite with the barrel of his gun to reveal the most basic of toilets lit by a single wobbling candle flame. 'Thank you,' said Daisy with a smile before tiptoeing inside and closing the wooden plank door. One of the men directed the others to another door at the back. With a deep breath, Michael braced himself and pushed in.

'Oh my God!' he gasped at the sight before him.

A short man with slicked back black hair sat at a grand desk, sipping on a large brandy. Beside him, a table was spread with plates full of food. In a wide stone hearth opposite was a large roaring fire, filling the room with a warm glow. Sitting comfortably beside the flames in two large overstuffed armchairs were Madame Fifi and Verity Van Cougar.

'Mickey!' Verity smiled, standing to greet him.

'Mum!' Michael cried, pulling her tearfully into a hug. 'It's so good to see you! We thought we were going to be executed.'

'Oh darling boy, I'm so sorry. That's Nils. He was trained in Special Forces. Has a penchant for drama.' One of the men stepped forward removing his balaclava to reveal another shaved head. He reached his hand forward with a grin to shake.

'Don't worry, you're very safe here,' said Fifi, rising to pat Michael reassuringly on the shoulder. 'Hello Chastity, Connie,' she nodded. Uncharacteristically lost for words, they nodded back, wiping a tear of relief from their eyes. 'Where's Daisy?'

'She's in the loo,' Chastity shrugged.

'And this is Hans,' she pointed, as the other man removed his disguise to reveal a third bare-skinned scalp.

'All these sexy bald men, it's like an infestation of Jean Luc Picards!' Connie smiled.

'You must be Chastity? We spoke on the phone?' said the man at the table.

'Gunter? Nice to finally meet you.'

'Please, eat, drink!' he gestured to the buffet table.

Meanwhile, Daisy was scared to come out of the toilet. After some time, he held back his shoulders with a gulp and bravely stepped from the cubicle, coming face-to-face with Luther. It was unusual to
296

meet someone larger than himself, regardless of the bulging muscles.

'Alright, sweet cheeks?' Luther blew a kiss and winked.

'Oh!' Daisy gasped with a blush. He hadn't expected this at all.

'Perhaps we could meet up some time for a drink?' purred the rugged hunk in a deep German accent. Daisy giggled, unsure what to say with little or no experience of gentleman callers. With an understanding bright white grin, Luther took his hand and led him through to the others.

'Ah, Daisy!' Fifi smiled as they entered. Realising for the first time that he was safe, he burst into floods of tears.

'It's OK,' said Chastity, reaching out to him.' Let me introduce you. This is Hans, Nils and Gunter, Daisy.'

'Hi!' Daisy waved, noticing for the first time the buffet table. Seeing his ravenous expression, Gunter signalled for him to help himself. And he did. Diving in head first, he pulled at roast chicken, Bavarian ham and knackwurst sausage, followed closely by Connie and Chastity. The men laughed and applauded at the spectacle. While distracted, Verity leaned to whisper in Michael's ear.

'Remember… Creighton is your father, not Fifi. These men are the guardians of his estate, it's them we need to convince.'

'Right,' Michael nodded.

'Once it passes to you, they can disband. It's a momentous occasion for them, but we've got to get this right!'

After welcome refreshments, lots of relaxed laughter and chatter and quite a lot of strong German beer, it was time to get down to business. Gunter opened the conversation.

'We have reason to believe that you are Creighton's son?' he asked Michael seriously.

'Yes… yes I am, Michael Small,' he confirmed. 'And Verity is my mother.'

'The only evidence we have is this.' He passed him a small folded piece of paper. Unwrapping it as Connie and Chastity looked over his shoulder, he attempted to understand what was stamped into the vellum.

'In th v nt of my d mis , I l av   v rything to my on tru h ir.'

'Is it in code?' said Chastity, squinting to check he was reading properly.

'No, the E's are missing. Creighton only had three fingers on his left hand,' Gunter assured.

'They're very hard to use, them old mechanical typewriters,' added Connie. 'I bet Agatha Christie had fingers like an all-in wrestler!'

'But it doesn't mention my name?' Michael noticed with disappointment.

'Which is why we must check further,' said Gunter. Standing from the desk, he drew back a red velvet curtain to reveal an enormous vintage safe. As tall as Michael and as wide as Daisy, it's dark green paint was scraped and worn to reveal a solid steel door held securely in place by three huge hinges. A large combination dial stood out from the centre, above which was the emblem Michael recognised from the keys around his neck: C.A.C. Three giant gold keyholes glistened in the firelight.

298

'Only Creighton knew the entry code, but we can open the door using the three keys he had entrusted to his beloved family. If you please?' Gunter gestured towards the safe. As tension mounted, Michael pulled on the two strings around his neck, pulling the keys from inside his jumper. Lifting the tethers over his head, he passed one key to Fifi. Verity pulled the third from her cleavage on a thick gold chain. Putting her key in the top lock, Fifi turned it clockwise to a loud clang.

'One,' said Daisy helpfully. Verity followed in the lock below. 'Two,' Daisy continued. Connie shot him an impatient look.

'It's not racing at Sandown, we don't need a running commentary!'

'And the third, please?' Gunter rubbed his hands together expectantly.

'Go ahead, honey,' said Verity, squeezing Michael's arm. With nervous anticipation, he reached forward and pushed the final key into the lock. With a turn, a series of loud metal thuds filled the room as the heavy door jolted and sprung slowly open with a loud creek. A collective intake of breath filled the room at the sight of hundreds of papers, scrolls and diaries jammed tightly onto its metal shelves.

Michael suddenly felt rather strange. His heart thumped in his chest and his fingers and toes tingled. Perhaps it was just the strong smell from the musty papers, but somehow the feeling in the air was electric. It was as if Pandora's box itself had sprung forth, bringing with it all the evils of the world. But like the legend, it also brought forth hope.

'Ah! The diaries. May I?' Gunter asked respectfully.

'Yeah, of course,' Michael nodded, as he pulled out a worn blue edition and returned to his desk. Taking a pair of spectacles from his top pocket, he began to slowly leaf through the bound scribbled pages, making occasional notes on a little pad. The room was silent as everyone took a seat and waited. Fifi swigged back the last of her brandy, Connie picked at his finger and Daisy reached for another chicken leg from the buffet table.

'We went to the Vindergurderbreurgenshaftenshitz Club,' whispered Chastity, patting Verity's knee.

'What did you think?' she smiled.

'It's amazing, exactly as you described. I'd love to work there one day.'

'You never know, you may get your wish. And we should persuade Fifi to perform, too. She won't like it, we'll have to bully her!'

After some considerable time, Gunter took off his glasses and signalled to the other guardians. One by one, they looked at the paragraph in the book that he had highlighted, each in turn nodding their response seriously.

'I can confirm that the evidence is clear,' said Gunter, closing the diary.

Michael looked up from his lap hopefully. 'What does it say?'

Asleep in Travis' large double bed in London, Jeanie awoke with a start as the telephone rang. Grasping her husband's arm with nervous anticipation, she shook him awake to stir him from his slumber.

300

'Is that the hospital?' she gasped, feeling for a small gold crucifix around her neck. 'Will you answer it, Hamish? I'm not sure I can.' Tapping his wife's arm supportively, he swung out of bed and picked up the receiver.

'Yes?' He looked back at his wife seriously. 'Yes, I understand. Thank you.' Jeanie held her breath as he put down the receiver and turned to face her. 'Put on your glad rags Hen, we've got to go. Travis is out of his coma!'

Back in the shack, Gunter stood from the desk and walked across to Michael. He jumped from his seat to speak eye-to-eye, adrenalin rushing through his veins.

'Creighton refers to you specifically as his son.' He took Michael's hand and shook it heartily. 'You are indeed the inheritor of his fortune and his estates, here and around the world. Congratulations!'

The room erupted with excitement, as everyone leapt to their feet and jumped up and down, cheering, shouting and kissing. Hans reached beneath the desk and pulled out two enormous bottles of Champagne, popping a cork with each hand and spraying everyone with its delicious golden fizz.

'It's all yours! It's actually all yours!' Connie laughed hysterically, pulling papers from the safe and tossing them into the air. As they zigzagged slowly to the ground, Michael could glance a flurry of property deeds, investment dockets and land titles.

'Congratulations, darling Mickey!' cried Verity, throwing her arms around his neck. Over her shoulder, his real father Madame Fifi grinned back at him calmly, catching some of the spraying Champagne in

301

her empty brandy glass and saluting him before taking a celebratory sip.

'Are you happy, love?' said Chastity, giving Michael a peck on the cheek.

'I feel a bit weird, actually. I wish Travis was here.'

'I know you do, Lu. I wish Nicky was here, too,' he smiled back. 'Come on, let's have some Champagne!'

Once the papers had been loaded into three large leather bags and handed one each to Creighton's henchmen, the party continued outside. Suddenly the cold winter wind didn't seem so sinister, as two large black limousines were pulled round from behind the shack. Connie, Michael, Chastity and Daisy carried the remains of the Champagne into one as Verity and Fifi took the other. Pulling away into the darkness, Gunter and Luther followed in the van.

'Well, that's our boy sorted,' Verity grinned, giving Fifi a hug.

'Yes, I'm pleased for him. He may as well have been Creighton's son, it really was the three of us together against the world, wasn't it?'

'Yes, it always was.' Verity could see a sudden sour look on Fifi's face. 'What is it?'

'It was Creighton who murdered Lettie's brother.'

'Really? How do you know?' Verity was shocked.

'There's evidence. But he wanted me to take the blame.'

'Why?'

'I don't know his reason. But I know just the psychotic bitch to ask!'

The cars didn't return to Big Dick's Halfway Inn as expected. Pulling into a brightly lit swish driveway, two smartly uniformed concierge doormen jumped forward to open the doors.

'Oh my God!' Connie gasped, looking up at the exotic building. 'It's the Ritz-Carlton. Can you believe it?'

'This is insane!' Michael laughed, stepping from the limousine.

'Your suite is reserved and paid for, Nils will collect your suitcases from big Dick,' advised Gunter. 'As Madame Fifi is on the run and you may be recognised as helping her escape from prison, you and your friends are booked in under a pseudonym.' He handed him the booking slip.

'Dirk Stardust?' Michael laughed.

'I think it is for the best. She is known by Interpol, and it is our job to keep you all safe until you return to London.'

'Thank you very much,' he replied, a little worried. 'Do you think the police will be looking for us, too?'

'It is possible.' He shook Michael's hand again. 'I wish you the best of luck. By the time you return to London, all of your documents will be with Creighton's solicitor.'

'My documents?' Michael couldn't quite believe what he was hearing.

'Yes. But it will take a few weeks before everything has transferred to you. Congratulations once more!' With a respectful nod, Gunter returned to the van. As it spun back down the long drive towards the street, Luther grinned and blew Daisy a kiss. Embarrassed, he covered his smile and gave back a little wave.

'Has our Daisy got herself an admirer?' Chastity whispered.

'Who knows? If he's lucky,' he grinned, turning to climb the steps to the front entrance.

Ascending in the high-class lift was like floating on a cloud. Connie kept licking his lips and pouting at the teenage attendant.

'Leave him alone, poor boy!' Chastity demanded.

'He likes it, he keeps winking at me,' Connie insisted.

'He's not winking, you're giving him a nervous twitch.'

'Not five seconds after we first met, he asked if I was going down. What did he expect?' Connie smirked. 'Luckily for him, I can't bend in these slacks!'

'He only asked if you was going down because you look like someone who should be ironing sheets in the basement!'

Their hotel suite was enormous and the absolute height of royal luxury. Connie could not take his eyes off the stunningly handsome bellboy as he showed them around.

'Your reception, Sir,' grinned the hunk, gesturing to a large lounge area with floor-to-ceiling windows overlooking Berlin's fashionable wealthy district. One enormous curved cream sofa weaved its way across the centre of a pure white carpet. Marble side tables bloomed with huge bouquets of fresh flowers in pinks and lavenders, and a large dining table and ten chairs with gold inlaid panels graced the other end of the room. A white grand piano sat elegantly to one corner beneath a huge oil painting of Bode Museum, and Grecian statues of antiquity silently guarded each corner. The bellboy picked up a remote from one of the tables and pressed the button. In an instant, the sunken ceiling lights dimmed as the wall lights rose, and the huge gold-framed mirror became a state-of-the-art television set.

'It has internet,' he advised, pressing another button to demonstrate.

'Wow, would you be looking at that? What time is Eastenders on?' said Chastity, glancing at his watch.

'And your bedrooms, Sir.' One by one, he opened four gilded doors to reveal enormous double beds with Egyptian cotton dressings in rose pink, daffodil yellow, emerald green and cobalt blue respectively. As they ran excitedly around to investigate, they discovered that each had its own marble en suite bathroom with gold taps and luscious fluffy white towels.

'Did you peek in that bedroom?' whispered Chastity.

'I always peak in the bedroom!' Connie quipped.

'Where's the kitchenette, then?' said Daisy, opening a cupboard to investigate.

'Anything you need, you call,' the man advised, pointing to a suite telephone behind the dining table.

'Thank you! Thank you so much!' Michael gushed, handing him a twenty Euro bill.

'Thank you, Sir,' he saluted. 'In your country, you are a rock star?' he grinned hopefully.

'Err…' Lost for words, Michael handed Chastity the booking slip.

'Yes, he is,' Chastity interrupted. 'Only the best for Dirk Stardust!'

'Can I get a picture?' Before Michael knew what was happening, the man had pulled out his phone and jumped next to him, snapping several shots. 'If you need anything… I mean anything,' he smiled suggestively. 'Just ask for Fritz, anytime.'

'Oh, err… yes, thanks!' Michael blushed.

'I'm famous too, you know!' Connie yelled after him as he left for the corridor, closing the door behind him.

'Dirk Stardust? Sounds more like a porn star!' Chastity whispered.

'I'll explain later!'

'Oh, it's alright for the rock star here with men falling at his feet, ain't it? What am I then, just his fuckin' assistant?' Connie sulked.

'No, I'm his assistant. And you're mine,' said Chastity, picking up the remote and flicking through the channels on the television. 'So just find the mini-bar and shut the feck up!'

By the time they had freshened up, Nils had returned with their suitcases from Big Dick's Halfway Inn. The other men, Fifi and Verity joined them in their suite for the real party to begin. Music blared and Champagne flowed as they danced and laughed
306

through the night till the early hours. Daisy even had his own buffet, delivered on a golden trolley draped with crisp white linen. He shared his bounty with equally ravenous Luther, as they chatted romantically together in one corner. Connie's attempt to drink the henchmen under the table with vodka shots failed miserably, as did Chastity's arm wrestle across the piano with Fifi. Verity tickled the ivories and sang melancholy Cole Porter while Michael rather unsuccessfully attempted drunken vocal harmonies.

He almost didn't notice his mobile phone vibrating in his pocket. Pulling it out, he squinted at the text on the screen, trying to focus his glazed eyes on the tiny words. Chastity noticed from across the room, as he suddenly burst into floods of tears and ran into his bedroom. Putting down his Champagne glass, he followed hot on his heels to find him lying face down on the bed sobbing.

'What's wrong? What's going on?' he asked, sitting on the bed beside him.

'It's Travis,' Michael gasped with joy. 'He's woken up!'

CHAPTER TWENTY TWO

The following morning, brilliant sunshine streamed in through the hotel suite windows as breakfast was served at the large white table. With his napkin tucked into the top of his jumper, Daisy picked his way through cereal, yoghurt and a selection of breads, Bavarian cheeses and German meats. Michael and Chastity settled for strong coffee and toast with marmalade.

'But I feel so guilty,' said Michael, holding his hung-over head in his hands.

'Why?' Chastity was concerned for his friend.

'I don't deserve all this. Travis is laid up in a hospital bed and I'm here living it up like royalty.'

'Remember you're Prince Philip's grandson? By rights, you should be living like this anyway.'

'But all this just doesn't feel right.'

'I'm guessing you'll get used to it, you got used to drag soon enough. And you can share it all with Travis, just think of the adventures you'll have!' Chastity swigged his caffeine. 'I think I'd be too nervous to live like this all the time. I'd be worried I was gonna break something. I even sat down to have a piddle.'

'When you wee do you shake, squeeze, flick or dribble?' asked Daisy, coming up for air.

'Well yes, all of those,' Michael giggled.

'I bet this is where all the celebrities stay,' Daisy added. 'Have you ever met anyone famous?'

'Yes, I once met Anneka Rice!' said Chastity excitedly. 'Well… she jumped out of a helicopter and ran past me.' He patted Michael affectionately on the arm 'Have you heard from Travis yet?'

'He hasn't answered any of my texts.'

'He's probably just resting, give him time.'

'I'm really happy for you that Nicky's coming home. I hope you can pick up where you left off?'

'Yes, I can't quite believe it! I always dreamed we'd grow old together. We're gonna just take it one day at a time.'

'And what about you and Luther last night, Daisy?' Michael chuckled. 'Are you seeing him again?'

'If he wants a piece of this, he's gonna have to work for it!' he answered sassily.

'Well, there's plenty for him to work with!'

Suddenly, Connie lunged dramatically from his bedroom, reeling at the bright morning light. With a white towel wrapped around his head in a turban and matching dressing gown, he slipped on a pair of Foster Grants to diffuse the glow, walking delicately across to the table.

'Look out, here she comes,' quipped Chastity. 'Norma Desmond on crack!'

'Can you chew your toast a bit more quietly? In my head, it's like an army squadron marching up a gravel drive!' Connie sat and poured himself a black coffee. 'Anyway, why are you up so early?'

'I went for a beauty treatment in the lobby,' said Chastity, posing with glee. Connie glanced over the top of his sunglasses.

'Was it shut?'

'Now we're all here, I've got something to tell you.' Chastity pulled his chair in closer. 'Verity thinks we should perform at the Vindergurderbreurgenshaftenshitz Club tomorrow night before we leave. What do you think?'

'But we haven't brought anything to wear,' said Michael.

'She said the dressing room is stocked like the BBC costume department.'

'I could sing with my mum?' Michael gushed.

'Yes,' Chastity agreed. 'We can go round and rehearse a few bits tomorrow afternoon. We'll get paid.'

'That's good, you'll be able to give me back that tenner for the mascara!' said Connie.

'Heinz will promote it as a one-off special event. And the best part is, Verity's going to persuade Fifi to do a spot, too.'

'Wow! Really?' Michael was excited at the prospect of finally seeing this legendary star in her element.

'Could be cool, Dolly,' said Connie. 'Let's have a look and see what the bitch can do. And working here makes us international cabaret stars! We can ask for more money back in London.'

'How can you do that if you haven't got a job to go back to?' asked Daisy, chewing on a large lump of cheese.

'She's got a point.' Chastity bit his lip. 'We've got to stop Lettie getting Sugar Sugar up and running again before Fifi's back at the helm. Connie, we need a plan.'

'Hmm…' Connie thought for a moment. 'Pass me that phone.' Michael reached back and grabbed the suite's handset, putting it on the table in front of him. 'It's time to carry out your threat, Tit!' Taking a mouthful of coffee, he picked up the receiver. 'Speaky English? Get me Westminster City Council in London, Health and Safety department.'

After some rest, Travis was sat up wide-awake in his hospital bed. Still a little bruised around the face and torso, he waited as two nurses checked his vital signs. They had told him that his parents were in town holding a vigil, but nobody had so far mentioned Michael. Having missed his opportunity to make peace with his boyfriend, he wasn't even sure that he knew he was in hospital.

Sipping from a warm cup of tea, he glanced up to see a grey-haired doctor entering the room. Well-dressed in a handmade suit and tie under a white coat, he peered over his steel-rimmed spectacles.

'Good morning Travis,' he smiled, taking the clipboard from the nurse.

'Morning, Doctor. How am I doing?'

'Very well, actually,' he said, leaning in to shine a small torch light into his patient's eyes. 'The brain scan shows no lasting damage and your cognitive tests all appear to be sound.'

'That's great, thank you so much for looking after me!' he grinned, feeling a little emotional.

'You're very lucky, you took quite a beating. But you're a healthy young man, I believe you'll make a full recovery in time.' He held a stethoscope against his chest and tapped his painful ribs.

'When can I go home?'

'If you continue like this, I'd say perhaps the end of next week? But take it easy for a while. Have you got someone who can look after you?'

'Yes… well, I'm hoping so.'

At that moment, Travis' parents arrived on the ward. As the doctor took his father aside to update him in the corridor, his mother leaned in happily to kiss him on the cheek before sitting at his bedside.

'I'm gonna be OK, Ma,' he cried.

'That's good news, Travis. I'm so pleased… and relieved!' she laughed.

'But there's something important I've got to tell you.' He bit his lip with hesitation, mind racing to find the right words. Jeanie could see how difficult this was for him.

'I've told Michael you're awake,' she said gently, saving him the stress.

'You know?' Travis was taken aback.

'Aye, that I do.'

'Me da? Does he know, too?'

'He does.' Jeanie's eyes sparkled. 'And he's fine, he understands. Your boyfriend is very handsome, but do you love him?'

'Oh Ma, yes I do, I really really do!' He jumped forward in his bed, forgetting his injuries. Holding his ribs with a grimace, he laid gently back. 'When did you see him? He is OK, isn't he? I wanted to text him, but my mobile's missing.'

'He's fine, but very worried about you. He'll be here soon enough.' She took his hand and looked him seriously in the eyes. 'Are you and Michael going to live together?'

'He was about to move in the day I was attacked.'

'Then your da and I agree, if you're going to live together you need to marry.'

Hamish returned, grasping the bottom of the bed frame. 'Aye, if it's good enough for your sisters, it's good enough for you, son.'

'Things need to be done properly,' Jeanie nodded. 'Do you want to marry the lad?'

'Aye!' His grin widened as his eyes filled with tears of happiness and relief. 'I do!'

With an afternoon free and time to kill, Chastity, Connie and Michael decided to see the sights on the Berlin tourist trail. Having picked up a map of the local area in the hotel lobby, they dropped Daisy at his lunch date with Luther before finding themselves in front of Charlottenburg Palace.

'Just think, you could probably afford to live somewhere like this now, Dolly,' Connie laughed, nudging Michael in the ribs.

'God, no,' he smiled. 'Imagine having to clean all those windows?'

'You wouldn't have to do them yourself, would ya? You'd get a team of fit young men in jockstraps to do that!' Connie lit a cigarette. 'You never pick up a cloth at my place, why start now?'

'Nobody can find a bloody cloth at your place, there's so much mess!'

'You're quiet for a change?'

'I'm just worried about Daisy,' sighed Chastity. 'Luther seems nice but he is a thug henchman, after all. And we're going home shortly, I just don't want her to get hurt.'

'She'll be fine,' assured Michael. 'He's treating her like a lady and stuffing her face at the same time, let her have her moment.'

314

'I suppose you're right,' he agreed. 'Come on, let's look inside the palace.'

'If we must!' Connie sulked.

Walking through the hall of sculptures, they stopped next to a white marble angel sitting on a rock.

'Ah, isn't that lovely?' Chastity smiled, rubbing it on the knee. 'Why haven't those others got wings?'

'Perhaps they're wood nymphs?' Michael suggested.

'I've been compared to a wood nymph,' said Chastity.

'Yeah, the fat one on the end!' Connie bitched. 'This is about as exciting as a piss in a bucket. Can't we find a gay pub?'

Without warning, a shrill scream rang out from the other end of the hall. Startled, they turned to see three teenage girls. 'Dirk! Dirk!' one of them shouted. Mobile phones in waving hands, they ran desperately towards Michael.

'What the actual fuck?' He shook his head in disbelief. 'Come on, we'd better leg it!'

They turned and ran towards the exit with the noisy girls in hot pursuit. By the time they had reached the gardens at the front of the building, the admirers had expanded to fifteen.

'Quick, this way!' Connie headed towards a large car park. They ducked behind a cake shop to one end, hoping to lose the crowd.

'Daisy would have loved this!' said Chastity, sniffing the delicious aroma. Suddenly, more screams ran out from behind them as they were spotted by yet another group of fans.

'To the cars!' Michael cried, leading the way. Squatting low in an attempt to not be seen, they weaved in and out between the vehicles towards the main road. But it was no good. As soon as they reached the pavement, another twenty young ladies simultaneously screamed, joining their fellow huntresses in pursuit across the busy road and up a side turning.

'Dirk! Dirk!' echoed from what had now grown to over a hundred pubescent voices, as residents and local business workers came to windows and stepped out of doorways to watch the spectacle. Running as fast as they could away from the terrifying avalanche of hormones, Michael and Connie each grabbed one of Chastity's arms to help him keep up.

'Exciting enough for you, yet?' Michael yelled above the din.

'Point taken,' Connie panted. 'Are you OK, Tit?' Chastity was so exhausted he couldn't even speak.

'Look, up there!' said Michael, pointing ahead to a small hotel. Pulling Chastity unceremoniously through its front entrance, they slammed it shut behind them and ran inside. The mass of teenagers hit the front wall like a human tsunami, banging on the windows and flooding the side alley to find another way in.

Arriving in a small empty dining room near the back of the building, they dropped Chastity into a chair before sitting themselves.

'Was ist los?' shouted a smartly dressed young woman, stomping towards them angrily from the kitchens.

'Please,' said Michael, trying to catch his breath. 'We just need to make a phone call? Someone will collect us, I'm really sorry.' He pulled his mobile out of his pocket and speed-dialled Gunter's number.

316

'Oh, you are Dirk Spangler?' she grinned shyly, batting her eyelids and plumping at her hair.

'He is today!' Connie puffed, tapping Chastity's flushed cheeks. 'Can we get a glass of water for our friend? I think she's having a heart attack!'

'Water, yes. Then selfie? Please?'

'Sure,' Michael nodded. 'Hi Gunter? We need help. Can Nils collect us from the Atrium Hotel? Thanks.' He turned to rub Chastity's back. 'Are you OK?'

'Aw my Gawd,' said Connie, looking at his phone. 'Dirk Stardust's got his own Facebook fan page!'

'Eh?'

'It's that bellboy, Fritz. He's a celebrity vlogger.

'What's a vlogger?' Chastity gasped, dabbing his damp forehead with a tissue.

'He does a German video log, like an internet diary? Here he is, Fritz Muller. He's got over six million views on YouTube doing short films about famous people that stay at our hotel. His clip of your selfie with him's already had over two-hundred-thousand hits!'

'That's insane!' Michael was gobsmacked.

'And look at this,' Connie grinned, showing them the screen. 'Someone's posted a video of us running away before we've even got our breath back!'

'That's the power of social media,' said Michael, pushing back his sweaty fringe. 'Dirk Stardust, the rock star who's never recorded a note!'

'It's the work of the Devil, that's what it is,' said Chastity. 'And we didn't even get a chance to do any shopping!'

The following afternoon, Connie, Chastity and Michael were familiarising themselves with the Vindergurderbreurgenshaftenshitz Club's backstage areas. The dressing room was ten times the size of the one they used at Sugar Sugar. Scenery, props and equipment from shows gone by stacked high against the back wall, intermingled with remnants of lighting rigs and sound systems. Eight huge elaborate gold-framed mirrors backed on to the stage, each with its own chair and table stacked high with makeup and accessories. Rail upon rail of costumes stood through the middle of the room, each topped with a shelf overflowing with wigs, headdresses and feather boas. To Connie and Chastity it was like a giant sweet shop, as they rummaged through excitedly, heads spinning with ideas for that evening's performance. Daisy delighted in trying on several outrageous hats, bellowing with laughter each time he looked in the mirror. And Michael sat to one end of the room with Verity, running through possible songs they could perform together.

'I'm so happy I can do this with you, Mickey,' Verity smiled.

'Me too,' he agreed. 'Ever since I very first met you, I've wanted to sing with you.'

'You know I've got to fly back out to Manhattan tomorrow?' she sighed. 'Back-to-back gigs are booked that I can't get out of. The show must go on! So we don't have much time together.'

'I know,' Michael nodded.

'But I'll be back as soon as I can. Or bring your new beau out to New York?'

'Yeah! I'd really like that!'

318

'So, tell me about Travis? I want to know everything!' Verity lit a Sobranie.

'Oh Mum, he's magnificent! He's handsome, he's sexy, I really want you to meet,' Michael gushed. 'And his eyes... my God, he has the most amazing eyes!'

'Sounds like love. Is he going to be alright?'

'His mum texted me, she said he's gonna be OK.' He furrowed his brow, thinking how unpredictable his boyfriend's recovery would be. 'It was very touch and go, I was so worried he wouldn't remember me.'

'How could he not remember you?' She put her arm around his shoulder. 'Always remember, never forget... you're pretty magnificent yourself, mister!'

Across the other side of the room, Chastity glanced through a costume rail to see a disgruntled Madame Fifi talking to the club's owner Heinz at one of the dressing tables.

'As soon as the posters went up, tickets sold out within an hour, you've got to perform!' he pleaded. 'You know how word spreads in this town?'

'Heinz, it is all in the past. I don't do that anymore,' she replied defiantly.

'But your people want to see your spectacular return!'

'You should have asked me first.'

'But Verity said... Argh!' Slamming his hand on the table, Heinz stood from his chair in frustration and stormed off.

Fifi turned to look at herself in the mirror. It had been such a long time since she had performed in Berlin, so much had happened since. Now she was the shining star of her own successful nightclub, she had no desire to return to her old life. Chastity stepped through the rail and walked across to join her. He pulled a chair from the next table and sat.

'Heinz giving you a hard time?' he smiled.

'You could say that,' said Fifi, pulling at wisps of hair in her reflection. 'Verity told him I would perform. I like Heinz, it is a shame to disappoint him.'

'Why don't you want to?'

'The name Lettie Von Schabernacket has brought me nothing but bad luck. That's why I changed it when I moved to London, but still it haunts me.' She sighed, turning to face him. 'And I'm on the run, remember? What if Interpol see the publicity, they already know who I am?'

'You've got a point,' Chastity shared her concern.

'Besides, my performing days are over.'

'But surely, that's what the great Madame Fifi is? A performance? Every night in Sugar Sugar you're still the greatest show on Earth. It's not the real you.'

'What do you mean?' she said, momentarily defensively.

'I've spent all these years believing you're nothing but a self-centred, hard-faced control freak. But in reality, you've saved all of us! You rescued me when my career nosedived and brought my Nicky back to me. You gave Connie a future when his dad threw him out. You care for your mother, allowing her to keep her independence. And Lord alone knows who else would employ Daisy!'

'Yes, poor Daisy,' Fifi smiled affectionately, looking across at his little fashion show.

'As for Hortense, she's anybody's guess! And you took Michael in when he was desperate. You didn't believe all that rubbish about him performing all
320

over Europe and being the best there is, did you?' Chastity laughed.

'Certainly not. I am the best there is!' she smirked, glancing briefly back to pout in the mirror.

'He wants you to perform, you know?' he nodded.

'He does? I can't think why.'

'Because you're a true living legend! And because he loves and respects you. Why is that so hard for you to believe?'

Fifi thought for a moment. 'Growing up without a family is tough. Yes, you can fight. You can battle on and you can win, but no matter how successful you become, you never belong. That is all I have given you, somewhere to belong.' Her look of thoughtful melancholy was something Chastity had rarely seen.

'And you belong with us, too.' He reached forward to squeeze her hand fondly. 'We are the Drag Queen Sisterhood and you are our matriarch. So, will you perform tonight? I know it's a risk, but surely that's what this club has always been about?'

She turned back to the mirror, staring at herself in deep thought. 'I'll think about it.'

CHAPTER TWENTY THREE

Back in Soho, Sugar Sugar's clean-up was still underway. People in white overalls mopped, scrubbed and polished every surface touched by the sprinkler system as Lettie marched around shouting orders. As one woman scrubbed the side of a big gold-framed picture of Chastity in a polka dot Little Bo Peep costume, a screw holding it to the wall came loose. She jumped back with a start as it swung to one side, bumping against the adjacent portrait of Connie dressed as Carol Channing. Embarrassed, she turned to face Lettie apologetically.

'Just take them all down,' he snapped. 'I'm changing the pictures, they don't work here anymore.' He walked away, pausing at the upper bar. 'And while you're at it, get rid of that hideous thing, too.' He pointed at the oil painting of Madame Fifi dressed as Queen Elizabeth the First hanging resplendently at the back of the counter. 'It makes me heave every time I see it!'

Spinning on his heels, he stomped through to his office. There waiting for him were three prominent local drag queens he had invited to replace Michael, Chastity and Connie. Sitting in jeans, jackets and t-shirts, they had already been waiting over twenty minutes.

'We ain't got all fucking day, you know?' moaned Chi Chi La Boom Boom, looking at his watch.

'Yes, I know, but as you can see I'm having a refit,' Lettie smiled apologetically, sitting behind his desk.

'Looks like they're just running a mop around to me!' sighed Ruby Tanya sarcastically. He ran his finger across the desktop, holding up the thick clump of dust before flicking it on the floor. 'So, what's the plan?'

'I've sacked the drags and Fifi's gone. I'm at the helm now, time for a new start, a fresh slate.'

'About time,' chipped in Ava Larf. 'Just how old is that Chastity Belt? She tells people those liver spots are a henna tattoo of the constellations but she can't fool everyone!' The other drags nodded in agreement.

'So, I want to ask if you'd be interested in replacing them? Regular work, no more hours on the phone trying to get bookings?'

'My diary's already full. Why would I want to get typecast in this dump?' said Chi Chi.

'The money's good.' Lettie slid a piece of paper across the desk to them. 'If you work here your careers will go stratospheric. You'll become Soho's guiding stars!'

'You think a lot of yourself, don't ya?' Chi Chi picked up the paper and showed it to the others, laughing. 'Is that per week or per show? You've been here too long sister, prices have gone way up since then!' Grabbing his bag, he stood up to leave. 'Why don't you ask Ida Know, since you're already licking butt? She'll do anything for a couple of gins and some arsylingus!' He turned to the two remaining drags. 'I'll be in Café Nero.' Blowing several air kisses, he left the room.

'We heard you've come into money,' said Ruby. 'So you're gonna have to do better than that!' He threw the paper back in Lettie's face.

'OK yes, we can up the money,' Lettie whinged. 'But I need a decision about the job now, we re-open in a couple of days.'

'I'm not sure we can trust her,' said Ava cynically.

'Look at me! This is a serious proposition.' Lettie was getting frustrated. 'A long term residency, enough already with carting costumes and sound systems everywhere.'

'Trouble is, all I see when I look at your face is the imprint of the last man who sat on it!' Ruby quipped. 'Who gets the flat above the club?'

'I'm keeping that for myself,' said Lettie. 'I need to be on-site.'

Suddenly, the door re-opened. In walked an austere looking middle-aged woman in a tweed suit and green hat carrying a large clipboard.

'Bernard Cohen?' she asked, looking at her paperwork.

'Bernard?' Ruby smirked.

'Yes? Who are you?' Lettie answered suspiciously.

'Marybeth Clang, Westminster City Council Health and Safety.' She looked at him diligently over half-rimmed spectacles.

'How did you get in?'

'One of your workmen opened the door. I've finished my inspection.'

'Your inspection?'

'Yes, following the complaint.'

'Complaint?' Lettie's mind was racing as his blood pressure rose. 'Chastity Belt! I'll have you for this,' he whispered to himself.

'Never a dull moment here, I'll give her that much!' said Ava. Clang continued.

'The sprinkler and fire alarm systems need completely updating. The customer areas have extensive water damage to the electrics, and the supply board is out of date it no longer meets regulations. I would therefore suggest that the entire building needs a re-wire.' She glanced at her hand-written list.

'Re-wiring?' Lettie was in shock.

'And the fire exit across the roof is lethal. The entire area needs to be re-surfaced and the parapets need re-building. The stairwell leading up to it is not sufficiently lit, and the fire exit signs need to be updated to the new European sizes, I would suggest you consider that during the re-wire.' She signed the bottom of her page, tearing off a copy and handing it to Lettie. 'I'll be back to check the fire extinguishers when you're more organised. Meanwhile, you are forbidden to open to the public until all works are completed and signed off,' she scowled disapprovingly. Pulling a calling card from her top jacket pocket, she placed it on the desk before leaving.

'I don't fuckin' believe this!' Lettie screamed.

'Have you tried that new orange and walnut cake in Nero's?' asked Ava casually, picking up his bag and walking towards the exit.

'Ooh, sounds lovely!' said Ruby, licking his lips as he rose to join his friend. 'Though as a rule, I'd kill my own grandmother for a custard donut!' Laughing, they left the room together as Lettie's phone began to ring.

'What?' he yelled, yanking it to his ear. 'Oh Billy, just what I fuckin' need right now!' Anger burned in his chest as he listened intently to the Essex thug. 'Fifi's still alive? How?' This was the last thing he wanted to hear. 'Oh yes, don't worry. If the sour little bitch turns up here, you'll be the first one I call!'

Later the same night, Michael stood nervously in the wings peeking through the tabs at the Vindergurderbreurgenshaftenshitz Club's massive audience. Every single table and alcove was overflowing with excited revellers, drinking and laughing, waiting for the cabaret to begin. Four barmen seemed to be pouring drinks non-stop, and Heinz was acting the perfect host, dressed in a black dinner suit and bow tie, grey hair slicked back and large moustache curled at the ends. With a broad grin, he swept from table to table thanking his old regulars for turning up.

'There's gotta be five-hundred people out there,' Michael gulped as Chastity joined him.

'And another thousand screaming girls outside in the street. Didn't Daisy tell you? Heinz saw Fritz's vlog, he's added Dirk Stardust to the posters.'

'That's insane!'

'Don't think about it. Once you get out there under the lights, you'll only see the first couple of yards like you do at Sugar Sugar.'

'What if I fuck it up?'

'You won't,' Chastity assured. 'It's no different to home. In fact it's easier to work to more people than it is to less, you'll see.'

'Is Fifi gonna do it?'

'We still don't know.' Chastity bit his lip. 'She's not talking to anyone, she's being very difficult.'

At that moment, Heinz finally made his way to the stage. Stepping up onto the catwalk, he walked back to the microphone and turned to face his patrons centre stage in front of the heavy red curtains. With a wide smile, he began to introduce the show in German.

'Is this is it then?' Michael gasped.

'Yes, you'd better get in position. Snap a lash, Lu!' said Chastity, running back to the dressing room.

Heinz finally left the stage to rapturous applause as the lights dimmed and the red drapes swung silently open. Michael glanced up from his position centre stage, kneeling in front of a large lit candle. Surrounded by plastic shrubbery as if outside, he wore a black jacket with a white neck scarf and a short brown wig. As gentle strings began to swell, he took a deep breath and launched into a Jewish aria, singing his best Yentl impression.

'*Oh God... Oh God... May the light from this flickering candle, illuminate this cruising ground so I can find myself another man...*' His audience screamed with delight at this quickly thrown together parody. Suddenly, retro seventies disco music began to play. Michael blew out the candle and ran behind the shrubbery for a quick costume change as Daisy pulled the whole scene backwards to make room for the next set. The stage lights came up and flashed as the heavy beat kicked in and Michael re-appeared dressed as a
328

man in an almost luminous silver and ice blue three-piece suit. With a hand on his hip, he thrust his finger into the air in true Saturday Night Fever style before rolling his hands and swinging his hips. The crowd leapt to their feet, clapping along and stamping their feet at this electric spectacle.

'I love you, Dirk!' shouted a hunk near the front. Fixating fiery eyes on the man, Michael pointed at him, moving his other hand to the front of his hip and thrusting to the beat. The man fell backwards with comic orgasmic judders into the arms of his friends. Chastity and Connie watched from the wings as they awaited their cue.

'Wow! Just… Wow!' Connie grinned.

'He's a natural! You can tell it's in his blood, can't you?' Chastity agreed. With a scream from the audience, they ran on to microphones either side of the stage behind Michael. Wearing co-ordinated silver waistcoats with matching skirts and white-blonde wigs, they stomped their knee-high platform boots and jigged to the music. Suddenly, Verity ran on to join Michael. Wearing a female version of the same costume as his, they grinned at each other centre stage. At the sight of this living legend, the audience became hysterical with joy as Michael began to sing.

'*There I was, minding my business, doing my thing, not bothering anybody. Then he walked, into my eye line, blowing my senses, now my life will never be the same.*' He turned to his mother as she began her part of the song.

'*And as he came to me, his spirit set me free, it wasn't hard to see, everything would change. An angel came to town. My life turned upside down.*

Was lost but now I'm found, I've been rearranged.'
Then holding hands, they began to sing together, as
Connie and Chastity joined in on backing vocals.

'*Then I saw him, the eyes of a demigod, burning
into my soul. Then I saw him, the eyes of a demigod.
Now I'm losing control, of love.*' They gyrated and
danced their co-ordinated discotheque choreography
as the crowd whooped and cheered, before Michael
began the next verse.

'*I could be, maybe a genius, maybe a king, I
could have been anybody. Till that day, I had a
purpose, I had a goal, but my life no longer is my
own.*' Then Verity continued.

'*He walked onto the scene, like something from a
dream, and now my world has been, spun out of
control. He's taken all of me. There's nothing left to
see. Now I'm in ecstasy, I'm in overload.*' Running
down the catwalk together, they high-fived their
admirers as the song drew towards its end.

'*Then I saw him, the eyes of a demigod, burning
into my soul. Then I saw him, the eyes of a demigod.
Now I'm losing control, of love.*'

'Thank you so much, it's so good to be back!'
Verity cried, blowing kisses to the throng. Then she
grabbed Michael into a hug. 'This is my son!' she said
proudly. Michael took a bow as everyone in the room
jumped to their feet once more. 'And these are our
girls!' She clapped her hands as Connie and Chastity
took a deep curtsey. With one final wave, they all ran
from the stage.

Jumping up and down in the wings with Daisy,
they clung to each other excitedly.

'That was brilliant!' laughed Connie, unusually
complimentary.

330

'That it was,' Chastity agreed.

'I wanna do it again!' Michael whined happily. 'And again! And again!'

'You really do make a great double act,' said Chastity.

Glancing over their shoulders, he was amazed to see Madame Fifi standing expectantly in the wings across the other side of the stage. Seeing his wide-eyed look of admiration, she smiled briefly before turning her attention back to the matter in hand. 'Look!' he gasped. Everyone turned to see what was drawing his attention.

'Go, girlfriend!' Verity shouted across, punching the air.

'She's gonna to do it!' Michael grinned. 'Fifi's actually gonna to do it!'

The lights dimmed once more and silent anticipation filled the room. Suddenly, a drum roll echoed out as Heinz's voice could be heard announcing the spectacular return of the great Letitia Von Schabernacket. Lively big band music began to play as Madame Fifi swished elegantly onto the back of the stage with bold defiance. Wearing a blood-red low cut two-piece jacket and skirt with bright gold buttons, she tipped her wide-brimmed hat to one side and glanced over the top of her large Gucci sunglasses. Her audience burst into a rapturous frenzy at the return of their goddess, falling over each other to get the best view. Spinning on her six-inch ruby stilettos, she walked like a supermodel to the front of the stage, swinging her matching handbag and snapping her fingers in coordinated kid leather gloves. Six young men in department store concierge uniforms followed her on, each carrying a large brightly coloured gift-wrapped box.

'Where the feck did they come from?' Chastity gasped.

'She probably keeps spares in her handbag!' Connie quipped, as Fifi began to sing her ode to the noble art of shopping.

I once bit the arm of a woman who reached for a trinket that I desired. A girl couldn't find one in my size, I slapped her face then had her fired. Nothing's gonna hold me down, when my credit card's in town. I love to shop! I love to shop!' The crowd went wild at this kitsch spectacle, as the acrobatic dancers leapt and spun, offering the boxes up to their impatient customer. One by one, she rejected them.

'I thrill to the rustle of a boutique bag and the register as it rings. Nothing and no one gets in my way as I prowl for gorgeous things. When I lay my money down, I'm the greatest show in town. I love to shop! I love to shop!' With utter delight, she took a wide diamond bracelet from the final box. She affectionately stroked the face of its delivery man before pushing him aggressively to the floor, rubbing the sparkling strap across her ample cleavage in ecstasy to whoops and whistles from her adoring public.

'My passion is delicious. My craving is divine. Insatiable my appetite, when I see what I want, it's mine! Mine! Mine!' Throwing her arms back, she thrust her hips and wiggled her breasts as another assistant ran to her aid with a large paper store bag. Holding the jewellery aloft, she dropped it in. Her onlookers screamed with utter delight.

'I haven't got time for the weaklings who have no stamina for the ride. If you can't keep up get out of my way, when I shop I never get tired. No one's going to take me down while I'm buying up this town. I love to shop! I love to shop!' Turning her back, she Monroe-wiggled to the back of the stage then revolved into a nineteen-fifties Vogue cover pose. With a loud snap of her fingers, the entire venue blacked out and the performance was over. The response from the club's patrons shook the building to its foundation. Standing in the wings open-mouthed, Chastity was stunned.

'What just happened here?' he panted.

'Genius, that's what!' Michael grinned proudly.

As the hall's wall lights brightened once more, a siren sounded.

'What the fuck's that?' said Connie.

'It means the police are outside!' Verity advised. 'It's saved a few criminal asses over the years. They've probably heard Lettie's back in town.' She glanced around the tabs into the customer area to see everyone sitting back in their seats on their best behaviour. 'This way!' She led them back into the changing hall.

Still in costume, Fifi quickly threw her belongings into a bag while her dancers helped Heinz roll the costume rails to one side.

'What's happening?' said Michael, beginning to worry.

'Grab your stuff… quickly!' said Verity, pushing them to the changing tables.

'But we're still in costume?' said Chastity.

'There's no time to change now. Don't forget to take your clothes with you, leave no trace that you were ever here.'

'Where are we going?' said Connie.

'You're taking the secret tunnels. They've been an escape route for hundreds of people over the centuries. They're pretty ancient. It's why the club was built on this site, they spread out all across Berlin.'

'Are they safe?'

'Safer than you are here right now.' Verity smiled reassuringly.

They did as they were told, grabbing some empty plastic carrier bags to contain their belongings. Rails out of the way, Heinz rolled back an enormous rug to reveal a trap door. Reaching down to its metal ring handle, he yanked it open on its hinges, crashing it backwards onto the floor behind.

'Quickly! Quickly!' he whispered, gesturing to a stone staircase leading down into darkness.

'We've got to go down there with all the spiders?' Daisy pointed at the steps with horror.

'There must be no trace that Fifi was ever here,' said Verity. 'You broke her out of prison, we can't take any chances. Interpol are not stupid. Hurry!' With his possessions under one arm, Michael grabbed his mother's hand to lead her, but she pulled back. 'I'll stay here to finish the show, it must look like business as usual.'

'You're not coming with us?' he cried.

'No, honey, I can't. I love you, Mickey!' She pulled him into a hug, kissing him on the cheek. 'I'll see you again soon, I promise. Now, go!' He ran across to join the others at the trap door.

'Ooh, I feel like Julie Andrews in The Sound of Music,' Chastity frowned, as Heinz took his hand to help him get his platform boot down onto the first step.

'The police are having trouble getting past Dirk Stardust's screaming fans out front. It's bought us a little time,' said Heinz, handing Fifi a battery lantern and giving her a hug. 'Thank you my angel. It was so good to see you again. Take route four, God's speed!'

'It was a blast!' she smiled, stroking the side of his face and tweaking his moustache affectionately before descending the stairs. They could hear a loud commotion echoing through from the customers in the bar.

'The police are inside the club. Hurry, everyone!' Heinz snapped. As the others followed behind Fifi, he reached into a large wooden trunk, handing them each a lantern of their own. 'I'm very grateful to you. Fifi was right, you are magnificent!' said Heinz, patting Michael's shoulder.

'Fifi said that?' He was moved by this unexpected revelation. Heinz nodded.

'You and your friends take route seven. Good luck!'

'Thanks for everything, your club's blinding!' Michael looked back to make eye contact once more with Verity, but she didn't see him. After fluffing her hair in the mirror, she took a deep breath and walked back towards the stage. He had expected to be able to spend more time with her. This sudden but necessary escape from the police had torn them asunder again far too soon. His heart filled with sadness as his eyes began to water a little. 'Bye, Mum!' he sighed to himself, taking a few more steps down into the musty abyss as the trap door closed ominously above his head.

CHAPTER TWENTY FOUR

Pausing to catch their breath for a moment in the pitch dark, everybody jumped when Madame Fifi switched on her lantern.

'Argh!' Daisy cried.

'Shhh! There's a button on the side.' As they lit their lamps and a dim glow flooded the tunnel, the sight before them sent a shiver down their spines. A low and narrow black stone arched corridor lay before them, running with damp and mould. A nauseous smell bit into their nose cavities, creating an unpleasant taste in their mouths.

'Aw my Gawd,' said Daisy, reaching into his pocket for an emergency Mars bar. 'You can see me coping with this with my nerves!'

'Don't eat that in here,' Connie advised. 'You'll get scurvy!' Reluctantly tucking the chocolate back in his pocket, Daisy began to gently sob.

'Follow me.' Fifi walked slowly ahead, wiping aside cobwebs and dust as she went. Clinging onto each other, they followed cautiously behind.

'Wasn't that a rat squeaking?' Chastity gasped, looking down around his feet. 'Watch you don't get bitten.'

'They wouldn't dare!' Fifi smirked.

After walking for some time, the tunnel opened out into a large cavernous atrium. They held their lanterns aloft to see multiple interlocking stone arches high above their heads. Below each curve was a different arched tunnel, above which was a copper plate with a number stamped into its green-tinged face. Michael looked above his head to see they had just exited number three.

'Where do they all go?'

'To secret locations around the city,' said Fifi, brushing dust from her suit. 'You can get changed here. Leave your costumes, Heinz will find them later.' She walked forward and hugged each one of them in turn, not something they were used to. 'Keep your wits about you, we are not the only ones to use these tunnels.'

'Shouldn't we stick together?' said Michael, touching her arm protectively.

'We have different destinations.'

'Aren't we meeting back at the hotel?'

'You can't go back there now.' Reaching into her bag, Fifi took out a knife and flicked it open. 'I will meet you back in Soho. There are a few things I want to ask Lettie before she's convicted for Creighton's murder!' With a final nod of self-confidence, she turned and disappeared into the darkness of tunnel number four.

'I don't like this. I don't like this one fuckin' bit!' Connie groaned, looking around at each of the black entrances surrounding them. He pulled off his wig and eyelashes before undoing the front of his costume.

'Me neither,' said Chastity, doing the same.

'We're gonna die, ain't we? We're gonna die!' Daisy grizzled.

'Nobody's gonna die, Daisy,' said Michael. 'Just stick close together and we'll be alright.'

'Yes, let's just get it over with as quickly as possible. Hold this for me while we get changed?'

338

Chastity handed Daisy his lantern. 'I've got some hand cream to get this drag makeup off, has anyone got a towel?'

'I was gonna have a dozen away from that hotel, but I ain't had the fuckin' chance thanks to this,' Connie whinged, unzipping his boots. 'You'll have to use the sleeve of your jumper.'

'Can't you just leave it on for now?' suggested Michael.

'But what if our tunnel comes out next to some kind of right-wing rally?' said Chastity, biting his lip. 'You remember what happened to Thora Niceberg in Birmingham? They stapled her big earrings to a wooden fence, she was there for hours before someone called the fire brigade!'

Half an hour later they had finally plucked up the courage to take on tunnel number seven. Leaving the costumes in a neatly folded pile by its entrance, they walked through the stone arch into complete darkness, clinging to each other behind Michael holding his lantern aloft. Bit by bit they edged their way forward, feet making little splashing noises in the puddles on the floor of the tunnel.

'It's so dark in here!' said Chastity.

'It suits you,' Connie smirked.

'How will we know where we are when we get to the other end?' gasped Daisy.

'If there is another end,' said Connie.

'Oh, don't say that!' Daisy began to cry again.

'Connie, you're making things worse!' Chastity scolded. 'Did you bring your map?'

'No, it's at the hotel. Why are you lurching to one side?'

'I didn't grab my belt,' said Chastity, one hand holding up his trousers. 'My legs are soaking up all the water.'

'You're always forgetting that!' Connie tutted.

'I can't see under my belly when I look down, so I don't realise I've not got it on.'

I told you to get some elastic braces, Dolly. Leave them clipped to your fuckin' trousers.'

'I can't wear braces, they make me look too old. It's like flat caps. On a twenty-five year old they look cool and trendy. If I wore one, I'd look like I've been hop picking!'

'Shhh! Listen…' Michael whispered. As silence fell, they could hear a distant knocking sound. 'What is that?'

'Aw my Gawd, they're coming for us!' sobbed Daisy.

'Nobody's coming for us,' Chastity sighed. 'Let's change the subject. How are things going with you and Luther?'

'He's very nice,' said Daisy, dabbing his eyes with the sleeve of his coat. 'That medium told me he'd be dangerous, but now Creighton's estate's sorted he's going to retire. He wants to move to London and open a fish and chip shop.'

'Sounds like the perfect love match,' said Michael, squinting his eyes in an attempt to see further forward in the darkness.

'Well don't forget to buy condoms if he gets frisky, love,' Chastity advised.

'Ooh, I couldn't! I'd be too embarrassed to go in a shop and ask for them.'

340

'And yet, you weren't too embarrassed to ask for them forty-seven Mars bars?' bitched Connie.

'Stop it!' Chastity scolded. 'We're all stressed enough as it is!'

'What do you think Fifi wants to ask Lettie?' said Michael.

'I'm guessing she wants to find out why Creighton set her up. And as soon as we get back, we need to get those photos to his solicitor. It's only so long before the police catch up with Fifi.'

'And we're implicated too because we broke her out of prison,' Connie added.

'It's all such a mess!' Chastity groaned.

'Oh my God, no! This is insane!' said Michael, stopping them in their tracks. 'Look!' He lifted his lantern high. Several yards ahead, their tunnel split into two branches. 'Which way do we go?' As they stood silently pondering their fate, they could hear footsteps.

'What the fuck's that?' said Connie nervously. All of a sudden, a deep menacing voice called out from somewhere within the darkness.

'Komm her!'

Lying in bed above his bar in Southend, Billy snored peacefully. It had taken him until the early hours to get to sleep with so much racing through his obsessive mind. In his dreams, he pictured himself at the end of the pier, one mile from the shore on the Thames Estuary. Beside him, Madame Fifi and Michael struggled to escape ropes tied tightly around their torsos, screaming for their lives but unable to run because of heavy concrete blocks encasing their feet.

With an evil rasping laugh, Billy put his foot behind each block and slid it over the edge of the wooden platform, plunging them helplessly into the freezing deep water to their deaths.

He was suddenly awoken, opening his eyes to find Archie Burke leaning over him. About to instinctively jump to his own defence, he realised there was a large kitchen knife held to his neck.

'How did you get in here?' he gasped.

'Where's our two grand?' said Archie, pushing the blade closer into the flesh of Billy's fat neck.

'It's not here, I don't keep cash on site,' lied Billy, beads of sweat forming on his brow. 'I'll get it brung in, piece of piss.'

'Fuckin' right you will!' growled Jed from behind his brother. Archie slid the blade slowly up Billy's neck towards his chin, shaving a bare patch in his stubble.

'We'll be back tomorrow!' Archie removed the knife and grabbed Billy's face, throwing it to one side aggressively. As the brothers left the room, Billy sat up and rubbed his hand across the raw route of the blade. The Burke brothers had a vicious reputation, they would surely be true to their word.

'Fuckin' amateur scum!' he spat defiantly. But with little money left in the safe and his bar failing, he knew he was in deep trouble.

After hearing an unexplained voice from the blackness of the tunnel under Berlin, everybody screamed in blind panic and utter fear as pandemonium broke out. Michael ran up one tunnel, Connie the other. Letting go of his trousers, Chastity tripped and fell forward
342

landing face down in a rancid puddle, and not knowing which way to run, Daisy clung desperately to the pillar of stone adjoining the two tunnels, gasping hysterically with his eyes squeezed tightly shut.

It took a few moments for Michael to realise the others hadn't followed him. Stopping to look back, the hairs on his neck and arms stood up sensing danger close behind. As he spun to defend himself, someone big and strong grabbed him. Crying out with horror, he dropped his lantern and struggled blindly against his captor.

'Help! Help!' he shouted desperately, punching and kicking the air as his feet were lifted from the floor. His mind raced, as he recalled awaiting certain torture and death in the back of the Billy's Daimler in Soho. And he remembered springing up from under the stage at Sugar Sugar to find himself confronted with the murderous phantom. He had already imagined himself being violently attacked in the alley to Connie's flat, the hideous assault on Travis had been meant for him. Perhaps this was fate finally catching up? Hidden away deep beneath the mysterious streets of Berlin, how long would it be before someone would discover his dismembered corpse?

As the tight grip released from around his waist, he turned and drew back to punch, but a strong hand grasped his fist in mid-air. To further frustrate his nightmare, the attacker began to laugh. Jumping back, Michael reached down to pick up his lantern. Lifting it high, he realised he was face-to-face with Nils.

'Oh, it's you!' Michael cried, embarrassed by his struggle.

'I come collect,' Nils grinned in broken English. 'You fight me?'

'No! No, I'm sorry. You just… scared the living shit out of me!' He panted with relief as Connie, Chastity and Daisy ran to join them.

'Follow?' Nils took Michael's lantern and gestured for them to go with him further into the tunnel.

Their eyes were blinded by early morning sunlight as Nils pushed against a large metal door to the outside. Screeching loudly on its heavily rusted hinges, it slowly ground open to reveal an abandoned concrete factory yard. An enormous derelict art deco building stood before them, with smashed windows and multi-coloured graffiti. Strips of rusty metal girders were visible here and there where the building had begun to fall apart, revealing its skeleton. Amongst abandoned litter and weeds growing from cracks in the yard floor, they were relieved to see a waiting limousine.

'It's dawn, how long have we been down there? I've lost all track of time,' said Chastity, stepping from the tunnel and shielding his eyes with his arm. Nils swung the heavy door shut against a wide concrete wall as they brushed each other down.

'What was this place?' asked Michael, looking around at several abandoned trucks and stacks of metal oil drums to one corner of the yard.

'Schokolade. Erm… chocolate?'

'Oh don't say that, I'm starving!' Daisy gushed.

'I have koffer from hotel? Suitcases? Many girls scream… argh!' Nils demonstrated comically, waving his hands in the air.

344

'They probably think Dirk Stardust is there,' Chastity chuckled.

'We go airport now, I take.'

'Now? But our plane tickets are for tomorrow? Aren't they?' Connie was confused. 'What day is it?'

'New ticket. First class,' Nils grinned, opening the limousine door. 'Plane one hour.'

Flying first class was a much-needed relief after their frightening ordeal. With facilities to freshen up and plenty of food and drink on offer, they truly had a chance to relax and reflect on their unhinged visit to Berlin.

'This is the life!' grinned Connie, sipping on Champagne. 'Unlike that other plane, where we had to pedal to help it get off the fuckin' runway.'

'Yeah, how the other half live!' said Daisy, gesturing to the seats in front. They watched with morbid curiosity as an ageing rich bitch drooled over her young male companion, plying him with bubbly, fresh strawberries and lots of sloppy kisses.

'Would you be looking at that?' smiled Chastity. 'He's thirty-five and hung, she's eighty-five with it all hanging!'

'I hope there's a doctor on board,' Michael chuckled. 'She's gonna need one if she carries on like that!'

'She don't need a doctor, she needs an archaeologist,' quipped Connie. 'I bet she's got a vagina like a half-eaten Pot noodle!'

'That's a lovely thought,' Chastity frowned, putting his chicken sandwich back in its box.

'I can't wait to get back now and soak in a hot bath,' Connie mused. 'I got a new shampoo specially, banana and mango.'

Just as they were getting used to the luxurious pampering, it was rudely snatched away from them. Arriving at Gatwick, they were promptly apprehended by airport police and taken to a small stark side room. Sitting gloomily on black plastic chairs at a long white table, they looked around the room as they awaited their fate. Strip lights on the ceiling flickered slightly, as if to accompany the frantic buzz of airport life in the background. On the wall facing them was a wide mirror.

'I bet they're all standing behind that thing watching us,' said Connie, trying not to move his mouth for fear of being lip-read.

'Ooh, yes!' Chastity agreed. 'Two-way mirrors, I've seen them on Inspector Morse.'

'Like that filthy old bugger in Clacton who set one up in his bed and breakfast to spy on honeymoon couples shagging,' Michael added, smirking through his reflection.

Suddenly the door opened and in walked a tall stocky bearded man with a dull blue suit and grey overcoat. Sitting before them, he opened a buff folder on the table and leafed through the pages, looking at each of them in turn.

'You're free to go,' he said, pointing a biro at Daisy.

'Go where?' Daisy gasped.

'Anywhere!' the man yelled impatiently. 'Just go home.' Bursting into tears, Daisy grabbed his suitcase and ran out of the door.

346

'Was that really necessary?' Chastity complained. The man ignored him.

'I'm Detective Chief Inspector Jim Cartwright,' he said, staring at Michael. 'And you must be Dirk Stardust?' A sarcastic grin spread across his face.

'You've seen Fritz's vlog, then?'

'It's gone viral, half of bleeding Europe's seen Fritz Muller's vlog. It's what helped us match you to CCTV footage from outside Holloway Prison.'

'Oh,' Michael gulped.

'Yes... "Oh!" The three of you have some explaining to do. Who's your accomplice, the infamous fourth man?'

'Nobby? Infamous?' Michael smiled with bewilderment. Cartwright made a note in the file.

'And how do you know the escapee, this Letitia Von... Scabbyknacker? Am I saying that right?'

'Eloquently,' retorted Chastity.

'But we've got evidence that she's innocent,' said Michael.

'And have the police seen this evidence?'

'Well no not yet, but...'

'So, you've broken someone out of prison and you're also withholding evidence?' Cartwright scribbled another note.

'But Lettie's not a murderer!' Chastity babbled. 'Well what I mean to say is, not this Lettie. The other Lettie's a murderer, but she did the other murder, not this one, that was someone else.'

'There's another murder?'

'I demand a phone call!' Connie cried, slamming his hands on the table and jumping to his feet. 'This is England, ain't it? I'm entitled, let me do that and I'll tell you everything.'

'Connie?' Michael questioned angrily. 'What are you doing?'

Cartwright closed his folder and stood from the table. He signalled through the mirror and a short dumpy officer with a bald patch, bucked teeth and glasses joined him in the room. Accompanying Connie out through the door, they sat him in an adjoining cubicle at a table with a telephone. Waiting for a while until the nosey coppers had left, he lifted the receiver and spoke.

'Hello? Get me Buckingham Palace press office!'

Ten minutes later, another police officer led Michael and Chastity out of the room and along a corridor to a large metal door deep within the airport complex. Turning a key in the lock, he signalled for them to enter and directed them in to a small holding cell, sliding shut behind them a wall of steel bars. Shaking with the horror of anticipation, they huddled closely together on a padded plastic bench as their captor turned and left.

A long hour later, they were still there. As each second ticked by, they were getting more and more worried that they would never again be released.

'Connie's been a long time, do you suppose she's alright?' said Chastity, wringing his hands.

'She's probably outside having a fag,' Michael sighed nervously. 'Have you ever been picked up by the fuzz before?'

'No, but I've been swung around by my left tit a few times!'

'Why didn't we just take that footage from the car park to the police before we went to Berlin?'

'That gets Fifi off the hook, but it won't help us. We broke someone out of prison, you get years for that kind of thing!'

'But she didn't do it, so in theory we were just rescuing somebody innocent... weren't we?' Michael knew he could be grasping at straws.

'Oh, I don't know.' Chastity put his head in his hands. 'I wouldn't survive prison. You hear such awful things about what happens to gay people in there.'

'We've lost our jobs, we've got hardly any money left, and now we're facing jail. I'm beginning to understand how Fifi must have felt,' frowned Michael.

'And where the feck is everyone? If only someone would just tell us what's going on. Ooh, I feel like Pola Negri in The Woman On Trial!'

At that moment, they heard a key in the lock and Connie marched in through the metal door followed closely by Chief Inspector Cartwright. Chastity and Michael jumped to their feet, grabbing at the bars desperately. In vast contrast to the sour look on Cartwright's face, Connie's impish grin told he had just done something rather naughty.

'You didn't, did you? Not with that little copper?' Chastity asked.

'Do me a favour, I'm not that fuckin' desperate!' Connie giggled. 'Just listen to this... go on Jimmy me lad.'

'No more questions, you're all free to go,' Cartwright groaned bitterly.

'Eh?' Chastity was confused.

'That's some Get Out of Jail Card you've got there. You've got friends in high places... very high

349

places! This came from the top.' Cartwright unlocked and slid open the bars. 'I want you off my compound in ten minutes, go on off you go. And if you've got evidence about this murder, that murder or any other bloody murders, for Christ's sake take it to the police!' Shocked, Michael and Chastity quickly grabbed their cases and followed Connie back towards the concourse.

'Came from the very top?' Chastity whispered. 'You phoned Buckingham Palace again, didn't you?'

'Fuckin' right I did!' Connie smirked. 'It's a nice idea being locked up with hundreds of horny blokes, but the thought of eating porridge every day just makes me heave!'

CHAPTER TWENTY FIVE

Having found Daisy waiting at Chastity's car in tears, they made their way out of the airport's parking complex and onto the road for London. After arriving back in Soho Square, Michael left his suitcase with them at the bottom of the stairs to Connie's flat before making his way towards St Thomas' Hospital to see Travis. About to climb the steps to his front door, Connie noticed something familiar poking out of a black plastic refuse sack next to the bins.

'Hold on a minute,' he said, walking across and pulling out a blue garment printed with bright pink flamingos. 'This is my shirt.' He rummaged through several other bags, his anger growing with each item he found. 'These are my fuckin' clothes! What the bugger's going on?' He ran up the stairs to find that his door key no longer worked. 'That flee-bitten manky old snake's thrown me out!'

'What?' Chastity took out his own key and tried for himself. 'Oh my God! I think she has.'

'Oi!' yelled Connie, banging hard on the door. 'That's my fuckin' banana and mango shampoo in there!'

'Have you got your keys, Daisy? Let's try the club,' Chastity suggested.

Helping Connie with the bin bags and Michael's suitcase, they took the alley to Old Compton Street and walked along to Sugar Sugar's front entrance. With a turn of Daisy's key and a push, the big glass

351

doors swung open, much to their relief. The venue was in semi-darkness as they tiptoed down the stairs and across the customer area.

'She's taken our pictures down,' Chastity gasped, looking at the bare walls. 'I didn't think she'd change things so quickly, you know how lazy she is?'

'I'm gonna smack her in the mouth so hard, her teeth'll bite her own arse on the way out!' Connie kicked the dressing room door open and stormed in. Flicking on the light, they dumped the bags and cases next to the costume rail. 'Nothing's changed in here,' Chastity observed, looking around. 'She can't have booked anyone new for the show yet.'

'Who'd wanna work in this shithole?' Connie groaned, lighting a cigarette.

'Well, us actually!' said Chastity, dropping into a chair.

All of a sudden, Edith arrived with Nigel in his cat carrier and a bag of shopping. Putting him gently on the floor, she swung the bag on the makeup counter and reached into her coat pocket to pull out a silver key.

'I can't get in your flat no more!' she frowned, holding it aloft. 'I was gonna have a dust round for when you got back.'

'He's been flung out,' Daisy added. 'It happened to my friend Mandy at bingo. When her landlord found out she was hookering on her afternoons off, he changed the locks. By the time she got back from Morrisons, all her stuff was on the front lawn.'

'Go on!' said Edith.

'No it's true, on my mother's life! The neighbours were picking through it all like vultures. That's why she took up with the bingo caller.'

352

'She never did?'

'As you know I don't repeat anything, but I've said it before and I'll say it again, she had it coming!'

'I got you a bit a shopping as you've been away, Connie,' Edith smiled, pointing at the bag on the makeup counter. 'Fresh milk and bread from Supersavers.'

'Which one? Only they're not all in good areas,' Daisy nodded wisely.

'And I noticed that little freezer in your fridge ain't working no more,' Edith continued. 'So I bought you two bags of ice. Put one in today and you can use the other one later in the week.'

'Thanks,' said Connie politely, shaking his head with despair.

'Look, this ridiculous situation we're in is only temporary,' said Chastity. 'We'll get the photos and that file we found in Creighton's office to his solicitor tomorrow and get rid of Lettie once and for all.'

'But the evidence is all locked in my flat, ain't it?'

'Miaow!' cried Nigel, sensing stress in the room.

'That's easy for you to say!' Connie replied to the cat. 'And we ain't got no money left, what are we gonna eat?'

Distracted by their trauma, they didn't notice Connie's baby monitor hidden amongst the wigs on the shelf above the costume rail. Silently listening in on their conversation with glee at the other end, Lettie stood in Connie's kitchen two floors above. Holding their evidence aloft over the sink with metal salad tongs, he clicked on his cigarette lighter beneath and set them aflame, wide eyes glaring as the fire rapidly consumed the file and photos. Within moments, all

353

physical proof of Lettie as Creighton's murderer was gone.

As Michael arrived in the corridor outside Travis' hospital room, he paused to compose himself. Nervously adjusting his fringe in the reflection of a glass screen, he pressed at his stomach, attempting to suppress butterflies. Having not been able to contact Travis by text, he didn't know whether or not he would still be remembered. And although his mother had briefly made contact as promised to let him know Travis was awake, he was scared at how Mr McBradey senior may respond to him just turning up. With a deep breath, he pushed gently against the door and tiptoed in.

Travis was sitting up in bed wide-awake talking to his mother seated beside him. His father was stood with his hands in his pockets looking out of the window at London buzzing in the streets below. They didn't notice Michael at first, as he slowly stepped closer towards the bed.

'Travis?' he gulped, bracing himself for the worst.

'Michael!' Travis cried excitedly, jolting forward from his pillows and holding out his arms. He ran into his embrace, sobbing with relief on his shoulder. 'I've missed you, handsome,' Travis grinned, kissing him tenderly on the neck.

'I've missed you, too,' said Michael, pulling him in close. After the longest time, he stood back, wiping tears from his eyes. 'Thank you for texting me,' he said to Jeanie. She smiled sweetly, her eyes watering at her son's joy. Hamish walked across from the window, holding Michael in his serious stare. 'Mr McBradey,' he nodded respectfully, waiting for trouble. He wasn't expecting his warmth.

'You're welcome, son,' he replied, grasping Michael's shoulder supportively. 'I expect they hae a lot tae blether aboot, Jeanie. Come on, let's get some coffee.' Joining her husband, she lovingly held his arm as they left the room.

'Are you alright?' Michael asked, taking Travis' hand. 'I love you!'

'I love you too. I'm going to be absolutely fine, I'll be home by the end of next week.'

'I texted you so many times after you woke up, but you didn't answer?'

'My phone's missing, I must have lost it during the struggle.'

'I need to tell you something about that.' Michael took another deep breath, kissing Travis' fingers. 'I'm so sorry, but… I think your beating was meant for me.'

'Then I'm glad it was me in that alley and not you,' said Travis, stroking the side of Michael's face.

'Really?'

'Of course! Who's git it in fur ye?'

'It's a long story but I'm innocent, I promise you,' Michael bumbled, looking down with shame. 'And I promise I'll never lie to you or keep anything from you ever again. But I've got some insane baggage. There's so much I've gotta tell you, I should have done it before this happened. I feel so guilty, and I understand if you don't want me anymore, but I do love you, and so much has happened since, and I just needed to know you were OK…'

'Stop,' Travis giggled. 'You're here, nothing else matters.' He lifted Michael's chin to look him in the

355

eyes. 'I would fight to the death to save you. I'm crazy about you, man! Whatever's going on in your life, I'm right there beside you.'

'Really?'

'What am I gonna do with you?' Travis grinned, ruffling Michael's hair affectionately. Then suddenly remembering back, his expression became more serious. 'Actually... someone did shout your name just before I was attacked.'

'Then it's true!' Michael gasped. 'I wasn't sure, but now I know who did this to you. Everyone in London calls me by my drag name, except for one man. Billy-no-nut!' He took his mobile from his pocket.

'What are you doing?'

'Telling the police who done it.'

'They came in here asking if I had any enemies,' said Travis.

'They're looking in the wrong place!'

'Wait, please. Before you do that, I've got something I want to do first.' Travis threw back his bed covers and painfully swung out his legs. Stretching across to his bedside table, he reached his hand inside the top drawer and took something out, grasping it in his fist. 'Get me out of bed?' he said, leaning on Michael for support.

'What are you doing? Should I get help?' Michael glanced to the corridor for a nurse.

'No, no! Just stay where you are.' Holding onto Michael's forearm, he lowered himself to the floor, wincing as one knee landed with a bump on the pale grey linoleum.

'Have you dropped something?' Michael stooped to look under the bed.

356

'Will you just stand still for a minute, ya bampot?' Travis laughed. Finally getting Michael's full attention, he opened his fist to reveal a platinum ring inset with three bright sparkling diamonds.

'Oh, my God!' Michael gushed as his eyes once again filled with tears.

'I love you and I want to spend the rest of my life with you, insane baggage and all!' Travis offered up the ring. 'Michael Small, will you marry me?'

A couple of hours later, Chastity and Connie were still sitting in the dressing room. Waiting for Michael to return from the hospital, the mood had calmed considerably as they drank several cups of coffee and munched on quite a few cakes, describing their adventures in Berlin to Edith. Nigel snored in his carrier as Daisy told everyone about his holiday romance with Luther.

'So, is it love?' Chastity asked with glee.

'Well, I do really like him,' explained Daisy. 'He's going to phone me tonight to make plans.'

'Ooh, that's lovely, Duck!' Edith grasped his hand affectionately. 'I knew today was gonna be special somehow, what with you telling me Travis has woke up and Nicky's coming home, an'all. I had one of them prominations!'

'A premonition?' Chastity corrected.

'Well, I dreamed last night that my dad was standing at the bottom of my bed. He looked younger than I remembered him, but he was still wearing that old green suit for when he did the garden.'

'Really? What did he say?' Chastity was intrigued.

'He said: "Everything's coming into bloom, Squitty". He called me that when I was a little girl on account of me wonky eye.'

'I didn't know you'd had a wonky eye?'

'Yeah, you couldn't tell if I was looking at ya or where you'd just come from. Then he said: "Come and look, it won't be long now". Chastity and Connie looked at each other with concern.

'What did he mean by that?' A cold shiver ran down Connie's spine.

'I dunno,' Edith shrugged. 'But it was nice to see him again. I do miss him, silly old bugger.'

'What was he like?'

'Quite austere, but you had to be in them days. We was poor but we was happy, though he didn't have much to do with me mother. The only place he ever took her was Norwood and that was for her own funeral.'

'He must have had something to do with her, or you wouldn't be here?'

'I think that was only cause of the blackouts!' Edith grinned.

'Well, I hope today is special for you. Though, we're not out of the woods just yet, Edith,' said Chastity. 'There's still so much chaos to sort out. We need to break into Connie's flat somehow to get that file and them photos.'

'And my banana and mango shampoo!'

'It's the only way we're ever gonna be rid of Lettie.' Chastity sighed, slumping in his chair. 'We've only just come back and I feel I need another holiday already.'

'Yeah, but next time let's go somewhere warm and sunny,' Connie mused, lighting a cigarette. 'Some

358

nice little whitewashed Greek villa overlooking the sea with sun loungers, a mini-bar and cock abundance!'

'Cock abundance?' Edith asked. 'Is that that bush you see in the photos with them really big pink flowers that grow up the wall?'

'Yes dear, that's it,' said Chastity.

'But you've already got a lovely tan.'

'Do you know what, thank you Edith,' Connie smiled. 'You're the first person who's said anything nice about it.'

'Well, it's calmed down a bit now, ain't it?' she nodded supportively.

'You still look like a nutter smeared in his own faeces,' added Chastity dryly.

'Yeah alright, don't crow on about it.'

'That's it!' Chastity cried. 'Fifi keeps that crow bar down the side of her filing cabinet in case someone tries to rob her, we may be able to prise your front door open? Go check her office.'

'Worth a try, I suppose.' Connie flicked his cigarette ash on the rug and left to have a look.

'Meanwhile Daisy, help me bag up as many of these costumes and wigs as we can. If Lettie's planning to re-start our show without us, I want to make it as difficult as possible.'

Connie listened at Fifi's office door before entering to check nobody was there. Quietly turning the handle, he slowly pushed it open and stepped into the darkness. Closing it behind, he grappled across the wall for the light switch. As he flicked it on, he leapt back in fright at what he saw.

'Aargh!' he screamed. Standing before him was Madame Fifi with the crow bar held above her head ready to strike. Next to her stood Fanny holding a chair out in front like a lion tamer. 'What are you doing creeping about in the bloody dark?'

'I could ask you the same question,' said Fifi suspiciously.

'We thought you were Lettie,' Fanny laughed, lowering the chair.

'Thanks a bunch! Do I look like a retard?' Connie snatched the crow bar from Fifi's hand before she had a chance to cause him any damage. 'I came for this, the deranged bitch has locked me out of my flat.'

'You're going to break in?' Fifi asked.

'No, I'm going to pick my teeth with it till the Lock Fairy brings me a new key,' he snapped sarcastically. 'Of course I'm gonna fuckin' break in! The evidence to lock her away is in there. Then I'm gonna squat.'

'Whatever come naturally,' Fanny grinned. 'By rights, she should give you a month's notice.'

'By rights, she should fuck off and die but I don't expect that'll happen, neither!'

Back in the dressing room, bin bags full of costumes were beginning to stack up against the toilet door.

'We'll do the wigs last,' said Chastity, leaning his weight against the empty clothes rail to kneel and begin packing shoes from boxes beneath. He looked up to see Connie arriving back with Fifi and Fanny.

'Mrs F, you're free!' Edith cried, hugging her around the waist.

'I'm not sure it was a good idea coming back here just yet,' said Chastity, climbing up from the floor. 'You're still on the run, this is the first place they'll look for you!'

'I had to return,' she replied seriously. 'I have decided that whatever happens to me, I'm going to begin again, make a clean sweep. And that begins with you all… my family.' She looked around for Michael.

'She's up the hospital seeing Travis,' Connie confirmed, laying the crow bar on the makeup counter and lighting a cigarette. Pulling up a chair, Fifi sat and took a deep breath.

'In prison and since my escape, I have had lots of time to reflect,' she began. 'And I realised that my entire life has been spent on the run. I have been forever seeking the approval of others, running away every time I did not get it. Over time, I have come to understand that those who did support me were only out for themselves. I have been used and abused by so many people… so many people.'

'Go on, dear,' said Chastity, sitting beside her with encouragement.

'After Greta Vin Derbar overdosed, our show in Berlin fell apart. Verity fled to New York and I came here. It was tough and took every ounce of strength I had with no real money of my own, which is why I relied on Creighton. I thought I could trust him.'

'Oh, I can't bear it!' cried Daisy, taking a tissue from his pocket to dab his eyes.

'I thought I had created my own perfect little world here at Sugar Sugar,' Fifi continued. 'Then Lettie came along and stole everything I had created, but that was only possible because none of it was real.

361

You made me realise that Chastity, when you said in Berlin that the great Madame Fifi was all an act.'

'You believed your own myth?' he nodded.

'Yes. So I have decided it is time to finally be true myself and to those who really are genuinely here for me.' She looked to Fanny for support.

'I'm taking her to the New Beginnings Clinic in Istanbul to have her penis removed,' she smiled, squeezing Fifi's shoulder. 'It's where I became a true woman, they'll take good care of her there. We'll be on our way this evening.'

In Connie's flat two floors above, Lettie had been listening to their entire conversation on the baby monitor. Grabbing at the phone, he dialled nine nine nine.

'Hello? I want the police, I've got information about an escaped convict.' Thinking as he waited to be put through, a sinister idea crossed his mind. 'No, returning to prison ain't enough for her. She needs to die!' he said to himself, quickly putting the receiver down and re-dialling. 'Billy? It's Lettie. I've found Fifi, she'll be at the New Beginnings Clinic in Istanbul. She's leaving London tonight. Give her a couple of stabs from me!' He slammed down the receiver and leapt to his feet. Grabbing a large knife from the kitchen, he ran for the front door.

In his bedroom above the bar in Southend, Billy put down the phone from Lettie and reached inside a small built-in cupboard for a suitcase. Throwing it on the bed and yanking it open, he began to randomly throw

362

in clothes from his tatty wardrobe and a small mismatched chest of drawers. Slamming it shut, he grabbed his jacket and carried it into his office. Dropping the case, he spun the dial on the front of his safe and opened its door as Knuckles walked in.

'Err... what you doing, mate?' he said cynically, as Billy took a large wad of cash from the safe and pushed it into his trouser pocket. He pointed at the remaining few notes before turning to pull on his jacket.

'They're for you,' he rasped.

'That's all we've got left!' Knuckles yelled. 'What about the fuckin' Burke Brothers, they're gonna be here expecting their money this afternoon?'

'Fuck 'em, I've got more important things to do.'

'Not that fuckin' bird in Soho again?' Knuckles ran his hand through his hair in frustration. 'Billy mate you're obsessed, you've got to let this go!' He grabbed the remaining cash from the safe shelf and slammed it shut. 'You've destroyed the bar, now you're fuckin' us up. Cause the Burkes ain't gonna bring flowers, they'll have fuckin' shooters!'

'And?'

'And? I don't believe I'm hearing this!'

'We won't be here, will we?' Billy coughed, picking up his suitcase. His faithful henchman hadn't noticed it until now.

'Where're we going?'

'Istanbul. I can't rest till I've got her!' Billy snapped, lighting a cigarette.

'Istan-fuckin'-bul? You're having a laugh, ain't ya?' Knuckles shook his head in disbelief.

'Yep, Istan-fuckin'-bul.'

'Nah, sorry mate, you've lost the bloody plot. I ain't going after her no more, you're on your fuckin' own!'

'Suit yourself.' Unperturbed, Billy picked up his cigarette packet from the desk and turned to face him off. 'Fuckin' stay here, then!' he growled, pushing past and heading for the Daimler.

CHAPTER TWENTY SIX

Billy jogged down the stairs and through the storeroom to the back door. Slipping the bolts, he pulled open the door and stepped outside to the yard. Knuckles was hot on his heels.

'Billy mate, you've gotta see sense,' he pleaded. 'She ain't worth it, not for everything you've got set up here.'

'You don't get it, do ya?' Billy opened the trunk of his car and threw the suitcase in. 'Nobody does me over... NOBODY!' He slammed the boot shut and walked across to a large tatty pair of wooden gates, lifting the bolts and swinging them open.

'This is obsessive, you've destroyed everything! We're ruined. You ain't right in the fuckin' head, you ain't!'

'Ah, fuck off!'

'Ya fuckin' nonce!' As Knuckles turned to walk away, Billy grabbed him by the shoulder, spinning him back and throwing a hard punch in to his face. He flew backwards, landing with a clang amongst several empty aluminium lager kegs. With a crack of his knuckles, Billy jumped into the driver's seat and pulled away, disappearing up the back streets.

A little dazed, Knuckles pulled himself slowly off the ground. Walking back across the yard, he pushed the gates closed and slipped the bolts. As he stepped back into the storeroom, he suddenly heard someone banging loudly on the bar's front entrance doors.

'Shit, the Burkes are here!' he whispered to himself, running through to the customer area and instinctively ducking behind the counter. Peeking over the top, he could see blue flashing lights shining in through the dirty glass of the windows and bouncing around the room. 'Thank fuck,' he sighed, stepping out and walking quickly across to let them in. 'I don't think I've ever been so relieved to see a copper in me life!'

Upon opening the door, he was swiftly arrested for the violent assault on Travis; Michael's phone call from the hospital had finally given the police the remaining pieces of the puzzle. They were more than happy to finally have something on the infamous small-town sidekick Knuckles. But of course despite searching the building from top to bottom, their prime target was nowhere to be found.

After being read his rights and led handcuffed to a waiting police car, Knuckles glanced across the road to see a Bentley parked in the kerb. He realised it was the Burke Brothers, come to collect in whatever hideous way they could. He smiled to himself. It was inevitable he would now be spending some time behind bars, but at least he would still be alive to fight another day.

In the car across the street, the Burke Brothers weren't happy.

'What'll we do now?' said Jed.

'They've got Knuckles, but they ain't got Billy,' his brother replied.

'So?'

366

'We go after him.' Archie took a cigar from his inside pocket and flicked open his Zippo to light it.

'Where?'

'We'll re-visit the scene of the crime.' Drawing back deeply on the smoke, Archie grinned. 'Get the gang together, we're going back to Soho.'

Back in the Sugar Sugar dressing room, Madame Fifi turned solemnly to Edith.

'I've got something to tell you, come and sit down,' she smiled gently. Chastity stood and manoeuvred Edith into his chair.

'What is it, Duck?' she asked, taking Fifi's hand.

'For all these years, you thought that your baby had died in childbirth. And even though I knew differently, I let you go on believing that was true. Well...' Fifi's eyes began to fill with tears as a lump came to her throat.

'I know, my darling. There, there,' she comforted. 'It's you, ain't it? You're my little Marvin?' Her crystal blue eyes sparkled with joy. Fifi was shocked at this sudden revelation.

'How did you know?'

'Well I didn't, not at first. You don't look like me, nor your dad.'

'She wouldn't, would she?' Connie smirked. 'She's had it all done. She's like Cher; plenty going on but not much of it her own!'

'Your premonition... you said today was gonna be special,' Daisy gushed, biting into an emergency Mars bar. Edith nodded in agreement.

'I just thought you was being kind, looking after an old thing like me the way you always did. But then at our Ethel's funeral, Lulu told me she was my grandson. I know people think I'm doo-lilly-wallop and a peanut, and I suppose I am,' she laughed.' But it didn't take long to put two and two together.'

'How?' Chastity asked.

'Well, I remembered when you got arrested. Ooh I couldn't sleep proper, I tossed and turned like no one's business. And then one night, the penny dropped... that night, Lulu called you her dad.'

'You're right, that he did!' Chastity recalled.

'Oh Edith, why didn't you say?' sobbed Fifi.

'You've been going through a lot, my poor darling. I knew you'd tell me in your own time.' She stood from her chair, stroking the side of Fifi's face affectionately.

'Can I call you Mother?'

'I do love a happy ending,' said Fanny, dabbing the side of her eye.

'We're all very fucking cosy, ain't we?' Everyone gasped with horror as they suddenly realised Lettie was standing in the doorway. 'This your little family, is it? Well make the most Lady, cause it ain't just your knob that's going under the knife!'

'How did you know we were here?' Chastity asked, grabbing Daisy's arm with fear. Lettie pointed at the baby monitor nestled amongst the wigs on the shelf above the clothes rail.

'You cunning fuckin' scab,' Connie snapped. 'You've been listening to every word!'

'We was just prawns in his dastardly plan!' Edith cried.

'I've been waiting for you,' Fifi glared, standing to face him off. 'Why did you kill Creighton?'

'There's no evidence to say I did,' Lettie grinned.

368

'We've got proof up in Connie's flat,' Chastity growled.

'Not any more, you ain't!'

'Why, you...' Fifi grabbed the crow bar from the counter, lifting it above her head as if to strike. In a flash, Lettie jumped forward and grabbed Edith from behind with his arm across her chest, pressing the cold blade of the kitchen knife against her throat.

'Don't do something you'll regret,' he panted nervously, backing away with Edith into the darkened customer area.

'How could I regret killing you? You've given me something to live for... revenge!' Fifi cackled defiantly. She followed him, holding the metal rod high in readiness for a window of opportunity. Everyone was close on her heels.

'Aw my Gawd,' Daisy cried. 'Edie's premonition... her dad was coming to get her... she's gonna die!'

'You'll never get away with it,' said Lettie, backing across towards Fifi's office. About to enter, he realised he would be trapped. Edith cried out with fear as he jolted her in the direction of the staircase to the roof.

'Why did you kill Creighton?' Fifi repeated.

'He ripped us off,' said Lettie, pushing against the fire door and pulling Edith backwards up the first step. 'That apartment building you live in? It was supposed to be ours. Me and me brother bought it off him, it was supposed to be our retirement nest egg. We saved for years, but he rinsed us good and proper, stole everything. Our money, our dreams... he took the lot, and you fuckin' knew it!'

'I didn't know about that,' Fifi insisted.

'Yes you did, you were in it together. Thick as thieves, that's what you were.' Nearing the top of the stairs, a terrified Edith stumbled. She began to cry as the knife dug closer into her neck.

'Let her go, you fool!' Fifi spat with fire in her eyes. 'This is between you and me, it has nothing to do with Edith.'

'Not on your fuckin' life!' Lettie yelled, pushing against the top door and yanking Edith out onto the roof. As everyone followed, he backed towards the edge of the parapet. 'Keep back or I'll cut her. I will, I'll cut her!'

Unaware of the drama unfolding above his head, Michael arrived back in Old Compton Street. Walking on a cloud of sheer happiness, he looked at his engagement ring with delight as he ducked through the alley and up the stairs to Connie's flat. Trying his key, he realised the locks had been changed.

'Clever girl, Connie,' he smiled to himself, pressing the doorbell.

He suddenly became aware of a commotion in the street. Jogging back down the steps and out through the alley, he could see a crowd forming in the street outside Sugar Sugar's front entrance. Pushing through to the front, he followed everyone's gaze up to the roof, gasping with horror at what he saw.

'This is insane!' He threw his hands to his face.

'Never a dull moment at this place, is there?' said a skinny queen, nudging him in the ribs with glee. In deep shock, Michael didn't respond.

'Oh my God, Nan! Dad!'

370

Back on the roof, Fifi stood her ground. Still holding the crow bar above her head, she slowly edged closer and closer towards Lettie and his terrified captive. Fanny held her hands to her face in fear for her friend.

'Be careful, keep away from the edge,' she gasped. Tightening her grasp, Fifi continued.

'I was never involved with Creighton's business dealings. He conned me too, we have that in common. Let go of my mother and we can talk this through.'

'He hated you!' said Lettie, beads of sweat forming on his forehead.

'Why?'

'When he tried to find his son and heir, he saw your name on the adoption papers.'

'Really?'

'I've never seen him so angry; he went as red as a rent boy's arse. I offered to help trace Michael, that's why he gave your inheritance to me. He was plotting his revenge.' He glanced down over the parapet into the street below, heart pounding in his chest at the sight of the sheer drop just inches away from his feet.

Chastity suddenly noticed that Edith was standing on the very edge of the loose sheet of roof felt. Perhaps this would give them a moment of opportunity to help her escape? While Lettie's attention was drawn away, he nudged Connie who in turn pointed it out to Daisy.

'We thought you'd had an affair with Creighton?' said Connie.

'Oh, fuck right off! That wrinkled old sack of bones? After he'd signed the paperwork, he walked over to the window. The opportunity was there, so I pushed him. And he deserved it, the thieving piece of shit!'

371

'You should have just told the police he'd stolen from you,' Fanny suggested over Fifi's shoulder.

'He had most of them on the payroll!' He turned back to Fifi. 'You think you've got it all sussed, but you're so fuckin' naive. He had it in for you and yet you still clacked off like his little lapdog and drove a car at my brother.'

'That wasn't me!' Fifi bellowed.

'Yes it was, I saw you.' Lettie's eyes filled with tears. 'I was there! Creighton phoned and arranged to meet us both to talk things through. My bus was late because of road works. As I turned the corner, there you were at the wheel heading straight for him. If I'd been on time, you would have killed us both!'

'You silly bitch! That wasn't Fifi, it was Creighton dressed as her,' Connie sighed.

'It's all making sense,' said Chastity. 'He plans to get rid of Lettie and Brian and then set Fifi up for their murders… kills three birds with one stone. It's genius!'

'I don't believe you!' A modicum of doubt was beginning to fill Lettie's mind.

'It's true,' added Daisy. 'They found the wig and everything!'

'I've got it on my phone… here.' Connie shoved his hand into his pocket and pulled it out, pressing play on the film clip and holding it towards Lettie. Although it was too far away for him to see, it was becoming clear that they were telling him the truth.

'If you'd have just come to us instead of lobbing Creighton out the window, we could have helped you find the evidence to put him away,' Chastity suggested. 'We were supposed to be a team.'

'My brother… he took my brother away from me, my only family,' Lettie rasped.

372

'We're your family... The Sisterhood.'

Harsh realisation hit Lettie like a locomotive. All of his underhand planning, scheming and fighting flashed through his mind like the recall of a nightmare. Lost in his own thoughts, he slowly lowered the knife away from Edith's throat. Seizing the moment, Chastity shouted.

'Now!' Stooping to grab the edge of the loose felt with Connie and Daisy, he pulled as hard as he possibly could. As the floor slid from beneath her feet, Edith dropped out of Lettie's grasp and landed with a bump on the floor in front of him. Thrown off balance, her captor dropped the kitchen knife, which bounced off the front of the parapet and plunged down into the street below with a loud clang. As he swayed mere inches away from the fatal drop, Fifi instinctively let go of the crow bar and reached forward to grab him. To the sound of the metal rod hitting the cobbles in front of the tense crowd below, they struggled to regain their balance.

'Argh!' Lettie screamed, putting his foot against the loose brickwork of the parapet. As masonry crumbled and fell, he lunged over the edge and dropped, still clinging to Fifi's arms. Fanny desperately reached for the back of Fifi's dress, but the sheer fabric slipped through her fingers and she fell backwards against the dormer. Daisy lunged forward and grabbed Fifi tightly around the waist, the weight of Lettie's drop pulling them both thumping to the ground.

'Help!' cried Daisy, sliding on his stomach closer to the edge. Shaken from their horrified insensibility, Chastity and Connie ran forward, each grabbing one of his legs. Fanny jumped to her feet and ran to grab theirs.

'Hold on!' croaked Fifi, stretched to capacity with the parapet digging painfully into her ribcage as Lettie swung precariously below. The crowd held their breath as his hands slowly slid further and further down her wrists. Suddenly his shoe came off, bouncing as it hit the pavement below. Maintaining eye contact, Fifi could see a look of melancholic remorse on Lettie's face.

'I needn't have done any of it,' he sobbed. 'The things I've done, I'm so ashamed.' Fifi tried to answer but could not draw air into her lungs. The best she could muster was a compassionate smile.

'Hold on, Lettie!' Michael yelled from the street below. But it was no good. His fingers finally lost their grip, and with a loud scream from the crowd, he dropped silently onto the street below.

'Oh my God, please no!' Michael gasped, running to kneel at Lettie's side. Lying on his back, he looked up at the sky as blood trickled from his mouth, nostrils and ears. He slowly turned his head to face Michael.

'Do I still look fabulous?' he sighed breathlessly. Michael looked down on his unnaturally twisted, broken body. One leg was snapped backwards from the hip underneath him, whilst his shoeless foot twitched at the end of the other. His right hand appeared to be facing the wrong way, and a small tear of blood trickled from the side of his left eye.

'You look as spectacular as you always do,' Michael gulped kindly, wiping the red droplet from Lettie's cheek.

'I'm sorry.'

374

'Shhh! You found my family for me, that's something I'll always...' Michael stopped mid-sentence. It was clear that Lettie had already gone.

To the sound of police sirens approaching Old Compton Street, Daisy managed to grapple Fifi back over the parapet to safety. Gasping for breath, she held onto him for a moment as the others joined their hug.

'Quick, the rozzers are coming,' said Connie.

'We need to go. Now!' cried Fanny, taking Fifi's arm and pulling her towards the rooftop fire escape walkway. As they stepped onto the metal platform, Fifi paused and turned back. She pulled her sobbing mother into a hug, kissing her on the top of the head.

'See you soon,' she whispered. Then, looking up at Chastity, Connie and Daisy, she smiled. 'Thank you.' Plumping her hair, she brushed the brick dust from the front of her dress, shaking it at the cleavage to get her breasts back in position before turning to follow Fanny quickly away across the rooftops.

'We did what we could,' said Chastity solemnly, straightening his jumper. Connie glanced over the parapet into the street below as several police cars pulled up next to Lettie's body. He could see Michael still kneeling at her side.

'Lulu's back,' he said, lighting a cigarette. 'What are we gonna tell the pigs? We can't lie, there must be a hundred witnesses down there.'

'All we can do is tell the truth,' Chastity advised. 'Fifi was here and now she's not. But in the name of all that's holy, for feck's sake don't mention Istanbul!'

Around the crime scene barriers on Old Compton Street, rumour and gossip was rife. Chastity, Connie and Michael stood amongst the buzz of solemn chatter and watched as Lettie's body was put into the back of an ambulance. Meanwhile, Edith sat on a chair by a police car wrapped in a silver thermal blanket. Daisy had popped in the bar and brought her a medicinal tot of brandy for the shock. He was now the last to give his statement of the afternoon's events to the questioning officers.

'That's that, then,' Chastity sighed sadly. 'Another soul gathered in the arms of Jesus!'

'She was Jewish,' said Connie. 'Would Jesus still love her?'

'He loves us all… but he don't like you, you poof!'

'Us drag queens are a dying breed.' Connie took another cigarette from his packet.

'You do suppose she has actually gone this time, don't you?' said Michael. 'She weren't a triplet or nothing?'

'No, I think that's all of them,' said Chastity, stealing Connie's cigarette. 'Though I wouldn't put anything past Lettie!'

'I got these,' said Michael, taking a hand from his jacket pocket to reveal a large bunch of keys. 'They were at her feet… well, by her foot! She must have dropped them when she fell. I reckon we can get back in the flat now, Connie.'

'Thank fuck for that, I need a hot bath.' He scratched at his crotch as if to demonstrate.

'Assuming she hasn't shut the water off, too,' Chastity smirked.

'Am I ever gonna get to use my banana and mango shampoo?'

'Will you just shut up about that fecking banana and mango shampoo?' said Chastity.

'Give me that tenner you owe me for the mascara and I might!'

'Ain't it creepy that you can be here one second and then without warning gone the next?' said Michael.

'Ooh, I know,' Chastity agreed. 'Like Jackpot Joyce? She won twenty-five grand on a scratch card then died in a car accident on the way home from the newsagent's. Eating at the wheel, you see?'

'Oh my God, that's terrible!' Michael gasped. 'Wasn't she paying attention?'

'It wasn't that, the crash was someone else's fault,' Connie explained. 'It was when the air bag opened. It rammed a Yorkie bar so far down her fuckin' throat she choked to death!'

'In a strange kinda way, I'm actually going to miss Lettie,' Chastity frowned. 'And I say that with a heavy heart and a heavy brow.'

'Does that include all those chins?' Connie quipped.

'I agree,' said Michael. 'She was one of us, after all.'

'Don't feel sorry for her,' Connie snapped. 'She made her choices and now she's got to live with them.' He drew on his nicotine. 'Well… you know what I mean?'

'Ooh, don't speak ill,' said Chastity. 'Remember what happened last time she died? She came back.'

'Bring it on, bitch!' Connie shouted into the ambulance, snatching the keys from Michael's hand and walking off toward the alley.

CHAPTER TWENTY SEVEN

After helping fetch the cases and bags from the dressing room, Daisy headed off home. Recovered from her ordeal a little, Edith was put in a cab to Bermondsey by Michael before he fetched Nigel from the dressing room and joined Chastity and Connie in the flat.

'What a day! I'm knackered,' Connie yawned.

'Ooh, don't set me off,' said Chastity, covering his eyes so as not to see. 'If I see you I'll start, and if we get caught in a yawn loop we could be here for hours!'

'What's on telly tonight?' Michael kicked off his shoes and picked up the paper. 'Return From The River Kwai? I didn't even know they'd gone!'

'That's last week's rag, the one with the photo of me as a granny basher,' Connie frowned. 'Lob it in the bloody bin.'

'Or open it to Connie's page and put in Nigel's litter tray,' Chastity grinned.

'Shut yer mouth and give yer arse a chance!' Connie retaliated. 'I'm not in the fuckin' mood.'

'You're right, we're all tired,' said Chastity. 'I'll make some tea.' Walking through to the kitchen, he picked up the kettle and reached for the tap. In the sink, he noticed the pile of ash Lettie had left after burning the evidence. A small corner of the buff folder had avoided the flames. He picked it up and carried it back through to the lounge.

'What's that?' asked Michael, taking clothes from his case and stacking them on the floor behind the sofa.

'It's a bit of that folder from Creighton's office. I found it in the sink, looks like she's burnt it all.'

'Oh, fuckin' great!' whinged Connie, taking a cigarette from his packet. 'How are we gonna prove she killed him now?'

'We can get other copies of the photos off Armitage, can't we?' suggested Michael. 'Though I'll probably have to take me shirt off again!' He reached out his hand to Connie. 'Lend us one of them ciggies?'

'Why does everyone keep poncing my fags?' whinged Connie.

'If you need nicotine, just have a suck on her nets!' Chastity chuckled, walking through to pour the tea. Handing Michael a cigarette, Connie suddenly noticed his diamond ring.

'What's that then, Dolly?' he pointed.

'Travis has asked me to marry him,' Michael gushed.

'Congratulations!' Chastity cried. 'Our Lulu a blushing bride, who'd have thought?'

'Great,' said Connie. 'When you moving out?'

'As soon as he comes home.'

'Don't forget that!' Connie pointed at Nigel, sitting on top of the telly licking his crotch.

'I was so happy till I saw what happened to Lettie.'

'Yes, it was so sad it turned out that way,' said Chastity, sitting on the sofa. 'It was as though someone switched the light off in her head so she couldn't see where she was going anymore.'

'She was a special kind of crazy,' Michael agreed. 'And she did seem regretful at the end.'

'Yeah, well we've all done things we regret,' Connie snapped. 'I should have bunked off school more, but that don't make me a murderer!'

'That's true,' Chastity sighed.

'But the way she landed, all twisted up like that.' Connie screwed up his face at the thought. 'It was only the skin holding her all together. It was a good job she'd had it all tightened, they'd have had to scoop her into a wheelbarrow just to get her in the fuckin' ambulance!' Chastity and Michael looked at him with disgust. 'Well, that went down like a fat kid on a seesaw!' He sulkily grabbed his suitcase and stomped into his bedroom, slamming the door behind.

'Let's just explain it to the cops and let them get their own bloody photos,' said Michael, sitting next to Chastity.

'I'm not so sure.' He bit his lip. 'She's dead, her brother's dead and so is Creighton. Do we really need to tell anyone? What difference would it make now?'

'You've got a point. Let's just concentrate on the living and prove Fifi's innocence.'

'After all, Lettie was a dear friend for a very long time… one of The Sisterhood. So let's just forget about it all, shall we?' Chastity crossed himself. 'Testicles, spectacles, wallet and watch… Bye bye, Lettie love. Rest in pieces.'

A day later, Michael, Chastity and Connie stood at Lettie's graveside looking down on his coffin.

'I don't know why we're here doing this,' Connie whinged.

'We're here because she had nobody else,' Chastity explained. 'She wasn't evil really, she was just sick in the head. Watching her twin brother murdered tipped her over the edge to insanity. But she was still one of The Sisterhood. And luckily, she was insured!'

'It was quick, weren't it?' said Michael. Chastity nodded.

'They believe that the soul stays with the body until after burial, so they have to get a wiggle on.'

'She ain't bloody here now, is she?' Connie looked around uncomfortably.

'Who's that?' asked Michael. He nodded towards a tall thin bespectacled man in jeans and a black shirt walking towards them clutching a Torah. At his side trotted a big brown bullmastiff, panting happily.

'That's Rabbi Bobbly,' said Chastity.

'Bobbly?'

'His real name's Bob Leigh, but everyone calls him Bobbly at the club.'

'He's a Sugar Sugar punter?' Michael was surprised.

'Yes, he's married but secretly bent as a nine-shekel note. Although he has got kids, there's a daughter called Porche.'

'Yeah, and a son called Vauxhall Vectra,' Connie quipped.

'Double barrelled… classy!' grinned Michael. 'Lucky you could get hold of him at such short notice, did you have his phone number?'

'No, I caught him in the tabernacle.'

'Ooh, sounds painful!' Connie winced at the thought.

'And that's his dog, Rolex. He's a watch dog...
don't ask!' Chastity smiled as they approached. 'Hi,
Bobbly. Thanks for doing this quickie for us.'

'Hi, ladies,' said Bobbly. 'It's a pleasure. Not in
drag today?'

'We weren't sure if it was appropriate, though I
did bring these?' Chastity reached into his bag and
pulled out three circular pink lace doylies.
Respectfully placing one on the top of his head, he
signalled for Connie and Michael to follow suit. 'It's
all I could muster at short notice, are they OK?'

'Your kippahs are magnificent! A little theatrical
but thank you anyway. Shall we get started?' Standing
at the foot of the grave, Bobbly opened his Torah and
began reading aloud in Hebrew with Rolex sitting
patiently at his side.

'We used to go out on the piss every night, now
all we seem to do is go to bloody funerals,' Connie
whispered.

'That's what happens as you get older,' Chastity
sighed. 'Then one day out of the blue, it'll be yours.'

'Oh, shut up, Tit!' A cold shiver ran down
Connie's spine.

'God has given, God has taken away, blessed be
the name of God,' Bobbly continued. 'Bernard Abashai
Cohen, sheltered beneath the wings of God's
presence.'

'Ah, now that's nice,' Chastity nodded. Closing
his Book, Bobbly walked around the grave to give
each of them in turn a hug.

'It was nice you came. You are officially the
chief mourners. See you all soon. When are you re-
opening?'

'Won't be long, love.'

'I'll bring Desmond down to see the show. Come on, Rolex!' With a smile and a tail wag, they walked off together back across the cemetery to his car.

'What did he mean by chief mourners?' Michael asked. 'We're the only ones here!'

'It's a family thing,' Chastity confirmed. 'I went to one of these before, we're supposed to tear a piece of clothing.'

'What, like this?' Connie grabbed the back of Chastity's jacket and pulled upwards. The entire panel tore away, leaving him standing in just sleeves and lapels. The force of the rip very nearly tipped him head first into Lettie's grave.

'Oops!' Connie chuckled.

'Aargh!' Chastity cried, waving his arms to steady himself. 'Not like that, you stupid tart!' he screamed angrily, snatching the loose remnant from Connie's hands. 'You're supposed to tear your own feckin' clothes, not somebody else's!'

'I'm not ripping this, it's Donna Karan,' snapped Connie, pulling his jacket in around him defensively. 'I wore it to her last funeral.'

'Yeah, I never get tired of seeing it!' Michael smirked.

Later the same day, Michael went to visit Travis at the hospital. Meanwhile, sitting in front of the telly in his flat above the club, Connie was exacerbating his boredom by flicking cigarette ash at Chastity, who was sitting beside him on the sofa.

'Don't keep bloody doing that,' he growled, brushing it from his sleeve. 'I could go up in flames!'

'I saw something on there called spontaneous human combustion,' Connie grinned. 'I just wanna see how much it hurts.'

'Yeah well, I don't want to lose another jacket.' Chastity picked up his mug of tea and moved away to sit in the armchair.

'I'm just so bored!' Connie dropped his cigarette on the carpet in front of the sofa and stamped it out with his foot. 'We can't do the show again till Fifi's back, there ain't even any pictures on the wall down there. And we ain't got no money left... I can't even go out on the pull tonight.'

'Perhaps we should have gone to the hospital with Lulu like she suggested?'

'And watch them two rubbing up against each other like a couple of randy cockroaches? No thank you!' Connie rammed his fingers in his mouth to feign being sick.

'Anyway, it's alright for you, living here free. I'm behind on my rent, if I don't pay something soon I'll get flung out!' Chastity bit his lip.

'You ought to leave anyway, that flat's a fuckin' death trap! Broken floorboards, mouldy walls and loose window frames? Your landlord should be strung up.'

'We're going to see Creighton's solicitor tomorrow about Lu's estate. She might get a little cash. Perhaps I can have a little lend till I get back to work?' Chastity sipped his tea.

'Don't hold your breath, she might get nothing for weeks!' Connie picked up the remote control and flicked through the channels. 'It's all just bloody repeats on here.'

'Wait!' Chastity cried. 'Look, it's Champion the Wonder Horse.'

'I ain't watching that old shite,' Connie whined. 'Whether it's a horse, a kangaroo or a fuckin' whale, it's always the same bastard story!'

'I like Skippy,' Chastity smiled. 'And Flipper's not a whale, he's a dolphin.'

'What planet are you on exactly? It weren't long ago you were rattling on about them little dogs that pick up rubbish.'

'The Wombles? They're not dogs.'

'Well what are they, then?'

'Wombles.'

'I give up!' Connie switched of the telly and lobbed the remote behind the sofa.

'Ooh, we could go down to the drag queen festival? Has it started yet?' Chastity was optimistic. 'We could have a go around all the market stalls? We could even offer to do a few songs on the little cabaret stage if you like? It'd be camp.'

'They won't pay and I'm not fuckin' working for nothing, not after paying ten quid to get in. It's all a con to get a free cabaret show.'

'Oh yes, I forgot about the entry fee,' sighed Chastity disappointedly. 'Ooh, I feel like Katherine Harrison in Cast A Dark Shadow!'

'Anyway, they'll only just be setting up today. It's on all week, Saturday's the day Drag Fest really kicks off when all the queens arrive in London. It'll be heaving with glitter, feathers, sparkles and acid bitchery as far as the eye can see,' Connie mused.

'I just hope Trafalgar Square can cope with the weight of all them sequins,' Chastity laughed. 'Poor old Nelson will be quaking on his column!'

386

'Ooh... I know what I can do,' Connie smiled, jumping to his feet and disappearing into his bedroom. After rummaging around for a few minutes under the bed, he retrieved two over-stuffed bin bags and dragged them back through to the lounge.

'It's a bit early for that, isn't it?' Chastity stood and dropped the empty mugs through to the kitchen. 'By rights you should do that next week, you don't want any bad luck.'

'Do you honestly think our luck could get any worse than it is right now?' Kneeling under the window, Connie pulled a large pink squashed up Christmas tree from one of the bags. Tipping the contents of the other bag out onto the carpet beside him, he took three plastic feet and slid them into the bottom of its trunk. Hearing the clatter of falling baubles and decorations, Nigel stirred from his slumber under the television and walked slowly over, sitting beside Connie to watch as he yanked the wire branches into shape. 'About there, I think,' he said, positioning the tree centrally under to the sill.

'I adore Christmastime,' Chastity gushed, sitting back on the sofa.

'You should, you were the original Midnight Mass!' Connie smirked.

'D'you know what this reminds me of? The last time that tree was up, you were seeing that big black bloke from Notting Hill.'

'Oh yes!' Connie reminisced, licking his lips. 'I spent Christmas Eve drinking hot chocolate.'

'He was a boxer, wasn't he?'

'Yeah, in a Christmas cracker factory.'

'And he nearly choked to death in your kitchen on that Brazil nut?'

387

'I remember,' said Connie. 'An arse you could crack nuts in and a nut allergy? It all seemed so unfair at the time!' Reaching across, he picked up a solitary pinecone and hooked it to one of the bottom branches.

'You can't put that there on its own like that,' said Chastity with a grin. 'It looks like your Christmas tree's having a shit!'

Fifi and Fanny's journey across Europe to Istanbul was arduous. They had decided to travel by land to keep Fifi under the radar in the full knowledge that the authorities would be looking for her. Having once been Interpol's calendar girl, she would be easily recognised, and although her disguise as Vladimir Tickleykoff was practically perfect, security checks on the railways were not as stringent as they would be if they were travelling by air.

They had taken a taxi from London to Ashford International and boarded a Eurostar train to Paris. From there they travelled east to Strasbourg and then through Munich to Salzburg and Linz without incident. Their arrival in snow-laden Vienna however was to prove a little more complicated.

A long and stressful delay due to a change of train was further exasperated by their discovery that their next train carriage was to be a draughty old wooden boneshaker with little or no heating and a distinct lack of refreshments. Fanny had managed to procure some bottled water and a few bags of crisps to sustain them a little for the next leg of their journey, but Fifi's costume was beginning to prove extremely uncomfortable after many hours under cover. She tried to console herself by remembering that her original flee from communist Eastern Europe to West Berlin had been much more difficult, although at the time she had been considerably younger and somewhat fitter. The only advantage on this journey was that, for the first time since leaving Kent, they had a carriage to themselves.

'How are you holding up?' asked Fanny sympathetically.

'Not good, but at least I can relax a little with nobody watching,' said Fifi, pressing her shoulders back against the tatty red seat velour and pushing her hands into the small of her painful back.

'Once the train's moving you can put your feet up.' Fanny pulled her black woollen coat in tight around her shoulders. 'At least you should be warm with all that padding.'

'I may have to remove the fat suit for a while, it's cutting in around my ribcage.' With a hand under either side of her fake belly, she lifted and moved it from side to side as if to find some relief. Fanny reached into her bag and pulled out a small paper map.

'According to this, the next big stop is Budapest.'

'How far is it?'

'About two and a half inches, so you've got plenty of time to take it off and have a good scratch,' Fanny grinned. 'Meanwhile if anyone sees you, just fold your arms over your tits.'

'The price we pay for being heavy-breasted,' sighed Fifi.

'I took my over-the-shoulder boulder holder off in the loo at Salzburg. I'm hanging loose and free, it was a relief to get it off, I can tell you. I felt like Julie Andrews running over them hilltops in the summer breeze,' Fanny laughed. 'Though there wasn't much room to spin round in that toilet.'

'The journey home will be easier without the disguise. Once the operation has been done, I don't care if they arrest me.' Fifi lifted her brow resignedly. 'It's inevitable that I go back to jail until my innocence is proven in court.'

'Try not to think about that now. Just imagine life without that willy cramping your style. Keep your pecker up… while you've still got one!'

Suddenly, a tall broad shouldered man in a station officer's uniform opened the door. Stepping into the carriage from the platform, he smoothed down his grey moustache with the back of his finger and checked his clipboard.

'English?' he asked in an emotionless Austrian accent. Fanny nodded. 'Papers, please?' He held out his hand expectantly as Fanny grappled in her bag and presented their passports and tickets. 'Why are you travelling to Istanbul?' he snapped.

'Just a short business trip,' answered Fifi in her deep male voice.

'What kind of business?' asked the man, looking at their passport photos. His question caught exhausted Fifi by surprise.

'Err… I err…'

'Research. My fiancé's writing a book,' Fanny offered desperately, mind racing for an alibi.

'A book about what?' came the austere reply.

'Err… Julie Andrews' tits!' Fanny gasped. Fifi looked at her with disbelief, nervous beads of sweat forming on her brow. The officer stopped and looked up from the paperwork suspiciously. 'She… err… she got them out in that film? You know?' Fanny rambled.

'And... err... it was very traumatic for us British, her being such an icon of propriety and high moral fibre and all. There were riots, it was in all the papers!" She could hear her heart beating hard in her chest. The man looked blankly at Fifi then back at Fanny.

'And this is taking you to Istanbul because?'

'Because? Err... he's going to interview a woman who fled the country and went into an electro psychiatric unit for therapy.'

'Because of Julie Andrews' tits?' There was an air of sarcasm to his question.

'The woman was a devout Mary Poppins fan, what can I say?' Fanny shrugged. After the longest pause, the officer reluctantly accepted their bizarre explanation and handed back the passports and tickets. Adjusting his cap, he silently stepped back out onto the platform. Fanny and Fifi quietly sighed with relief, but as he turned to close the carriage door, he looked back at Fifi and paused. The bitter breeze whistling against her fake beard was lifting a small flap at the side that had come unglued from her sweat. As his angry stare burned into her soul, Fifi held her breath.

'Is something wrong?' asked Fanny with a casual smile. The man signalled for two backup officers to join him. He reached in to confiscate Fifi's suitcase, handing it to one of the officers before stepping back into the carriage and taking her by the arm.

'Herr Tickleykoff, I must ask you and your companion to alight from the train and come with me.'

CHAPTER TWENTY EIGHT

Huddled alone beside each other in a small dingy interview room at Vienna's train station, Fanny and Fifi were fidgety with nerves. They quietly awaited their fate, the only sound in the room coming from an enormous clock on the wall between two high barred windows behind them. Fanny finally broke the silence.

'That clock's not tick-tocking properly. I'm not sure if it's tocking or ticking?'

'Julie Andrews' tits?' Fifi asked sarcastically.

'It was the first thing that came to mind,' Fanny gushed. 'I was desperate. You didn't say anything!'

'I was thinking.' Fifi paused, rubbing her hands together to ward off the cold. 'This is not good. Running from Interpol is one thing, but presenting forged papers is a whole different level. You are a dear friend Fanny, I cannot draw you into this. You must make your excuses and get the next train home.'

'I'm not leaving you here alone, we're in this together!' She patted Fifi's hands supportively. 'We just have to think of something. You and me have gotten out of scrapes before.'

'Yes we have, haven't we?' Fifi smiled as she thought back to more carefree times.

'Do you remember that time in Manchester when we missed the last bus and hopped on the back of that passing fire engine?'

'Yes, it had slowed in the traffic. We only wanted a lift to the end of the road, our stilettos were killing us.'

'Then they suddenly got a call and we shot across town, swinging off the back with the blue lights and sirens going,' Fanny giggled. 'They didn't even know we were there till we arrived at the fire!'

'We only got away with it because they thought you were a drag queen.'

'Well, I was still wearing a wig then. It was before I'd had me winkle picked.'

'You know, I've been thinking?' Fifi whispered poignantly. 'I'm not sure I can go through with this.'

'Don't worry, we'll think of something. We'll be back on that train in no time.'

'I don't mean that, I'm talking about the operation,' Fifi sighed. 'I mean, it is what it is and I am who I am. It was different for you. Your surgery removed something that was detrimental to your wellbeing, like a growth or a cancer or something. You came out of it as your true self. For me, this a part of what has made me strong and given me defiance.'

'Is that how you see it?'

'I'm having trouble seeing it any other way.'

Suddenly the door opened and the officer returned with a colleague. He held up a small plastic evidence bag containing Fifi's spirit gum, placing it on the table before her.

'Herr Tickleykoff, I need you to explain to me why you have glued on a false beard,' he said cynically, smoothing his moustache as they both took a seat before them. A short silence fell on the room. 'Can you explain this?'

394

'I'm afraid I lied to you about Julie Andrews' tits,' said Fanny, covering her eyes with her hand to feign despair. 'My fiancé is ill. This journey is our last attempt to save my poor darling's life.'

'What is wrong with him?' The officer's expression changed to one of concern.

'He has cancer.' Fanny crossed her fingers behind her back superstitiously, not wishing to tempt fate with such a hideous lie. 'The chemotherapy resulted in massive hair loss. He was so ashamed.'

'I was so ashamed,' Fifi repeated, shaking her head.

'I'm very sorry to hear that,' said the officer gently. 'Is there evidence of this?'

'Do you speak Turkish?' Fanny asked. The officers shook their heads. Relieved, she reached into her stocking top and pulled out Fifi's clinic appointment letter, handing it across the table. 'And now we have missed our train. We must get to the clinic on time or we may be too late!'

The officer looked at the document. Across the top of the page in big medical-green letters was the heading: "New Beginnings Clinic", with the Istanbul address next to a small cartoon diagram of a grinning doctor. The remainder of the letter was typed in Turkish.

'Do you know what this says?' He passed the letter to his colleague, who shook his head and shrugged.

'He had to glue on a fake beard to disguise this hideous, unforgiving disease from our dear children,' Fanny continued.

'You have children?'

'Oh Lord have mercy, the children!' Fanny screamed, throwing her head into her arms on the table before her and sobbing uncontrollably.

'Little Colin is only three years old,' frowned Fifi, rubbing her back supportively.

Clearly moved by their plight, the officers offered them coffee and food before putting them on an express train to complete their journey with an upgrade to business class. Settling back in their comfortable seats with table service, Fanny and Fifi could not help but laugh to themselves as they roared through Budapest and Bucharest towards their final destination.

'I can't believe you lied about something like that!' Fifi chuckled. 'You do know, if you ride bareback with the Devil, you're gonna get burned?'

'Let's face it sister, if the Bible's to be believed, I'm already damned.' Fanny smiled. 'So what's a little white fib to help a dear friend?' Fifi reached across to grasp her hand affectionately.

'Little Colin would be so proud!'

The following morning, Michael, Chastity and Connie walked up Threadneedle Street in the City of London looking for Creighton's solicitor's office. The heavy traffic filled the air with clouds of dry pollution, catching them in the back of their throats as they wove their way between suited businessmen and women hustling and bustling in all directions.

'If one more bitch bumps into me, I'm gonna smack her into next January!' Connie whinged.

'I've had my toes trodden on four bloody times now,' agreed Chastity.

'That's cause you've got them fuckin' great clodhoppers on. Why don't you just wear normal shoes?'

'I have to wear a broad fit nowadays. It's all those years wearing stilettos, my toes don't all point in the same direction anymore,' Chastity explained with embarrassment. 'Pulling socks on over my toenails is like trying to get a duvet cover on a tree.'

'Can't you wear flip-flops?' Michael suggested.

'I haven't got the grip between my toes.' Chastity coughed. 'This traffic's like that busy junction where Olivia Piper lives. She's forever dipping her nets.'

'Does she still shack up with that loopy geezer who ate her sofa cushion?' said Connie.

'I said fat mate not flat mate; they didn't live together. Last year she had a one night stand on a hen night in Blackpool and now she's got a baby.'

'Breeders, eh?' smiled Michael.

'A little girl. She's called it Maris. If you saw it's little potato face, you'd understand why.'

'That's what happens when you fertilise a vegetable plot with your own shit!' Connie laughed.

'She doesn't?' Michael screwed up his face at the thought.

'She's very self-defecating,' Chastity nodded.

Turning a corner, they paused to look at the mass of unrelenting activity that surrounded them. The noise of chatter, cars, buses and taxis echoed all around, bouncing off the walls of the surrounding high stone buildings.

'Where to now?' Connie sighed.

'There!' said Michael, pointing to a narrow street opposite. Dodging dangerously between the slow traffic, they crossed the road and headed up the

397

cobbled street between two red brick office blocks. After a few hundred yards, it opened out into a small paved square. Wooden park benches sheltered between tall birch trees with branches softening the drone of City life. 'That's it,' said Michael, directing them to a huge modern glass-fronted building to one side. A brass plaque read: "Smythe, Saxon & Smythe".

Pushing through the revolving door into a vast minimal entrance hall, they were a little overawed. Shiny white stone floors and matching walls reflected the sparse light from the square, highlighting thousands of silver flecks in the tiles. A tall marble sculpture dominated the centre of the lobby, majestic in its sheer scale.

'What is it a statue of?' whispered Chastity.

'It's probably Creighton in drag,' Connie quipped, walking around the back to take a closer look. Chastity could see the uncomfortable look on Michael's face.

'Are you nervous, Lulu love?' he said, holding his arm supportively.

'Shitting myself, to be frank,' Michael gulped.

'Well don't be. It's your inheritance, your money. It's them who should be quaking in their boots, not you.'

'Yeah but look at this place, you could get a jumbo jet in here! And who the fuck am I, some little two-bit drag queen from Essex? They're just gonna laugh at me! Suppose it's all a mistake? Or worse still, just someone taking the fuckin' piss?'

'Calm yourself Dolly! If they laugh, we give them a little slap then we leave. Nothing gained but nothing lost.'

'Connie's right. We can't let them intimidate us. The Sisterhood must prevail. Come on.'

They walked across to a solitary escalator against the back wall and stepped on, slowly lifting thirty-feet above street level to the next floor. But what they found at the top was not what they had anticipated. The steps terminated into a tiny white lobby, just the width of the escalator with a low ceiling from which hung a single white pendant lamp. Ahead of them was a solitary wooden door.

'Is this it, then?' Michael laughed.

'I expected a palatial reception desk with some skinny bitch in a tight miniskirt filing her nails,' said Chastity.

'Intimidated, my arse!' smirked Connie, rapping hard on the door.

'Enter,' came a voice from inside. They pushed through to a tiny office littered untidily with papers, documents and files. Behind an oversized desk sat a small elderly insignificant looking man with scruffy grey hair wearing wire-rimmed spectacles and a black three-piece suit. 'Please sit, sit.' That would be a challenge with so little room.

'I'm Michael Small, I've got an appointment?'

'Yes, yes of course. I'm Saxon, of Smythe, Saxon and Smythe.' He leaned forward to shake Michael's hand. 'I'm the last now, Smythe and Smythe are both gone.'

'Yeah, we remember one of them going,' said Connie.

'Quite, quite,' Saxon fidgeted. 'You are my final customer before retirement.'

'We expected something more substantial?' said Chastity, looking around at the dusty archives.

399

'Ah yes, the entrance hall? At one time we occupied this entire building, but it's mostly sold off now. Just this little room left. And me!' he laughed. 'Everything is in order, I just need you to sign a few bits of paper and everything from the estate of the late Creighton Cross will transfer to you.' He pushed a stack of papers across the desk to Michael.

'Do I need a solicitor to look at these before I sign them?' he asked cautiously.

'Perhaps I didn't explain myself properly young man?' Saxon smiled. 'I am your solicitor, as I was your father's. It's my job to ensure you are safe and protected. Since receiving word from Germany, I have been preparing everything especially for you before I close this firm down.'

'Does he get much, then?' asked Connie.

'Well yes, he does. There is a substantial cash sum spread over three international accounts, stocks and shares in a dozen or so businesses and real estate in London, Germany and Switzerland, to name a few.'

'Really?' Michael could not quite believe his ears.

'There's even a castle in Scotland, should you care to visit.'

'Ooh, I feel like Susan Littler in Spend Spend Spend!' said Chastity.

'I've prepared a dossier to explain everything in greater detail. With wealth and property comes responsibility so you will need to study this.' He handed a blue folder to Michael. 'I'll be on the end of the phone for another few weeks should there be anything you need. I still have a few loose ends to tie up.' Opening the front of the folder, Michael glanced inside. Halfway down the front page, he noticed something quite extraordinary that sent a shiver down his spine.

'Oh my God, this is insane!' he gasped.

'What? What is it?' said Chastity.

'I'll err… I'll tell you later.' He closed the folder. 'So it's as simple as that is it? I just sign these and it's all done?'

'Yes, as simple as that.' Saxon handed him a pen.

'The thing is, he ain't got no cash in his pocket right now,' added Connie. Do you know what I'm saying? Can he have fifty quid or something?'

'I can transfer just a little cash into your existing account immediately, if that helps?' Saxon offered.

'Yes please, if it's not too much trouble?' Michael nodded.

'Certainly. Would one-hundred thousand do?'

The sudden shock was too much for Michael as he burst into floods of tears. Not ten minutes before, they had pooled their loose change at a small café beside the tube station to buy a cup of coffee between them. Now suddenly he could afford to treat his loyal friends to lunch in Paris by private helicopter without even noticing a dent in his bank balance.

Connie and Chastity screamed, clinging onto each other and jumping up and down ecstatically. Wiping his streaming eyes to see, Michael rapidly went through the papers one by one and signed where indicated.

'That's it, all done. Congratulations!' Saxon reached across to shake his hand once more. Michael's hand was already shaking of its own accord.

'Thank you! Thank you so very much!' With a broad grin, Michael joined the others in their excited hug.

Leaving the office a few moments later laughing and giggling like three schoolgirls, Chastity pushed a button to send the escalator into reverse as he joined Connie on the way back down. But Michael held back.

'Are you coming?' Chastity asked.

'I'll be with you in a minute,' he replied, turning back into Saxon's office.

'Mr Small?'

'You said I could ask if I needed anything? There are three things you could sort out for me?'

Hot and sweaty from his desperate flight across Europe, Billy finally arrived in Istanbul. As vengeful as ever, he was practically foaming at the mouth with the prospect of destroying his nemesis. Racing through town in the back of a taxi, his throat was raspy and dry making it difficult for him to swallow, further exaggerated by the dry heat and dust blowing in through the open window. Looking at palm tree after exotic palm tree lining the road as they whizzed past, an evil smile of anticipation spread across his chubby unshaven face.

Stepping from a vehicle outside the New Beginnings clinic, he put down his suitcase and pulled a small piece of paper from his pocket to check he had the right address. It was a large single-story white stucco building with a low-pitched grey slate roof. Bright pink flowered shrubs lined the exterior walls under large picture windows to either side.

'That fuckin' bitch is in here somewhere,' he muttered under his breath. 'She's gonna rue the day she crossed me cause I'm gonna slit her throat from ear to ear!' After paying the driver, he climbed the concrete steps to the front entrance and pushed cautiously inside.

The entrance hall was high-ceilinged and spacious, walls and floor lined entirely with white marble. Relieved to be out of the blistering sunshine, he wiped his forehead with his sleeve and pulled at the large wet patches under each armpit. To one side of the room was a decorative fountain. Two large alabaster dolphins leaping back-to-back from a wide trough spurted clean clear water from their mouths into the pool below. Glancing around to check nobody was watching, he scooped his hand into the trough and splashed his face, rubbing the soothing cool liquid around the back of his neck and through his slicked back hair. A little refreshed, he stepped back and listened. Though nobody was in sight he could hear activity seemingly from sets of double swing-doors either side of an un-manned gold and red reception counter.

'Where's she gonna be?' he asked himself, tiptoeing closer to the desk. As he approached, he noticed a sign above the doors to the left. He couldn't understand the Turkish writing, but next to it was a small cartoon symbol of a man. 'That must be the geezer's ward,' he whispered. The sign over the other doors had something similar for women. 'That ain't a lot of help,' he grinned. 'She could be in either fuckin' one of them!' Deciding to try the female ward first, he took the doors to the right.

Walking along a wide corridor, he glanced in through the open door of each private room as he passed looking for his prey.

'Merhaba? Merhaba?' came a woman's voice from behind. Startled, he turned to see a pretty young

403

nurse, olive skin and chestnut hair framed by the stark brilliant white of her uniform and hat.

'Err... I'm visiting a friend?' Billy smiled. The nurse shook her head with confusion.

'Kimsin?' she asked tetchily. 'Ne istiyorsun?'

'Friend?' Billy repeated. 'I visit friend.' He put down his suitcase and tried to demonstrate with sign language.

'Doktor? Doktor?' she shouted up the corridor. A few doors away, a short bearded man in a white coat and spectacles walked out.

'Evet?' He asked as he approached.

'I'm looking for a friend? Madame Fifi?'

'Ah, evet! Madame Fifi, seni bekliyorduk,' smiled the man with a happy nod.

'Eh? English... do you speak English?' Billy huffed. 'Only I ain't got a fuckin' clue what you're on about, moosh!'

'Iste, iste.' The man signalled for Billy to follow. Walking up the corridor together, they entered a large hospital room at the end. Billy was disappointed to find just an empty bed surrounded by medical monitoring equipment.

'No, you don't understand!' he growled, dropping his suitcase. Still exhausted and jet-lagged, he fast was getting frustrated. 'I need to find Madame Fifi.'

'OK, OK,' said the man apologetically, taking hold of his arm as the nurse removed the suitcase.

'Get off me!' Billy yelled, pulling away. Hearing the raised voice, two uniformed male orderlies ran into the room and restrained him by the arms. Both younger and considerably fitter, his struggle against them was futile. Screaming with anger, he pulled, shoved and kicked, but their grip was too strong for
404

him to overcome. 'I'll fuckin' kill the lot of ya!' he bellowed, as the nurse ran back into the room holding a hypodermic needle.

'Evet,' she smiled kindly, pushing the needle into his left buttock and squeezing the trigger. Billy gasped, drawing in breath as a relaxing tingly warmth flooded through his veins.

'I'm gonna… I'm gonna…' Suddenly the room began to spin and his breathing slowed, the chatter around him echoing into the distance. As the room gently blurred and faded to black, he collapsed unconscious face down on the bed.

CHAPTER TWENTY NINE

A little light December drizzle fell from the sky as Daisy made his way up the stairs towards Connie's flat. Tapping on the door, he closed his umbrella and gave it a shake, standing it in partial shelter up against a drainpipe.

'Hello, Daisy love,' Chastity smiled, opening the door. He followed him through to the lounge, taking off his coat.

'Hi, Dais,' said Connie, looking up from his sewing machine.

'Hi,' he replied. 'What ya making?'

'New costumes for Drag Fest, we're going Saturday. It's gonna be fab. I'm so excited I'm dripping like a three-minute egg!' He picked his cigarette up from an ashtray beside him on the table and took a puff before running a swathe of azure blue sequinned fabric under the needle.

'I could see it from the bus as we went past Trafalgar Square. It looks better than last year! I could hear the music they was playing... Leif Garrett, I Was Made For Dancing.'

'He was made for punching!' quipped Connie. 'You coming, Dolly?'

'I'd love to but I haven't got any money left, we ain't been working have we?' Daisy sighed.

'Well, that's what we wanted to see you about,' said Chastity, walking through from the kitchen and handing him a cup of tea as he sat on the sofa. 'Lulu's got some of her inheritance money and she's promised to help us out a bit till we get sorted.'

'Really? That's very kind, ain't it?'

'Yeah, and we can pay her back once we get back to work,' said Connie through a mouth full of dressmaker pins.

'She's gone clothes shopping so she looks nice for Travis. He's coming home on Friday,' said Chastity excitedly. 'She'll be back in a while. Talking of clothes Daisy, you must dress up for Drag Fest. Connie will make you a costume.'

'I was going with my mate Mandy from bingo, but I'm not now cause she's a fuckin' nightmare!' said Daisy, taking a bag of smoky bacon potato chips from his pocket.

'How so?'

'Well, she phoned me at three o'clock this morning after being out on the piss saying she couldn't get her car started. So I turns up and she's sitting in a skip holding a manky old tin tray for a steering wheel.'

'At least she wasn't drink-driving,' Chastity giggled.

'And then she was sick in the taxi. It was like that girl off The Exorcist, all green and slimy cause of the Crème de Menthe. The driver went off alarming! So I'd rather go with you.'

'So what costume do you want, then?' said Connie.

'I've always wanted to do Britney Spears,' said Daisy through a mouthful of crisps.

'Ha ha!' Chastity laughed. 'Perfect!'

Suddenly, they could hear banging from the club below.

'There it is again!' said Connie. 'You heard it too that time, didn't you?'

'Yes,' said Chastity, biting his lip. 'There's not anyone down there, what do you suppose it is?'

'And I swear there was someone walking round on the roof earlier.' Connie nervously lit another cigarette.

'You don't suppose it's Lettie's ghost, do you?' Chastity clutched at his chest defensively.

'Oh shut up, don't say that!' Connie gasped.

'You can see me coping with that with my nerves, can't ya?' whined Daisy, putting down the empty crisp bag and taking an emergency Mars bar from his other pocket. Chastity stood and picked up his coat from the back of the armchair.

'It can't be Fifi, she's still in Istanbul having her wanger clangered. Whatever it is down there, we'd better go see. Come on.'

Arriving at their plush hotel in Istanbul, Fanny and Fifi were relieved to be able to freshen up and change their clothes. After making the most of a hot shower, they put on towelling dressing gowns and got down to some serious pampering.

'I shan't be needing this anymore. Bye bye Vladimir,' Fifi grinned, stuffing her disguise into a large waste paper bin.

'That'll be a nice surprise for the maid when she empties it in the morning,' laughed Fanny, blowing her hair with a dryer at a small console table. 'It's nice to see finally the old Madame Fifi back. I was beginning to believe I really was engaged to Herr Tickleykoff. I look far too young to be anyone's mother.'

'Since you've had it all pulled back behind your ears, yes!' Fifi smirked, taking a bottle of blood-red nail varnish from her bag. But the mention of surgery suddenly turned her mood more sullen. Sitting at the table beside her friend, she breathed a deep serious sigh.

'What is it?' Fanny switched off the hairdryer.

'I'm so very grateful for everything you've done for me,' Fifi began. 'You put your own safety on the line to help me hide in London. You helped with my disguise to get me to Berlin, then you lent me money and smuggled me out of the country to come here. You even stood by my side when we got apprehended in Vienna. I'm not sure I deserve such loyalty.'

'Nonsense!' Fanny grasped her hand. 'Who was it that phoned me five times a day when I had my breakdown? And who was it that sat up all night with me through tears and tantrums when I was trying to decide whether to go ahead with gender reassignment? I only survived all that because of you. I'm alive now because of you. You old soak!'

'I'm sorry, but I've decided not to go ahead with the operation.' Fifi looked down at the floor as if ashamed.

'There's nothing to be sorry for.' Fanny lifted her chin and looked her in the eyes. 'I kind of guessed that's what you'd say, anyway.'

'Really? And you still came all this way with me?'

'Of course! Going on this journey was the only way you could figure it out for yourself. You were going ahead with surgery because you thought others expected it of you, not because you wanted it for yourself. It's almost like peer pressure, but you have to
410

be careful when you follow the Masses because sometimes the M is silent.'

'Perhaps you're right.' Fifi looked at herself in the mirror. 'I think it was finding my son that made me begin to question my imperfections. But strangely, being forced to masquerade as a man has made me realise how glad I am to be exactly who I am.'

'Come on,' said Fanny, running fingers through her hair. 'Let's glam up to the nines and go tell that clinic we're cancelling. Then we'll go out to celebrate; there's an obscenely large bottle of Champagne somewhere out there waiting for us. Let's teach Istanbul how to really party!'

As Daisy put his key into the glass door of Sugar Sugar's front entrance, they were alarmed to discover that it was already unlocked.

'Aw, my Gawd,' he whispered nervously. 'Perhaps it is her ghost?'

'Ghosts don't unlock doors, they walk through them,' Chastity advised.

'D'ya think it's burglars, then?'

'Worse than that Connie, it could be Billy-no-nut. So stay alert, girls!' Pushing inside, they huddled closely together as they walked cautiously down the darkened staircase towards light from the customer area. Reaching the bottom, they could see two men removing curtains from the back of the stage. Another two were packing glasses and bottles of drink into wooden crates. All of the furniture was missing and three further workmen were ripping up the carpets.

'What the feck's going on?' said Chastity.

'Surprise!' shouted Michael, leaping out at them from under the stairs.

'Argh!' they all cried, throwing themselves back against the wall.

'I've decided to use some of that money to get Sugar Sugar sorted for when Fifi gets back,' he gushed. 'They're doing everything! That dodgy wiring, new curtains, even new carpets. And that rank fuckin' loo in the dressing room.'

'We thought you was a burglar!' Daisy sobbed.

'I got Saxon to organise everything. They're gonna do a complete refit so we can all get back to work. And I told him where to find the evidence to get Fifi's off. He's got her a barrister.'

'Aw my Gawd!' Connie was in awe. 'Was that them on the roof earlier?'

'Yeah, they're doing that too, and front of house. You're getting new bullet-proof glass doors, Daisy!' He pulled him into a hug.

'I'm gobsmacked, I don't know what to say!' said Chastity open-mouthed. 'Where's all the chairs and tables?'

'It's all gonna be new. Same as before like, just newer. But that's nothing, wait till you see this!' Giggling like an excited schoolboy in a sweet shop, Michael ran across to a small cardboard box under the stairs. Dipping his hand in, he ran back to show his prize, holding it up for all to see.

'What is it?' Connie squinted.

'A bottle opener shaped like a drag queen! It's fuckin' awesome, aint it?'

Chastity laughed. 'It looks like Connie in that hideous rubber Emma Peel costume.'

'You're just bitter cause there weren't enough rubber in the whole of London to make one for you!' Connie bitched with a smile.

'Oh, and there's this.' Michael reached into the back pocket of his jeans and pulled out three envelopes, handing them one each. Chastity slid his finger under the flap and pulled out a greeting card. Emblazoned with a big glittery rainbow, it was decorated with the words: "Thank you." He gasped with shock when he discovered inside a banker's draft for ten thousand pounds. 'There's the same for each of you, I hope it helps a little?'

'Bloody hell, Dolly! It'll take years for us to pay all this back.'

'I don't want it back, Connie. It's a gift, to say thank you for everything you've done for me over the past couple of months.' Michael took his hand. 'You let me and Nigel stay at your place even though you're allergic to cats. You've taught me how to do drag, you even gave me your prize money from the fashion competition. And if it wasn't for you taking me out that night, I'd never have met Travis.' He turned to Daisy. 'And you've stood by me through everything, looked out for me through thick and thin. You even got on a plane for me when you're so terrified of flying.' Then he turned to Chastity.

'No don't, I'm going to cry!' His eyes welled with tears, but Michael continued unabated.

'You've been so kind to me through everything. Whenever I've needed help or advice, you've always stuck up for me. And that means a lot, you know? Before I met you, no one had ever done that for me.'

'But you've just got all this money and you've given the whole lot away to other people?' Connie snivelled. 'You don't have to do this, you know?'

'I ain't just given it to other people, I've given it to me family. Ten weeks ago, I didn't even have one! And I can and I did, so I have and I have and that's that.'

'I'm just speechless,' Chastity rasped.

'That's a first!' quipped Connie.

'I'll be able to bring my rent up-to-date now.'

'Yeah and give me that tenner for the mascara,' said Connie. 'I'll be able to get my pink diamond Cartier earrings!' Daisy meanwhile was in pieces. Bursting into floods of tears, he grabbed Michael for a tight bear hug, lifting him off the ground.

'Put him down Daisy, his ears are turning blue!' Chastity yelled. Freed from suffocation, Michael fell backwards with a slight cough.

'Oh, and there's something else. You remember that folder Saxon give me in his office?' Chastity and Connie nodded. 'Well there was something really spooky in it, but I wanna wait till Travis is with us before I tell you.'

Fanny and Fifi arrived at the New Beginnings reception desk looking every bit like movie stars. Head to foot in glamorous couture, they totally owned the room. Fanny wore a sugar pink two-piece suit with a matching fascinator and shoes, while Fifi worked her signature devil-red in a knee-length dress with co-ordinating jacket and wide-brimmed hat. Fanny tapped a bell on the counter and a petite, perfectly groomed blonde nurse appeared from the swing doors to the left.

'Ah hello, hello,' she grinned, recognising Fanny instantly.

'I'm glad we've got her,' she laughed, 'She's the only one here who speaks any English!'

'You back at last, Miss Hardbastard?'

'Hardcastle... Fanny Hardcastle,' she corrected.

'I think she was right the first time,' Fifi smirked.

'This is Madame Fifi, she used to be my friend,' Fanny batted back. 'She's here about the operation?'

'Yes... double sausage?' the nurse nodded.

'You got two for the price of one?' Fifi asked.

'It's a deal they do for men who want to become lesbian couples. It's only been six months since my op and I do love a bargain!' She turned back to the nurse. 'There's been a change of plan.'

'Ah yes, operation complete success!' The nurse smiled.

'Eh?' Fanny and Fifi looked at each other baffled.

'All good, all good. Come, come!' They followed her through the swing doors to the right and down the corridor to the large hospital room at the end. There, lying unconscious in the bed surrounded by tubes and wires, was a sight that Fifi had utterly not expected.

'See! Madame Fifi.' The nurse pointed. Fifi drew back a deep intake of breath and staggered wide-eyed into Fanny's arms.

'What? What is it? Do you know this man?'

'Yes. It's Billy-not-never-nut!' Fifi rasped in disbelief.

'Really? That's him?' Fanny was as taken aback as she was. 'Well, what's he doing… Oh, my! Are you thinking what I'm thinking?'

'I believe I am!' Fifi's look of shock melted into a broad vengeful grin as she gently lifted the side of Billy's blanket to confirm their suspicions. 'How absolutely delicious!'

The day had finally come for Michael to collect Travis from the hospital. His parents had said their goodbyes on the ward before heading back to Glasgow. Jeanie had given Michael the keys to the apartment and handed her son's care over to him as promised. Still a little sore, Travis was walking with a very slight limp and needed a helping hand into the waiting taxi.

'I feel so fecking horny! I think it's the painkillers?' Travis whispered, grabbing hold of Michael on the back seat.

'The doctor said you've got to take it easy for a while,' Michael giggled, pushing him away.

'He said I've got to keep active.'

'I don't think that's what he was suggesting! Connie, Chastity and Daisy are going down to Drag Fest at Trafalgar Square tomorrow. I've gotta collect Nigel and my stuff from Connie's so I thought we might go down there with them first? Give you a bit of gentle exercise?'

'There's nothing gentle about the exercise I've got in mind!'

'That's as long as you think you're ready for Soho after what happened to you there?' Michael held his hand supportively.

'Aye. Aye, I think I'll be OK,' he answered cautiously. 'I won't know unless I try. And I can't become a hermit just because of something like that.'

'Well, let's just take it one day at a time.'

'Ma told me you had to go to Berlin?'

'Yeah, I've got so much to tell you. My head's all over the place, you're not gonna believe everything what's happened to me!'

Arriving at the flat for the first time since before the attack, Michael was thrilled to see the luxurious cat bed Travis had bought for Nigel. And Jeanie had kindly replaced the flowers with a brand new bunch, which lay in a plastic sheath on the kitchen island beside the card Travis had originally written.

'They're beautiful, thank you very much,' smiled Michael, giving his fiancé a hug.

'Now you'll have to open your legs!' smirked Travis.

'Why, haven't you got a vase?' Michael laughed. 'Go freshen up and I'll put the kettle on. And you'd better make that shower a cold one!'

A short while later, Travis walked from the bathroom to find his lover singing to himself while putting the flowers in water. He stopped from drying his hair with a towel for a moment to listen. He had never before had a proper opportunity to hear just how good his voice really was. The one and only time he had seen him perform was fleeting because of insecurities arising from his past. Now knowing he had over-reacted, he was wishing he had stayed and heard more.

417

Suddenly realising Travis was watching him, Michael's melodic joy turned to acute embarrassment.

'What?' he asked, cheeks flushing.

'You're voice is awesome,' said Travis, sitting on the sofa. Michael took a seat next to him with two mugs of coffee.

'Thanks. It's so great you're finally home, ain't it?' he smiled lovingly, leaning across to peck him on the lips.

'Home is wherever you are, handsome!' Travis took a sip from his coffee.

'Like I said, there's something I've got to tell to you.'

'Before you do, can I just say this?' Travis put his mug on the coffee table and took Michael's hand. 'Sitting up there day after day, I've had a lot of time to think. You're my world and I want to look after you and take care of you. I earn more than enough to support both of us and I've got money in the bank.'

'What are you saying?' Michael swept back his fringe.

'I know you didn't really want to be a drag queen, and it's fine if you want to continue, but it's also OK if you want to give it up. I can easily support us both.'

'I'm not sure what I'd do with myself all day,' said Michael with a smile.

'Well, that's the other thing,' Travis continued. 'I thought perhaps I could sell my flat and we can get somewhere together… somewhere that's ours? You decide where. We've both had a hard time in the past, so we could put it all behind us and make a fresh start. So you could go shopping and make a home for us both?'

418

'That's really sweet.' A lump came to Michael's throat.

'Or you could just stay at home and be my sex concubine?' Travis grinned devilishly. 'But seriously, I just want you to be happy, I really do. What's mine is yours. We'll set up a joint bank account: Mr and Mr McBradey!'

'Wow!' laughed Michael.

'Oh, sorry,' Travis gasped apologetically. 'I'm not saying you've got to take my name after we're married.'

'Sounds just perfect to me.' A little tear of happiness came to Michael's eye. 'As you say, let's move on and make a fresh start.'

'Oh man... It would be such an honour if you did!'

'And what's mine is yours, too,' Michael added. Travis picked up his mug and took another swig.

'Would you want to stop doing drag, though? I'm not sure you should when you look and sound so fantastic.'

'I don't know.' Michael remembered back to the horrific circumstances that had first put him in costume. But even despite recent events, the idea of bringing his new career to an end had so far not even occurred to him. 'I'll have a think about it.'

'Anyway, what was it you wanted to say to me?'

'Erm... I don't really know where to begin,' Michael sighed.

'There's nothing wrong, is there?' Travis looked concerned.

'No, in fact quite the opposite,' Michael grinned excitedly, eyes twinkling. 'The thing is... How d'ya fancy getting married in a castle in Scotland?'

419

CHAPTER THIRTY

In his hospital bed at the New Beginnings clinic, Billy slowly opened his eyes. Still weary from anaesthetic and extremely tired, he ran his tongue around his dry mouth and coughed. Noticing a kind hand holding a small plastic cup of water in front of him, he took a much-needed sip. As his vision slowly focussed, he realised the angel of mercy before him was Madame Fifi.

'You!' he yelled, swiping the beaker from her hand. He attempted to lunge forward and grab her by the throat before realising he was too drugged to do much of anything. Laughing, she sat in a chair by the bed next to Fanny.

'Well well, and what are you doing here?' she smirked knowingly.

'I'll get you, you fuckin' circus freak!' he growled, clenching his fists.

'You haven't got the balls for it,' Fanny grinned.

'Well... ball,' Fifi added spitefully. Looking around, Billy suddenly realised he was laid in a hospital bed attached to a drip.

'What the fuck?' He sat up in bed and ripped the tube from his hand.

'There's another of those one down there,' said Fifi, pointing to his crotch. He looked at a catheter pipe draining urine into a plastic bag attached to the side of the gurney. Then, lifting the blanket, he glanced down to where his penis had once been. Slow

421

realisation turned to blind panic as he began to thrash violently on the bed, screaming with absolute horror at the top of his voice. The orderlies ran into the room, restraining him by the arms on the mattress as the nurse re-inserted the drip into his hand.

'You know, he looks a little upset to me?' Fanny smiled casually.

'Do you think?' Fifi replied, plumping at her hair with disinterest.

'You warped bitch! What have you done to me? What have you fuckin' done to me?' he spat, slowly relaxing against his captors as his eyes filled with tears.

'You came here to hunt me down and now you've had your comeuppance. You've only yourself to blame.' Fifi stood from her chair bitterly and picked up her bag, walking toward the door as Fanny followed. 'So when you crawl back into your little cave in Essex, remember you did this to yourself!' As she pushed the door to leave, Billy's desperate sobs made her stop in her tracks.

'I can't go back! I can never go back, ' he cried pathetically.

'Come on, leave him here, he's not worth it,' Fanny advised. But instinctively, Fifi could not just walk away. As the nurse and orderlies left the room, she turned and walked slowly back to his bedside.

'My life's over now ain't it?' He rubbed his eyes with the bed sheet, looking cynically up at her. 'Yeah go on, fuckin' gloat!'

'That operation was meant for me. Do you know why? Because I am deliciously different and now so are you,' she said calmly, perching on the foot of his bed. 'We all belong in the circus. So what? That's what life is, isn't it? A circus? We're all just doing what we can to get through, whatever it may throw at us?'

'But I'm not even a man anymore, how the fuck am I supposed to go on like this?' he snivelled, responding to her wisdom.

'You are and you will,' Fifi nodded, patting his leg sympathetically. Listening from the door, a slow and rather uncomfortable realisation came over Fanny.

'You're gonna take him in, aren't you?' she said tetchily, joining her at the bedside. 'After all he's done to you and your son, you're actually gonna bloody well take him in?'

'He's no threat to me now,' Fifi sighed. 'In fact he might be useful in Soho. Besides, where else can he go?'

'You'd take in any old rabid stray, wouldn't you? You deranged cow!' Fanny shook her head despairingly.

'That's what us circus folk do... stick together. He's one of us, now.'

'I don't know what your Mickey's gonna say?'

'I'll call him.' Fifi stood from the bed, taking her diligently by the arm. 'Meanwhile my dear friend, you'd better book another plane ticket.'

It had taken some time for Travis to get over the shock of hearing about Michael's vast inheritance. After several stiff vodkas and a good night's sleep next to the man he loved, winning the lottery had given him the courage to venture bravely into Soho again. After stepping from a taxi outside Sugar Sugar, he was a little nervous as Michael led him slowly through the alley towards Connie's flat.

'Are you sure you're OK?' Michael asked caringly.

'Aye, I'm fine. I'd rather face it head-on.' Though, after climbing the steps to the front door, he did sigh with relief at being past his uncomfortable challenge.

As Chastity invited them into the lounge, Nigel leapt into Michael's arms.

'Hello, mate!' he said, kissing him on the forehead. 'We're going to our new home today.'

'Yeah, it'll be nice to walk around naked again without that cat gawking at me!'

'Nobody wants to see that Connie, not even Nigel,' Michael giggled.

'I'll have you know men are falling over each other to have a go on this.' He struck a theatrical pose.

'Only cause you're convenient in the West End,' Chastity smirked. 'If you lived in Catford they wouldn't even bother to get on the bus!' He turned to Travis. 'How are you doing, love?'

'Aye, OK thanks. A bit bruised.'

'I expect you are, but it's lovely to see you back on your feet again.'

'This one's been going on and on and on and on about you,' Connie whinged playfully, jabbing Michael in the ribs. 'I was tempted to put superglue in her fuckin' lipstick.'

'Ooh, do you remember when Porky Pauline had her jaw wired up to stop her eating?' said Chastity. 'Well, her real name was Tarpauline… her birth was a cover-up.'

'Yeah, and she had to suck that green sludge through a straw that gave her really bad flatulence?' Connie remembered. 'Her arse was so big, every time
424

she farted it was like a sonic boom! She nearly took her own windows out.'

'And they gave her that suppository diet pill to soak up all the fat? She didn't get her knickers up in time, let rip and knocked all the ornaments off the sideboard!'

'See what I have had to put up with?' said Michael apologetically to Travis' laughter.

Suddenly Edith arrived with Daisy, a little flushed.

'Don't panic, we're here!' he gushed, giving everyone an air kiss. 'Our bus took ages to get through Trafalgar Square with all them drag queens down there, there's fuckin' millions of 'em!'

'Hello, dear,' said Edith, giving Michael a peck on the cheek.

'Hi Nan. How are things with Gerry?'

'Ooh, lovely! She's got a job in some play down the road called The Mousetrap, though I don't know how long it'll run for. But it's smashing, we laugh and we laugh.'

'I'm so pleased for you, Nan.'

'She keeps giving me money, loads of it, she won't take no for an answer. I've had to buy another tin to keep it all in! We brings in all them weeds from the garden and have a cup of tea with the wireless on while we chop 'em all up and put them in little plastic bags.'

'Really?'

'Yeah. I said to her just put 'em out for the dustman, he won't mind. But instead she takes a few with her every time she goes out to save him the trouble. Kind, ain't it?'

'Yeah, it sounds very kind indeed,' Michael smiled knowingly. Then Edith turned her attention to Travis, looking him up and down suspiciously. 'Are you this geezer who's asked my grandson to marry him, then?'

'Aye, is that OK?' Travis smiled.

'You'll do,' she grinned, throwing her arms around his waist affectionately before turning back to Michael. ''Ere… He turns an eye, don't he?'

'Innit, tho?' he replied.

'He's well cut, as we used to say in the old country,' Chastity agreed.

'We used to have one of them down the caravan in Whitstable when I was a girl,' said Edith.

'What?'

'A whelk hut,' she grinned mischievously.

'Welcome to the family, Travis.' Chastity patted his shoulder sympathetically. 'Best of luck with that!' Edith stood on tiptoe and tapped Travis on the chest to get his attention.

'You'll look after him for me, won't you? Only he's had a hard life.' Her blue eyes twinkled up at him seriously.

'Nothing is more important to me than your grandson, Edith.' He grasped her hand reassuringly. 'I promise you I will.'

'Right then,' Connie interrupted, slipping into his denim jacket. 'Shall we get downstairs and get our slap on for Drag Fest?'

'Oh, just before you do that there's something I want to show you all,' said Michael, grabbing Travis' hand excitedly and leading the way towards the front door.

426

Walking across Soho Square holding Travis' hand, Michael was on cloud nine. Although the soft December breeze was a little chilly, it was warm in the brilliant sunshine as people sat all around on benches and grass eating, reading, chatting and laughing. Michael giggled to himself.

'What's tickled you?' Travis asked.

'This is just so perfect! Only a few weeks ago in Essex, I couldn't even tell anyone I was gay cause of how they'd react. And now look at me here with you, holding your hand out in the open and no one's even flinching.'

'Then I guess this is where we belong,' Travis smiled, grasping his fingers tighter.

'Where are you taking us then?' Connie called out from just behind, catching them up with a small bag of shopping.

'Over here,' said Michael, exiting through a side gate and crossing the road.

'Armitage's Photo Studio?' asked Chastity. 'Are we all having a photo done together? Ah, that's nice! But I wish you'd have said. I've got this tatty old jumper on, I'd have worn something better.'

'Oh it's not that bad... for someone so beamy,' Connie quipped. 'Though the colour's not very flattering. Dog anus brown?'

'Yeah, like your fake tan.' Chastity grinned.

'Are we nearly there yet?' said Edith, catching them up as they paused on the cobbles. 'Only Daisy's hungry.'

'In a minute, Dais,' said Michael, stopping in front of the photo studio. 'It's not this one we're going to, it's the one next door.'

427

They shielded their eyes from the sun's glare and looked up. Now the scaffolding had been removed, the full glory of the beautifully restored vintage building could be seen in all its white stone majesty. Four floors each had two large Georgian sash windows to the front overlooking the greenery of the square, and a wide sugar-pink front door adorned with shiny brass furniture glistened in light.

'The pink was my idea,' Michael laughed. 'What d'ya think?'

'What is this place?' asked Chastity.

'Me and Travis own it!' he beamed.

'We do?' Travis was dumbfounded.

'You remember that file Saxon gave me in his office? That's where I saw it, it was part of Creighton's estate. It's where we're all gonna live.'

'Eh?' said Connie, lighting a cigarette from the one he was already smoking.

'I knew it was meant to be as soon as I read it cause it's where I found Nigel the day he ran away.'

'Ooh, cats can be psychic like that,' said Daisy. 'He knew he was gonna live here so he came home.'

'Ah, bless!' Chastity smiled.

'You could be right.' Climbing two small steps to the front door, Michael ripped a piece of card from the portico to one side, revealing a large brass plate which read: "Sisterhood Towers." 'That was my idea, too! Blinding, ain't it?' he beamed proudly. Reaching into his pocket he pulled out a big bunch of keys. 'Come on!'

'Am I allowed to smoke in there?' Connie asked.

'Connie this is me you're talking to,' Michael nodded. 'You can do whatever the fuck you like!'

428

Stepping in through the front door, they entered a long wide hallway painted brilliant white. Ahead of them was a beautifully restored Georgian staircase, winding up past the high ceiling to the floors above. Michael turned a key in a big door halfway along the corridor and stepped into a large room with polished dark-wooden floors and a huge fireplace.

'This one's for you,' Michael said excitedly, taking two keys from the ring and handing them to Daisy. 'I've put you near the front door cause you can look after us all. You've gotta try and imagine it with all your furniture.'

'What's going on?' Daisy was confused. 'I can't afford to live here.'

'It don't cost nothing, we're not going to charge you rent,' said Michael. Flapping his hands excitedly, Daisy began to cry like a baby, sitting on the floor with a thud and throwing his face in his hands, too shocked even for an emergency Mars bar.

'Oh, thank you! Thank you!' he grizzled as Edith knelt beside him, cradling his head against her chest.

'They'll be alright down here for a minute, come on,' said Michael, leading everyone else back out into the hall. Chastity scratched his head, trying to understand what was happening.

'So you're saying you've bought us all an apartment each? Together in this block?'

'No I didn't buy it, it was just here.'

'But why are you giving them to us?'

Michael stopped, taking Chastity by the shoulders to look him in the eyes. 'Because you're my family. And I love you.'

They walked further down the hall to double doors behind the staircase. Pushing a button to one side, they drew open to reveal a lift. Stepping inside, Michael pushed for the first floor. Chastity and Connie were now themselves crying. Connie reached into his shopping bag and pulled out a toilet roll.

'Oh, you can't do that in here!' Chastity scolded through tears.

'I'm not having a shit you dozy bitch, give me some fuckin' credit,' Connie snapped back. 'I just wanna dab my eyes.' He tore off a long strip and handed it to Chastity.

Stopping at level one, Michael handed Connie some keys as the lift doors slid silently open. 'This is your floor, away from us so I don't have to listen to you shagging anymore!' he laughed. Giving him a hug, Connie ran excitedly along the landing to his door as the lift continued up.

Arriving at the second floor, Michael took Chastity's arm and walked him to his new front door.

'And this, my friend, is for you.' He handed him his keys. 'You won't have to worry about that bastard landlord of yours no more. And you can walk to work from here.'

'I don't know what to say,' Chastity sobbed, pulling him into a hug.

'And there's something in there I think you might like?' As Chastity turned the key, Michael pushed the door slowly open. Standing looking out of the front window over the square was a man. He was a little difficult to identify at first through the glare of sunlight streaming in, but as he turned to face them, Chastity realised exactly who he was.

'Nicky!' he gasped, running desperately into his arms.

'Hi, Chas,' he answered with a broad grin.

'What are you doing here?'

'This is where I live, with you. Lulu's paid for me to come home, so now we can be together.' Chastity collapsed to the floor with him in floods of tears, looking into each other's eyes and kissing passionately. Pulling the door shut behind him, Michael re-joined Travis in the lift.

'I can't believe you've done this for your friends,' said Travis gently, wiping away a small tear. 'You've changed their lives. You truly are a remarkable man. How lucky am I to be with you?' He took Michael into his arms and kissed him as the lift doors opened on the top floor.

'And this one's ours,' said Michael excitedly, taking him by the hand and pulling him along the hallway.

The penthouse was enormous, made to look even larger by the lack of furniture. Similar to the other apartments, it had the advantage of being over the stairwell, giving the lounge at the front more space. Chalk-white panelled walls and flat ceilings surrounded with deep elaborate plaster mouldings broke light from the front windows, casting playful shadows around the room. Through a large arch at the back was a modern cream minimal kitchen with a breakfast bar and brown leather stools below matching alabaster worktops. Double doors to the back opened onto a large terrace overlooking the rooftops of London's glamorous West end.

'Through here's where the magic's gonna happen!' Michael laughed, leading Travis across the terrace and through another set of French doors to a spacious, high-ceilinged bedroom. 'There's an en suite and a dressing room through there off the hall,' he gushed, pointing to a side door. 'What do you think?'

'I'm feckin' gobsmacked!' Travis smiled. 'It's incredible, amazing, profound!'

'Only you said about us getting a place that's ours from the beginning, like? Something we could own together when we're married?'

'It's astounding!'

'Could you call this place home?' Michael whispered seriously. Travis took him into his arms.

'I could call a cardboard box under a railway arch home, as long as you're there with me.' He kissed him tenderly on the lips. 'But I guess this old dump will have to do for now!'

'I didn't think I could ever been so happy.' Michael rested his head against Travis' broad chest. 'Nothing could ever upset me ever again!' Suddenly, his mobile phone rang. Reaching into his pocket, he looked at the screen. 'It's Fifi,' he said, answering. Travis watched as his blissful expression diminished to one of horror. 'That's insane!' he cried, ringing off.

'What? What is it?'

'Billy-no-nut's with her. She's bringing him back to Soho!'

CHAPTER THIRTY ONE

In the dressing room a short while later, Chastity and Connie were in costume with a full face of makeup ready for their visit to Drag Fest. Daisy sat in his Britney schoolgirl costume while Connie filled his lipstick line, watched intensely by Edith and Michael. Hammering, banging and drilling rang in the background as the last of Sugar Sugar's fantastic re-fit continued.

'You know, I've got a good feeling about today!' said Chastity, pulling on a lilac beehive to match his gingham ball gown.

'Just don't let anyone pinch your handbag like they did last year,' Connie advised, putting the lipstick down on the counter.

'Ooh, it was terrible, Lu,' Chastity remembered. 'I lost my bus pass, my house keys, everything. At two o-clock in the morning I had to wake up next door to borrow their ladder. Then I had to climb in through an upstairs window in a gold lamé dirndl dress with a six-foot train. Everybody came out, I don't think the neighbourhood knew what hit them!'

'She ripped all down the front. I tried repairing it, but in the end we had to lob it out.'

'Well, without the matching handbag it was useless anyway!'

'Yeah, well now that-an-a-cat is moving in with Travis, I'm gonna pick up a yummy bit of trade for a night of unbridled rampant shagging before my hymen grows back completely!' Connie reached into a small plastic box of jewellery and pulled out several elasticated bracelets, sliding them onto his skinny wrists.

'Last year, she got off with a baker. We had fresh crusty bloomers for a week.'

'Speak for yourself,' Connie grinned, fluffing the azure blue puffball skirt on his corseted frock. 'Do you know, he could kneed two cob loaves at the same time? My nipples were like tinned strawberries!'

'Then just after that, she met a sailor at the Titanic Exhibition in Greenwich.'

'I've always been a fan of seamen. Rough and ready, he was.' Connie reminisced with a lick of his lips. 'Though every time he climaxed he shouted, "Ship ahoy!" But he was every inch a gentleman.'

'Just how many inches was that exactly?' Chastity batted his eyelashes in the mirror.

'I'd have a go on that Bennybatch Cumberditch given the chance,' Edith giggled impishly. 'That dark brown voice of his makes my knees go all wobbly!'

'Really Edie, I'm surprised at you!' Chastity laughed.

'And that one that sings on there with all them tattoos? *I've gotta move like bugger, I've gotta move like bugger*!' she warbled, shaking her hips.

'Moves like Jagger? Adam Levine from Maroon Five,' Daisy corrected.

'For an old lady, you're a bit of a goer on the quiet, ain't you?' Chastity suddenly noticed her pungent smell. 'Have you been eating peppermints?'

'No duck, it's my new bubble bath Listerine.'

'Edith, that's not bubble bath, it's mouthwash!'

434

'I wondered why it didn't foam up any good,' she grinned. Chastity raised his eyes at Michael in the mirror.

'I still think you should have gone to your first Drag Fest in costume, Lu?'

'I don't want to in case I have to take Travis home quickly,' he said. 'He seems to be OK, but he's gets tired easily.'

'Best be safe than sorry after the fact has gawn, 'said Edith intelligently.

'Besides, there's something else.' They turned to face Michael as his tone turned serious. 'Fif's on her way back from the airport and she's bringing Billy with her.'

'Eh? What's going on?' Chastity was confused.

'There's been a mix up. They've cut his willy off instead of hers.' After a brief moment of silent shock, Connie fell to the floor in hysterical laughter.

'Oh my God!' Chastity gasped. 'How the be-Jesus did that happen?'

'I don't know, but she reckons he's not going back to Southend. The boys are upstairs at the door looking out for 'em.'

'Has he still got his odd bollock?' Connie rasped, trying to catch his breath. 'Just hanging there on its own like a soggy balloon after a party?'

'Can't they cut of Fifi's willy and stitch it on him?' asked Edith.

'It doesn't quite work like that,' Chastity advised. 'Perhaps we should leave before they get here?'

'That's what I was thinking.' Michael bit his lip disconcertedly. 'I really don't want to see him. Can we go now?'

'Yes, come on.' Chastity kicked Connie. 'Get up, you!'

Travis and Nicky laughed as everyone joined them at Sugar Sugar's front entrance.

'You all look amazing!' said Travis.

'*Oh baby, baby,*' sang Daisy, swinging his arms and spinning around to demonstrate his best Britney.

'For feck's sake don't attempt the back flip, they've only just repaired the pavement since Lettie fell!' Chastity grinned.

'Can we just get out of here?' said Michael anxiously, looking up and down the street. But it was too late, as a black cab drew around the corner and stopped beside them. Out climbed Fifi, looking fabulous in a blue two-piece Chanel travelling suit.

'Mrs F,' cried Edith, running to give her a well-received hug. Travis put his arm protectively around his fiancé as Billy stepped out onto the pavement. Paying the driver, he turned to face them.

'Michael,' he nodded with a forced smile.

'I've got nothing to say to you,' he replied, holding onto Travis.

'Where's your willy now? In a glass case above the mantelpiece?' Connie snapped sarcastically.

'You fuckin' little bleeder!' Edith suddenly lunged forward, unexpectedly slapping Billy hard across the face. 'Do you know what you've done to my family?' She stared up at him angrily. 'I've met your type before, sunshine. You're nothing but a two-bit bully who thinks he owns the world, stomping about in your clicky shoes like you fuckin' own the place!'

436

'Come on, Mother,' said Fifi gently, pulling Edith back.

'If I had a knife I'd cut ya, I would, I'd cut ya!'

'It's OK, she's right,' said Billy. 'I deserve it.'

'Deserve it?' Edith continued. 'You've already lost yer willy and yer odd bollock, I'll take your fuckin' face off, an'all!'

'Way to go, Edie,' Connie added. With a resigned nod, Billy turned to Michael.

'Is he your boyfriend, then?' He reached out a friendly hand to shake but Travis did not reciprocate. 'I've made mistakes, I know. But I'm gonna put them right, I promise,' he said sheepishly.

'What the feck did you bring him here for?' said Chastity, poking Fifi's arm.

'Because he has nowhere else to go,' she sighed. 'He needs us.'

'Well I don't need him!' Michael's eyes filled with bitter tears.

'We used to get on really well, didn't we mate?' said Billy, trying to build a bridge.

'Yeah, before you accused me of conning you out of that fuckin' drug money. It was nothing to do with me!'

'I know that now. It was a mistake and I'm sorry.'

'Oh I can't bear it! I can't bear it!' Daisy sobbed, pulling an emergency Mars bar from inside his bra.

'You can't just fuckin' waltz up here and say sorry. Six weeks ago you was gonna kill him!' Connie yelled, standing defensively in front of Michael.

'Why would he trust you now?' said Chastity, jumping to Connie's side. As Billy fell silent, they were shocked to notice a tear running down his cheek.

Maybe he had changed? Perhaps his remorse was genuine? But how could Michael be sure?

'I… erm… I need time,' he rasped.

As the cab pulled away, his attention was suddenly drawn to a Bentley pulling into the curb opposite. A sudden lull seemed to fill Old Compton Street. Instinctively, he knew something was wrong. He shielded his eyes from the light and squinted, looking to see who it could be, but it was nobody he recognised. However as Travis followed his gaze, a cold shiver ran down his spine. He knew exactly who these men were.

'Feck!' he cried, grabbing hold of Michael protectively and throwing him back inside the entrance lobby.

'What's going on?'

'It's them… The bastards who kicked the shit out of me!'

'Bloody hell,' Connie gasped, as the thugs stepped from the car, each holding a vicious tool of violence.

'Quick, get back inside!' yelled Nicky, hustling Chastity behind the newly installed glass doors. Connie, Daisy and Edith followed.

'I owe 'em money, it's me they're here for!' Billy growled. He pushed Fifi inside from the pavement and bravely turned to face off Jed and Archie Burke and their three henchmen.

'Oh my God, we need the police! We need the police!' Michael panicked, trying desperately to get his mobile out of his pocket.

'No. We can do better than that,' said Chastity with defiance. 'Connie… we need reinforcements. Call for backup. Now!' Connie took out his phone and
438

began group texting. Glancing to Michael for a nod of reassurance, Travis stepped back outside and took Billy by the shoulders.

'Don't be a fool, man. They're gonna annihilate ya!'

'This is my fuckin' problem, just protect Michael. And Fifi... make sure she's OK, too.' Billy took a deep breath and braced himself for the inevitable. 'It's fate, this is. I've got nothing left to live for.'

'You've got everything to live for,' Travis cried urgently as the men slowly approached. 'We're all in this together!'

'Are we?' For the first time in as long as he could remember, Billy recognised true compassion. His emotion swelled and his fight-or-flight instinct kicked in as his adrenalin began to flow. Suddenly turning, he grabbed Travis and pulled him inside. Slamming the big glass door shut behind them, Daisy attempted turning his key in the lock, but his hands were shaking too much as he sobbed uncontrollably.

'It's OK, stand back,' said Travis, snatching the fob to take control.

'Here,' said Nicky, grabbing one end of the cloak-check desk. Billy took the other and they slid it behind the doors as a barricade.

'Everyone keep back,' Travis advised, lifting a fire extinguisher from the wall as a weapon while Nicky ripped the thick metal coat-check rail from its brackets. Billy stood defiantly in front, hands poised ready to fight, beckoning through the glass.

'Come on then you bastards, fuckin' bring it on!' he bellowed, as everyone braced for the worst.

Stepping ahead of the others, Jed swung a thick metal chain around above his head and slammed it against the door. The noise inside was deafening, but the glass held unaffected. Expecting it to shatter on impact, Fifi looked to Michael for an explanation.

'They're bulletproof,' he nodded nervously. Frustrated, Jed took another swing to no effect. One of his henchmen smashed a baseball bat, but still nothing.

'Not so fuckin' clever now, are we?' Billy laughed gruffly.

Archie stepped forward with a machete, staring Billy down and swishing it around in the air as if to demonstrate slicing him to pieces. Then he jammed it into the gap above the door, sliding it rapidly back and forth in an attempt to cut the lock from its bolt hold. As it jutted into the room, Travis rammed it with the fire extinguisher, snapping off its end. The metal point dropped to the floor inside behind the barricade. Anger building in his face, Archie threw the weapon to one side and began kicking at the door violently, as Jed and the henchmen unleashed their full might against the glass.

Everyone screamed with utter fear, as Travis and Nicky joined Billy with their shoulders against the back of the cloak-desk to hold them off, the doors vibrating from the impact. Chastity snatched the Mars bar from Daisy and took a bite himself.

As suddenly as it had begun, the onslaught stopped. The unexpected silence was deafening.

'What's going on?' said Nicky, peering over the barricade. They watched as the thugs stepped back. Running across to the Bentley, Jed jumped into the driver's seat and started the engine.

440

'We've won!' Chastity cried with relief. 'They're leaving.'

With a screech of tyres, Jed bumped the vehicle onto the opposite curb before reversing to align the back of the car with the glass doors.

'No they're not, he's gonna ram us,' Travis screamed. 'Quick, everyone get downstairs!' Fifi and Chastity each grabbed one of Edith's arms, lifting her from the ground to run her into the club below closely followed by Connie and Daisy. But Michael stayed behind. 'Go! Go!' shouted Travis.

'No!' said Michael, eyes filling with tears once more. 'I'm staying here with you. I'm not gonna lose you again. If you go, I go!' Travis grabbed him by the arms and kissed him.

'I love you,' he whispered, looking Michael in the eyes.

'I love you, too,' Michael answered, as Jed revved the car loudly.

'Here we go,' said Billy, putting his back against the barricade. Nicky joined him.

'Are you ready?' asked Travis tenderly.

'Thelma and Louise, ain't it?' Michael grinned lovingly as they both leaned hard against the cloak-desk.

With a loud shriek of rubber on cobbles, Jed released the clutch and the Bentley left the ground, flying backwards and slamming violently against the front of the glass doors. With an unbearably terrifying crash, their hinges snapped from the brickwork as the car shoved them backwards, sending the barricade and its defendants tumbling across the room to the back wall with a painful thud. Travis pulled Michael's head into his chest protectively as the doors finally

441

disintegrated and shards of shattered glass rained down upon them.

A stunned silence followed. Seconds seemed like hours as everyone tried desperately to catch their breath. Michael could hear Travis' heart thumping loudly. In his other ear, he could hear something quite extraordinary that made him question his own survival. Softly from somewhere in the distance, angels were singing.

'*Go on now go!*' It rang out, getting slowly louder and louder.

'Can you hear that?' he asked Travis.

'Aye, I can,' he replied. 'Is that "I Will Survive"? Where's it coming from?'

'Connie's text?' Michael looked up at him with a grin. 'It's our reinforcements!'

As Jed pulled the car forwards back into the street, they pushed the broken cabinet away and stood up.

'Is everyone OK?' Travis asked. Billy and Nicky nodded as the chorus of voices got louder and louder. Hearing the singing, Chastity and Connie peered around the corner from the top of stairs.

'What is that?' said Billy, staring out through the crumbling doorframe.

'It's The Sisterhood,' giggled Chastity. 'Bring it on, girls!'

In the street outside, Jed jumped from the car and re-grouped with his brother and their henchmen ready to attack, but they were distracted from their plan by the growing sound of an army approaching.

'What the fuck?' said Archie, as twenty exotic drag queens suddenly marched around the corner from Charing Cross Road onto Old Compton Street.

442

Twenty more followed, then another fifty. Their eyes were drawn to a side-turning a short way up the street as another fifty turned the corner towards them, glistening and sparkling in the brilliant sunshine, every shape, size and colour of the rainbow. More appeared from opposite and others from the side. The eccentrically attired Drag Fest participants had surrounded the Burke brothers from all directions.

'There's fuckin' millions of 'em!' Jed cried, backing up against the side of the car. Stepping over the glass from the entrance lobby, Chastity held aloft a large rainbow flag. Thrusting it into the air with glee, he shouted at the top of his voice.

'CHARGE!'

'Oh, shit!' gulped Archie, cowering against the Bentley as the fierce troupe of feathers, sequins and bows launched their glittering attack. The defenceless thugs cried out in pain as fist and stilettoes rained down upon them. Sharpened talons scratched, enamelled teeth bit and jewellery-laden hands punched and ripped as they were slapped and kicked in places they never knew they had. From every direction, the vicious onslaught was relentless.

'Hell hath no fury like a drag queen scorned!' Connie laughed, lighting a cigarette.

'Five hunky bad boys versus three-hundred man-hungry girls?' Chastity smirked. 'They'll never get out alive!'

Despite the Burke's best efforts to defend themselves and fight back, every attempt to win history's most glamorous battle was completely futile. Now completely naked, bruised and bleeding, they tried desperately to climb back into the car.

'Not just yet you don't, baby!' said a huge Kim Kardashian lookalike as two strong queens grabbed Archie's arms from behind, forcing him to his bare knees and backwards, shoving his head up the skirt of an enormous Dorothy.

'I don't think we're in Kansas anymore,' he smirked to his glove puppet Toto as he bounced up and down on Archie's face. His brother Jed meanwhile was forcibly bent forward over the bonnet of the Bentley with a feather boa stuffed in his mouth, as a brazen Cynthia Payne parody ripped off one of its windscreen wipers and whipped his bare arse. Their muffled, blood-curdling screams could hardly be heard above the riot. One of the nude henchmen attempted to save himself by climbing a lamppost, but three drag queens pulling on each leg was too much for even him to escape. With a horrified cry for help, he lost his grip and fell backwards, disappearing into the slavering throng.

As Fifi, Daisy and Edith joined everyone at Sugar Sugar's entrance, their laughter filled the air.

'Lettie would have loved this,' Chastity sighed, squeezing Connie's arm.

'Yeah, she couldn't have planned it better herself!' Connie grinned.

Finally inside the car, the thugs shielded their faces against flying glass as handbags smashed through the windows and knocked out the headlamps. Jed started the engine and the sea of sheer gorgeousness parted as the vehicle jolted a few times before tearing desperately up the street and away into the distance. A loud cheer filled the air as wigs, hats and hand handbags were tossed victoriously towards the heavens.

444

Relieved their ordeal was over, and utterly amazed by what he had seen, Travis pulled Michael into a hug.

'Have you decided yet? Do you still want to be a drag queen?' he said, eyes sparkling. Michael looked up at him and laughed through a broad grin.

'Fuckin' right, I do!'

As the excitement died down, the drag warriors picked up their belonging and slowly trickled back down towards the festivities at Trafalgar Square. Fifi put her hand on Billy's shoulder.

'Are you alright?' he asked.

'Yes, thanks to you. Still got balls, then?' she grinned. He walked over the loose rubble on the pavement towards Michael and Travis.

'Thank you,' he smiled, reaching out a hand once more. This time, Travis accepted the invitation and shook. 'I've seen some gang fights in my time, but I've never seen anything like that!'

'Well, just remember that next time you're thinking of stepping out of line, Dolly,' Connie smirked, lighting a cigarette and pointing in his face. 'Don't fuck with the drag queens… cause we is fuckin' invincible!'

CHAPTER THIRTY TWO

Two weeks after Drag Fest, Connie, Chastity and Daisy had finally moved into their lush new apartments on Soho Square. Michael had been nesting like crazy, taking his time mixing and matching things from Travis' flat in Pimlico with new furniture for their spacious penthouse. With only a week to go until his wedding, it seemed he hadn't had a moment to rest. With so many decisions to make and arrangements to put into place, it was only his excitement carrying him forward.

Sitting at his breakfast bar with coffees from a new machine, Chastity and Connie helped him go through his wedding lists.

'I really love the suit you've made for me, thank you,' he gushed.

'I'll take it downstairs with me before Travis gets home from work,' said Connie. 'It's bad luck for him to see it before the big day.'

'And which napkins did you choose for the wedding breakfast?' Chastity squinted at the scribbled notes. 'The ones folded like a swan or a lotus flower?'

'Neither,' Michael confirmed. 'I found an origami design on Google for a Scottish thistle.'

'Oh, that's nice!'

'I still think you should have gone for the one shaped like an erect penis,' mused Connie, looking at the photograph in the catering catalogue.

'I can't do that to Travis' parents!' Michael laughed, fumbling through his pile of paperwork to show them the printout. 'I think they've had enough to cope with recently.'

'And the soup… Minestrone or Chicken?'

'Oh, chicken… I can't be bothered with croutons.'

'And what are they for?' said Connie, pointing at the crockery page.

'Ramekins? They're for the Crème Brûlée,' Michael advised. 'Posh nosh, innit?'

'I've always wondered. I got some in Poundland, I use them for ashtrays!'

'So, I've just got to pick up my new stilettos,' said Chastity methodically. 'Then I've got to pop into the workshop and see Mr Clutch.'

'Is there something wrong with your car?' Connie asked.

'No, the catch on my handbag's broken.'

'Thank you for agreeing to be my groom's maids,' Michael smiled. 'At least your costumes are better than we wore at Frenchie's wedding.'

'Yeah well, anything's possible with a fuckin' budget!'

'I saw Billy moving into your old flat yesterday morning, Connie,' said Chastity, sipping his coffee. 'Did you invite him to the wedding, Lu?'

'I wasn't going to, but Travis said I should give him a chance,' Michael sighed. 'I guess he's right. If I hold onto grudges it's only me who's getting hurt, ain't it?'

'With that multiple personality disorder of his, he'll be a bugger to buy Christmas presents for!' Connie bitched, lighting a cigarette. As he leaned in
448

across the counter and drew back on his nicotine, Michael's new automatic air freshener ignited sending a puff of fire into his face. 'Argh!' he screamed, grabbing his head as a strong odour of burning skin filled the kitchen. 'My bloody eyebrows have gone!'

'Ha ha! You look like Herman Munster!' Chastity reached into his pocket and pulled out a ten-pound note, slamming it onto the surface in front of him. 'Here's the money for that mascara,' he smirked. 'Buy yourself some new ones!'

'What stupid bastard put that there?'

'It's lavender and chamomile,' said Michael apologetically.

'It's fuckin' lethal, that's what it is!' Snatching the cash, Connie shoved it up the end of his sleeve and darted out to the bathroom.

'Take no notice of her,' said Chastity, noticing a worried look on Michael's face. 'It wasn't long ago she singed my eyebrows. They'll grow back.'

'It's not that. I've invited my friend Tamara to the wedding.' Michael bit his lip. 'If Billy's gonna come, there could be trouble.'

'Don't worry yourself, she's a big girl. And we'll all be there, won't we? What could possibly go wrong?'

'Perhaps you're right,' Michael sighed resignedly.

'Tonight's Sugar Sugar press launch will be your last show as a single lady!' Chastity tapped Michael's hand affectionately. 'I think Fifi was wise to save the grand re-opening until we get back from the wedding. I expect she'll be holding court as usual this evening? Like Marie Antoinette before her face landed in that basket! Let's hope it puts her in a good mood for a change.'

'I hope so,' said Michael, biting his lip. 'Cause there's something really important I've gotta ask her.'

Sugar Sugar was bursting at the seams. All the old regulars had arrived dressed in their most fabulous outfits for the wildly anticipated press launch. Michael had wisely suggested from the beginning that the much loved venue stay looking practically the same as it had before. He had remembered back to when he had worked at Billy's bar in Southend-on-Sea. The owners of a nearby club had spent a fortune updating the look and layout of their madly successful haunt only to realise upon re-opening that their customers didn't respond well to change, shutting the place down within a month. Happily, it was clear to tell on Sugar Sugar's press launch night that everything would be business as usual.

All of the club's big elaborately gold-framed drag pictures were back on show around the walls in their original positions, except for one... Lettie's. Now draped in red velvet, Michael, Connie and Chastity stood with a glass of pink Champagne in their opening costumes with a resplendent Madame Fifi before it, ready for its public unveiling.

'A few words, Fifi?' said one member of the press, snapping a photo. She took a radio mic from the butch lesbian nearby.

'Since I was a slip of a girl in gingham and pigtails, I have always wanted my own cabaret nightclub,' she began dramatically.

'Can she remember that far back?' Connie smirked under his breath.

'And now here I am, surrounded by my adoring public in the middle of London's glittering West End.' A loud cheer went up from the audience. 'But any such venue is only as good as the stars that perform on its stage.'

'She's finally admitting that, is she?' Chastity quipped back.

'So it gives me great pleasure to reveal the portrait of our newest, brightest shining star. What do you think of my new discovery? I found her in the gutter the last time I visited gay Paris...'

'Oh, fuckin' get on with it!' Connie shouted, much to the delight of the onlookers.

'I give you Lulu L'Amore!' Fifi tore away the curtain. The entire club erupted with cheers and whistles at the sight of Michael's new picture. Standing tall and proud, he wore a brilliant-white silk and lace ball gown, corseted at the torso with a long skirt and yards of glistening fabric generously gathered at his feet. Long red curls lapped his bare shoulders and chest, framing a huge pure diamante necklace. Standing defiantly with white-gloved hands on hips, he looked every inch a glorious, glamorous diva of the stage. Staring proudly out at the world for all to see, his coronation was complete. He had finally been crowned a fully-fledged drag queen.

'Wow, it's fabulous!' Chastity gasped. 'He should be getting married in that!'

'Lu-lu! Lu-lu!' the crowd chanted. Michael looked through the sea of thrusting arms to find Travis, proudly clapping his hands with admiration. The audience lulled as Michael took the mic.

'I just wanna say thank you to everyone,' he rasped, voice wobbling with emotion. 'To my dear friends Chastity, Connie and Daisy. My gran Edith and my da...' He stopped himself mid-sentence to a glare from his father. 'Erm... I mean Madame Fifi. And last but not least, my gorgeous fiancé Travis who I love very much.'

'Here, here!' yelled Chastity, throwing Travis a wink as the press cameras flashed.

'This last eleven weeks since I've been here have been insane, you wouldn't believe,' Michael continued. 'But I ain't dead yet, so here's to the next eleven. The show must go on... cheers!' He thrust his glass in the air as the room screamed with admiration.

'OK, let's get the show underway,' said Fifi, swishing back her long orange gown to turn. 'If you'd like to follow me, boys?' she smiled, holding out her arms to direct the journalists and photographers.

'Err... before you go, can I just ask you something?' asked Michael, lowering his voice to keep his question private.

'Quickly?' said Fifi, smiling back at the press and looking at her watch.

'I want you to give me away at my wedding?'

'Me?' Fifi was clearly moved by his request. 'Are you sure?' Michael thought he could notice her bottom lip wobble a little.

'Of course!' he whispered. 'Whatever we put on for the cameras, you're still my father.' Fifi smiled, grasping his hand affectionately.

'It would be an honour,' she nodded quietly, giving him a hug before turning back to her fans. Throwing her arms in the air like a movie star on the red carpet, she bellowed at the top of her voice. 'Let the show commence!'

Stepping through the dressing room and out onto the stage, Lulu L'Amore, Chastity Belt and Connie Lingus looked stunning in their matching floor-length chiffon gowns. Cerise at the feet fading to pink at the shoulders, they sparkled with hundreds of tiny crystals reflecting the stage lights. Walking forward together to three microphones on stands at the front, Michael took the lead to a gentle piano as they sang their heartfelt anthem to friendship.

'There I was at a crossroads in my life. Had no choice but to crumble up inside. From the dark a voice called to me. Someone took the time to save me. When my head's against the storm, cold and all alone. And my shoulders bear the burden of decline. Then I know that I can always turn to friends like mine. Friends like mine.' He looked to either side at dear friends. They had been through so much together in such a short time. There had been one or two occasions when Chastity had frustrated him a little and quite a few times when he was very close to punching Connie's lights out, but ultimately they had stood by him through thick and thin. With a smile, he grabbed their hands as he continued.

'Like a fool I stood boldly in denial. Stupid pride running circles in my mind. Then a hand reached out to lead me. Gave the food of life to feed me. When my head's against the storm, cold and all alone. And my shoulders bear the burden of decline. Then I know that I can always turn to friends like mine. Friends like mine.'

453

Just over a week later, the day had finally arrived for Travis and Michael to wed. A light snow lay silently over the vast moors surrounding the castle as if to usher in a new dawn as Michael and Fifi's white Rolls Royce arrived from a local hotel.

'I'm really pleased I can do this for you,' Fifi smiled, taking his arm.

'So am I,' he grinned.

'I just want to say I'm sorry,' she sighed regretfully.

'What for?'

'You've had such a terrible life and it's mostly my fault. Things needn't have been that way.'

'Forget the past,' Michael nodded. 'This is our new beginning.'

As the car pulled under the wide stone portico at the front, Chastity and Connie stepped out from the entrance, a picture in matching figure-hugging violet silk gowns and short blonde wigs. As the chauffer held open the door for them to climb out, butterflies began to flutter madly in Michael's stomach. He looked up at the magnificent relic before him. Tall slate-roofed turrets towered each corner and grand crenellations ran across the wide parapet. The winter sun reflected off of more windows than he could count. He took a deep breath and puffed a few times to calm his ever-growing nerves.

'He is here, ain't he? Travis is here?' he flapped.

'Yes, he's here,' Connie confirmed. 'Calm yourself, Dolly!'

'You look gorgeous!' said Chastity, taking a step back to admire his shot silk ivory suit. Tanned and with his dark hair slicked back, Michael fiddled with

454

his violet necktie nervously. 'You look like Gary Cooper.'

'You look like Donny Osmond!' Connie giggled.

'Thanks... I think,' said Michael.

'And you don't look bad neither, considering your advanced years,' said Connie, brushing a loose hair from the shoulder of Fifi's fuchsia-pink two-piece suit.

'So that's what sluts are wearing this season?' shot back Fifi, flicking Connie's breast.

'You're finally here, marrying the man you love. It's all just so perfect!' Chastity grizzled, dabbing his eye with a small lace hankie. 'Weddings are so romantic: "Do you take this man?"' he quoted.

'You'd need a forklift to take her!' Connie smirked at Chastity.

'It's been such a frightening journey for you, I know. But we're very proud of our protégé, aren't we Connie?'

'I guess. On the bright side Dolly, you could write a book about everything that's happened.'

'Nah, nobody would wanna read that!' Michael laughed.

'Keira Knightley could play me in the TV mini-series,' Connie plumped his wig.

'Ooh yes!' gushed Chastity. 'Who could they get to play me?'

'Susan Boyle!' Connie lit a cigarette. 'So are you taking Travis' name then? Or just keeping you own... Dirk Stardust?'

'I'm gonna be Mr Michael McBradey,' he said proudly.

'Ooh... so if we're all your family, that makes us The McBradey Bunch!' Chastity chuckled.

455

'And gay couples can adopt kids now, you know?' Connie advised.

'If I want to hear the pitter-patter of tiny feet, I'll buy Nigel some tap shoes!'

He looked around at the castle's grand entrance lobby. High walls of huge clean grey blocks decorated with white flowers and bouquets towered all around, meeting at the top in an arch above a massive crystal chandelier. Through a stone arch beyond was an immense hall with a carved wooden gallery high up to either side. From just inside the huge entrance, seats had been laid facing forward creating an aisle to the largest fireplace Michael had ever seen. To its right was a huge fifteen-foot spruce Christmas tree decorated in white and violet garlands, baubles and lights. Enormous gold-framed ancestral portraits hung all around amongst an array of stuffed animal-head trophies and displays of ancient armoury. The pageantry of this regal old building was simply staggering.

'This place is insane, ain't it?' he laughed. 'How many bedrooms has it got?'

'I lost count at eighteen,' said Connie. 'I had to go outside for a fag and couldn't find me way back to the same corridor.'

Michael looked in at the friends and family seated to either side, each one dressed in their very best for his big day. The daunting thought of having to learn the name of everyone on Travis' side alone filled Michael with apprehension. But what really had been worrying him was how Tamara and Billy would react to each other. He had been so cruel to her for so long, Michael wanted to be sure she was OK.

Stretching his neck, he looked down his side of the church. There was his mother Verity chattering with Fanny. Edith was wiping away a tear between Gerry and Nicky. Daisy sat hand-in-hand with Luther, who had travelled over from Germany especially for the occasion with Heinz. Frenchie cooed with her young husband Shaun, and Rabbi Bobbly sat in a rainbow-striped kippah next to his boyfriend, Desmond. A splattering of their most loyal Sugar Sugar fans filled the back. And sitting at the front next to an empty seat reserved for Fifi was Billy. Just a couple of feet away on the same pew sat a well-groomed young man Michael hadn't seen before. But his dearest, oldest friend was nowhere in sight.

'She's not here is she?' he cried. 'Did Tamara leave? Was it Billy?'

'Yes she is here,' Chastity smile kindly. 'And she spoke to Billy over dinner last night. Everything's fine, she's probably just in the loo.' He leaned in closer. 'Connie thinks she might be pregnant, her tits are massive!'

'Really? Oh, wow!' said Michael.

'We think that's the father.' Connie pointed at the hunk next to Billy. As Michael looked, he was relieved to see Tamara teetering in from under the gallery pulling at the back of her skirt. Seeing Michael, she grinned back and blew him a kiss before sitting between Billy and her new beau. At that moment, Travis' parents walked back from their seats to greet him.

'You look wonderful,' Jeanie smiled with pride. 'Everyone's here. I'll introduce you to Travis' sisters and their kin later.'

'Best of luck, son,' said Hamish, shaking his hand warmly. 'And this must be your father?' He nodded at Fifi with a smile. 'Travis has explained everything.'

'It's nice to finally meet you,' she replied.

'I wish you both a very long and happy life together,' said Jeanie, wiping away a tear. 'And you'll look after him for me, won't you? After all… he's just a man.'

'*Stand by your man,*' Connie and Chastity warbled in unison.

'Yes, of course,' said Michael giving her a hug. 'What do you think of the castle, then?'

'It's magnificent,' she answered, looking around. 'I've never been inside before, but we have been in the grounds.'

'Really?'

'Aye.' She moved in closer. 'When Hamish and I were a-courting, we used to sneak up here to be alone. I would sing to him and he would pick me flowers. He's a romantic old fool really.'

'Haud yer wheesht, woman!' His cheeks flushed.

'I was only fifteen, if my da had ever found out he would have shot him! So you can imagine how delighted I was to discover you'd wed here.'

'Well, I'm glad you feel that way,' said Michael, taking her hand. 'Because me and Travis have decided to give it to you as our wedding gift.' A moment of stunned silence filled the room.

'You can't do that, son,' said Hamish emotionally.

'Yeah we can and we did, so it's done and that's that! Our life's in London, it'd just sit empty. You could live here, or run it as an hotel of something if you like?' He put his hand on Hamish's shoulder. 'A castle needs a strong character to take charge cause it comes with a title. You'd be the Laird... I looked it up on Google.'

'Oh, Hamish!' gasped his wife. 'For the grandchildren?'

'Aye,' he said sharply, trying desperately to hide his flood of feelings. 'Come on Hen, we're about to start.' Holding out his arm for her to take, they hurried back along the white-carpeted aisle to their seats.

Michael could see the priest arrive as three uniformed Highland drummers took their place to the left of the fireplace. As their rhythmic beat filled the hall, a solitary chorister stepped forward. Also in traditional dress, he stroked his long white beard and moustache as he began to sing a wedding march especially composed for the happy couple by Slasher.

'Home is where my heart lies, o'er the heather'd fold. Where a true man waits for me, in my arms to hold. And as the years embrace us, I will stand with he. Till the angels call me, to the great eternity.'

A single bagpipe player arrived at the arch in front of them to lead Michael up the aisle.

'This is it? Are you ready to become Mr McBradey?' said Chastity excitedly.

'Aye, that I am,' Michael grinned, taking Fifi's arm.

His walk down the aisle with Fifi behind the piper was like a dream. Followed closely by his two groom's maids, the sumptuous carpet beneath his feet felt like a cloud. Looking ahead he could see his darling Travis, resplendent in traditional dress of jacket, kilt and sporran, beaming with delight as his husband-to-be marched slowly towards married life.

'I think the wrong groom's wearing the skirt,' whispered Connie.

'Ooh, I feel like Katherine Heigl in Twenty Seven Dresses,' Chastity sniffed.

Reaching Travis' side, Michael looked up into his sparkling eyes.

'Hiya, handsome!' he said, stroking the side of Michael's face.

'Hello, baby,' he replied, eyes welling with tears of happiness.

The ceremony was perfect. After years of trauma, trial and tribulation, Michael's life was finally complete. Happier than he had ever been, he gazed longingly into his new husband's loving eyes as he uttered the words, 'I do!'

Printed in July 2019
by Rotomail Italia S.p.A., Vignate (MI) - Italy